BLACK MAMBA

TIERNEY JAMES

Owasso, OK

DEDICATION

To my incredible brave friend who fought
the enemy until the end.
Glenda Mitcherson Coleman
I will miss you forever.

ACKNOWLEDGMENTS

This is the time I get to thank all those who stepped up and made this book possible. Your encouragement and support means the world to me. Without you, I may have given up on Captain Hunter and Tessa Scott. Your hilarious comments and ideas kept me in stitches while giving me inspiration to keep the chaos going between these two.

Lipstick and Danger Street Team – You guys never fail me. A big hug and lots appreciation to all of you who promote, read and review my work. My heart is full of love for you. Thank you.

Wizards of Publishing – Sometimes it is painful to have you as my editors. However, you are always right and because of you I am a better writer. I feel like I'm going to a writing class every time I jump into your life. A big, big thank you to Kate and Nan.

Sleuths' Ink Mystery Writers – These writers have encouraged me for a number of years. They have educated, promoted and encouraged me when I didn't believe I could get the job done.

Writers of the Purple Page – Every day we meet in cyberspace over coffee and the latest news in our lives. Along the way, we push each other to be better writers, find new ideas and laugh at ourselves when we screw up.

Paperback Press – Thanks for being my number one hand-holder when I get paranoid or my technical skills fail me. You give my book life in all that you do on the publishing end. I shudder to think how hard this journey would be without you.

BLACK MAMBA

Black mamba: With coffin-shaped heads, this is one of the most dangerous snakes in the world. They are brownish in color and get their name from the color of the inside of their mouths. Black mambas have been found as large as fourteen feet long. Capable of striking a victim multiple times, it only takes two drops of venom to kill a human. Their potent venom shuts down the nervous system and paralyzes the victim. Death can occur in twenty minutes if not treated with anti-venom.

CHAPTER ONE

The woman paced then glanced toward the mirror to admire her image. Sometimes she paused long enough to fling her black tresses back then push out her full lips to appear pouty. The call of peacocks in the garden drew her to the second-floor window. A dark-skinned man in a suit stopped his evening security check to stare up at her half-naked form. Even from this distance, such admiration could get him killed. He waited in some kind of expectation for only a few seconds before moving into the darkness. She broke off the connection as her bedroom door opened.

"Where have you been?" She pivoted and moved toward the man she'd married. His stocky physique hid an agility that could strike a man to the ground with little effort.

"I am the president. I am always busy." His eyes traced her tall, slim form with admiration.

An impatient stomp of her foot started her pacing again. "I have been waiting for hours. You ignore me when I return and complain when I leave. What do you want of me?"

"To be a mother to our son instead of a spoiled socialite." The calm, even tone was a warning sign.

She moved toward him and circled his neck with a tender embrace. "I have missed you." He set her aside, walked to the window, and looked down. She pulled him back to her and pressed her body closer. "Come to bed. It is late."

"Did you visit our son? He has been asking for you." He allowed her to remove his jacket.

"I will see him in the morning. I'm sure that old woman can manage one more night. Besides, I have other plans for you, my husband."

He buried his smiling mouth against her throat and whispered, "And I have plans for you."

President Baboloki dressed in comfortable clothing and returned to his office on the first floor of the mansion the government of Botswana had provided for him. He poured a brandy before lighting a cigar, having dismissed most of the staff for a surprise night off. His son's caretaker remained in the attached cottage, seeing to his needs. The chief of security also stayed on property to do some training with his men in one of the classroom buildings.

After staring out the window for nearly twenty minutes, the president phoned someone outside his inner circle.

"Is everything ready?" He puffed a cloud of smoke toward the ceiling.

"Yes. The package is wrapped and waiting, Mr. President. It will be given to her at the designated time."

He clicked off and decided to go to his bedroom to get a few hours' sleep. Glancing down at the newspaper on his desk, his attention shifted to the obscure article about a missing diamond called the Kifaru; nonsense about some legend and ruling Botswana. Tomorrow, he'd focus more on that problem.

~ ~ ~

The plane bounced a little as it always did when it crossed the equator, alerting the wife of President Baboloki they were over the Democratic Republic of Congo. She had been in Botswana for only twenty-four hours before flying into one of her rages about living in a Third World country. It was too much to bear. She reminded him she was French and Ethiopian, raised in Europe, not some dried-up watering hole in Southern Africa. The president had suggested she fly back to Paris, do some shopping, and return in a couple of days. Her ability to control the pompous dictator gave her great satisfaction.

She admired her slender fingers and manicured nails before twisting her diamond ring off. "No need for that." She dropped it in her designer handbag and kicked off her shoes.

Her male companion, or Baboloki's snoop as she liked to call the middle-aged servant, brought her a beautifully wrapped box, trimmed in gold. "What's this?"

"A gift from your husband. I was told to give it to you when we crossed the equator, ma'am." He waited for a thank you. He got none.

Like a delighted child at Christmas, she tore the ribbon off only to pause with her hands on the lid of the box. His gifts in the past were expensive and in good taste. Maybe this first lady job would have to be endured a little longer. She threw the lid on the floor to find black tissue paper covering a curled object. With abandon, she reached in and grabbed something slick and cold.

A scream of revulsion escaped her throat as the black mamba struck her twice, once in the face, the second time on her collarbone. She staggered out of her leather seat and cried for help.

Her companion dropped the tray of coffee he carried when the snake raced forward. He backed toward the cockpit, shrieking for help. The serpent followed him and lifted the front third of its body, striking the arm he held in front of him.

The wife extended a hand toward the cockpit when the sound of chaos brought the pilot into the danger zone. In the throes of agony, she watched him fall victim to the venomous snake's repeated strikes until he fell backward inside the cockpit. Her body rolled to the side when the plane turned into a lopsided plunge toward the rainforest below. Her last conscious thought was the jungle would swallow up one of the president's problems…the bastard.

Chapter Two

Tessa felt a rocking motion against her shoulder then a touch to her cheek. Darkness refused to release its hold on her dreams as she adjusted her body by stretching out her legs. When her bare toes touched something long and hard, she felt a hand grasp her foot. A finger slid from toes to heel and brought her to a state of fitful consciousness.

When she tried to jerk away and push to a sitting position, her eyes fluttered open to stare into the amused expression of Captain Chase Hunter who sat across from her. He held her foot, flexing his hand to tighten and release. She relaxed enough to trick him into loosening his grip then immediately landed a kick to his lower leg.

He emitted a quiet, almost-throaty chuckle. He'd reminded her of the Big Bad Wolf on more than one occasion. He grabbed her again before she could land another kick and ran his finger up and down the bottom, tickling her into uncontrollable laughter. Attempting to escape, she slouched down farther into the leather seat she'd secured when boarding the plane.

"Stop it," she gasped then slapped at his hand.

Others of the Enigma team roused from their slumber as well and cast sleepy glances at her and Chase. Two years ago, they would have gathered around and watched their boss act more human than cyborg. These days, they expected the two of them to make each other uncomfortable.

Chase slid his finger one more time before she jerked away. "I said stop." She tried to catch her breath then landed another kick on his knee.

"I tried to wake you up, but you were in your usual coma-state. You sleep sounder than anyone I know."

"I'm catching up. You try being at the beck and call of three kids and a demanding husband."

Chase winked. "No thanks. You're enough of a pain in the neck for me. Are you saying, if I get you out of my life, I'll sleep again?"

Tessa yawned and nodded.

He leaned closer when she lowered her head to rub her face. "Fire me, will ya? I have no business going on these ridiculous trips." His nearness reminded her of his interest.

Creases formed at the corners of his eyes. "What would be the fun in that, Tessa? I have too much fun saving your butt every time you get into trouble. And whether you admit it or not"—he searched her face— "you like being rescued."

The overpowering urge to deny the accusation washed over her. She decided to surprise him. "You're right about that, Chase."

"Maybe I can do it again when we get back home. This time something a little more personal."

"I've got the perfect idea." She met the amusement in his eyes with what she hoped reflected her distrust and annoyance.

"Care to share?"

"I'm thinking you can rescue me by babysitting my three kids and ensuring Robert does some of the honey-do jobs he never has time for so I can go shopping with my girlfriends." She tapped him on the nose as his amusement faded.

"Ouch." He leaned back in his leather chair. "I can do that. You'll see what a prince I am."

"Prince of Darkness, maybe." She stood and edged out into the aisle, smelling coffee. "Want a cup?"

He nodded before slipping his hands behind his head and stretching out his long legs. The flight attendant hired for their private charter arranged a tray of the chocolate chip cookies Tessa had brought along for the trip. Cups of steamy brew caused her to inhale deeply. She volunteered to take it herself.

"Thanks, Tess," he said pulling his legs back for her to sit across from him. He turned up a small shelf table and watched her add cream and sugar to her cup. He scarfed down two cookies then sipped from the Styrofoam cup. "So, how exactly did you get Robert to be okay with this trip?"

"Sex," she said bluntly.

He choked on his coffee then spilled it down the front of his red tee shirt. Tessa couldn't resist letting one corner of her mouth turn up. "It's for the good of the country."

"You're getting to be a little bit of a smart-ass."

"I'm trying to fit in, Captain Hunter," she mocked with a salute then grabbed a broken cookie off the tray.

His mouth widened into a genuine amusement. "What kind of sex?"

"Do you want the truth, or should I make it up?"

"Make it up. I'm sure it is better than the real thing in Robert's case." Chase's solemn face hinted he wasn't kidding.

Tessa narrowed her gaze at him. "Touché." She wasn't sure why conversations always gravitated toward things more personal with him.

Why did he insinuate he might be interested in her? Ridiculous, since he didn't want any part of Enigma agents or married women. Tessa represented everything he avoided to remain footloose and fancy-free. At times, the two of them seemed so close: sharing books, music, ideas, and personal stories of their private life. He'd become her best friend. Muddying the friendship waters with a physical relationship wasn't something she cared to explore. For both of them, this crossed the line between right and wrong.

"I'm waiting on the sex talk," he teased then took another sip of the hot liquid. "Trying to figure it out, my sweet babe in the woods?"

"I'm not sure you can handle it."

He set the cup down and propped his feet on the seat next to her as if to block any kind of retreat, a habit she'd acquired when things got uncomfortable between them. "I'm not sure I could, either." The wolfish chuckle unnerved her. "Maybe we should stick to business." He nudged her with his sock-covered foot but gave her hip an extra rub, drawing a frown back to his amused dark eyes.

Dangerous ground. Was he teasing her to see how fast her comfort level would tank, or did this back-and-forth they practiced have meaning? She shoved his foot away then grabbed it to pop his toe, forcing an angry groan.

"You deserved that. Why can't you be normal for once?"

"It's a little early in the morning to hurl insults at your captain, Miss High and Mighty. I didn't know talking about sex made you uncomfortable. That explains so much."

His tone resembled a scientist discovering a new chemical compound. Tessa bit her bottom lip but couldn't hold back a warm chuckle. "I despise you, Chase Hunter."

"Ditto, Tessa Scott."

They paused long enough to try and stare each other down. "Friends?" he asked.

"Forever," she said, lifting her cup in a salute.

Longtime agents, Zoric and Sam appeared at their side.

"Are we interrupting anything?" Zoric smirked then motioned for Tessa to slide across to sit next to Chase. The Serbian edged over to the window seat. Sam sat across from Chase, offering the captain her own brand of smoldering come-hither expression.

"As a matter of fact—" Chase started.

"Not at all," Tessa finished. "What's up? Sleep well? Did you get some cookies? I brought plenty. Vernon still sleeping? Where's Carter?" Stopping her bombardment of questions to cover her guilt grew impossible. Did the heat spreading across her neck and jaw show red in the dim light? The others really didn't understand their back-and-forth insults and friendship.

"My. My. Aren't we a chatterbox?" Sam always sounded as if she might be ready to interrogate Tessa. "Slept great. I don't eat sugar. Vernon is playing on his computer. Carter is in the cockpit trying to tell the pilot how to do his job. Or maybe hitting on the flight attendant." She curled her legs under her, settling in. "What were you talking about?"

"Sex mostly," Chase quipped and folded his arms across his chest.

Tessa squirmed under their stares.

"That isn't exactly true. He's making that up." Tessa took a nervous sip of coffee.

Chase turned his head toward her and bit his bottom lip before shifting his focus back to the two agents. "Oh, right. Sorry. We were talking about the weather."

Even though Zoric appeared amused, Sam's frown deepened as she leveled a penetrating glare toward Tessa. She didn't appreciate the concern Chase gave the newest recruit for the last two years. The senior agent had never shared the limelight with another woman, ever. This remained Tessa's ace in the hole. If bodily harm mysteriously happened to her, Chase would make sure Sam paid the price. On the other hand, Tessa continued to admire the woman for her guts, beauty, and ability to control men with the curl of her little finger. Tessa sometimes wished to be more like her.

Vernon and Carter sank into the leather chairs across the aisle.

"We've started our descent," Carter offered.

"Tessa, what did you learn last night when you were working?" Chase's voice switched to his professional, no-nonsense tone, a signal given when their workday had begun.

This created a safe cocoon for her. At least when she talked shop, the captain wouldn't be messing with her head.

"In February, Handsome traveled to Canada where we lost him in Vancouver. We spotted him at the Quebec airport a month later."

"No one tried to stop him?" asked Carter.

"Negative," Chase chimed in when Vernon handed him a map of Southern Africa. "According to Tess, he believes the Kifaru diamond is the key to regime change in Botswana. That sweet little lump of carbon could destabilize the entire region. We want to know if the diamond is really all that important to the people of Botswana."

"Why would he care? He's a drifter contracted by the CIA when it pleases them." Zoric took the last cookie from the tray and shoved it in his mouth

"My research shows he's had multiple aliases throughout his life." Tessa glanced at her notes then handed the tray to the passing attendant, taking note of how Carter enjoyed her backside. He winked with a kind of mischievous delight that made it difficult for her to hold back laughter.

The former astronaut had found the boot to his behind at NASA for his womanizing. She couldn't help but think him adorable in a bad-little-boy way.

"So how much truth to the fact he was in the foster care system?" Zoric continued.

Tessa shrugged. "None that I found. Oh, there were kids meeting his description and history, but the pictures didn't match or the trail went dead. As a matter of fact, I couldn't find anything that hinted he'd ever been in the United States until he became a legal adult. He enrolled in an engineering school in Rolla, Missouri and was a so-so student, although the professors I talked to said he always knew more than he let on."

"Meaning?" Chase said.

"They suspected he purposely failed or didn't answer all the questions. At any kind of project or group work, he always excelled. He didn't like to show his work on some tests. Said he didn't see the point if he could give them the answer. They thought he didn't show the work because he might be cheating. Maybe it was an attempt at rebellion."

"But he graduated?" Zoric asked.

"Yes. But the bottom of his class. One more thing of interest is he worked part-time at a fast-food place and managed to graduate debt-free."

"No way he paid for college working at a place like that," Chase added.

"Exactly. He kept a small bank account under the name Louis Girard Jones." Tessa retrieved her laptop from a satchel under the seat and powered up. After scrolling, she found the file with the details of Handsome's life. "He drove a late-model Chevy, stayed off campus in a nondescript apartment complex where other students rented. He wasn't a partier, as far as I can tell, and no serious relationships during college."

"What about afterward?" Sam asked. "Did he get a real job in engineering?"

"Yes, but not the typical job. For about three years, he served in the Canadian Forces Reserves before switching to the Canadian Military Engineers. Their job is to provide survival, mobility, and combat effectiveness for the rest of the military."

"So, what you're saying is he took that fancy education and used it to study land mines and demolitions." Zoric took out his pocket knife to clean his fingernails but returned it when Sam pushed it away with a hateful smack on his arm.

"That is true, but Canadians also use that kind of expertise in maintaining lines of communication, bridging and setting up utilities. There are a lot of jobs in that field. He bounced around a number of them for another five years, received commendations for excellence before leaving. After that, there seems to be a lack of information."

"Any friends, relationships, or trouble with the law?" Sam quizzed.

"With one man. A Dr. Andre Girard, originally from Montreal. He and his wife opened a practice there in pediatrics. Here is a picture of them at the clinic, Mrs. Girard looking very pregnant." She paused for effect, but no one seemed impressed, so Tessa continued, "Anyway, Dr. Girard traveled to Africa several times in the late seventies and early eighties to volunteer in a clinic supported in part by his parish."

"His wife didn't go?" Tessa wasn't surprised at Carter's question since his interests centered on the female factor.

"From what I gather, she miscarried the baby and wasn't physically able to go to the international conference on health care in Africa at that time. Dr. Girard, being a keynote speaker, decided to attend. He took a side trip to Botswana to go on a photographic safari."

"What does this have to do with Handsome?" Sam yawned.

"I'm getting to that." She tried to contain her excitement. "When the doctor returned, he and his wife pulled up roots and moved to a small community on the north shore of Lake Superior, helping First Nation communities with health care. Six years later, Mrs. Girard died of complications from a blood clot." She continued to talk as she searched for another file on her computer. "The doctor then moved back to Toronto to open a practice there and to raise his son."

"Were the son and Handsome connected somehow?" Chase asked, leaning in to catch a glimpse of her computer screen.

"No." She turned the screen around, displaying a picture of a man walking into a church, holding the hand of a boy about the age of eight. "This is Dr. Girard and his son."

Everyone leaned in to get a better look. "But that child is black."

CHAPTER THREE

Vernon, who already knew the information Tessa provided the group, took the opportunity to retrieve his own laptop. He'd passed the job off to her months ago because he needed to send new tech people into the field with teams from other universities. When she'd get sidetracked or lost in the information universe, he would pull her back and redirect her search. Tessa used the geography skill of human-environmental interaction to finally open doors to discovering Handsome Jones.

When the others dozed off the night before, she'd finished up her presentation and double-checked facts that sounded preposterous with him to make sure everything made sense.

"Black?" Sam took the computer to peer closer with Zoric. Even Carter leaned out into the aisle to get a better look.

Chase's brow creased after taking a second look at the picture. "And Dr. Girard's other child?"

"There was no other child. His wife miscarried at five months and was told she'd never be able to carry a baby to term. It was her second loss." Tessa took the computer from Sam.

"So, this black child was adopted, I'm assuming." Sam's voice grew softer. Tessa thought she noticed a little moisture at the corners of the woman's eyes. Maybe Sam had a heart after all.

"Not exactly. Well, not until the child was in his teens. Then the paperwork magically appeared on record including a birth certificate that said the child was born in Biloxi, Mississippi. My research indicated he was an American citizen, given up for adoption when the good doctor volunteered at a clinic there. That child was John Girard. We know him as Handsome Jones. Most of their friends knew nothing about John—I mean Handsome, until about the time you see him in this picture with Dr. Girard."

"How did they keep it a secret and why?" Chase accepted another cup of coffee from the flight attendant.

"Living on an Indian Reserve in rural Canada can keep your friends at bay. The Girards worked hard and didn't really stay in touch with their former friends. I think the reason has to be because Handsome was really the son of John Kabo, born in a small village in Botswana where the good doctor vacationed on safari shortly after his wife miscarried their child."

"You make it sound like he brought home a puppy to replace the one his wife lost." Sam smirked then cocked her head and slid her hand down her long black ponytail. "How could that even happen?"

"Africa. Back in the 1970s and 80s, a lot was going on. The camp Dr. Girard stayed in was hit by General Baboloki's men, killing almost everyone, including the tourists staying in the safari camp."

"How did he survive?" Chase asked.

"I was able to track down a bush pilot who flew tourists to various camps along the Okavango during the seventies. After the camp was destroyed, he moved his family to Harare, Zimbabwe for several years before taking a position at a vineyard in South Africa. Again. Flying tourists in from Johannesburg and Cape Town, South Africa. I tried to talk to him before we left Sacramento, but he died several years ago."

"A dead end," Sam interjected. "Sorry. No pun intended."

"Not exactly. I located his daughter, who didn't know her father may have been involved in the rescue of our good doctor and a baby. Said the last years of her father's life he had Alzheimer's and often rambled about saving the future of Botswana from the butchers of the bush. He talked about a doctor taking a baby from his father's arms and escaping with him. Because the pilot feared for his life, he moved his family a number of times."

"And you think Handsome Jones was that baby?" Chase asked.

"It certainly looks that way. The doctor currently is in Gaborone working in a clinic. He has spent the last few years working with UNICEF and Doctors Without Borders. He also built a clinic in the bush where he spends a lot of time. Actually, it's not far from where we plan to go later in the week."

The flight attendant announced they were landing at Victoria Falls Airport and everyone needed to be buckled up. Tessa closed her laptop and shut her eyes when the thump of landing gear went down. Memories of all the Tarzan movies she'd watched as a kid flooded her senses along with the image of the old black-and-white movie of Stanley and Livingstone, and even George of the Jungle.

Africa—a dream come true or a nightmare waiting to happen? She stole a sideways glance to find Chase staring at her with narrowed eyes. Whatever lay ahead, he would be beside her. He blinked a kind of reassurance.

~ ~ ~

President Baboloki admired himself in one of the many mirrors through his mansion. The wide mouth stretched across his face to appear pleased when he lifted his chin to check for lines of age. When he found none, the president ran his hands down the front of his khaki-colored uniform pinned with a variety of ribbons and medals to remind people of his accomplishments over the last thirty-eight years.

Women had often told him his eyes were the color of obsidian and feared they might drown in their depths. The narrow nose reflected his Tswana heritage, but the short stature and jet-black skin spoke of the Zulu of South Africa. Great kings came from that tribe, so he felt honored when some compared him to the tribe from the south. And like the Zulu who assumed they would be in charge, President Baboloki never considered anyone might second-guess his decisions concerning Botswana.

The army followed him blindly, so he rewarded them with salaries that could feed their families and give them prestige in their villages and clans. They remained loyal and crushed resistance whenever it reared its ugly head.

The parliament continued to hold some ideas from the old days, thanks to the wealthy landowners and safari companies, but the diamond business flourished under his deregulation and favoritism, thanks to their propensity to make cash deposits in several accounts he kept in Switzerland and the Cayman Islands.

However, the world was changing, and the United Nations questioned whether the Kimberly Accord kept the diamond business from funneling money to areas of conflict throughout Africa. Groups of do-gooders from the United Kingdom and the United States seemed to think with the new stability and productivity, there should be more infrastructure, schools, medical facilities, and technology. He believed in withholding technology from the people indefinitely. Exposure to the wider world might give his people the idea they had choices concerning their destiny.

Some snoops from the US State Department had arrived on his doorstep to discuss avenues of mutual concern with an eye to the future.

To President Baboloki, this meant meddling in things that weren't their business. They landed in Harare two days earlier to speak to the new Zimbabwe president who quickly reported to Baboloki what they had to say. Zimbabwe's economy was on the verge of collapse and wanted to secure some loans from Botswana with their tattle-tale diplomacy.

There had been a time when meeting such influential foreigners would have given him pause. He took it upon himself to find the best teachers to educate him in the ways of the world, including mathematics, science, and finance.

He gave his image one more inspection in the mirror before turning at the sound of one of his assistants entering.

The man dressed in a suit and tie snapped his heels together before giving a quick nod of submission. "They have arrived, sir."

"Show them to the veranda and serve them some refreshments. I will be there shortly."

"Of course."

~ ~ ~

Chase checked the time again then let his eyes follow Tessa who moved about the gardens off the veranda. They had been waiting over an hour for the president to make an appearance. Was it a power play, or did matters of state keep the president from joining them? The man was known to enjoy a grand entrance. Someone pulled back a curtain from a second-story window and stared out at them. Tessa might have an admirer.

What wasn't to admire? She meandered around the grounds, the breezes catching the hem of her blue cotton dress. She lifted the blonde curls that fell to her shoulders in disarray, baring her neck in the process. The urge to taste her nape was almost always in the back of his mind. Apparently, someone else enjoyed watching her absentminded stroll amongst the flowers.

His instincts whispered he should pull her back, keep her closer so he could protect her from interested parties. But then again, Tessa had a way of drawing people out and maybe this pie-in-the-sky demeanor could work to their advantage. She continued to be the most unassuming person he knew—too trusting, too innocent, too gullible to believe people might be evil and have ulterior motives.

This remained the exact reason he'd fallen in love with her long ago. He feared Afghanistan might have destroyed that goodness in her, but if anything, she came back stronger and more convinced a guardian angel was never very far from her. Chase accepted that role in spite of her love for someone else. They kept their relationship professional, no harm, no foul or so he tried to convince himself. He'd play her superhero or her knight in shining armor for the duration of their friendship. But one day he was going to have to do something about her husband, Robert Scott.

"I should have left him there," he mumbled, thinking of the time he rescued the man from a potentially damaging situation that could have gotten him thrown in jail or disbarred.

"What?" Tessa approached him, smiling.

"Our host is putting us off," he said, eyeing her head to toe without trying to cover his admiration. Something about the way the breeze moved the hem of her dress reminded him of a Monet painting.

"African time. You need to enjoy the day. It's beautiful here." She picked up a glass of cool lemonade and pointed to a nearby tree. "Look at those birds. Aren't they incredible? And these plants. I've never seen anything like them."

"Yes. They are quite spectacular," came a voice with a British accent. Chase and Tessa turned to see the president walking toward them. His eyes did a quick appraisal of Tessa's figure without being vulgar as he took her hand and kissed it tenderly. "Welcome. I apologize for the delay. There seemed to be some confusion regarding proposed legislation coming before our parliament." He gazed into Tessa's eyes and continued to show admiration.

She eased free from his grasp. "No need to apologize. You left us in a most beautiful garden, President Baboloki. It is such a pleasure to finally meet you. I am Tessa Scott, and this is my assistant, Captain Chase Hunter."

He shifted his eyes to Chase, offering a more narrowed expression as he appraised the competition. The men clasped hands for only seconds. "Captain? Military. Are you here in a professional role or"—he turned a warm gaze back to Tessa—"protection for the lovely lady?"

"A little of both." Chase chuckled. He laid a hand on her back, marking his territory. "We're a team, for sure."

Tessa flashed both men a patient smile as a blush crept up her neck and face. "Thank you for the lemonade. Was it freshly squeezed?"

The president moved toward the garden path. "Yes. We actually have our own lemon trees."

"Will your wife be joining us? I'd hope to speak to her about how she can assist in some of the women's programs that have been successful in other parts of Africa."

He held out his arm, inviting Tessa to his side. "No. I'm afraid when shopping is involved, she drops off the face of the earth. Come. Let me show you the grounds. Are you interested in gardening?"

Tessa slipped her arm through his as a sudden breeze twirled her hair across her face. "Yes, and that would be lovely. I have many questions about some of these species. I never figured a military man such as you, would be interested in such a pastime."

"Well, I find that it soothes the soul," he said, patting her arm. As they headed down the path, Chase moved to follow, but was cut off by a security officer in a three-piece suit. "We'll be back in a few minutes, Captain Hunter. I'll take good care of Ms. Scott. No need to worry about her safety while she is here with me." He leveled a warning glare at the captain.

Tessa didn't react to the heavy scent of testosterone. "Tell me about this one, President Baboloki, the purple one with the chartreuse leaves." She touched the flower before smiling up at the Botswana president who beamed back at her.

Chase relaxed as he took a step closer to his guard. "How about you and me have a little something stronger than lemonade. Your boss got anything like that?"

Chapter Four

"The grounds are lovely, President Baboloki. Thank you for sharing your knowledge of these unusual plants." Tessa withdrew her hand from the president's arm once more. This time he accepted her retreat as they joined the captain at a small table on the veranda.

Twice during her tour of the garden, she caught a glimpse of a woman staring at them from a downstairs window. She didn't shrink from her observations when they made eye contact. Dressed simply in a pale-blue shift, the woman didn't appear to be one of the maids she'd seen carrying out tasks in president's home. They were all dressed in black dresses with white aprons. Her short-cropped hair might have been gray. Maybe she was a tutor for the president's young son or an assistant for his wife. She quickly dismissed the curiosity when the president spoke.

"It was my pleasure, madam. Let's talk business for a little while before dinner. I expect you are tired from such a busy itinerary."

Did he really know anything about her itinerary, or only assume as much since the US State Department sent her?

He poured both of them another lemonade then nodded at Hunter sipping a drink that differed in color from theirs. "I see my associate brought you my best Scotch."

Chase eyed his glass then gulped the rest of it down and gritted his teeth. "I'm not sure it was your best, but it was damn good."

The president laughed good-naturedly. "I assure you it was, Captain Hunter." He motioned for Tessa to take a seat. "What shall we talk about?"

~ ~ ~

Surrounded by twenty guests from various walks of life, mostly business and government appointees, President Baboloki enjoyed their admiration along with cocktails served on the candlelit veranda. Tiki torches burned along the garden paths. The irritated call of alarm from a male peacock perched in a nearby tree wove itself into the soft conversations floating on the African breezes. It seemed to chase away the heat so pressing earlier in the day.

"Mr. President?" came a familiar voice. The leader moved to the edge of the covered veranda. "How did it go with the two State Department people from the US?"

Baboloki stirred his drink then captured the olive at the bottom of his glass and popped it into his mouth before facing the white African owner of the Camelthorn Diamond Mines spread throughout Southern Africa. "The woman was quite lovely. Her escort impressed me as intelligent, but you never know with the Americans. Their CIA keep getting smarter and smarter."

"CIA?" A touch of panic in the man's voice caused the president to chuckle.

"Relax. They are snooping. Nothing more."

"For what?"

"Seems there's some concern about possible instability in our country. They are concerned the upcoming elections might not be fair, and I could be a dictator who has you and Parliament in my pocket." The man opened his mouth to speak, but the president raised his hand to stop him. "Mr. Opperman, I mean no disrespect. The candidate you and the others have put forth is a worthy opponent who under normal circumstances could easily defeat me. But we both understand that isn't going to happen."

Kirk Opperman pulled his shoulders back then raised his chin. "You have outstayed your usefulness to us, Baboloki. Power has made you drunk on your own inflated importance. It is time to show the country change with a new face. The world is leaving us behind."

"Not so many years ago, you wished for me to keep the world at bay, and I have done that for you and your greedy mining operations. You get rich while our neighbors wallow in war and poverty because somehow you allow them to have enough conflict diamonds to keep things stirred up."

"You have turned a blind eye to such practices, and we've lined your pockets with incredible wealth."

"And for that price I have kept tribal interference to a minimum, not to mention their demands for better health care, education, and technology. Can you imagine what would happen if the outside world reached into the Kalahari and delta regions?" The president paused as a waiter stopped to take his empty glass then continued, "It makes no difference to me if legislation would tax you at a greater rate to make these things happen. I would simply disappear with all my millions and leave you to stew in your own sludge of corruption."

"You seem to forget there are those of us who remember your dirty secrets, the imprisoned teachers and community leaders who dared speak out against you," Opperman snarled. "Do not threaten me."

Tessa Scott and Captain Hunter entered the dining room and were ushered toward the veranda. The conversation needed to be concluded. "One more interesting note for you, Kirk." The president let a smile spread across his face. "The lady coming through the door says she believes the Kifaru diamond has returned to Botswana." He enjoyed the look of horror on the man's face. "If that is true, then I suspect you are in for some extreme changes around here."

"You've got to find out who has it," he snapped.

"Ahh. So you need me again. Touching." The president patted the man on the shoulder as he stepped toward his new guests. "I'm always willing to serve my people and my country, Kirk. Remember that stability in Africa comes with a hefty price tag."

"And an inflated ego is no match for the man who possesses the Kifaru," Opperman growled through clenched teeth. "Introduce me," he ordered as he joined the president moving toward the Americans.

Chase laid a hand on Tessa's back, sliding his hand up and down her soft, cool skin several times before she turned a narrowed gaze toward him. The strapless white dress hugged her figure enough to make him stumble into a library table when she'd joined him in the lobby of their hotel. Fortunately, she hadn't reacted to his discomfort and admiration. She'd tied her blonde curls into a knot at the base of her neck, but a few still managed to escape to frame her face. The pearl earrings and bracelet added an elegance he appreciated on such a beautiful woman.

He leaned down to whisper in her ear. "Here they come. Do not, and I mean do not, get far from me tonight." She turned her blue eyes on him and for a second, he lost his train of thought. Her lips were close to his since he hadn't withdrawn from her ear. He wondered if Tessa might be teasing him when she shifted her gaze to his mouth. Then she broke the spell.

"Get your hands off me," she whispered sweetly. "You don't need to mark your territory. I'll stick to you like glue."

He offered a chuckle as the two men stepped closer. "That brings a whole new image to mind."

"You're impossible," she growled then faced their host, smiling. "President Baboloki, you've created a beautiful atmosphere for dinner."

The president lifted her hand to his lips for a short kiss then hooked it through his arm. With a gentle shove, she left Chase's side. "This is Kirk Opperman. He owns the Camelthorn Mines throughout Southern Africa."

Chase shook hands, and small talk ensued for a few minutes before the president drifted away, introducing Tessa to several couples. With drink in hand, he trailed them at a respectable distance, trying to listen to Opperman while keeping track of Tessa. It would be typical of her to forget President Baboloki left a bloody trail of people who dared oppose him or got in his way.

"I understand you believe the Kifaru diamond has surfaced?" Opperman finally got Chase to stop and focus on something other than Tessa.

"Rumors mostly. I read the diamond has great significance to the Tswana people of this country. Why is that?"

Opperman took out a cigarette, offered one to Chase who shook his head, and lit up. After taking several drags, he nodded. "Superstition, mostly. The original owner of the diamond found it and convinced his clan such a rare gem meant prosperity and health to the tribal people, that they would rule the country."

"Well, President Baboloki has ruled for thirty, or is it thirty-five years? You aren't at war with any tribal clans. Terrorist groups have been kept at bay, and tourism has returned. Sounds like you're doing fine." Chase quickly located Tessa talking to a man wearing the white collar of a priest.

"True. However, all good things come to an end, do they not?"

"Is that Desmond Tutu my friend is talking to?" Leave it to Tessa to find a holy man.

"Yes. I believe it is," Opperman said before taking another sip of his drink. "And although good things do come to an end, it makes sense to see if improvements need to be explored. If the people decide they want change, it is usually best to find out why and how you can make that happen, hopefully with little conflict."

Chase took a glass of champagne from a tray offered by a passing waiter. After downing the drink, he examined the remaining drops. Would Tessa ever try such a delicate drink? She could use a little loosening up.

"Our people want the changes people everywhere want: better infrastructure, health care, and technology. At the same time, some of the things we lack are exactly what brings tourism and needed dollars into this country. Adventure seekers don't want to go on safari and see a satellite dish or microwave tower jutting up out of the savanna or delta. They want the adventure of a lifetime, the National Geographic postcard version of their dreams." Opperman gulped down the rest of his drink and gritted his teeth. "Baboloki buys good whiskey; I'll say that for him."

"Maybe I'll try that later."

Tessa excused herself to freshen up. After such a delicious meal and heavy dessert, she wanted to escape the nonstop questions from strangers about her work, American politics, and her favorite television drama from Hollywood. The powder room had been created for events such as this so multiple women could use it. There was another across the hall for men. When she washed her hands, a tall black woman entered and set a basket of paper towels on the counter.

"Good evening." Tessa recognized the woman who had watched her from a window earlier in the day. Up close, she looked older than she'd thought. "Oh. I saw you today. Do you live here?"

"No," she said taking one of the paper towels and wiping down the drops of water.

Tessa did the same. "Sorry. I didn't mean to make a mess. I had to step away for a few minutes."

She nodded but said nothing.

When the woman stretched out her arm to throw the towels in the trash, she revealed scarred forearm. She pulled her sleeve down and leveled a glare at Tessa.

Tessa turned to face the wallpaper with its intricate design of tiny black rhinos jammed together in circles.

"Kifaru," Tessa said. The woman gazed at her with new interest. "Black Rhino."

The woman's eyes watered. "The Kifaru killed everything and everyone I loved. It is vile. You best not mention it in these halls." She stiffened her back, raised her chin, and left.

Tessa turned to run after her, but paused to grab her purse. When she entered the hall, the woman was nowhere in sight.

~ ~ ~

"You smell like a brewery," complained Tessa as she and Chase walked to their rooms in the boutique hotel. She decided to discuss the encounter with the woman later. He was a handful at the moment.

Chase stretched his arms out then, touching his nose successfully. Next, he walked an imaginary straight line and managed to pull it off until the last step when he stumbled and nearly fell. Tessa hurried to his side then pushed in front of him before relieving him of his key. When she attempted to slip it into the lock, he pressed up against her and took a deep whiff of her hair.

A disgruntled growl escaped her clenched teeth as she swung open the door and slipped her arm around his waist. "Come on, big guy. You're a bit tipsy."

He leaned into her as they passed through the door and kicked it shut with the sole of his shoe. "I'm not tipsy. I'm on the short road to being drunk." He grabbed Tessa's hand and tugged her after him toward the bed. "You were beautiful tonight. Did I tell you that?"

Tessa pried at his fingers and sighed. "Yes. With each drink you took, I became closer to being goddess of the Universe, I'm sure."

He chuckled deep in his throat, reminding her the man was not to be trusted unless you believed werewolves were misunderstood characters who needed some TLC.

"I like that. Goddess of the Universe. It's good to have a nickname." He eyed her hungrily as he loosened his tie. "Maybe you should help me get undressed and tuck me into bed since you think I need to be taken care of."

Tessa crossed her arms across her chest since his gaze lingered a little too long there and then huffed out a retort. "Well that is a fine howdy-do, Chase Hunter. You have to get drunk to make a pass at me. You're despicable and a coward." She watched him flop down on the edge of the bed.

She pivoted on her heel and moved to the interior door to her adjoining room. The squeak of bedsprings drew her sideways glance back to Chase who stalked like a lion toward her. At the touch of his hand on her shoulder, she fell back against the door, weak in the knees, and staring up into his dark eyes.

"Don't be like that, baby. Stay and talk to me a while. You know, like we used to do before you went to—well—" His hand brushed her cheek, but she jerked her face away.

"Afghanistan?" she interrupted. "Everything always comes back to that, doesn't it? Is that why you've been giving me the cold shoulder for months?"

"I wanted to give you some space. Some time to heal." He leaned into her, a lopsided pout on his mouth. "Here we are in Africa. Alone and—"

"Drunk."

"Not quite, but close. Watching you tonight with Baboloki drove me crazy. I don't trust the guy, and he kept checking you out. You and that sexy dress of yours." He slid his hand down her arm but she quickly knocked it away.

"What about the Captain Hunter code—no married women or Enigma agents?"

His voice lowered. "Rules were made to be broken."

"Ugh!" She shoved at his chest with more strength than she believed possible. He stepped back.

Tessa reached behind her for the doorknob and twisted. A gush of warm air hit her in the face from her open windows. She froze, as a shadow moved toward the sheer curtains that lifted like ghostly fingers. A shattering noise preceded the man's escape to the outside, and she screamed Chase's name.

Chapter Five

Chase raced for the window but stumbled over clutter on the floor, giving the intruder precious seconds to escape into the night. The light spilling in from his room illuminated Tessa standing inside the door with her hands covering her mouth. He turned on the bedside lamp and took a quick survey of the room. With everything in disarray, he came to the obvious conclusion they'd either been robbed or someone wanted information. Chase guessed the latter.

He stumbled back to Tessa who trembled, stripped of her snarky attitude. She fell against him and circled his waist as he wrapped his arms around her. Resting his chin on the top of her head, he inhaled the fragrance of her warm hair as the touch of her fingers spread out against his back. Her rapid heartbeat reminded him he'd nearly lost her once and had no intention of ever letting that happen again.

When he tried to step back, Tessa pulled him tighter and shivered. Even though she pretended to be brave, she considered spiders a serious terrorist threat to women everywhere. This time he ran his hands down her arms before stepping back to arm's length.

"It's okay. Thank goodness you didn't go in the front door. You do understand we share a room from here on out. Right?"

She nodded like a scared little girl.

"Good. Let's figure out what they wanted, but I think I already know. Then we'll call the front desk. Do you mind fixing me some coffee? I'm not all that clearheaded." She nodded and stepped back into his room and soon heard her pouring water into the single cup coffee maker. A few minutes later she brought him a cup.

Chase eyeballed the room again while the steam from the coffee curled upward toward his nose. He rested his lips on the rim of the porcelain cup, waiting for the brew to cool enough to sip the black goodness. "Better check," he mumbled.

Tessa moved to the desk where she kept her laptop and notes. "Gone. They were after the source of the Kifaru."

"They didn't waste any time taking the bait. But to come here—I didn't expect they'd be so brazen. Somebody is a little too anxious to find our guy."

Tessa returned to his side, hugged her body. "I hope we haven't put Handsome in danger."

"He can take care of himself. We need to make sure the people of the outer villages don't suffer from Baboloki's insecurity." He took a drink of the coffee. "Nothing like a little adrenaline to sober a guy up." He dropped a narrowed gaze on Tessa who put on a good show of calm. "You okay?"

"Of course." She turned to go back in his room, but he cut her off.

"Call the desk. Sound hysterical. I promise to be the irate partner. We're not staying in these rooms tonight."

Tessa lifted the phone and dialed the front desk.

The coffee woke Chase up enough that he felt wired. He stepped to the sofa in the second-floor room where Tessa slept and watched her for longer than he should have. She tossed and turned while he contacted the team and Director Clark back in the States to catch everyone up on the day's events. Jet lag never got easy, and Tessa seemed to suffer from that as well. After he insisted she take some Benadryl, it didn't take long for her to fall into a deep sleep.

The air-conditioning held the room to about seventy. He liked it cooler but it kicked off when he tried to lower the thermostat. Tessa drew up her bare legs and snuggled into the pillow she'd taken from the full-size bed. He covered her with the blanket. The white dress left too much skin exposed.

There remained the effect on his body from her helpless gratitude toward him. She'd stayed at his side when he flew into a rage at the desk manager, demanding different rooms. When the man announced only one other was available, she'd looked up at Chase with gratitude.

"Let's share." She'd slipped her hand in his and squeezed before turning back to the anxious manager and security guard. He drew her close and kissed her temple. This cooled his heels almost instantly. The manager sighed, offered his apologies several times, and rubbed his hands together. Tessa sniffed back a tear and laid her head against Chase when the hotel security guard offered to walk them to their new room. Her acting ability remained top-notch.

This could be the perfect opportunity to take advantage of her hero worship. But making love to Tessa Scott would mess with his ability to think straight. When and if that ever happened, his next move would be to get her out of Enigma and some place safe—forever. Such a scenario involved her kids and her lame brained husband, who he should have taken care of months ago. He clenched his teeth multiple times, wanting to remove Robert Scott from Tessa's life. Had he really sunk so low he'd consider bodily harm to an innocent to get what he wanted?

When she took a deep breath, he touched her shoulder then toyed with the blanket, pretending to make sure she remained comfortable, when in reality he longed to create a world where she became obsessed with loving him.

He bolted the door then pushed a chest in front of it for extra protection in case he fell asleep.

The springs squeaked when he sat on the foot of the bed. Removing his shirt and tie helped him relax even as he stared longingly at his newest agent. The belt came off next along with his trousers before he slipped into lightweight khakis. Normally he slept in boxers or nothing at all, but he needed to be ready to move fast in an emergency. Besides, the more clothes he wore when Tessa occupied his space, the better things stayed in perspective. He ran the palm of his hand over his face as fatigue washed over him. A yawn followed a roll his shoulders.

His mental checklist turned to Handsome Jones. What was he up to, and why? Did he have connections to the village where almost everyone had been slaughtered? Was the Canadian doctor somehow involved? They would know soon enough. The State Department made plans for them to visit a new clinic in a remote part of the Okavango Delta after coordinating with UN personnel in the Nairobi, Kenya office. They didn't need any more trouble in Africa. Botswana remained stable for the time being, and the rumors of discontent created a sense of urgency.

Whatever Handsome planned, it involved the Kifaru diamond. How he'd found it remained a mystery. Why did he care what went on in this part of the world? Did he have something to gain by interfering in the politics of a relatively stable country? He had the Kifaru months ago and entrusted it to Tessa. Why not sell it for the millions it would bring instead of opposing a thug like Baboloki? Tessa's research failed to uncover any connection between the pair.

Taking a deep breath, he walked to the lamp near the window and clicked it off. Then, he pulled back the curtain to survey the lighted grounds below. Nothing appeared out of sync with the surroundings. A step away from the window, he turned to gaze down at Tessa who'd rolled to her side. Her arm dangled over the edge of the sofa and a bare foot pushed out from under the blanket. He remembered how ticklish her feet were and guessed if he touched a toe she would kick even in a deep sleep. Moving up to where her head lay, he could see her lips parted, and her breathing came a little too fast for someone supposed to be sound asleep.

With his index finger, he pushed several curls away from her delicate face and considered kissing the spot he'd freed from their unruliness. He withdrew to the bed, afraid one thing would lead to another if he didn't rein in his pathetic attraction to something he didn't deserve.

He lay on top of the covers, hands behind his head, staring at the ceiling, still unable to shut off his thoughts. The sound of Tessa tossing and turning drew his attention again. She mumbled in a language that sounded like Pashtu, the language of Afghanistan. He recognized some of the words. Was she dreaming of the tribesman who'd kidnapped her or the terrible things she'd done to survive?

The Enigma psychiatrist kept him informed of her progress without jeopardizing the confidentiality rule. According to him, Tessa had forgiven herself and put those days behind her. Nightmares had become fewer as the weeks and months passed. If that were true, why did she grow more agitated by the second?

Tessa jumped off the couch and ran to the blocked door. She frantically tried to move the chest of drawers, panting between sobs.

Chase came to her side. "Tessa. Tessa," he cooed. "It's me. Chase." When he dared lay a hand on her arm, she swung around and landed a fist on his shoulder then aimed at his jaw. Catching her small hand in his, he witnessed terror filling her wide eyes. "Tessa. Come back to me," he said in a reassuring voice. "You're having a nightmare."

Her body went limp, and she dropped her hands to her side. Leaning forward, she rested her cheek against his chest. Stroking the back of her head, he waited for her to swim up from her tortured dreams. He felt the sweat on her neck and back and once more blamed himself for abandoning her in Afghanistan. If he had a redo he would shun his duty and evacuate her to a safer place.

"I'm sorry," she whispered. "It was so real."

"Does this happen often?"

"Not for a long time. Maybe the stranger in my room triggered it. Guess I'm a coward."

Chase chuckled and rubbed her back vigorously. "A pain in the butt, yes. A coward, no."

Landing a gentle fist to his abs, Tessa pushed away. "Sorry if I woke you."

"I hadn't gone to sleep." He took her hand and led her to the bed. "Sleep here. You'll be more comfortable. I don't mind the couch or the floor."

"Is this going to be one of those times when you say that then in the morning I find you next to me?" She tried to cover a yawn. "I'll take the couch. Thanks for the rescue." She slipped away from him.

"It's what I live for," he mocked in a deep voice, drawing another chuckle from her as she lay down.

"Good night, big guy. I'll try not to be so needy the rest of the night. One of these times I'm going to save your hide. I promise."

"And I promise to give you a reward fit for a hero."

"Code for inappropriate, I'm sure," she spoke in a low voice.

"Absolutely."

They talked for a while longer until conversation gradually fell away. Chase stopped fighting sleep and imagined the two of them ending each day like this, only with her next to him. This picture often formed in his mind and kept him from going to the dark place he'd been before they'd met. Even if this was all they ever shared, it was better than nothing.

CHAPTER SIX

"Here is the information pulled off the woman's computer, Mr. President." His head of security laid a plain file folder down on Baboloki's uncluttered desk then exited the room as the president turned from the large window overlooking the palace gardens.

President Baboloki resisted picking up the folder since he already knew most of what it contained. He'd waited up for the first bits of information to be brought to him in the early morning hours despite dozing off several times. He'd refrained from drinking too much alcohol during dinner, but after turning fifty-eight, the temptation to steal a nap here and there had become a habit.

His toned body appeared strong and fit for someone his age, but he knew better. The dark-black skin was free of the wrinkles and scars that came with stress, manipulation, and deceit. This part of his job gave him pleasure rather than concern. The euphoric sensation of power bestowed a fountain of youth on his calm exterior.

Only when events, people, or overcooked food failed him did he notice creases around his large round eyes. He'd trained his staff to recognize when his wide nostrils flared, to expect condemnation or retribution swiftly. It proved better to beg for forgiveness than to explain. Even this gave him pleasure in a peculiar way. Better for them to fear and respect him than to take matters into their own hands and cause a coup or, worse, a free and legal election. How absurd would that be in Africa?

Another tap at the door preceded the entrance of a skinny girl of no more than fifteen. She slipped in, burdened with a tray holding a silver coffee service and a china plate stacked with biscuits and jam. He pointed to a table in front of his leather couch then picked up the file folder. When the sound of the door closed, Baboloki moved to the couch and flopped down like a tired lion then slipped on a pair of reading glasses he kept on the end table then opened the folder.

One section, highlighted in yellow, jumped out at him immediately. He leaned forward to read it a second time as his blood pressure increased. Heat flushed his cheeks. In seconds, he'd called Kirk Opperman.

"We have a problem."

~ ~ ~

"You look a little green, Tessa," Carter Johnson said, leaning in front of her to look out the window of their small plane. He sat between her and Samantha Cordova. Chase was in the front with the pilot, over Carter's objections. After all, he was a pilot and Chase wasn't. If push came to shove, taking over the plane would be no big deal for him. But sandwiched between two of his favorite ladies, he decided he'd come out ahead.

In such tight quarters, Tessa's cheek touched his when she turned to look at him. He wrinkled his nose in mischief and pressed a little closer. "You okay?" he continued.

Tessa grabbed his hand when the plane bounced. "I'm going to be sick."

Chase stole a glance back at her and then passed a small brown paper bag to Carter who immediately folded it. "I'm going to tuck this into your shirt, sweetness, so don't slap me. It will make you feel better within a minute or two."

"Okay," she mumbled with a nod and raised her chin and opened her collar.

"No worries." He smiled like a little boy then spread open her collar wide enough that two more buttons popped open. He could see her black lacy bra and puzzled once more what Chase Hunter was waiting on to claim this little piece of heaven.

"The plane is bouncing because of turbulence, not engine problems. The heat rises up from the savanna floor in the afternoon and causes this uneven motion." He patted the bag and adjusted it so that it slid down slightly. Reaching into her blouse, he slowly pulled it up as his eyes caressed hers with the kind of come-hither look that got him into trouble from time to time.

She lowered her chin sharply and pushed his hand away.

"Just trying to make you comfortable."

"Stop it," she groaned.

Chase turned around in his seat again. "Problem?" he growled.

"Carter is getting a little handy," Samantha snapped, shoving an elbow into Carter.

Carter's body twitched at her jab, his laughter suddenly filling the plane. "No worries, boss. She'll be right as rain in a minute."

"Tess?" Chase inquired. "Did you see the elephants below?"

She shook her head. "I don't care," she breathed.

"Coming in," Chase informed the group. "We're landing on that strip of land next to the delta."

"Thank you, Jesus," Tessa mumbled.

Carter was amused once more as Chase offered encouragement with a sympathetic nod. Tessa gave a thumbs-up indicating improvement. He didn't understand those two. Best friends, or at least they pretended to be in public, drew a great deal of speculation at Enigma. Chase still managed to have a string of women at the university interested him and didn't try to hide the fact those relationships were more physical than emotional. But when it came to Tessa, he morphed into a knight in shining armor, her constant protector and companion. How did he do it?

Carter glanced over at Samantha, his partner on missions like these, and hoped he didn't slip in his drool when he exited the plane. She continued to be the most beautiful woman he'd ever known and the most frustrating. No matter how many times he'd suggested they get better acquainted, Sam continued to rebuff him with a mixture of annoyance and apathy.

But there had been moments when she'd touched him, pulled him from the fire of disaster, defended him to the director or Chase. Maybe he would eventually win her affection, if not her heart. Baiting her into anger was a pastime he enjoyed and, if truth be told, he believed she took pleasure in the activity, too. She bordered on being sadistic, so she gave as good as she got. Playing hard to get might be a good strategy.

The wheels touched down, rocking the plane slightly, as Samantha pointed to the blue delta. "Oh look, Betty Crocker, there's your twin."

Tessa leaned forward to see her pointing to a hippopotamus slipping into the water. "Bite me," she moaned, still a bit pale.

"Gladly," Carter said then chomped his teeth together. "How ya feeling, sweetness?"

Tessa liked him, bad humor and all, but it was because he'd been an astronaut, and in her head that meant hero, smart, risk-taker, badass. She nodded and pulled the bag from her blouse. "Better. What is in the bag to make the motion sickness disappear?"

"Nothing," Carter said, taking it from her. "You focused on the bag instead of the motion, and you got better. Simple trick. Works every time."

"Amazing. Thanks, Carter," she said bumping his shoulder with hers.

He winked at her. What a nice lady she was; one that had no business in Enigma. "I'll make a pilot out of you yet. Lessons begin when we get back."

Samantha offered an exasperated "humph" as she unbuckled her seat belt. "Be careful if he wants to put the plane on autopilot."

Carter wrinkled his nose at Sam. "Then, next time, don't be sending me mixed signals."

Samantha rolled her eyes. "You wish."

"On every star I see, Agent Cordova."

"Enough," warned Chase. He thanked the pilot for a safe trip and informed them he'd fly to their end destination to drop off their luggage so it would be waiting for them when they arrived.

"Oh. My. Gosh." Tessa looked around her in awe when her feet touched earth. "I'm really in Africa. I'll check this off my bucket list."

Carter watched his boss roll his broad shoulders after being in such tight quarters and understood more than their innocent Mrs. Tessa Scott, this wasn't just an African adventure. Both he and Chase carried weapons, and he for one didn't like the idea of hippos, elephants, and crocodiles moving in the same geography as them. The real concern could be the trouble brewing between the villages and Gaborone, the capital city. A man walked forward from the edge of a stand of trees and waved his hat in big wide movements.

The instinct to take Tessa's hand as they approached the white man in a pith helmet standing at the tree line, forced Chase to keep shifting his glances at his team to make sure they were alert. Of course, Tessa had that pie-in-the-sky look about her like she'd fallen into a Tarzan movie and would soon be the target of adventure and the main character of a story around the campfire. She even pointed to a pile of elephant dung like it might be the Holy Grail and giggled like a schoolgirl.

"This is so great," she said with excitement. None of the others expressed any enthusiasm for pachyderm poop.

Chase took her elbow to guide her after she stumbled over a branch the size of a baseball bat. "Watch where you're going. This ain't Disney World's Animal Kingdom."

Instead of jerking away like she ordinarily would, Tessa hooked her arm through his. "I know! Right?"

He couldn't resist a grin at her wide, excited eyes that matched the blue of the Okavango water. "Try to show a little restraint," he warned.

"You guys can be restrained all you want. I've dreamed of this since I was a little girl. This is fantastic." She laid her other hand on his arm, and he flexed his muscles under her tender touch.

He loved how life inspired her, but Africa was a combination of mystery, danger, and death. She probably would think the bite of a black mamba an educational experience. He stole a glance down at her feet to make sure she'd worn boots instead of those sparkly flip-flops she'd brought along. It would be like her to want to dip her toes in the Okavango and end up stepping on a disgruntled snake.

"Good afternoon. I'm Dr. Girard. I've been expecting you." The man at the tree line greeted them with his hand outstretched toward Chase. "Flight a little bumpy? Watched that bird dip a couple of times as you were descending."

"Not too bad or unexpected." Chase put on his friendly expression then introduced the others. The doctor inspected Tessa for a few extra seconds as if in some kind of recognition.

"Mrs. Scott. May I call you Tessa?" the doctor asked as he fanned out his hand toward a path leading through the trees.

"I wish you would." Tessa sounded cheerful and moved up alongside the doctor, leaving the protective arm of Chase. "We've been excited to meet you and see the work you've been doing here." She twisted her head around, sometimes bending down to look through brush and trees. "Are we safe to walk through here?"

"Quite safe," the doctor encouraged. "There is so much activity that the animals don't come around in the day. The nighttime is another matter. Mostly small game, an occasional hippo or elephant but other than that, nothing to be concerned about. Most of the big game will be where you're headed later today. You probably spotted some movement from the plane."

"I'm afraid I was too queasy to open my eyes," she admitted.

The doctor chuckled. "Well, no matter. You'll see plenty by the time you arrive at Camp Kubu. Come. We've prepared a small lunch for you. Then we'll have a tour of our clinic and school."

"Sounds perfect." Tessa sounded enthusiastic. Chase zeroed in on her, willing her to be careful, but she turned away and continued chatting with the doctor.

She wanted things to be right with the world, exciting to explore and nothing to worry about in spite of the scare at the hotel. That characteristic remained one of the many things he loved about her, but this wasn't the time or place to get careless.

He remembered earlier in the morning when the rays of light pushed through the windows. The image of tangled blond hair and a sheet half-draped across her body... She'd accepted his mandate to stay with him without complaint. While he made coffee, Chase had watched her come to life. The awareness he needed to stop kidding himself about having a relationship with her weighed heavier each day.

He caught the are-you-kidding-me look in Carter's eye. His friend believed he should take what he wanted. But he couldn't break his own rules. She was a married agent. The agent thing was an easy fix; the husband, not so much. A frown seemed to get Carter back on track with observing his surroundings. Sam never wavered, always the agent he could bank on to go by the book.

"Some of the villagers have planned a surprise I hope you'll enjoy." Dr. Girard raised his voice so everyone could hear his announcement.

The doctor led them to a white cinder block building in a clearing where the ground had been stomped down so little vegetation grew. A few chickens searched for food and scattered when a couple of near-naked little boys chased them. The smell of smoke and meat cooking over an open fire drew them to a pergola-like structure covered in vines and thatch where a long table had been prepared with cans of Coca Cola, plastic cutlery, disposable plates still in their cellophane bags, and centerpieces created from tin cans filled with nature's adornments like twigs and flowers from nearby bushes. The simplicity of it all drew praise from Tessa as some ladies stood nearby waiting to begin serving the meal of boiled potatoes, okra, and onions, along with barbecued beef steaks and something that looked like chicken.

"Hmm. Smells wonderful, Dr. Girard." Tessa swung a leg over one of the benches as several little girls rushed up and pointed to her hair. She laughed and untied the ponytail that had begun to come loose then shook her head, and the mass of curls fell like gold ringlets over her face and ears. The girls giggled and covered their mouths as one attempted to touch her hair but jerked her hand back when a woman admonished her. Tessa took the little girl's hand and placed it on her curls. The others eased up and did the same while the women laughed at the effort Tessa attempted toward friendship.

Dr. Girard clapped his hands, and the girls scattered. "You have made them very happy. They say your hair feels like the cotton in my clinic." He motioned for the three ladies to begin their tasks. "You have won their hearts. Thank you. Not many of our guests put up with the children."

Chase straddled the bench next to Tessa, wanting to draw her close. "Tessa used to be a teacher. She's great with kids."

"Yes. So, I understand." Dr. Girard popped open a Coke.

"And how did you hear that?" Chase's radar went up.

"When your State Department inquired about a visit, the UN provided me with some background on you." He lifted his chin toward Sam who sat across from Tessa. "Dr. Cordova is an economist, interested in the geo-political movement of goods and services in Africa and has been a frequent advisor to the UN in Nairobi and Bangkok. Dr. Johnson, former astronaut, has been studying the effects of global warming and the ozone layer on the increased desertification of Africa."

Carter nodded with a finger salute.

"And me, Dr. Girard?" Chase took one of the Cokes and popped it open, irritated there was no fizz or sound of freshness.

"It is my understanding that in addition to being a literature professor and doing research into the folklore of desert tribes, your former military training has put you in the unique position of offering protection to Mrs. Scott—sorry, I mean Tessa—especially since she is a representative of your State Department. The UN suggested we have someone who could handle a situation if one arose."

As a plate of food was placed in front of each guest, the doctor hurried away to attend to an emergency. The team ate in silence as the heat of the day begin to press upon them. A slight breeze stirred up an occasional wall of dust.

"Delicious. Good as Baboloki's feast." Tessa licked the sauce from her fingers and managed to get a drop on her shirt.

"You really are a hillbilly, Tessa," snorted Sam who had managed to be perfect.

"And proud of it," she cooed, swinging her legs over the bench. The ladies pointed out a washroom inside the clinic once Tessa displayed her messy hands to her new friends. "I'll be right back and bring some wet towels for the rest of you hillbillies."

Good-natured laughter filled the air as Tessa disappeared inside the building. Chase wanted to follow but decided he'd give her some space since she only meant to wash up.

~ ~ ~

Tessa splashed some cold water on her face after running some water over her hands. Having read up on the geography element of the area for months, she read this water was the purest in Africa because it came straight out of the Okavango and most likely safe. She ran wet fingers through her hair since a single stained towel hung lopsided on a hook next to a toilet. As she walked out the door, she tied her hair up to cool her neck.

"I didn't know how long it would be before you found me, Tessa." A large figure emerged from the shadows.

Tessa gasped then stole a glance out the door to see if she could spot her friends. "H-Handsome," she stuttered.

"You don't have to worry. I mean you no harm."

Dr. Girard walked briskly into the hall and stopped so fast Handsome had to grasp his arm to keep him from colliding into him. "Oh. I didn't see you, Son." The doctor patted Handsome on the back.

"Son?" Tessa whispered.

Chapter Seven

"Yes." Dr. Girard turned to Handsome and patted his much-larger arm. "Louis is my son." His eyes held questions as he glanced between the two. "Didn't he tell you?"

"I may have left that part out." Handsome slipped an arm around the doctor and hugged the man. "No worries. Please do not be telling people that. We've talked about this."

"Oh. Right. Sorry." The doctor patted his son on the cheek. "It's, well, here all seems right with the world, like we've come home. And I believe your Tessa Scott has your confidence." He offered Tessa a rather sheepish look. "You do understand the importance of keeping this quiet?"

Did her eyes reveal the shock she felt, even though she had suspected the truth all along? "I'm beginning to, Dr. Girard. This is a very dangerous situation."

"Yes." The doctor hung his head. "I'm very aware. It has been a long time coming. My son trusts you, and so do I."

"With all due respect, Dr. Girard. We've just met."

The doctor suddenly frowned at his son.

"Don't worry, Father. I'll take care of this. Why don't you go back to see to our guests and have something to eat? Soon you'll need to get back to your patients."

He offered a weak smile then nodded toward Tessa before exiting, leaving a heavy silence to well up between the two.

"The Kifaru?" Handsome's voice turned cold, void of the warm emotion shown to Dr. Girard. "Where is it?"

"Safe." Tessa rubbed her hands down the sides of her khaki shorts until Handsome let his focus drop to her nervous motion. "I mean"— She lowered her voice; someone might be listening—"I don't think we should be talking about this here."

Handsome raised his chin and peered down his wide nose at her. Perspiration trickled down one side of his brow until it dripped off his jaw. "Perhaps you're right." He looked behind him then to each side. "I am glad you're here."

"I'll bet you are." Chase stepped out of a shadowy hall with his Glock leveled at Handsome's chest. "I have a bone to pick with you." He nodded to Tessa. "Frisk him."

"But—"

"Do it," he growled without taking his glare from Handsome.

Tessa huffed her protest then stepped closer to Handsome. "Sorry," she sighed.

Chase stopped her from reaching out by holding up his free hand. "Assume the position, Handsome, or whoever you are."

With a chuckle, he faced a wall and leaned in obediently.

"Go ahead," Chase ordered Tessa.

This was her first time to perform a search on anyone besides one of her kids hiding a frog, cricket, or princess ring supposedly found on the sidewalk in front of the Old Fashion Mercantile in downtown Grass Valley. Something about running her hands up and down the inside of Handsome's legs didn't make her feel like Jethro Gibbs on NCIS like she'd imagined.

"He's good." She took a step back so he could turn around.

"Thank you, Tessa, for giving me something to think about when you're gone." Handsome cooed as his eyes became hooded and his lips pooched out before shifting his contempt toward Chase.

Chase squinted as if the sun blinded him then holstered his weapon under his loose tee shirt and safari vest.

"Where's my diamond?" Handsome asked for the second time then pushed past the two agents.

"We agreed to not talk here," Tessa gasped as she hurried to catch up with him.

He stopped and turned around so suddenly she crashed into his chest and bounced off into Chase who caught her in his arms. He quickly stepped in front of her. "You're dealing with me, not Tessa."

A smirk toyed with his thick lips. "I don't suppose I have a choice, since you hold my future."

"Your future?" Chase chuckled. "Guess you have let the expectation of power go to your head. Oh, wait. You think you're going to unseat the most respected man in Southern Africa and change everything because of a glorified rock that used to be a lump of carbon," he laughed.

"He is a thug who walks on the backs of these people."

"Ahh. And you're such a good guy." Chase took a threatening step closer, his body becoming rigid. "I know this because you left us stranded in the Sierra Mountains."

"Looks like you did okay."

"No thanks to you. It might surprise you to know an avalanche knocked the cabin off its foundation and nearly killed us."

Handsome looked at Tessa.

She nodded to confirm the truth.

"Yet you survived as always. This poses the question: how many lives does an Enigma agent have?" His frown deepened. "And the diamond?"

"Handsome!" Tessa pushed forward and between the two men. "Please. Not here." Her voice dropped to a loud whisper. "You have nothing to worry about." She touched his arm. "But you're going to have to fill us in so we can help you."

"Help him?" Chase snapped. "Why don't we swim with crocodiles while we're at it?"

Tessa rammed her elbow back into her boss's midsection. "I'm on your side, Handsome. You've got to trust someone. It might as well be us."

His mouth widened, revealing good teeth, unlike the people she'd seen outside; an obvious sign of overall health in the Western world. "Go finish your meal. Some of the people from the village have prepared entertainment for you. Then my father will show you around the clinic and the work we've accomplished." He lifted his eyes over her head to stare at Chase. "I will take you by boat to your camp. We can talk safely along the way."

~ ~ ~

Although they'd left sunny California at the beginning of the summer season, here in the Okavango it was winter. Most people believed Africa a hot dry place, picturing the Sahara Desert or dense jungles where tribal people danced around naked with a bone in their nose.

Chase could not understand how the most powerful country in the world could be so ignorant of all aspects of geography. Schools in the US chose to focus on reading and math for better test scores. In taking that path, American students became more focused on their own self-importance than ever before.

Even those who served in the halls of government in Washington remained clueless as to the domino effect their decisions had on the world. Ask a soldier about geography. Their world view would be far different than what you got on the evening news.

Their boat cut through the calm waters of the Okavango Delta with Handsome at the rear guiding them into a postcard sunset. The eight seats available, thankfully, had failed to fill. Chase wasn't sure if Handsome orchestrated their solitude, or if any other guests had already arrived at Camp Kubu. The women sat next to each other, covered in a blanket, their cheeks rosy from the dropping temperatures and wind coming off the water.

The purr of the motor sounded almost soothing until it suddenly died and the boat rocked gently.

Carter, next to him, turned to inspect his surroundings, but Chase slipped his hand into his vest to touch his weapon, keeping his focus on Handsome.

Their guide flashed him a condescending glare. "We always stop not far from camp to let our guests drink in the beauty of the sunset on the Okavango." He lifted a Thermos and poured steaming liquid into four small porcelain cups of various colors and condition. "Temperatures drop quickly this time of day, so I brought you some tea." He served it to Carter and the women from a weathered tin tray that back home would be sold in a hobby store. Chase, declining a cup, remembered seeing a similar one in Tessa's apartment.

"Thank you, Handsome. Delicious." Sam beamed up at him then winked. "I needed this."

"Me, too," Tessa chuckled. "I was getting a little cold. This is incredible." She turned to watch the sunset. "So beautiful. How often do you come home?"

The man set the tray on a vacant seat and settled next to the women. "Not enough. After my mother died, my father tried to bring me at least once a year. As I got older, we stayed longer. He was instrumental in building the medical clinic. At first, I didn't appreciate the work he did, but, fortunately, he let me find my own way."

"What changed?" Carter asked Handsome.

Chase remained frozen and tight-lipped.

I was around fifteen when some of Baboloki's men came to the clinic to make sure we weren't treating some suspected poachers who had been spotted by the parks department during an aerial sweep. Back then, poaching the last of the black rhinos was a serious problem."

Tessa spoke in Swahili. "Kifaru."

"Yes. Every few years, rhinos would be introduced and then they would disappear. You have to understand the money obtained from taking the horn of a rhino can help a poor family survive for months in Africa."

"Still, it is tragic to lose such a magnificent animal," Sam interjected before taking another sip of tea.

"The villages couldn't understand why this kept happening. They respected the black rhino for its strength and promise to our people. Then came the day when soldiers came into the clinic and accused my father of harboring poachers."

"What happened?" Chase decided to take the last cup of tea.

Handsome squinted at the sunset before speaking. "They beat my father. He had treated a man with a wound consistent of someone who had been gored. It wasn't life-threatening and, trust me, if a rhino gores you or even steps on you, it is life-threatening. Several from a Doctors Without Borders group who'd arrived the day before, intervened and convinced them it was a mistake."

Tessa covered her mouth in shock. "Oh, Handsome. And you witnessed this?"

"Yes. Several of the villagers who volunteered at the clinic would not let me go to him or call him Father. I didn't understand they were protecting me. My father was a kind and gentle man who loved these people and had always taught me how important it was to help them. He used to say some day I would be able to make life better for them."

"No one knew you were the doctor's son?" Chase asked.

Handsome shook his head. "No. I was just someone he brought with him each time to assist. I resented it because I believed he was ashamed of me. But, that day, everything changed."

Tessa laid her hand gently on the man's arm, and he in turn patted her hand and sighed then smiled. She had a way of soothing the fiercest beast. Her techniques had worked on him in dark times. The sincerity in her touch and trust in her eyes once again activated the ache in his chest. Somehow, people always spilled their guts to her, rewarded with sympathy and understanding. Sometimes he questioned if she was human or an angel.

"Please, Handsome. Tell us," Tessa whispered.

"I ran outside and climbed a tree as the soldiers went through the clinic and stole things. They took all the drugs we had, so lifesaving surgeries had to be postponed. Several of the men met up under the tree where I hid to watch the mayhem unfold. Several of the young women who worked there joined me because they were afraid that..." He swallowed hard.

Chase nodded. "We get the picture. Go on."

"Anyway, my Tswana wasn't all that great, but good enough to understand there wasn't any poaching that day. And the rhinos' disappearance was the soldiers' doing, not the locals. Apparently, Baboloki wanted the people of the bush to understand there would never be a black rhino to ever rescue them from his leadership. The people finally stopped believing in the Kifaru. My father finally told me the story of how my birth father sacrificed everything to save me. My life really did have meaning."

"Why the hell didn't you tell us that back in the States?" Chase felt an ounce of guilt for giving the man such a hard time in the past.

"Baboloki heard rumors over the years that the heir of the Kifaru had survived the attack on my village. He was obsessed with finding the truth. I have skirted his henchmen a number of times. I'm used to hiding in plain sight."

"How does Reeva Kaplan play into all of this?" Tessa frowned.

The Enigma team had caught the South African woman in a San Francisco hotel room with Tessa's husband, Robert. His story continued to be he'd planned to purchase some high-grade diamonds for pennies on the dollar. He'd managed to secure a deal for his law firm to represent her client's interest.

Chase's team had been sent to kidnap Kaplan in order to track down her business partners and possible ties to the funding of terrorist groups. Out of loyalty to Tessa, they'd removed the half-dressed Robert from the scene before Reeva could do him any more harm.

When the FBI got involved, things went sideways. Two experienced US Marshals ended up dead. Out of thin air, Kaplan showed up to help Handsome escape his hideout in the mountains near Lake Tahoe and avoid further interrogation as to why he had gotten involved in conflict diamonds.

"Reeva Kaplan is an opportunist." Handsome shifted his gaze from Chase to Carter. "Much like Enigma and the financial dogs that fund your operations."

Tessa withdrew her hand from his arm, but he pulled it back and stroked it. "I'm sorry. You actually have a right to know. She duped your husband, by the way. His only mistake was trying to get something for little to nothing from a woman like Reeva."

The man might be lying in order to give Tessa a reason to forgive her worthless husband, especially when Handsome cut his eyes to him to see his reaction. It wasn't something out of the question, of course, since Robert liked to save a buck where he could and cut corners in order to accomplish the goal. Even if Handsome was a semi-good guy, it didn't erase the fact he'd left them stranded with no way out of a bad situation.

Chase also suspected Handsome had a soft spot for Tessa.

"Thank you for telling me that, Handsome. But why you? Why Robert?"

"Robert was in the wrong place or law firm at the wrong time. Turns out your son liked to snoop with his computer and access things he didn't understand. Those pranks led Kaplan to you and eventually your husband. I'm hoping that problem was resolved."

"Yes." Tessa squeezed his arm. "But why you?"

"Have you heard of Camelthorn?"

"We met the owner at Baboloki's when we were in Gaborone," Chase offered.

"They have always believed in the stories of the Kifaru and the power it has among the people of the Okavango and Kalahari. They want that diamond in order to put the person in power who can best represent their financial interests. At this time, it isn't clear if that would help these people. Baboloki and Camelthorn seem to be at odds for some reason. Rumors are, they believe Baboloki has become too powerful. The army listens to him, and he pays them very well. He visits them often and even, at his age, goes with them on training missions."

"A good ole boy, as we say in Texas," Carter chuckled.

"Something like that." Handsome removed Tessa's hand so he could rest his arm on the back of her chair, a movement that drew Chase's attention.

Chase hadn't decided if the man was developing a crush on his Tessa or wanted to keep him on edge. Chase arched an eyebrow at the man, but he didn't react.

"Baboloki understands the meaning of the Kifaru diamond. He wants it, but he also wants to find out if a relative of the man they called John, my birth father, still exists. That could change his comfortable lifestyle and make his army think twice about their support. Even they have family away from Gaborone, and in many parts of Africa, we remain a tribal society."

"Meaning?" Carter took his and Chase's cups and placed them on the tray.

"You don't go against your tribe, and you certainly don't turn on your clan. If they find out who I am, then all may be lost, depending what the president has promised the one who finds me. Financial security for the ones you love is a powerful motivator."

Darkness sank toward the horizon when Handsome returned to the wheel and started the engine. At a loud splash behind them, everyone turned to look. A large bull elephant moved out into deeper water and shook his head. Tessa gasped then rose to her feet, but the thrust of the engine pushed her clumsily back down.

Handsome smiled, turning to her. "That is Rambo who usually has a couple of other males with him. He likes to come into camp from time to time."

In about ten minutes, lights from a settlement appeared out of the swamp. He piloted the boat to the dock where several natives waited with warm greetings and secured the lines then helped the guests disembark.

Laughter filtered down to the group as they walked up a small hill toward a large open-air pavilion. Chase held back until Handsome came alongside him, aware of how much bigger he was. They glared at each other until Handsome spoke offhandedly.

"Did you buy any of that story I told, Captain Hunter?"

"No. Sounded a little rehearsed to me."

"I want my diamond. You're on my turf, and it is a dangerous place. I wouldn't want you wandering into a dangerous situation out here in the back end of nowhere."

"As you previously said, Enigma agents have nine lives."

"Hopefully, you haven't used yours up."

Chapter Eight

"Welcome to your first dinner with us at Camp Kubu."

The camp director stood before a blazing fire facing his guests, who were seated on cushioned rattan chairs arranged in a circle. He looked like a character from a Charlton Heston movie dressed in his olive-colored clothes with his pant legs stuffed in scuffed hiking boots. The pencil-thin mustache seemed out of place on such a wide, weathered face creased with wrinkles around the eyes and cheekbones. Salt-and-pepper hair and a toned body made it difficult to guess the age of the man who stood with his hands behind his back.

Besides the Enigma team, Chase counted six others. An older couple and a married daughter with her husband from the UK, along with two men in their late forties with German accents. Including the team, that made ten guests.

"I'm Peter Morgan. We are never strangers here at our little slice of heaven," the speaker began, pointing to the Okavango behind them. Even though darkness engulfed the landscape, everyone dutifully turned toward the intended scenery. "Let's introduce ourselves before dinner. Our American guests arrived, so we'll hold off serving until they have had a chance to refresh themselves in their quarters." He nodded toward Sam. "Why don't you go first?"

In their introductions, the Enigma team sounded like nondescript Americans who had planned their vacation months ago. A mining conference in Johannesburg and some work for the United Nations coinciding with their trip helped them choose Botswana over Kenya. The mature British couple asked some questions the kind of work brought them here, but Chase dumbed it down, explaining they were gathering statistics on the impact of the recent drought on the Okavango Delta.

With introductions concluded, the camp director insisted Handsome escort the team to their tent lodgings. He remained silent as he lumbered down a worn path, swinging his two-foot flashlight in search of danger in the brush on either side.

On a raised platform of about six feet, a white tent with a mess-screen door that zipped from top to bottom, reminded Chase of something featured in an adventure movie. A canvas camp chair sat on each side of the door next to small rattan tables the size of five-gallon buckets. The deck of their new home extended six feet with a railing formed from crude branches nailed together to look as if someone had thrown them together. All part of the charm, he guessed. At the top of the steps a lantern blazed, as well as another on one of the tables.

Tessa unexpectedly took his hand as they moved through the darkness. Surprised at her gesture, he stole a glance at her and got a timid wrinkle of her nose. Was she blushing? When they stepped up on the deck, she released his hand.

"Is this where Sam and I will stay?" she asked, walking to the tent. Silence greeted her words, and she paused to look back at them.

"No," Handsome announced. "You two are in a relationship and Carter"—he raised his chin at the other two Enigma agents— "has already made it clear he and Sam are an item." Sam elbowed Carter to move away from her.

"This is inappropriate." Tessa sounded a little more relieved than she probably would admit.

"It's me or Carter," Chase snapped, unzipping the door.

"Don't you girls go fighting over me, you hear?" Carter chuckled. "There is plenty of this"—he motioned up and down his body— "to go around. Hell, I'll take both of them."

Sam bristled. "You never cease to amaze me, Carter."

Handsome motioned for Carter and Sam to follow him to the next deck some ten feet from theirs. "Dinner is in an hour. I'll be back for you. There are flashlights in the dresser. Don't go out without taking one. Leave the lanterns on all night, even if the light bothers you. You can always drop one of the door flaps. Last week two college kids from Italy turned theirs out, and Rambo and his buddies pushed a tree on top of their tent."

"Sure. Thanks, Handsome," Chase said pulling back the door for Tessa before asking, "What's it going to be, Tessa?"

"Take a hot shower while you can," Handsome went on. "The workers built a fire under a large drum of water for you. In the morning, it will be cold. Only at night will you have hot water."

Handsome led Sam and Carter into the darkness as Tessa rubbed the sides of her capris and moved to go inside. Chase could sense her nervousness at being alone with him once more. A whiff of her body lotion touched his nose when she pushed by him, causing another one of those nagging pains in his chest. Having her alone for several nights might be a bigger challenge than keeping track of President Baboloki and Handsome.

Light spilled into the tent from the lantern outside their door. He stepped inside and zipped it back down before turning to watch Tessa inspecting their new abode. The tent interior was roughly fourteen-by-sixteen feet. Long, screened windows with outside awnings on each side of the room would keep the cool night air flowing. She stopped in front of the beds piled with white comforters and pillows.

"Twin beds," she sighed as her hand trailed across the comforter. "Soft."

Maybe the twin beds might help her relax and feel more secure with him. But the beds were butted up against each other in spite of being made up separately. There was a dresser in one corner of the room that might have been an antique. She found the flashlights and laid them on the bed. One nightstand on each side of the bed with a basket of various soaps and shampoo. She lifted one of the bars and sniffed it.

"Nice that they brought our bags," she said walking to one of two laden luggage racks. "I'm covered in dust and Okavango spray." She felt nervous and forced a laugh. She pulled out some clean clothes.

Chase went to his own suitcase and dug through his clothes. "Shower together or separate?" he asked casually. She took a step back and gasped. His resolve to be hard-nosed evaporated as she held up a clean blouse when a lacy black bra fell to the floor. Before she could snatch it up, he rescued it and handed it to her on one finger. "I vote together. Save water. Save the planet." She opened her mouth to speak, but he unzipped the back door and stood aside. "I know. I'm despicable, rude, a Neanderthal, sexist, obstinate, and, on a good day, I'm arrogant."

Her eyelashes batted, a nervous tic she displayed when unsure of herself or of him. In the last two years, he'd learned to read her body language. "On a good day, you like to be a hero."

There wasn't a possibility he hid his surprise at her comeback. "Yeah. There's that. Come on. Let's see how this shower thing works."

He grabbed one of the flashlights before exiting. He led the way through an open space leading ten feet back, framed on each side with an eight-foot bamboo wall. In the rear, they came to an open-air bathroom with walls but no ceiling, divided into three cubicles. On one side was the toilet, the middle a sink, and on the right, a shower. He turned the handle on the copper faucet, and water sputtered then flowed.

"I'm laying the flashlight on the sink. Can you see?"

"Yes. Thanks."

"I'll go get my things. Don't use it all up or next time—"

"I know. We will shower together."

Chase wanted to order her to use it all up, but suspected he'd shared enough clever insinuations for one evening. Scaring her into a snarky, unruly attitude wasn't what he wanted. It didn't take him long to gather his things.

He realized Tessa hadn't taken a towel. If he'd concentrated on the task at hand instead of a naked Tessa in the shower this wouldn't have happened. Once again, he pondered the possibilities out of his reach. They were working. If he remembered that, then maybe he wouldn't make a fool out of himself.

The squeak of the water faucet reached his ears. He guessed Tessa had finished.

"Chase?"

He snatched one of the robes folded on the ends of the beds. He didn't answer until he stood outside the bath enclosure.

"So help me if you used all of the hot water—"

"No. No. There's plenty. I-I forgot my towel."

"I guess I could dry you off with mine," he forced himself to be nonchalant.

"Or I could file a sexual harassment suit when we get back to the States."

He reached around the shower partition and tossed her a towel. "Here. I brought you this, too." He dangled the khaki colored cotton robe with the Camp Kubu logo. Grabbing for it, her damp fingers touched his.

"Okay. Harassment suit dropped." She stepped out and shivered. "Lordy, it's getting cold."

"Probably warmer in the tent." He handed her clothes to her. "You can dress there. I'll be out in a couple of minutes. Did you leave the soap?" She handed him her bar and hustled toward the tent.

The night orchestra of mysterious sounds created a surreal joy mixed with trepidation. Tessa hurried to dress in her jeans and sweater. The dappled lantern light from outside cast large shadows to further engulf her in a sense of in-over-her-head. Why hadn't she protested harder about sharing the tent with Chase?

Evidently, the man would shed his officer-and-a-gentleman cape and take advantage of the hero worship she'd found increasingly harder to hide. Admitting the truth could potentially close the gap between them. This alarmed her the most. His ethical line in the sand glowed with danger, throbbing and beckoning her to explore something she had no business even considering.

His reputation with women paralleled Carter Johnson's. Carter's cavalier attitude, however, didn't suggest there would ever be more than a one-night stand. Something about Chase hinted at a rock-solid catch who could be molded into a husband and father. Intelligent, ruggedly attractive enough to suggest he'd gathered a few battle scars in life, a quiet demeanor for the most part, and a wide mouth that drew her eyes at the most inopportune time, gave the man ample dating opportunities, if you wanted to call it that.

But Tessa knew other things about Captain Hunter, things that might scare all those doe-eyed brainy bimbos from the university away. She'd seen him shoot a man in the head after pretending to take advantage of her to lure him into a dark alley.

There were times she'd seen him use his fist like a pile driver to pound a terrorist into a bloody pulp. He had no qualms about torture or mayhem, if it helped him meet his goals. Life lessons he'd experienced had turned him cold, callous, and left him standing on the edge of disaster more times than she could remember.

Never been in love. Never cared to be. Loyalty to his country unquestionable, his belief in God needed some work as did his patience with those, like her, who failed to follow orders. But Tessa couldn't imagine her life without him since she'd experienced life at Enigma.

Sitting on the edge of the twin bed nearest the back door leading to the shower, she propped her foot on a small stool. She recognized the squeaky faucet turn off. She tried tying her boot laces over and over as she stole glances toward the bathroom enclosure until Chase emerged. His strides, although hard to make out, were not unfamiliar to her so she closed her eyes to envision him.

"Are you all right?" he asked as he unzipped the door and pushed inside. Barefoot and wearing faded jeans, his open bathrobe revealing a muscled chest still damp from the shower. Maybe she imagined the damp part.

Tessa sucked in her breath and mumbled, "I'm going straight to Hell."

"Anytime soon?" he quizzed then turned away and dug through his duffel bag.

The heat of embarrassment creeped up her throat and face. He heard that. "I'm good."

"What were you staring at when I came in? Something spook you?"

He pulled a San Francisco Giants sweatshirt over his head before putting his hands on his hips in that stubborn stance he sometimes took.

"If I'd known you were going to wear that ridiculous sweatshirt, I would have brought my St. Louis Cardinals one," she huffed trying to change the subject. Unfortunately, he didn't bite and continued that penetrating gaze that made her swoon and shiver at the same time. "Listen." She pointed to the screened window and stood up.

"Sounds like a bunch of puppies complaining."

"Fruit bats sound like puppies. They're hanging in the trees. I was concentrating on that sound is all."

"And how do you know they're fruit bats?"

"Haven't you ever read Stellaluna by Janell Cannon? My kids loved that book." His dark eyes narrowed as a cocky expression played around the corners of his mouth. "It's about a fruit bat."

"Oh. I'll be sure to put it on my reading list. Maybe you can give me a summary when we get back from dinner. It's been a while since I've had a bedtime story."

"I'm not surprised," she quipped in her most impatient voice. "I'm starved. Can we go?"

"When Handsome comes for us. What's your hurry?" Chase checked the back door then locked their luggage before turning back to her. "We could sit outside and wait if you like." When she plowed toward the front door, her foot caught on the metal leg of the bed, sending her into a clown-like stumble. Chase grabbed her and spun her body around. She landed smack against his chest.

Chapter Nine

Chase's rock-hard body pressed against her chest. His jaw clenched as Tessa stared up into his face. The friendliness in his expression immediately changed to simmering interest, his hands splayed on her back. A dignified retreat might appear clumsy at best. The warmth of his body took the chill away from her own. She tried to convince herself this was a normal reaction.

Who was she kidding? If she were a pan of cookies coming out of the oven, his hands would have third-degree burns. She tried to pull up the image of her devoted husband waiting patiently back home. Considering his shenanigans in the last few months, that wasn't going to work.

Before she could do anything foolish, Chase gently pushed her away, letting his hands slide to her arms. "You're trembling."

No kidding, Captain America. "It's really cold." A trembling voice followed by a fake effort to rub her arms was a feeble attempt at normal. He cocked his head then arched an eyebrow as if he didn't believe her.

"The water could have been hotter," he confessed.

"Yeah. I like it really hot," she chuckled, trying to hide her nervousness. When a grin lifted one corner of his mouth, she blurted out, "I mean the water." A sudden rush of heat filled her face.

"Of course. What else would you mean?" He nodded toward the bed she'd tripped over. "The leg has a slight bent angle. Probably how you caught your foot. Hard to see in the dark." He moved around her and peered out the screened front door. "Do you want me to lower the flaps for us tonight so the light won't be a problem?" When he turned his head to get an answer, Tessa let her hand go to her throat then let it slide down her chest to her waist. Chase's gaze followed the movement.

"I don't think the light will bother me. How about you?" Tessa hoped she sounded confident and blasé.

"I think having a little light would be good tonight," he offered in an even tone.

"Why do I get the feeling we're talking about two different things?" Tessa wished she could be more like Sam in these insecure moments.

"You tell me. You're acting like you have your finger in a light socket." He faced her. "There are two beds. Two. Count them. One. Two."

A wave of embarrassment forced a nervous stutter. "I-I'm not concerned about that at all."

"Then what? Tessa, we are working. You understand the way I feel about mixing business with pleasure. Your Bobby will never find out we shared a tent. Relax."

"His name is Robert. Again. I'm not concerned."

"Besides, you're not my type." Chase turned away to look back outside then unzipped the door.

Tessa bristled. "Type? You have a type?" His low chuckle was a clear warning to be careful. "Pray tell, what is your type?"

"No. I wouldn't want you to stop being your perky little self to please me."

Tessa stormed toward the door only to be cut off by Chase's tall frame. "Why do you delight in making me uncomfortable?" She exhaled an angry breath.

"Because I can. You really think because we're friends and colleagues I'll take advantage of you, Tess?" He raised his chin slightly then glared down his straight nose. "I have too much respect for you to do that."

"Oh," she whispered, ashamed of her Victorian concept of how a man and woman should act around each other. "It's, well, I don't know how I'm supposed to act with all of this. If Robert ever found out—"

"He won't," he insisted. "Be yourself." He sounded like a patient father. "I'm sorry if I make you uncomfortable. I'm not going to force myself on you. We kid like this all the time. Means nothing."

She refocused her eyes to the floor.

"I would do anything for you, baby." He always called her that when he got sentimental. "I care for you and, whether you admit it or not, no matter how many names you call me—you care for me, too. You are the one person I didn't have to worry about taking me the wrong way."

Now she couldn't resist meeting his gaze. How could she speak frankly without sounding like she had a serious crush on him? "I would do anything for you and yes, we kid around a lot. Sorry. I'm a little uneasy." The anticipation in his eyes didn't help with her rapid heartbeat. "You've always been there for me when I needed you most."

"Yeah, and it's turning into a full-time job," he mused. "We're going to sleep together tonight, Tess. Nothing will happen. I tease you a lot when no one can hear us, but I would never take advantage of you."

"Guess I knew that. I have a certain amount of guilt because I enjoy these moments a little too much." She tried to resist but could feel a suppressed grin spreading across her mouth.

"Me, too. We're going to have to have a serious talk about that one of these days. I'm not a saint, Tess. You know that. If you ever give me the sign you want more than what we're doing..."

"Good evening." Handsome ran up the steps of their deck and came straight for the front door. Tessa and Chase increased the space between them. He pulled the door open for Tessa to join him, but dropped it when Chase tried to exit. "I hope you are hungry," he said, pulling Tessa to the railing. "I'll get your friends and we'll be off." But Carter and Sam were already descending the stairs of their own place, each carrying a flashlight.

Chase's expression had grown solemn. She wished they'd been able to conclude their conversation, but the moment had passed. She stretched out her hand, and he came to her, taking it as if it were a common gesture then led her down the steps to join their friends. The charade had begun.

~ ~ ~

Baboloki read the intel one of his aides dropped off an hour earlier. He chewed the inside of his jaw after scanning it a second time. The cries of the peacocks in the garden drew him to the window to see if there might be a disturbance. A guard patrolled the grounds with a rifle cradled in his arms, sensors flipping on a dim light as he passed. Another guard stood outside the veranda, posed statue-like.

The information he'd received confused him. The ridiculous story of the Kifaru diamond had resurfaced months ago, stirring up interest among the tribal people in the bush and Kalahari. For years, he'd been able to control such gossip by removing the person who dared repeat the story of long ago. The details of the day he led his soldiers to round up troublemakers still haunted him. His men were only supposed to find the one they called John and any of his family and friends who tried to protect him.

Such a man brought too much education to his people, put ideas in their heads of needing more than the government was willing to supply.

A school and medical facility in the area could never be properly staffed. Improved communications and a voice in how Gaborone ran the country would only give them too much power.

The men with money promised him a position in the government if he would silence such resistance. John was loved and respected among the people of the Okavango. His father and grandfather were trailblazers in uniting the country. But other men took over and pushed back so their pockets would remain full. And his own desires to be something other than a soldier drove him to be ruthless that day.

If he could bring John to Gaborone, show the tribes how complaints might change their lives, then their voices would grow silent once more. The story of the Kifaru diamond and its worth convinced Baboloki if he could secure that prize, then he could begin a new life, one with dignity and respect. But the diamond remained elusive.

"Find the one they call John," he'd ordered his men. "Bring him to me."

But all along the Okavango, the word went out that soldiers were coming. The people waited for them with clubs, rocks, and clumps of elephant dung to throw at them. They came by boat and put in a mile downstream. The village men waited near the water, preventing them from gaining the upper hand. By the time the smoke curled upward from their torched village, there was little to save. Yet they fought in spite of guns mowing them down.

Women screamed and ran with crying children in tow. Several of his men took advantage of the young girls before killing them. The youngest men who were caught were beaten and promised protection if they led them to John. Either fear of the soldiers or a rebellious nature remained an obstacle until one woman was dragged before him.

"Where is your husband, woman?" Colonel Baboloki growled as he raised her chin with the barrel of his gun.

"She just had a baby, Colonel," the soldier who captured the woman informed the colonel. "The child is missing."

The colonel smirked at the woman who glared at him boldly. "Where is the child?"

"My baby died. My sister took the body to bury. Have you no mercy?"

"None. And apparently your husband doesn't, either, or he wouldn't have left you to us."

He raised his chin at the soldier. "Take her to the boats."

Though frail, she fought like a lioness to escape then cried and screamed until a soldier slapped her down. With some effort, he managed to get her up and into the bush where they disappeared.

Baboloki turned to his aide. "He can't be far. Torch all the huts. Hunt down the ones who escaped and leave them for the hyenas."

"Colonel." Another soldier approached but kept his distance. His uniform had splotches of dung on the stomach area mixed with blood. "We have found him. He runs toward Camp Kubu where the foreigners are."

"Kill them. We don't need witnesses. He'll hide among them."

"Yes, sir." He turned and left.

The crackling of fires, the reek of death and fear hung heavy in the air, and the voices of begging for mercy swirled around him, but all he could think about was where the Kifaru diamond might be.

He remembered that day as if it were yesterday, still longing to discover the location of the Kifaru. Why wouldn't the woman tell him?

"President Baboloki?" His head of security entered with a tall woman in her early sixties.

"Yes, Dage?"

The steely-eyed woman wore her gray hair so short it resembled a cap pulled tightly about her head. She was still beautiful after all these years in captivity: skin the color of mocha, obsidian eyes full of wisdom and resistance.

"Oh. Thank you, Dage." The president extended his hand toward the leather couch. The woman lifted her chin. "I mean you no harm, Keeya. Please. Sit down. You look tired."

She did as instructed and tucked her long flowery dress tightly beneath her. Sitting stiff-backed on the edge of the leather cushion, the woman stared across the room at nothing, revealing little about her mood.

"You look lovely tonight."

She shifted her blank expression to him. The full lips narrowed into a frown.

"Are you well?"

"Yes."

Baboloki moved to the couch and sat next to her. She didn't move when he slipped his hand onto hers. The weathered skin felt cold as he wove his fingers through her bony ones. "I have news."

The lack of interest did not change her focus on something across the room. Given the opportunity, would she kill him? After all this time, the woman still hated him for killing her husband, even though he'd shown her nothing but kindness.

"I have found your son."

"My son died the day you murdered my village." She turned her eyes toward the emptiness of the room.

"I have told you many times, that is not true. I discovered your husband, John, carried him into the bush and tried to save him. And for all these years, I have searched for the child throughout the land, thinking one of your people managed to get him away."

She said nothing. The woman had worn a mask of indifference for decades.

"Are you not curious?"

"No, because he is dead." Keeya's voice remained void of emotion. "What do you want of me tonight. Surely you have younger women to amuse you. I am an old woman, and cannot possibly interest you. What of your wife?"

Baboloki sighed. "My wife is away, and you are correct. There are younger women to satisfy me." He ran his hand up her arm. She had learned to withhold a flinch of revulsion. "You and I have passed the days of physical intimacy. But we are still friends."

This did draw her attention back to him, and she dared remove his hand before turning to stare back at nothing.

The president stood. "I brought you here to ask you one more time about the Kifaru diamond."

"I know of no such diamond."

Walking to his desk, he lifted a picture and brought it to her. It was a large diamond lying on a Time magazine cover with a date from two weeks earlier. She squinted at it then up at the president.

"What is this?" she demanded in a voice that sounded like she'd gargled gravel.

"The Kifaru."

Tears welled up in her eyes and threatened to spill down her cheeks.

"And your son has returned to Botswana." He offered a patient gaze. "You soon will be of no use to me at all."

CHAPTER TEN

During small talk among the guests and Carter's hilarious stories about his space adventures, Handsome took it upon himself to keep glasses filled with water. After the plates were cleared, bread pudding and hot tea were served. He spoke if addressed, but never interjected a comment or advice on a topic. It wasn't his place, and doing so would be a good way to lose his job. Smile and nod. That remained his priority for this particular night.

He wanted to evaluate the guests more than anything. Were they weak, a threat, on vacation, or something else? From what he could find out, these people had no interest in the politics or economics of Botswana. Nothing in their conversations hinted at anything but enjoying the Okavango as it should be experienced, with a camera and a lust for adventure.

When they moved to the deck firepit surrounded by camp chairs reminiscent of Hollywood movie sets, their conversation became quieter. Some stared out into the darkness. A lion roared in the distance as something splashed into the nearby Okavango. Discussion followed about what it might be.

"A hippo often visits the camp. We call him Amadeus. Don't be fooled by them. Cartoons would have you believe they are lumbering, sweet creatures"— the camp director lit his pipe—"but more people are attacked or killed by hippos in Africa than any other animal."

"Even more than lions?" the older British woman asked.

"That's right. Don't try and get between them and their path to the water. They are very much a part of the eco-system of the Okavango. We put up with their short tempers. Not uncommon for them to come onto land at night to feed. Stay in your tents until morning, please."

Tessa rubbed her arms and gave a little shiver. The crackling fire glowed on her face, and Handsome suspected she might be falling in love with this place. He knew of her geography background, and a camp like this was swathed in classic textbook adventure. With her hair pulled back in a ponytail and face makeup-free, she looked almost like a woman in her twenties. He also noticed her pretty blue eyes and the sideways glances she gave her boss.

He hadn't planned on putting them together in the same tent, but someone had paired them together during the reservation stage of the trip. At least, this way, she'd be safe from the human beasts that could descend upon them.

The California housewife had affected him more than he'd remembered. Their conversations back in the States had been few, but she'd ended up on his side and believing in him. People like Tessa wanted to believe there remained a certain amount of good in the world. He didn't buy into that logic.

Besides being easy on the eyes, she had a funny way of listening to you, like every word out of your mouth was coming from God. Even the sassy, obstinate side of her gave him pleasure. The way she loved her kids and tried to comfort them during a difficult experience they'd shared in the States, gave him insight to her sincerity.

He regretted abandoning her at Lake Tahoe with Captain Hunter. Leaving the diamond with her could have blown up in his face. The avalanche Hunter spoke of was unexpected.

Yet there were several things he didn't like, including her husband, Robert Scott, and her boss, Chase Hunter. One of his contacts, Reeva Kaplan, had told him all about the husband, a flirt and womanizer for sure. Maybe Reeva had it wrong, but his own observations let him conclude Robert was more interested in a successful career than being a good dad.

Then there was Hunter, a sometimes-rogue agent who took matters into his own hands whenever it suited him. Hadn't he suffered from the brute's actions on a number of occasions, like the time in Tunisia where he landed in jail on the captain's orders? Yet, Tessa appeared to have some kind of control over the man.

Handsome had never known him to show affection or interest in anything more than loyalty to country and his team. Hunter demanded nothing less from them. But he'd seen the look in the man's eyes when Tessa nearly drowned in Lake Tahoe, and how he'd fumed like a raging maniac when it looked like she'd been taken against her will. The woman held her boss in the palm of her hand. Could she be in love with him or flirting with danger? More likely the poor sap of a captain had fallen for someone totally out of his reach and control.

The captain stared into the fire while others continued polite conversation. Even Carter and Samantha had quieted, looking a little exhausted from their trip. Once, the captain took Tessa's hand in his large dark one without meeting her expectant gaze. He rubbed the back with his thumb for a few seconds. She laid her hand on his without diverting her eyes from the camp director who was listing the activities for the following day. Even when he withdrew, she never looked away. It all seemed a little rehearsed. Enigma trained its agents in deception.

Samantha, probably the most beautiful woman he'd ever met, appeared aloof and mildly irritated at her partner, Carter. That relationship was most definitely rehearsed. She'd not give Carter Johnson the time of day. She was one chick he didn't trust, and he decided to keep a closer watch on her. Did the rift he'd detected between the two women have anything to do with the sleeping arrangements? Sam had little to no conscience and could be a deadly opponent.

Carter took the role of good-time-Charlie or comic relief among the four. The other guests seemed quite taken with him, and as an astronaut with a colorful past, the spotlight never seemed to faze him. Carter might be a distraction and paired with Sam, the chances were good, the handsome couple would draw anyone's attention and imagination.

"Time for bed, Tess," Chase said rising from his chair and stretching. When she stood, he dropped his arm around her shoulders and pulled her close.

She placed her hand on his abdomen. Still no surprised expression, no narrowed looks of contempt or even an ounce of hesitation on Tessa's part.

"See you folks in the morning." He nodded to the Brits and the Germans as Carter stood and pulled Sam to her feet.

"Handsome will escort you to your tent." The director passed out the flashlights they'd left on a table. The rest of the group stood, yawning, and agreed it was time to turn in. "Very good. Did everyone approve of their accommodations? I neglected to ask."

"Quite good." The older British woman sighed sleepily. "Glad we're in the nearest tents. I don't think I would like being down where you Americans are staying."

"Too far from the kitchen, right?" her husband teased then moved up by Handsome.

The two German men clicked on their flashlights and moved on down the path. They swiftly approached the third tent, swinging their lights back and forth. Handsome instructed them to call out when they were inside. By the time the Brits entered their tents, the Germans called a "Guten Nacht."

"We can talk at your place." Handsome tilted his head toward Sam and Carter. He glanced at Tessa, who appeared to be a little spooked and hooked her arm through Chase's. He pulled her along. Their flashlights brightened the fivesome's way to the tent deck.

Sam immediately took a chair by the door, crossing her long legs. She reminded him of one of those Vogue models who absently stared into space for all to admire. Carter and Chase leaned against the railing, and Tessa remained at Chase's side. All the flashlights were extinguished since the lantern glowed near Sam. He figured that was the reason she sat there, to make sure she could be observed and adored.

Chase crossed his arms in front of his chest and arched an eyebrow. "Someone broke into Tess's room and stole her computer while we were in Gaborone. We planted the information about the rightful heir of the Kifaru diamond and that it had been located."

"Were you there during the break-in, Tessa?" he asked. She seemed smaller than he remembered.

"I was just getting back. Chase and I returned from dinner at President Baboloki's to find the room had been ransacked. He escaped through a window." She rubbed her arms and shrugged. The woman had spunk, but he doubted her cold disregard for danger. She wasn't like them yet. There remained too much light in her eyes for that kind of black heart.

"You took a risk. I thank you," Handsome said extending an arm to give her a brief hug. He shifted his disgruntled frown to the two men and noticed Chase straightened to a more agitated stance. The man really did have a thing for Tessa Scott. This amused him to no end. "Why wasn't it in your room?" Glaring at the captain didn't faze the man much.

"I expected them to come at me first. I could pretend to protect it. Make a show of resistance—"

"No matter. It's done. We wanted them to take it, and they did," Tessa interrupted.

"And the Kifaru?" Handsome lowered his voice, paranoid the bush had dangerous ears.

"Safe for now. Do these people understand who you are?" Chase inquired, relaxing against the railing once again.

"Some people in my village remember the day the soldiers came. Most were killed, but others survived to tell the story. They escaped into the bush. One man remembered Dr. Girard who tried to save his badly injured father.

"My research said no one survived," Tessa spoke in a soft voice.

"There were a few, but they scattered to other villages for shelter and even then, the villages were afraid to take them in because of the soldiers. Gradually, they have returned and rebuilt, but it has taken many years. My father, Dr. Girard, made it his mission in life to bring medical care to these people. He raised money over the years to keep the work going." Handsome stared up into the sky for a few moments as if trying to piece together what to say next. When Tessa laid a hand on his arm, he glanced down at her. "He and my adopted mother were fine Christians who put their faith into action. By taking me in, he risked his life, his career, and his fortune. I, of course, never knew my real father, but I believe God placed me in his hands that day when Baboloki killed my family."

"He is an angel," Tessa said, squeezing his forearm. Handsome laid his large hand on her tiny one, and felt the coolness of the night seeping into her skin. He massaged her fingers to warm them then clamped down on it while she stared up at him. He liked to think she believed in him.

"As are you," Handsome confessed.

"I think I'm going to throw up," Chase growled.

"Don't listen to him, Handsome. Continue with your story." Tessa shot an annoyed look Chase's way.

"We moved around a lot when I was a kid. Changed my name a number of times for the sake of safety. Maybe it was paranoia on my parents' part. I never knew for sure. Never had a chance to make many friends. They were pretty protective. As a teenager, I rebelled."

"Not uncommon," Tessa consoled.

"My father used to say it was due to my intelligence."

"Boy did he get that wrong," Chase quipped.

Handsome ignored the insult. "He, of course, knew all about my real father being an engineer and figured I needed some challenges. When I was around fifteen, he finally told me about where I came from. All those years he'd slipped into the country to work here, I'd never understood why. From that point on, I tagged along to learn."

"How did you hook up with the CIA?" Carter asked.

"Who says I was with the CIA?" Handsome frowned.

"Just the way you're denying it, is pretty much an admission of guilt. Don't forget your little episode in Tunisia," Chase reminded him.

"At one point, I made connections with people who I hoped might teach me a better set of survival skills than my father or the engineering university I attended in Missouri. It didn't take long to attract some interest. I speak four African languages. I was ripe pickings out of thousands. But then Tunisia happened, and I ended up owing a debt to

Enigma, thanks to you, Hunter."

Carter smirked. "We're one big happy family. Maybe I should suggest that as our motto."

Tessa chuckled and stepped away from Handsome's continued touch. "So, exactly what is your plan, Handsome?"

"To rule Botswana as my birth father planned to do."

CHAPTER ELEVEN

The slow and easy conversation about Handsome's plan to rid Botswana of their dictator continued for another half hour. He then lumbered off into the darkness, swinging his flashlight to guard against wandering animals from the bush. There was a chance the camp director needed him to finish up some kind of preparations for the following day. According to him, his quarters consisted of a tent not so different than theirs, but without the comfortable furniture and sweet-smelling soap.

"Just the basics. It's enough. I go back to the village on my days off to help out at the clinic."

Carter and Chase remained outside while the women slipped into the tents to prepare for bed. Tessa dropped one side of the tent flap across the door for more privacy. They remained quiet for only a few minutes.

"He's taking a big risk. Baboloki gets wind of this, and he's a dead man," Carter spoke in a low voice. "I'm betting he's aware the diamond is real and somewhere close enough to threaten his hold on power. It won't take him long to locate him. My concern is another massacre like the one that started this whole story."

"He's under a microscope. Probably won't come to that, but you're right." Chase could see the outline of Tessa undressing in the tent. "Removing Baboloki could create a vacuum where someone worse could step in. Just because Handsome owns the diamond, doesn't mean he is the best man for the job."

Carter agreed and tried to interject more opinions until he followed Chase's line of sight and elbowed his friend. "Maybe you'd better go take care of business. You've stopped listening to me anyway."

Chase straightened and moved toward the tent. "See you in the morning."

The slow sound of a zipper opening helped Tessa lose focus on tying the string on her pajama bottoms. Even in semi-darkness, he took her breath away when his six-foot-one frame came through the door. He turned in slow motion to offer one of his intimidating gazes at her as a stream of light from the outside lantern fell across the upper part of his face.

I'm in a freakin' romance novel where everything is about to go to Hell. Was that where she would end up?

"What? You're staring at me," he said with all the emotion of a piece of dry toast. He stripped off his shirt. She couldn't tear her eyes away, and managed to tangle her fingers in the string of her pajama bottoms. Maybe double-knotting was overkill. She undid it. "What did you think about Handsome's story?"

He sat down on the end of the bed and patted the covers for a second then untied his boots. He quickly stood and placed them neatly under a camp stool. She liked a man who could pick up after himself.

Had she really been reduced to this? Next, she'd be daydreaming about him painting the house or weeding the garden instead of throwing her across the bed in a wild night of passion. How sick was that? When he dropped his pants and tossed them on his leather bag, she snapped back to reality.

"It matched up, for the most part, with what we already knew. He seems a little more reserved and less threatening here. What did you think?" she asked, wondering if he would slip pajamas over his boxer shorts or at least, put on a tee shirt.

Please, God, don't let him. Yep. I'm going to Hell.

He turned around and put his hands on his hips like he might be ready to inspect the troops. His face remained shrouded in shadows. The deep voice sounded a little dark, too. "No. I can't say I noticed that." His step closer brought his features into focus. "I see you brought your sexy pj's." That condescending smirk reminded her of a creature in Alice in Wonderland.

She tried a little too hard to appear nonchalant as she shifted her weight to one hip and dropped her hands to her side. When she did, her finger caught in the drawstring and completely untied the pajamas, causing them to slip farther down on her hips. She tugged them up and tied them again.

He arched a brow. The cold seeped through her thin tee shirt. She folded her arms across her chest to hide her body's embarrassing reaction.

"Victoria Secret for Moms had a sale. Couldn't resist."

"Would that be the hot-momma section or the don't-get-too-close-momma section?"

"Shut up," she huffed, pulling the comforter down far enough to slip in with a little grace and a big flippant attitude.

Her toes touched something hairy and warm near the end of her bed. With a scream, she threw back the covers to scramble out to a standing position and jumped onto Chase's bed butted up against hers. He moved to his side of the bed when she leaped into his arms.

"There's something in there!" She pulled him tighter against her body. She could feel him chuckle as he pushed her to arm's length, which took several tries before she released her hold around his neck.

"You're imagining things. But hey, I'll play the hero if it gets me another close encounter of the Tessa kind." Loud laughter followed his comments.

"Stop it. Do something!" she demanded, and stomped impatiently on the mattress where she remained standing.

Chase returned to her side of the bed and laid his hand on top of the comforter. Immediately, his expression changed from amused to a frown. "I see what you mean. Not good," he whispered.

Tessa brought two fists up to her mouth. "Oh. My. Gosh. Chase! Be careful. What are you going to do?" she asked breathlessly. As he lifted the covers ever so gently, she repeated, "Be careful."

He jerked his hands back.

Tessa gasped again and shivered.

"Stop talking, woman, and let me do this."

"Sure. Sure." When he frowned at her, she clamped her lips shut and waited for him to move again.

Chase reached under the layers and grabbed something. He struggled to hold on, grunting with trying to keep control of whatever had found its way into her bed. "I've got it!"

"What is it!" she screamed.

Chase continued to fight as he dragged the thing out and lifted it into the air. "I'm pretty sure it's a hot water bottle." He smiled then laughed. "A hot water bottle covered in a furry wrapping to keep your cold feet warm."

"What?" she fumed then jumped to her side of the bed and eyed the monster she'd imagined. Touching it proved once more she remained a coward at heart. "It felt like an animal."

Chase handed it to her. "Nice water bottle. Go ahead. Pet it. It won't bite," he teased before breaking out in laughter again.

She took it then slapped him in the chest. "You knew all along what it was, didn't you?"

"When I sat down to take my boots off, I felt one at the foot of my bed. I also heard the camp director tell the staff it was time to warm up our beds." His laughter subsided to a chuckle mixed in with his words. He wiped a tear from below one of his dark eyes.

"I despise you." She tried to appear annoyed.

"No, you don't," he said returning the water bottle to the foot of her bed. "Oh, and thanks for the vote of confidence I could save the day, even if it meant my life," he mused as he tucked the covers back in. "Unless there is something else you require of me, I think we should call it a night."

"Well," she teased. "There is one more thing."

His eyebrows arched in expectation, Chase stepped close enough to move the bed. She was still standing on the mattress, so he had to shift his eyes up to meet hers. "I'm yours for the night. Name it."

"I need to go to the bathroom. I want you to go with me."

His expression changed from anticipation to aggravation. "You want me to go with you to pee?"

"There might be a snake or something out there. Anything could get in that bathroom."

"Way to spoil the mood," he sighed and lifted her off the bed only to set her feet on the floor. "I'll get the flashlight."

Gentleman that he was, Chase escorted her to their bathroom and flooded the area with light as he stood outside and waited. Returning to the tent, he shone the light all around the inside to alleviate any further fears she might have about uninvited guests. He even pulled back her sheet one more time for a closer inspection before letting her climb into bed.

"Thanks, Chase. Really." Tessa watched him circle to his side and slip between the covers.

He grunted, "You're welcome," and turned his back to her.

"Do you want to talk?"

"Nope."

"I mean about Handsome?"

"Still nope."

"Don't you think we should? I mean, I have some concerns." Tessa rolled to her side to stare at his back. He remained silent. "I wanted to run something by you that I found." Still the silent treatment. "Maybe we could talk while we're having sex," she fumed.

His shoulders shook. Was he holding in a laugh? "Not much on talking while I do that," he offered in an even tone.

"Well, that isn't the gossip among your brainy bimbos at the university," she quipped. "According to them, you are—"

Chase turned over to face her. This conversation was the equivalent of gas being thrown on a fire. "I'm all yours," he said calmly.

"Good. Thank you."

"I haven't done anything. Yet." The wolfish expression wasn't lost on her. He tucked his arm under his head.

He kept her off guard by saying suggestive things. What could she expect when she'd hinted at a physical reward for his bravery? The tit for tat meant to get his attention might backfire if she wasn't careful.

"Last night when we were at Baboloki's, I ran into a woman in the bathroom."

"That's a relief. No hot water bottles? No other men?"

"I'm serious."

"Me, too. I would hate to have to kick in the door to rescue you in such a magnificent place."

"Are you going to listen to me or keep poking fun?" she huffed.

"Both. Go ahead. I'm all ears. You met a woman in the bathroom..." He propped up on one elbow, lying on his side, facing her.

She scooted a little closer. "Something was strange there." She launched into a quick retelling of their awkward meeting, the wallpaper and then the warning from the woman with the scars. "I saw her earlier in the day watching Baboloki and me walking through the garden."

"Girlfriend?" he yawned.

"A little old to be a girlfriend, considering I've seen pictures of his wife who is about twenty years younger than him and pretty close to looking like a supermodel. Where was his wife, anyway?"

"The president has a reputation for being a ladies' man. Maybe he sent her away for a few days. She probably jumped at the chance. He was certainly checking you out." Amusement etched his face.

"A lot of help you would've been if I needed you. You were on your way to being intoxicated."

"What can I say? The man has some good booze. You should try it sometime."

"You aren't listening to what I'm saying. The woman warned against talking about the Kifaru in Baboloki's house. Why would he have black rhinos in the wallpaper? Or a collection of them in a display case in the hall? On the way out, I spotted rhinos sculptured in the chandeliers hanging on the front veranda."

"It is Africa, Tessa. There were also elephants and giraffes." He rolled to his back and placed his hands beneath his head, staring at the ceiling. "Who do you think she was?"

"No clue. But she said something curious when I mentioned Kifaru." He turned his head toward her, still wearing an amused expression. "She said, 'I know the Kifaru killed everything and everyone I loved. It is vile.' I think she might be someone from Handsome's village. Maybe she has information about his parents. Many of the people weren't identified. Maybe part of his family escaped."

"I asked him about that earlier. He said none of the few who came back to rebuild knew anything of his family, and most of the people there now were not even around when the massacre occurred."

"Still, there could be someone who didn't return. Possibly escaped. Maybe more than one." Tessa scooted closer, again, and whispered, "Wouldn't it be amazing if a relative still existed? I would love that for Handsome."

Chase frowned. "You two are a little too chummy for my taste. And you are too trusting. Let me refresh your memory about how he left us to die at Lake Tahoe."

"He didn't know there would be an avalanche," she defended.

"Maybe. But keep in mind he worked dark ops for the CIA, not that he admits to any of that, and he has a reputation for violence. He isn't the sweet guy you're imagining. Not much of what he's told you is true. Remember, he lured you to Tahoe with a false narrative and you could've been in serious trouble. What am I saying? You ended up in the lake with the car nose down."

"Did I ever thank you for saving me?"

"Not properly. No," he fumed. "You think everyone has some good in them and to be honest, I've seen very few who do."

"Maybe you need a break from Enigma because there are many good people out there."

"Well, besides you, I doubt it."

Tessa stared at him. "I'm not that good anymore," she said softly. "Remember what I did in Afghanistan?"

"I remember you saved a bunch of little girls from the Taliban. The cost didn't matter." He let his voice quiet. "Handsome is still using you to get what he wants. We have the diamond, and he needs it to give Baboloki the boot." He took a deep breath. "Who do you think the woman was? I'm betting you have some wackadoodle theory."

"Not sure. But maybe…"

"Here it comes. Drum roll."

"She was old enough to be Handsome's mother or aunt. He has this haughty way he looks down his nose at you when he stiffens his shoulders then pooches out his lips."

Chased sighed but nodded.

"She did the same thing. And she definitely looked like she was of the Tswana tribe."

"Tessa, almost everyone around here looks like they're from the Tswana tribe—because they are," he retorted.

"Baboloki isn't. He's from South Africa, if I remember right—shorter, darker, and stockier. She was lovely, very lithe, and almost genteel."

"Don't be putting ideas in Handsome's head. He's dangerous enough as it is.

"At least we need to check it out."

He yawned again. "I'll get the satellite phone up and running tomorrow. Vernon and Zoric can take care of that end. In the meantime—"

"We should go to sleep." She couldn't suppress a yawn after watching him. Quiet rose up between them. "Chase?" she murmured.

Silence.

"Carter and Sam. Are they…"

"They're working. This isn't a honeymoon."

"So, they aren't…"

"Having sex?"

"Yeah. I mean, Carter is always on the make and, well, Sam is the poster child for nymphomaniac."

"I guess it could happen. Don't care as long they do their job…" His voice faded.

"Chase?"

"I swear, Tessa, if you don't go to sleep, I'm going to— Last question. Shoot."

"Do they think we're having a—a fling while we're here?"

He chuckled. "Everyone thinks we're having a fling, Tessa." Another yawn.

"And that doesn't bother you?"

"Nope." He turned to face her again. "You know why? Because I think about it all the time."

"Oh. You do?" she whispered.

"Don't you?" His eyelids drooped.

Tessa quickly moved away from his nearness. "Never."

"You're a terrible liar, Tess."

CHAPTER TWELVE

A chubby woman dressed in a teal blouse and black skirt entered President Baboloki's office. He glanced at a nearby mirror to watch her fuss with straightening his desk after setting a cup of hot tea on the table near where he had been standing to gaze out the French doors into the garden. A small embroidery pillow with rhinos, lions, and giraffes lay on the floor near the couch. Picking it up, she made eye contact with the president in the mirror then placed it the middle cushion.

"I forwarded your itinerary to your computer, Mr. President. A new shipment of your favorite tea arrived, so I brought you a pot straightaway."

He glanced over at the fifty-something woman who wore her hair pulled back in a bun. The streaks of gray-and-black reminded him of a zebra. Her face remained smooth and clear even after staying by his side for so many years. Her devotion and loyalty enough to spy on other employees who failed to live up to his expectations had been rewarded with a good income to support her seven children. She even kept an eye on Keeya for him and gave the woman small jobs of responsibility to keep her occupied and out of trouble.

"Thank you, Naledi," he said returning to his desk. "And how is Keeya this morning? She was very upset last night."

"I let her sleep in, Mr. President." Naledi emptied an ashtray, removed a glass he'd used for bourbon the night before, and cleared the coffee table. "Should I wake her?"

"Soon. There's been a change of plans concerning my trip. I want to take Keeya with me. The change will do her good."

Naledi stopped and stared at him. "But, sir, she can't be trusted not to run."

"She is too old to run, Naledi," he offered patiently, ignoring her questioning his decision. "The election is coming up soon, and I want people to remember who she is to show that I have her support. The tribes may not appreciate my wife who wears designer clothes and jewelry. Her European ways tended to give the impression she thought herself better than the people of the bush and Kalahari. She never missed a chance to look down her nose at anyone who wasn't part of the fashion world or Hollywood. Soon, I will have to replace her. My son will be better off with us. Has there been any word from my wife? Inform her I'll be gone for a while if she wants to stay in Paris a few more days."

Naledi nodded. She had more often than once expressed appreciation of Keeya who played with the young boy and kept tutors on track with his education, unlike the wife. "I will always be available to help."

"Tell Keeya of my plans as well. We leave day after tomorrow. Change our reservations to include one more. When you leave, inform Dage of the change so he can adjust the security needs."

"Sir, what if Keeya refuses to go? She is a stubborn one."

"Then, I'll have to convince her." He smirked as he sat at the desk and opened his laptop. "I've done it before," he said offhandedly. "I think maybe this time she'll be a little more willing. Be sure to tell her we'll be traveling to her old village, rebuilt to include, a medical center and small school."

Naledi bowed her head again and left the office to complete the tasks set before her.

~ ~ ~

Vernon Kemp drummed his thumbs on the steering wheel. His passenger didn't like crowds, traffic, or new places; especially when it involved Africa. Taking the keys away from the Serbian allowed his friend to play lookout and bodyguard all in one.

"Are you sure about this?" Zoric quizzed the young tech genius as they drove through Gaborone. "How do you know the security systems along with the computer network are down?"

Vernon drove cautiously through the streets, dodging scooters and smoke-puffing trucks. "Because I made it happen. Looks like after all this time you'd trust me. Relax. I got this." He whistled to pretend he didn't have a care in the world. It wasn't often he got to boss the intimidating interrogator into submission.

Vernon, only in his twenties, was the youngest of the Enigma team.

Trouble with the Pentagon and Homeland Security got him a second chance at Enigma. They didn't much care about his illegal off-the-grid stuff, only that he could perform when they needed him. His dark-red hair pulled up in a ponytail revealed pale skin and an abundance of freckles. He swaggered when he walked and could be mistaken for a surf bum.

Because Vernon wasn't a slave to fashion, Director Benjamin Clark often referred to him as their resident hippy with no respect for authority. That wasn't exactly true because he'd throw himself on a landmine for Captain Hunter and never deviated from the plan laid out for him. It was the captain who got him out of trouble with the Feds and the military some years earlier, and he'd paid that favor back. It wasn't that he never broke the law again. He just didn't get in trouble for it anymore.

"So why does the boss want us to get into the president's residence? I could have snooped around for information from my basement in Sacramento."

"Tessa thinks a woman is being held against her will who might have a connection to all this." Zoric gripped the seat as his partner weaved in and out of traffic.

"What kind of connection? Did he say?"

"You know Tessa. She gets an idea in her head and if we don't listen someone gets in a jam. Chase thought we should check it out. The woman has an uncanny ability to see things we don't."

"And those things only happen to her. Makes you want to be a believer, doesn't it?" Vernon pounded on the horn to get a truck pulling a small trailer out of the way.

Zoric took a deep drag off his cigarette then exhaled the smoke. "You're not going to bring up all that walking-with-angels stuff, are you?"

"You have to admit somebody is looking after her."

"His name is Chase Hunter, and we both know he is no angel." Zoric pointed to a right turn, but Vernon took it too fast. The tires squealed on their van. "Slow down, will ya!" he shouted as he dropped his cigarette in his lap. "Can you drive like a normal person for once?"

Vernon presented their credentials at the security gate then followed the drive through the manicured grounds of the president's office. Since the men were on the list of visitors and their vehicle passed inspection, they were soon cruising to a maintenance entrance.

"Creepy shit." Zoric squinted his beady eyes.

"What?" Vernon pulled into a parking spot.

"See those snakes wrapped around a rhinoceros on the gate? Even their uniforms had what looked like a snake choking the thing. I'm sure that isn't by accident."

"Sounds like you're afraid of snakes." Vernon moved his hand like the head of a snake and snapped it at Zoric.

They exited the van and moved to the back to retrieve their tools.

"I don't like them." The Serbian had committed a great deal of torture in his life, and nothing usually fazed him.

"Maybe they're one of your relatives." Vernon snapped on his tool belt then swung a backpack over his shoulder. The Serbian dropped his cigarette then ground it with his toe. "You're goin' pick that up, right?"

"Sorry. I forgot you were an environmental-terrorist wannabe." He bent down to pick up the butt.

"Watch out. Snake!" Vernon jumped back causing Zoric to trip over the curb and fall flat on his back. He crab-crawled backward when the tech laughed and bent to pick up a stick. "My bad. Only a stick." He continued when Zoric's eyes turned black, lending him an even more evil look than usual. Vernon tossed the stick at his friend as he got to his feet.

Zoric growled through gritted teeth, "You are very funny, my little genius. I hope you are amused when I come into your room some night and gut you like a pig."

Vernon sobered. "Can't you take a joke. No sense of humor at all," he moaned as he stepped around him. "You mess with me, you mess with Tessa. You want that?" He stopped with his hand on the doorknob. Everyone knew she had a tender spot for him. When the Serbian remained silent, Vernon felt more confidence to taunt his partner one more time. "I didn't think so." The handle twisted in his hand, drawing his interest. "Even the doorknobs are snakes. Cool."

After checking in they were led to the security office where the two men were never left alone. It didn't really matter to Vernon because he could cause mayhem with anything electronic while someone watched and he recited the "Gettysburg Address" in Klingon.

The security guards on duty were more interested in Zoric who could have played Dracula in anyone's most recent nightmare. The guards postured a little too much, and Zoric kept smiling at them with his crooked mouth.

Vernon addressed the two short guards. "I need to check some connections throughout the house. That okay?"

The guards frowned and refused.

"Look here." He showed them that their security cameras were back on. "You can follow us like a stalking lion. It's not like I'm going to do anything to lose my job. Okay?"

They nodded, but one put his hand on his weapon in a threatening manner. "Do not go upstairs to the residence or I might have to use this.

Understand?"

Vernon shrugged and quickly answered. "Of course. Sure. Whatever, dude. Just want to make sure there are no more loose connections. Are we cool?"

A bewildered expression crossed the guard's face.

"I mean, are we good? I can look around?"

"Don't touch anything but the things connected to this." The security guy pulled out a drawer and gave Vernon a map of all the wiring, boxes, outlets, and security camera placement he might need. "Understand?"

Vernon agreed.

"Bring the map here when you're done, and give me a report."

"No problem. Let's go," he said elbowing Zoric who looked like he did before doing one of his interrogation jobs for Enigma. Vernon believed the man liked his job a little too much. If he began salivating over the prospect of sticking someone with that knife of his, he would have to send him back to the van. "Look normal, would ya?" he whispered. "Oh, wait. This is normal."

In some rooms, Zoric helped him, and in others he wandered around so the security would focus on him rather than Vernon doing a little adjustment. There was a lot more coming and going of personnel near the offices, but they spotted only one woman who wore a badge indicating she worked for the president.

"Can we get a glass of water, ma'am?" Vernon asked in a polite and respectful voice. "Warmed up a bit today. Guess it will be freezing again tonight, though."

She pointed toward a hall. "There's a kitchen down there where the staff eat. I'm sure you can find something." She seemed to be in a hurry or maybe didn't want to stop and chat with contract workers. Either way, she moved on toward the staircase leading to the residence.

They ducked into an alcove when the angry voices of two women lifted from the staircase.

"Keeya, it is about time you came downstairs. The president insists you tell him why you're refusing to go to your old village in the Okavango. Don't you want to see how it has flourished?"

Vernon slipped out enough to observe the women.

The tall lithe woman continued down the stairs, holding her head high. "I do not owe the man who killed my husband and my child any explanation. It is another one of his sick tricks to get me to go. My heart is broken in so many pieces that whatever he does to me can never be as bad as losing my family, friends, and way of life. He's kept me in this gilded cage so long I have forgotten how to fly."

The bossy woman turned to catch up with her. "Please, Keeya. Go with him," she begged. "It will do you good to go back."

The tall woman with closely cropped gray hair stopped and turned to look at the secretary with contempt. "You have stopped my escape many times. Why do you want me to go with him this time? What is happening?"

"Because he needs you to do this. Can't you see he cares for you? Why else would he have brought you here to live under the nose of each wife he took then discarded. The only one who endured was you. If you had shown him the same kindness given to you, then you would be mistress of this house instead of that prancing idiot who spends his money so freely."

The corner of Keeya's mouth tilted upward. "I will continue to endure—but not with him." She took one more step then turned back. "And I will find a way to leave forever." She continued down the steps and toward Vernon, who escaped back to the alcove with Zoric and motioned they needed to leave.

Before they could exit she crashed into Vernon, who choked on his words. Of all times for him to freeze up with a woman who needed him.

Zoric bowed his head quickly, seeing the startled, almost fearful look in her eyes. "Go to Camp Kubu. There are people there who can help you," he whispered then touched her arm as if trying to steady her.

Keeya jerked away. "Who are you? How did you know that is where the president is going?"

"We are friends of the Kifaru."

"There is no such thing," she snapped raising her nose in the air.

"What was dead thirty-eight years ago, has returned, ma'am. Please," Zoric spoke softly while Vernon pretended to check an outlet. "Go with the president."

"Humph!" she retorted and strode away toward the kitchen.

"Hey! You! What are you doing?" The security guards hurried toward them. "Are you all right, ma'am?" They got only a dismissive hand wave. "Are you finished?"

"Yep. Headed to get some water," Vernon said taking another glance at Keeya.

The guards took the men's arms and quickly escorted them outside. "Get your water somewhere else."

"What about my report? I need you to sign this or I don't get paid," Vernon, said fumbling with a yellow ticket. He presented it with a pen that looked like a toddler had been chewing on it.

The guard signed the form before shoving it back at Vernon. "You've got one minute to leave the grounds or you'll be needing a cork to plug the hole I plan to put in you."

Vernon glanced at the bill then smirked up at the guard. Zoric was already opening the van door to leave. "Thanks! Call us again next time you screw things up."

"Get in the van," Zoric ordered.

After he slammed the driver's side door, Vernon couldn't resist calling them some colorful names as he offered a gesture of disrespect.

CHAPTER THIRTEEN

The Enigma team spent the morning in a mokoro, a canoe-like boat with a flat bottom narrow enough that Tessa had to sit in front of Chase on a bench with a stadium-style back. One of the guides stood on the back and poled them through the Okavango Delta at a leisurely pace. He stopped once and fished several soft drinks from a cooler to give them. It seemed a good time for him to rest.

The whispering wind pushing through the papyrus and an occasional frightened marabou stork taking flight reminded Tessa she most certainly wasn't in Kansas anymore, or California or anywhere resembling home. The silence engulfing them brought a kind of peace to the troubled thoughts plaguing her for many months. How difficult would it be to live off the grid here, forever? She lifted her face toward the sky and closed her eyes, loving the warmth on her skin.

Removing her pith helmet, she twisted around to see Chase surveying the area. His dark sunglasses hid what she guessed might be a security scan. When he turned his head back toward her, she couldn't resist a smile of contentment.

"I love it here, Chase." Her voice remained low in her awe at such a magnificent show of nature.

His mouth thinned to a straight line, and he nodded some kind of agreement but said nothing. Taking a sip of his orange-flavored drink, he returned to his military-style observation.

The guide pointed to the tall grasses where a bright-red object moved in slow, jerky steps.

"Saddle-billed stork." He dropped his hand to his pole as if to steady his stance on the back of the mokoro.

"Beautiful. That has to be everyone's favorite."

The guide agreed.

How many times had he been told that about the creature standing gracefully at about four feet tall. "How many species of birds are here?"

"Four hundred, maybe. Many."

Tessa opened the pamphlet the camp director passed out at breakfast with names of birds they might see. She checked the saddle-billed off and counted ten others she'd already marked. When she sighed and let her gaze rest on the still waters of the Okavango, Chase laid a hand on her shoulder.

"You okay?"

Tessa reached back to touch his hand, and he immediately withdrew. She looked over her shoulder at him and became aware of his breath on her cheek. "I'm good. I love the quiet."

"I could get use to this," he mumbled. "Let's run away."

It wasn't often Chased teased her about the future. "Okay. No hot water bottles, though."

"Forget it, then. I don't want your cold feet rubbing up against me. You're such a pain in the neck sometimes."

Tessa clicked her tongue in mock annoyance. "No wonder you're single. Such a baby."

He kissed her on the cheek. She twisted around, and their noses touched. Tessa could see her surprised reflection in his mirrored sunglasses.

"Do you enjoy being a temptation?" He continued to speak low as he lifted a curl away from her face. When she didn't answer, he continued, "Because I'm getting pretty tired of it. Any advice?"

"Think of me in footy pajamas, crazy hair, and walking like a zombie with donut crumbs on my chin first thing in the morning."

His lips twisted to one side. "Yeah. Sounds sexy to me."

"Stop it." She frowned. "You might think flirting is funny, but did it ever occur to you I find it distracting? I don't appreciate you toying with my affection, Chase." She turned away, but he wrapped his arms around her, bringing his mouth to her ear.

"And I don't appreciate being held at arm's length while you decide whether or not you love Robert or some tribesman in Afghanistan." Tessa stiffened and tried to lean forward, but he held her in place. "I'm not toying with your affection. I'm holding myself in check."

"I'm not ever going to be your next one-night stand." She briefly considered whether the guide listened to her low-pitched growl.

"You most certainly won't ever be that."

She turned and found her face touching his. She waited for him to withdraw. He didn't.

"I'm playing the affectionate companion slash bodyguard. Wouldn't want anyone to get the wrong idea about us." His amusement spread across his generous mouth when their lips brushed against each other. "Damn, woman," he whispered then leaned back in his seat.

"Ready to go?" their guide asked.

Tessa wanted to jerk the pole away from the guide and shout, What I'm ready for is to strip naked and make a complete fool out of myself. It wouldn't be the first time. But she remained quiet with her tumultuous yearnings and fought to refocus on the business at hand. How could he say one minute they were best buddies and in the next voice things that scared her to death?

"Moremi," Chase addressed their guide, "how deep is the water here?"

What difference did it make? She wasn't going for a swim anytime soon.

"Most places along here can be walked across. A few places are two or three meters deep. Not a good place to swim. The open water is deeper for this. Fishing is better, there, too. But we do not encourage straying but a few feet from the motorboats and mokoros. The crocodiles grow bigger each year. Then there are the hippos who feed on the bottom." Moremi closed the cooler and stowed their empty cans in a mesh bag.

"How is the hunting?"

The mokoro glided through the water again. The movement restored her calm enough for her to face forward and soak up the sunshine.

"There is no hunting, now," Moremi sighed. "President Baboloki stopped big-game hunts."

"Too much environmental pressure from the outside world?" Chase inquired.

"I do not understand it, sir. All of that is beyond me. I know my people are hungry part of the time, and the lack of jobs forces the men to leave their villages to live in the city."

Moremi might not be telling them everything. She had read where ten years earlier UNESCO had labeled the Okavango a World Heritage Site in the hope the vast number of big-game animals would be protected so that ecotourism might flourish. If that were true, why did the people coming and going at the medical clinic appear so poor and unhealthy? The nearby village they'd toured had not been one of progress. Maybe Handsome could shed some light on her concerns.

Before she could return to emptying her mind of geo-political conflicts, Chase touched her shoulder and whispered.

"See that stand of trees to our right?" She shifted her gaze to find it before nodding. "Swim hard."

Even before she could protest such a ridiculous idea, something pinged off the front of the mokoro. The shrill sound of a bird taking flight followed the second shot hitting Moremi. She turned to see him fall into the water. A flood of confusion and fear washed over her.

"Now," Chase yelled then rocked the mokoro to flip it over. Tessa had already leaned hard to the right, and his movements added momentum to her tumble. In a split second, the mokoro came crashing down in front of her, barely missing her head. Panic gripped her as she twisted around to search for Chase, only to find him gone.

A shot echoed across the water, thumping against the mokoro. Another shot hit the water. Tessa cried out, and tears welled up in her eyes. Panic gripped her ability to think beyond pushing under the mokoro. Her feet touched the soft bottom of the Okavango, and so she tried to scrunch lower in the water. A terrified scream escaped her throat when something grabbed her thigh then her arm.

~ ~ ~

Handsome stopped working on the repairs in the camp kitchen when shots echoed across the Okavango. His assistant walked to the door and stared with wide eyes. He turned back to Handsome and shrugged, but the assistant's pinched brow drew Handsome away from his work to stand next to him.

"That sounded like gunshots to me," Handsome mumbled. "Think we've got some poachers?"

"Maybe. Not usually around here." His friend turned back to look out across the tranquil waters of the Okavango. "How many mokoros are out?"

Handsome wiped his hands on an already-soiled towel. "Two. The Germans are on a walking tour, the Brits in one of the Land Rovers."

"The Americans took the mokoros. The smiley one with the beautiful dark lady, left about twenty minutes ago. Got a late start."

Handsome nodded before pushing out into the late morning sun. A troop of baboons hurried through the stand of trees near the camp's edge. He stopped and took a closer look. Three of the bull elephants that liked to visit were backing up at his approach, tossing their giant heads in a show of irritation. They must be spooked at the gunshots. He guessed they'd moved closer to the camp, detecting danger. No one ever bothered them within the campgrounds, and they usually kept their distance. But today they had wandered in close to the observation deck and dining area. He kept an eye on the giants as he approached the office hut. Elephants could charge suddenly, and he didn't want to spook them further.

"Mr. Morgan?"

The camp director looked up from his tidy desk. "What is it, Handsome? You look worried."

"Did you hear gunshots?"

Peter Morgan stood suddenly and grabbed his rifle out of the glass gun case. "No. I was trying to get a message to the main office about supplies. The shortwave radio is acting up again. "Fill me in."

"I want a gun." Handsome straightened his large frame, stopping Peter in his tracks. He came only to Handsome's shoulder and his eyebrows rose with his caution. "Please. A gun. If poachers are out there, the campers could be in trouble. I can help."

Peter retrieved another rifle and a box of ammo. "You sure you can use this?" He checked the weapon then loaded. They locked determined gazes. "Yes. Well I see that was a silly question." They moved to the outside where several other workers had gathered. "Has the motorboat been fueled up today?"

"Yes, sir." A young man motioned for them to follow as he ran toward the boat dock. "I tried to call the ones still out in the delta, but they aren't responding."

Handsome got into the boat last. Peter fired up the engine then took the wheel. "We've got our radios. Call the others if you can and get them back. No need to go into details."

"Right away, sir." He turned and hurried back to camp.

The roar of the engine drowned out the possibility of hearing another gunshot. The water was shallow in the channel they chose to search. The boat moved steadily, both men keeping a vigilant watch on the shorelines.

"There." Peter pointed to a mokoro headed their way. The pole man frantically pushed the pole from side to side, increasing the momentum of the boat.

Handsome spotted Carter and Sam's tight expressions as they turned their heads to look back then to the shore. Had they seen something? At least they were unharmed.

Handsome idled the engine as the mokoro pulled alongside and Sam stood awkwardly. Blood created a widening stain on the arm of her blouse.

"Are you all right?" Handsome grabbed Sam's hand then helped her into the larger boat.

"Yes," she moaned, touching a trickle of blood on her arm. "Grazed me is all." She and Handsome helped Carter aboard. "I'm good. You?"

Carter sighed then touched Sam's cheek and nodded. "Good."

The usual sarcastic banter between the two had evaporated when the situation grew serious. She laid a hand on Carter's for a brief moment. The former astronaut then turned to Handsome. "What's going on?"

Handsome leaned over to address the poleman in the mokoro. "Can you make it on your own? It will be faster without the passengers. Are you injured?"

He assured them he could make it and pushed off. Handsome addressed the passengers. "Do you want to go back? This boat is faster than the mokoro."

The camp director frowned at Handsome. "They don't have a choice. I'm responsible for all guests. She's been injured."

Carter shook his head angrily. "We're staying. Our friends are out there. They were ahead of us by about two hundred and seventy-five meters. The shots came from there."

"You can't deal with these people," Peter shouted over the engine as it roared back to life.

Carter pulled out his weapon from inside his safari vest as Sam removed one from hers. "I said we're going. I think my partner agrees," he growled. "She's tough. She'll be fine."

"Let them come," Handsome insisted. "They are more than UN people, Mr. Morgan." Handsome leaned in to Peter's ear. "We may need their help." He withdrew and leveled a dangerous glare at his boss. "We may need their help."

"Very well," Peter agreed. His mouth turned down as he stared at the extra guns then squinted at Handsome. "You had better be right."

The boat powered up as the three found a seat. They scanned the area for trouble, muscles visibly tensing when an elephant jumped into the water. The boat swerved out of the way. A wave rocked them wildly, nearly flipping them over. Peter powered down once more and took a white-knuckled grip on the steering wheel.

Handsome retrieved the binoculars out of a console then handed them to Carter. "Here. See if you can find them."

His first concern was for Tessa Scott. He had convinced her to join him on this excursion into madness. She believed in him, and he'd jeopardized her safety. A woman like her should not be working for regime change in an African country. She had a family to think of. He'd never meant for any of them to get hurt.

A fire burned in his belly as he thought about the urgency to find her. Crocodiles were his biggest concern then hippos. They were vicious and resisted being intimidated, even by elephants and crocodiles. But there hadn't been any hippos in this channel for weeks. They'd moved onto better feeding areas, leaving the crocs to sun themselves on the banks without fear of being stomped on by the cantankerous mammals.

These backwaters of the Okavango were perfect for snatching birds, fish, terrapins, and small mammals. Crocodiles sometimes worked together to ambush antelope or zebras, chomping them in pieces and sharing the meaty delights. Humans were easy prey if caught unaware. Natives remained vigilant, but tourists needed constant reminding not to get too close with their cameras.

"Slow down," Carter ordered. He pointed at something in the water.

"I see it," Peter called as he killed the engine and floated up to the overturned mokoro.

Handsome handed Sam the rifle, knowing she was a dead shot. "Carter, can you jump in to help me right the mokoro?"

Even before the last words were out of his mouth, Carter had removed the binoculars from around his neck and vest. He handed off his weapon and went over the side after Handsome entered the water.

Both men plunged beneath the mokoro and in seconds resurfaced. They flipped it over before spinning around to face the boat.

"Well?" Sam called.

Handsome pulled a safari vest from inside the mokoro then turned it for her to see.

It was covered in blood.

Chapter Fourteen

A strangled scream escaped Tessa's lungs as she fought to remove whatever had clamped onto her leg. In the chaos, her feet floated out from under her, and she sank under the water. Frantically, she slapped and clawed to free herself. When she regained her footing, she jerked herself upright and brought the large beast with her.

Her fists pounded on the body.

"Tessa! It's me! Stop." Chase squeezed her arms tight enough so she couldn't move.

Tessa gulped and sobbed. Falling against him, she wrapped her arms around his neck. "I was so scared," she wailed. "I thought a crocodile had my leg."

"I didn't mean to scare you. Guess you couldn't see my hand with all the silt you stirred up." He stopped and pushed her back then lowered his eyes to meet hers. "You're okay, babe. Pull yourself together. We're not out of this yet."

Her neck moved like that of a bobble-head doll when she tried to convey her willingness to continue.

"We need to swim out of here. It isn't far to land. I had to take Moremi to safety. He's badly hurt."

Chase was covered in blood. "Are you hurt?" she gasped running her fingers over him like a mine detector. Even as she asked him, he pulled off her heavy safari jacket. She slipped her arms from the vest and watched the blood transfer to her jacket. He pushed it aside. "This will weigh you down, Tess. It's only about chest-deep here. Swim the first twenty feet or so then you can walk the rest of the way. I'll be right there with you."

"You are bleeding. Chase!" she cried. "Where are you hurt?"

"Just a flesh wound. But I need to get out of this water. I don't know if crocs can smell blood, but I'm not willing to find out. Let's go." He pushed the jacket aside before putting his hand on the top of her head. "Ready?" Before she could answer, he shoved her under the water. She surfaced on the other side of the boat almost instantly.

Chase surfaced next to her and swam hard with vigorous kicks. She followed even though she'd never been a good swimmer. Her arms ached, and her lungs burned. All the advances in exercise over the last year didn't seem to matter when trying to keep up with Captain American. Even wounded, Chase continued to surprise her with his strength.

After he rose up out of the water, he stopped long enough to jerk Tessa to her feet and hold onto her hand. They trudged ahead through tall papyrus grass. She held tightly, thinking any second she would stumble and fall or be snatched up by a disgruntled beast.

The grasses soon opened up and they walked out onto dry land. Tessa staggered after Chase when he ran to help Moremi, who lay sprawled on the sandy ground. He lifted the guide's body into his arms. "Let's find shelter. I don't know where those gunmen are. We've got to get to a safe place."

"But, but, but," Tessa protested between gasps for air. "Where? How?"

Chase halted suddenly and she crashed into his back. "Hear that?" he asked.

Tessa hunkered down as she cocked her ear toward the direction he stared. "Something is moving in the bush."

Moremi groaned. "There." He pointed toward a dense stand of trees where several mounds of dirt towered like sand castles. A disgruntled group of carmine bee-eaters created a blur of orange as they flew up from the sandy banks. "Safe there."

It felt like walking in quicksand as they tried to find a safe place. Once inside the ring of trees, Chase laid Moremi down then pulled him up to rest his back against one of the palms. He took some fronds to dust away their footsteps, backed toward the bush in the opposite direction then circled back to where Tessa waited. She exhaled in relief when Moremi stirred.

He coughed through his garbled words. "Supplies." He pointed to a pile of rocks. "Buried there. You'll find what you need."

Tessa and Chase kneeled and removed the white stones, some weighing at least ten pounds, piled about two feet high, uncovering a hole, four feet wide. Once they were removed, she helped him lift two metal containers. Rust had formed on the handles and around the latch.

The slow crash of brush toward them continued. Moremi turned his head toward the sounds. "Do not worry. I think elephants are nearby. We are protected by the trees and rocks. They can't get to us. They get nervous when the scent of blood is in the air."

"That didn't take long." Tessa turned her attention to the metal box. Chase flipped it open.

Moremi moaned a note of caution. "It isn't my blood they smell. Poachers must have brought down a larger animal and may be butchering it for food or market. You must be still if the elephants come this way. Even if they can't get to us, they may throw a stone or branch. A smaller tree would not be difficult to push on us." He cringed as his eyes squeezed shut followed by a moan.

Chase jerked a first aid kit out. "Tess, I may need your help." He opened a package of gauze soaked with some kind of chemical.

"What is that?"

"We use this stuff on the battlefield." He handed her a piece of gauze he'd torn off then he ripped open the pouch. "This contains kaolin. It accelerates blood clotting." He applied it to the gauze. "Let me try and clean the wound." In quick order, he ripped open Moremi's flimsy tee shirt and tossed it aside.

Located under his shoulder, the gunshot wound revealed ripped skin and a sizable hole. Normally a bit squeamish at the sight of blood, Tessa swallowed hard and watched Chase disinfect the area with some kind of cleaning pad. "Push that gauze in here and apply pressure. I'll get more packing for it and try to tape it when we slow the blood flow. With any luck, the bleeding will stop in five minutes. He's going to need a doctor."

When Tessa applied pressure, he bolted upright then fainted, his body sliding to the side. Chase caught him and laid him flat before propping his head on a blanket roll Tessa handed him from the container. He continued to apply pressure for a few more minutes then bandaged the area. The knowledge he had been a medic with the Rangers and later on, used those skills when serving in Delta Force, gave Tessa some reassurance Moremi might survive. His parents had been medical missionaries in China and had often been forced to assist in an emergency.

An elephant's trumpeting startled her. Several of the giants swayed outside their ring of protection, raising awareness there remained a number of other dangers facing them. Chase opened the larger of the two metal boxes and found a rifle that may or may not work. It didn't matter since there was no ammunition available. The handgun appeared newer and was already loaded.

"Get that other blanket, Tess." He slid over to a large rock and sat, leaning his head back.

Tessa tossed it to him then grabbed the first aid kit. She eased over to him on her knees and set the kit down next to him. "Let me take a look," she said, pulling his shirt up to examine his side where the blood oozed enough to make a spot on his clothes. His smirk indicated a possible flirtatious comment, but it never came. She didn't know a flesh wound from the real thing, but it needed cleaning nonetheless. After applying some antibiotic cream and a small bandage, she pulled his shirt back down.

Chase shook the blanket out then held it up enough for her. "Get under here with me." She hesitated when their gazes locked. "It's green. We'll be camouflaged."

Tessa laid a couple of palm fronds across Moremi before moving under the blanket. Chase pulled it up to their chins. He turned his head toward the throaty rumble of the elephants, moving to the delta side of their hideout.

"I'm not sure whether to be scared of these big guys or the ones with guns." She couldn't help pushing herself closer to his body. Somehow, his proximity reassured her.

He dropped his hand down on her thigh and squeezed. "I'm going to trust the elephants. These are females so they aren't likely to let some guys walking around get close to their calves. I counted eight females."

"That makes fifteen then, with the little ones," she whispered. A snort from one of the elephants and several others lifting their trunks, silenced Tessa's chatter. She leaned her head against his shoulder then laid her hand on his.

The sound of a distant engine floated over the waters. Tessa couldn't decide if it was a car or a boat. Chase stiffened under her touch then pulled away to check his weapon. Moremi moaned again, alerting the elephants to their presence. A guttural rumble then a protest trumpet sound by the matriarch; the largest female followed. She watched them move away but not before the matriarch charged at them then quickly turned and joined her herd. A sigh of relief escaped Tessa as she leaned her head back against the boulder then grabbed her nose.

"I think the ladies left a large deposit of pachyderm crap for us." Chase threw off the blanket and crawled over to Moremi to check on the bleeding. He stole a few glances between the rocks as if looking for trouble. "We're some ways from the water. If someone comes looking for us, hopefully the boat hasn't drifted too far from where we came ashore." He tried to stand. Tessa scampered up and grabbed his arm.

"Where do you think you're going?"

"I'm going to see if I can drag the mokoro ashore. If they send up a drone, they might spot it."

Chase frowned when she pulled his arm to stop him.

"Absolutely not. What if a croc gets you? Or the poachers? Or that elephant, who I'm pretty sure would love to sit on you. Do you honestly think the camp keeps a drone? Nonsense. No. No. No. You stay out of the water."

"Your concern is touching," he said, laying his free hand where she'd gripped his arm. "I figure it's past noon. They'll be expecting us for lunch. Moremi had a radio, but it ended up in the water. I didn't try to retrieve it. Things were happening pretty fast."

"If those were poachers…"

"They may not have been. Why would they be shooting our way? Game is over here, not out in the water."

"But Moremi said…"

"Yes. I remember what he said. He may know something more. If those men meant to scare the tourists, then it will affect the bottom line for these people. You're the one who told me how that massacre affected tourism for years. It's becoming prosperous again. Maybe someone doesn't like it."

"Like President Baboloki?"

"Right."

"But why? Killing tourists would make him look bad, like he wasn't in control of his country." Tessa pondered the possibilities.

"Not sure. Maybe Handsome will have some insight to this."

A gunshot broke the quiet sound of the wind moving through the dry grasses. Both Tessa and Chase retreated back down to adjust the fronds over Moremi. He looked nearly invisible. They'd managed to secure a few fronds for themselves and huddled together as they waited. The sound of voices drew near and added to the uneasy trumpet of unhappy elephants. Whoever approached had picked up on their trail.

"Over here." Someone shouted loud enough to cause the elephants to turn and stomp through the bush away from where they hid behind the anthills.

Chase gripped the pistol then rested his wrists on the dip between the anthill towers. With the fronds placed against their chests, Tessa convinced herself, it would be difficult to spot them.

"You need to get down, Tessa. I don't want you to get hit by a bullet meant for me." Chase pushed her back. Tessa grabbed his fingers and squeezed. "I'll be okay. Trust me."

She swallowed hard then licked her lips. Wanting to share a word, a moment, she longed to share how much she admired him. Why not admit she cared about him even in the middle of the night when he suffered from nightmares and might take a swing at her attempt at comfort? Before she could offer even one encouraging word, he turned away.

"Whoever it is, I think they've moved farther away," Chase whispered. "I still don't see anything."

She stood beside him when he moved enough for her to see through the gap. "Maybe they just gave up and decided we weren't a threat or got scared at what they'd done."

"Always the optimist."

"Chase, I want to tell you—"

Another shot cut through the silence, followed by elephants stampeding back toward them, trumpeting loudly. The matriarch stormed at them, running into the anthill tower. They jumped back as it collapsed. Chase raised his pistol in the air and emptied the chamber.

"She doesn't seem intimidated by this." He tossed the gun aside and dragged Tessa back as she stared in horror at the advancing elephant. More shots followed from outside their protected circle. The matriarch rocked her head then like a choreographed dance, the herd rumbled away in quick order. Chase picked up the rifle and shook his head before squinting at the area beyond their enclosure. "No more ammo," he confessed. "But whoever is out there won't know that."

"Chase. Tessa." The familiar voice grew louder. "Chase. Tessa. Where are you?"

Tessa let a light laugh escape her throat and tried to step out through the opening the elephant created, only to be jerked back into the safety of the circle. "Where are you going?"

"That is Handsome. I'd recognize it anywhere."

"Who says he didn't instigate this?"

"Chase. Tessa." Handsome lumbered forward, holding a rifle.

"Where did he get that shiny new toy?" Chase growled and pulled her behind the remaining anthill tower. "I don't trust him."

Tessa pushed at his arm around her waist to free herself while straining to see the people gathering behind Handsome. "Do you trust Carter and Sam? Because they are with him."

<h1 style="text-align:center">CHAPTER FIFTEEN</h1>

The boat roared through the waters, occasionally sending up a spray of water when called upon to dodge something in the Okavango. Handsome stood at the helm, focused on getting Moremi and Chase to the medical clinic. He'd dropped the director, Peter Morgan, at the camp to reassure the guests and talk to authorities if they could be contacted by radio. The waters here remained deep and clear, allowing him to open up the throttle.

"How much farther, Handsome?" Carter yelled over the roar of the engine. "Moremi has lost a lot of blood."

"Twenty minutes. Less if hippos don't get in the way." Handsome stole a glance over his shoulder at his unexpected partners.

Chase had emerged from their hiding place while trying to restrain Tessa from lunging forward in pure delight at seeing him. She amused him even then. The woman continued to amuse him with her child-like enthusiasm. Seeing them together reminded Handsome of how dangerous it could be to cross Captain Hunter, and most certainly a death sentence for anyone who harmed the housewife from Grass Valley.

The whole idea she had thrown in with this group reminded him of a jail inmate who was given a puppy to train then release to a worthy recipient. Only with Tessa, the chances were, they'd get her killed before being released. Maybe he'd take it upon himself to make sure that didn't happen. Good people like his father and this woman needed someone to protect them from the world.

Finally, the village of his birth came into view. His father and several men waited on the dock. Trickles of sweat trailed down the back of his neck. The afternoon sun could be brutal even this time of year. The boat slowed as he maneuvered it alongside the dock.

"Peter got through to us after you dropped him off." His father helped his men tie up the boat then extended a hand to the women to join him.

A gurney lay on the faded, splintered boards of the dock. With the creak of rotting planks, Handsome half expected each step he took would cave in with his bulk. He moved back to where Carter and two other men who'd jumped in the boat, lifted Moremi up.

When Chase tried to help, Carter pushed him aside and let loose some colorful words to order him away. The man had to be in on the action, no matter if he was injured or not. Other than a slight squint in the captain's eyes, he didn't exhibit any pain from his own wound.

After helping get Moremi onto the gurney, Handsome turned in time to see the women pull Chase from the boat. He quickly shook them off, but his father refused to be rebuffed as he lifted his shirt to examine the injury.

"I thought this was supposed to be a flesh wound," Dr. Girard mumbled then pulled the shirt back down.

"Guess I got it wrong." Chase cut his eyes over to Tessa who had taken on the look of a deer in the headlights. "I'll be fine. Let's take care of one problem at a time."

"Very well, then." Dr. Girard nodded and motioned for the men to carry Moremi toward the clinic. "But you're next, then, Samantha."

Handsome waved the women off when they tried to assist the captain. "I've got him. You go on ahead. Tessa, I want you checked out, too."

"No. I'm fine." She stepped toward Chase, but Handsome held up his hand. "Do as I say, woman," he demanded.

Even Sam stopped dead in her tracks before taking Tessa's arm. "Let's go, Betty Crocker. Chase is a big boy. Stop mothering him."

Tessa let herself be dragged away by the one person she professed to not trust. He sincerely doubted the idea they were enemies. To his knowledge, Sam had no lady friends, only men, but she may have found her match in the Grass Valley housewife. He walked alongside Chase, careful not to touch him unless assistance became necessary.

When the women were out of earshot, Chase turned to him and spoke through gritted teeth. "What the hell was that all about?"

Handsome stared ahead. "When we came looking for you, a call came over the radio about a group of poachers in the area. They don't usually get so close to the camps. Too many things can go wrong like today."

"So poaching is a problem?" Chase stumbled but righted himself when Handsome grabbed his elbow. He missed a step and pitched forward. Handsome grabbed his arm. Chase stopped for a split second and took a deep breath before he pulled free. "You were saying?"

Handsome didn't try to object to Chase being prideful, and even enjoyed that the man probably suffered from more pain than he let on. "The poachers. The world gets outraged at the big game hunters coming into Africa. They say safaris are antiquated and encourage the killing of endangered species."

"You sound like this was a good thing. I'm surprised."

Handsome ignored Chase's condescending tone. "I admit some of those hunters did take unfair advantage of big game even when warned not to. For decades, these safaris brought much money to the villages. Jobs at camps, artwork, guides, and start-up businesses were created because these wealthy hunters came for trophies."

"What about the other safaris? Didn't they make an economic impact?" Chase stopped on the edge of the medical compound. Both men paused and watched the chaos of an injured patient being carried into the clinic. Handsome noticed the labored breath of his charge and his dark skin beginning to turn ashen.

"Yes. Of course, photo safaris added even more jobs. There always seems to be an abundance of Western tourists looking for adventure. That isn't the problem."

Chase cringed as he moved toward the clinic. "Does any of this have anything to do with us being shot at?"

Handsome shrugged. "Hard to say. Before Baboloki came to power, there was poaching, but at a level manageable by agencies put in place to curtail this kind of activity. When he fell for the world view to do away with big-game hunting several years ago, he shot up in the polls of world opinion."

"But not with his own people?" Chase took a deep breath as he stopped at the steps to the clinic.

"No. Jobs dried up. Tourists with disposable incomes moved to other hunting grounds in countries that cared little about world opinion. It didn't take long for the people to become hungry and desperate. Poaching a rhino for his horn can sustain a family for a year or more. Soon the meat of Cape buffalo, kudu, and a number of other animals became a necessity for rural people."

"And the poaching…"

"Is out of control. Animals that were once only threatened have moved closer to being on the endangered list. Although I am against killing elephants and rhinoceros for their tusks and horns, there does come a time for good conservation. We have to find a way to live peacefully with the beasts of the earth. And we have to provide for these people if the animals are to continue living among us."

"What does Baboloki say about all of this?"

"He is protecting the animals. Yet, he goes on safari each year at different camps where that tourism has returned."

"Which he decimated to begin with."

"Exactly."

"You still haven't given me a straight answer on why someone shot at us."

Chase was taking the steps slowly when Tessa came rushing out and put an arm around him. Chase's snarl transformed into a smile at her touch.

"Don't just stand there with your bare face hanging out, Handsome. Help me," she demanded.

"He's refused my help," he protested, but he pushed Tessa aside and forced his arm around the captain.

"Oh. And he is so much bigger than you," Tessa snapped with more indignation than he expected. "Your father is waiting." She stomped inside then pivoted and watched them enter.

"Is she always such a pain in the ass?" Handsome mused.

Chase cringed at Tessa when she tried to adjust her hold on him. "You have no idea."

She pushed out her lips as if trying to mask amusement when they moved past her. "Both of you shut up."

The medical clinic had limited resources for serious injuries. Dr. Girard stabilized Moremi, but he needed surgery. And Handsome received word from Peter at the camp that they'd caught a break.

"A plane is diverting here, Dr. Girard." He couldn't bring himself to call him Father in this place. He feared danger would rob him of the one person who truly loved him. If the wrong people found out he was the owner of the Kifaru diamond, the whole village might suffer. "We were expecting some important people from Gaborone at the end of the week. They moved up their arrival to today."

"God is good." The doctor covered Moremi with a dingy sheet. "Now you, Captain Hunter." The doctor patted an empty examining table then shooed everyone else out the door. Tessa and Handsome remained. "You, too, young lady." The doctor pointed to her then the door.

"I'm not leaving him." She spread her legs out enough to take a stubborn pose before she crossed her arms in front of her chest. "I'm not squeamish, Dr. Girard."

Handsome turned his head toward the door when Sam and Carter burst into laughter.

"We'll wait here in case you need us," Carter managed to say through gasps of amusement.

Sam pursed her lips together and narrowed her eyes with a loud "humph" that sounded a great deal like mocking. Dr. Girard had already attended to Sam's injury.

Tessa ignored them and took Chase's bloody hand. His eyes lifted to meet hers, and Handsome witnessed some kind of connection between the two. It faded quickly when they pulled away from each other.

"Let's have a look," the doctor mumbled as he cut Chase's shirt away.

Once the bloody clothing had been tossed aside, the doctor examined the entry wound. Chase flinched ever so slightly. Handsome chuckled, drawing an angry expression from the man.

"Tessa?" Chase switched his focus to his champion. "You need to leave. Remember Afghanistan when I got shot up? You didn't handle that very well."

"I was surprised to see you is all," she said, fanning herself. "Is it hot in here?"

Everyone turned and noticed her ashen-colored face. She pushed her hair back then wiped her brow. Her rapid blinking and rolling of her shoulders indicated distress.

"Get her out of here," Dr. Girard demanded, looking to his son.

"Carter." Handsome grabbed Tessa by the arm, who appeared to be a little wobbly. The man hurried into the room with Sam at his side. They slipped their arms around her and tugged. This time, all her stubbornness evaporated.

"Okay. I'll leave," she said through a cough. "I'll be right outside, Chase, if you need me." She tried to push helpful hands away unsuccessfully.

"Good to know. Sam—" Chase moaned as the doctor examined his wound.

"I'll take care of her," she complained. "I'm getting used to having a pain in my neck all the time."

Without missing a beat, Tessa looked up at Carter. "Are you going to let her talk to you like that?" He burst into laughter.

"Always the comedian," Sam said as they disappeared back out into the hall.

"Thanks, Dr. Girard." Chase slid off the table and accepted one of the doctor's tee shirts to wear. "Glad it wasn't something serious."

"It looked worse than it was. I thought for sure more than one bullet had lodged in there, but it went through without nicking anything important. You're a lucky man. Since you've a number of scars, you understand how stitches work and that they'll be more aggravating than the wound. However, do rest today, maybe tomorrow." He handed him a baggie of pills. "The white ones are nothing more than Tylenol, and the pink ones are an antibiotic. Take all of them. I gather you've had a tetanus shot in the last year or so?"

"Six months ago." Chase pulled the shirt over his head. "How many months of the year do you work here?"

"Maybe six. I do have a practice in Florida and although I'm officially retired from it, I need to keep an eye on things. Always good to keep sharp and see what the younger doctors are doing these days."

"Who takes care of this while you're gone?"

"I have an arrangement with Doctors Without Borders and several medical mission groups. I'm here two months and then back to the States for two. Soon I will be here full-time."

Chase took the bottle of water the doctor offered to him and drank deep. "Does that depend on whether Handsome takes over the country with his diamond?"

The doctor busied himself with organizing a cart of supplies. "My Louis is not trying to take over the country."

"Could have fooled me. He seems pretty determined to see a regime change in Botswana."

"That is only wishful thinking. There are always people who would prefer a different leader. The United States is a prime example of that. My Louis only wants the best for these people."

"His people, it seems."

Dr. Girard whirled around with panic flooding his eyes. "You must never say that out loud. No one here must ever know who his real father was or what treasure—"

An aide knocked on the door and entered in a state of agitation. "Dr. Girard, the plane has landed. We have Moremi ready to go."

"Very good. Thank you."

"Doctor." The aide's eyes widened. "The plane belongs to President Baboloki."

"B-Baboloki," the doctor stammered. "Are you sure?"

"Yes. Yes. Come see. The president is here." He motioned for them to follow and hurried out the door.

"Where is Louis?" The doctor rushed into the hall.

"He went to help with Moremi," Sam spoke in her usual apathetic tone. "What's going on? The whole compound acts like we're about to be stampeded by a herd of elephants."

Chase nodded to Carter. "We need to get him inside. Now." They were already out the door when he remembered Tessa. "Where is she?"

"With Handsome. She wanted to check on Moremi and say a prayer over him." Sam gave a disapproving eye roll.

"That woman and her higher power will be the death of me."

"I think we're too late." Carter halted on the bottom step as Handsome and several other men carried the stretcher out across the dusty lawn with Tessa tagging along, holding Moremi's hand.

Dr. Girard bounded down the stairs and raced toward the men carrying the stretcher just as President Baboloki strutted into the compound with his entourage. He stopped to survey his surroundings before letting his eyes fall on the approaching Americans.

Carter nudged Handsome away and took his place, whispering who the guests entering the compound were. Dr. Girard joined them to check Moremi's vital signs.

Handsome refused to leave his father's side. "This must be stressful for you. It is time I met the man who changed both our destinies," he whispered to Carter.

"President Baboloki." Dr. Girard stepped aside and let the men make their way toward the seaplane. "Thank you so much for sharing your plane with this man. With your generous offer, he will have a chance to survive."

President Baboloki arched an eyebrow when his eyes fell on the tall black man before him whose face masked any emotions. "But, of course. My people come first."

Chase pulled Tessa to his side. "Mr. President. We meet again. I didn't expect to see you so soon. Such a pleasure." But the president appeared unhappy to see him.

"I did not expect to encounter you, either, Captain Hunter." Chase wondered why his hand gripped more tightly than necessary. "I heard there were other casualties."

"Only a flesh wound. I was lucky." Chase smirked.

"Yes." Baboloki frowned. "I think you were." He ushered the rest of his group forward. "I understand you will provide boats to take us to our camp?"

"I have a boat ready, Mr. President." Handsome's voice gave Chase a chill. Did he maybe have a fever? The man he'd met in North Africa years ago, glared at the president.

"Very good." Baboloki turned and motioned several people forward, one, a woman a little younger than Dr. Girard.

With bowed head, the woman crossed her hands in front of her and stopped behind the president. She appeared thin and frail next to the stout leader. Her simple yellow dress of Kenta cloth reminded Chase of a wildflower. Her gray hair closely cropped around her face, revealed delicate features, still beautiful for a woman of her age.

The doctor stepped forward. "Welcome, President Baboloki. I'm Dr. Girard. I run this clinic."

At that moment, the woman jerked her head up and stared wide-eyed at the doctor. He, too, appeared spellbound. She extended her hand toward him.

"I am Keeya."

They clasped hands while staring into one another's eyes.

Handsome moved next to his father in a protective stance.

The woman's eyes darted to him then staggered back as her hand covered her mouth.

"My—"

Before she could say another word, Keeya's eyes rolled back in her head. Her knees buckled, and Handsome rushed to catch her. Lifting her up into his arms, he glanced at his father who appeared stunned.

"Dr. Girard?" Handsome questioned when his father laid his hand on his heart.

CHAPTER SIXTEEN

Even before Handsome laid Keeya down on an examining table, her eyes fluttered open and searched the room while others moved in and out. Chase followed Handsome into the clinic while Tessa walked beside the doctor who lowered his head to listen to the shorter President Baboloki explain Keeya's condition.

"She has been losing weight. Her appetite seems to be nonexistent of late."

"And who is she, President Baboloki?" Dr. Girard slowed his steps.

"Keeya is my companion, friend, and helps with my son. She has been a part of my family for many years." His voice showed concern. "Please see that she has what is needed. If I need to send her back to Gaborone, I will do so straightaway."

"It could be nothing. I will check her out." The doctor motioned for one of the aides to step forward. "Take the president to the dining area along with his people and serve some refreshments." The aide nodded and extended his arm toward another area of the compound. When he moved away, Dr. Girard halted and rubbed his face with his hand. "Dear God in Heaven," he whispered.

Tessa rubbed the doctor's arm. "What is it? Are you okay?"

"No. I am not."

Sam returned to inform them Moremi was on the plane about to leave. The doctor ignored the announcement and continued to stare at his newest patient.

He moved to Keeya's side to stare down at a woman who batted her eyelashes and stared with confusion at the doctor. Chase stood back experiencing a sense of protection toward the doctor. In spite of his misgivings toward Handsome, the fact this unselfish doctor took a black child to be his own, without considering how it would affect his own life or career, led Chase to realize maybe there really were more good people in the world than he'd once believed. Tessa had been the first one, followed by Dr. Girard.

"Chase, you need to sit down. You're as pale as me. Come on. Let me get you something to eat." Tessa stood in front of him and laid a gentle hand on his arm that managed to distract him for a few seconds.

"I'll be there in a minute. Go ahead. I want to make sure everything is okay here." He laid his hand on hers then rubbed her fingers tenderly. "Go on. Make sure Sam and Carter are with you. I don't trust the president. He seemed a little too surprised to see us."

"You think he was behind the ambush?"

"I wouldn't put it past him." He took a chance and stared into her blue eyes. That familiar pain in his chest forced him to stand up straighter instead of leaning against the wall. Rubbing the spot might alarm her. "His head of security, Dage I think his name is, was eyeing you like a piece of meat. Be careful."

"When we get back to camp, I'm putting you to bed," she declared only to turn scarlet. "I mean…"

Chase chuckled. "I know what you meant. But let me have my moment, will ya?" He led her out the door. "I'll watch you until you get to the dining area." He lifted a hand toward Carter who shaded his eyes then waved. "Tessa?"

"Yes?"

He leaned down and whispered in her ear. "Thanks for being at my side in there. I'm glad you're not squeamish," he mocked.

She surprised him by laying a soft hand on his cheek then rushed down the steps.

Handsome lumbered past him in the doorway and announced his plans. "I'm going to make sure the boats are ready. Peter is sending a second one, so we'll head out in an hour or so. The president probably will want to get back before dark. The camp will be in chaos with the president arriving sooner than expected."

"Are you going to be able to handle this?" Chase grabbed his arm.

"I'm not going to kill him, if that's what you are concerned about. I want him to be afraid like my people were on the day he slaughtered them along with my parents. If it hadn't been for that good man in there, all hope would be lost. I'm not going to jeopardize everything he's sacrificed, for my own chance at revenge."

"There may be hope for you yet, Handsome."

Dr. Girard took the woman's hand in his and bent close to speak to her.

Chase waved Handsome off. "Go on. I'll wait here to make sure things are okay. I don't like that guy Dage who protects Baboloki. Be sharp."

Handsome pursed his lips then continued down the stairs.

Returning to the examining room, Chase stood in the doorway in order to see anyone approaching from the hall or outside. He didn't like those kinds of surprises. He heard the woman whimper when he stepped back into the hall to listen to them.

"Dr. Girard," she said kissing his hand. "Dear Dr. Girard."

Chase's body tensed as a story unfolded before his eyes.

"I believed you were dead," the doctor spoke softly, with a catch in his voice. "I'm so sorry. We were told everyone died, Keeya. I'm mortified I trusted them. I beg your forgiveness."

"Was that my son, good doctor?" She grabbed his hand with both of hers.

"Yes. He resembles his father but also you."

As she struggled to sit up, the doctor slipped an arm behind her back to assist. "I thought he was killed with his father. John snatched him away soon after his birth and said he would try and find you. I was told everyone died, including my husband and the innocent tourists at the camp."

Dr. Girard's eyes took on a faraway look as he explained what had happened so long ago. Chase listened, mesmerized.

Laughter floated into the darkness along with the tinkling of silverware against china, and glasses lifted in toasts as stars emerged to form the Southern Cross. Roasted pork simmered with pearl onions and creamy potatoes surrounded by sliced red tomatoes satisfied appetites until the bread pudding arrived with more champagne.

"Join us, John!" one Australian invited as he pointed with his glass to an empty chair. "Tell us more stories."

The guide glanced at the white camp director, Clive, who frowned and gave a small head shake. "I think I will clear these dishes and call it a night. My wife is expecting a baby any day. I hate to leave her too long." John offered a wide, almost mischievous smile.

"A baby! How marvelous," a middle-aged Englishwoman said as she pushed her gray-streaked hair away from her face. "Do you have names picked out, John?"

"Yes. But, after meeting all of you, I think, perhaps, I should add a few more to the list."

Laughter burst forth, adding another layer of relaxation to the gathering. Dr. Girard couldn't help but ponder about how well John was treated when tourists weren't around. Congratulations were offered and in return, the guide promised to keep them informed of any good news concerning his family then he slipped away.

Dr. Girard leaned back in his chair and listened to the conversation continue.

"John is full of such incredible stories and information, Clive. Was he educated at a university?" The Australian slipped a beefy arm onto the back of his wife's chair.

Clive drained his glass and stood to hunt for another bottle. "Yes. His father and grandfather came from the village nearby and rose through the ranks of government in the early days. They were instrumental in the creation of our democracy. Their hard work pulled in the surrounding tribes. It was a tough go at first, but, today, we are a stable country. John was given the opportunity for an education in engineering. After graduation, he decided to come home and marry his childhood sweetheart."

"I've read the Autonomy Party is trying to change things. What is it all about?" interjected Dr. Girard.

"Yes, it's all rubbish, of course. They fear the minority of whites who occupy the Workers' Party have too much control over the minerals industry and don't pay enough taxes that would shore up schools and medical services in rural areas like here."

The guests nodded as if they understood.

"Can you imagine getting a doctor to come here? Or teachers?" Clive asked.

"I'm a doctor, and I'd gladly donate my time to help these people several weeks of the year. I'm sure mission groups from countries like the United States would love serving time in such a stable country." Dr. Girard covered his glass when the director tried to refill it.

"Do-gooders come and go, but they mostly do more damage than good."

"How so?" The doctor took another nibble of his bread pudding.

"They put ideas into the heads of these people. The natives begin to think they can have a better life. Next thing you know, they are poaching the black rhino to have enough money to send their kids away to school or buy a satellite system to watch CNN. Then they will want highways to drain the Okavango. The tourists bring in lots of money that filters to the villages. These people need to work, not dream about impossible things unavailable in this part of the world for another fifty years."

"What of the diamond mines?" The English lady held her hand up to let the light bounce off her diamond. "Surely, there are jobs there."

"The current government shut some of them down when it surfaced the diamonds were being used to sponsor rebels in neighboring countries who wanted to take down their governments. So, for now, this is not an option. There is trouble in Gaborone. The military has threatened to take over if the elections aren't held soon to seat a more moderate leader, who will stimulate the economy with foreign investments and exploratory mining. Some even want a dam along the Okavango to generate more electricity for a growing population."

"And all of this wild land?" Dr. Girard leaned forward, thinking of John and his village.

"Would be underwater. The animals displaced or drowned. Tourism dried up. Villagers homeless and moved to urban areas where they'd be exposed to drugs and other criminal endeavors. This hope generates conflict. We don't need any more nonsense. John came here to escape the discord. He was expected to go into politics or mining, but he chose to help his village and family here. Good man, although I suspect he is into something else at times. I keep an eye on him."

The conversation drifted into less controversial topics as a breeze from the Okavango River swept across the camp and fruit bats made their puppy-like barks from high in the trees. The fire pit glowed with dying embers when the group separated with huge flashlights in hand to guide them back to their tents. They were reminded of an early wake-up call as they said good night to rest for another adventure at morning's first light.

With the rising sun, two Tswana girls of not more than twenty brought trays for the campers. Pots of hot tea and a small plate of biscuits was placed on a folding chair outside each tent. The girls offered a warm greeting in hopes of stirring their guests awake. Dr. Girard was already dressed and ready as the sun rose above the horizon. He watched the blue waters of the Okavango turn to blades of wavy silver. When a troop of baboons wandered through camp, the rapid click of his camera hurried them along.

When the last of the campers entered the dining area, Clive rushed in to speak to the group. "I'm so sorry to tell you this."

"What is it, Clive?" the Australian woman asked as she stepped forward.

"Three of our workers were attacked by a Cape buffalo on their way to camp this morning."

"Oh Lord, not John!" fussed the English lady, laying her hand on her heart.

"Thankfully, no."

A sigh of relief went up among the group.

"Two managed to climb trees, but the third man was gored severely. I must ask you to be cautious of your picture taking. Animals sense when something has gone wrong. Your morning activities must be postponed for a short time."

Dr. Girard placed a hand on Clive's shoulder. "Take me to him. Maybe I can help."

"I hope so. I've put a call in on my radio. A seaplane will be here within the hour. Come. He's on the outskirts of camp."

"How did he get there?" Dr. Girard asked as they jogged toward a shack where several men stood nervously, speaking in whispers.

"Other workers came along with pistols they used to scare the animals away in cases like this. Usually they travel together, but these three set out early and got caught off guard." He opened the door wider to let the doctor pass through. "I'm going to check on the plane. Tell these men if you need anything that isn't already here. Thank you, Doctor. Mose is a trusted worker. I wouldn't wish this on anyone."

The doctor stared at the unconscious man covered in blood and knew, even before he drew closer, the seaplane would do him no good. The wounds were deep and in all the wrong places to survive. Dr. Girard decided he would go with the man to offer what comfort he could, though. A few of the men asked him questions, and he offered encouragement but remained vague.

"He is my father," one man confessed. "I have no money to save him."

The doctor frowned and took the wounded man's pulse. "I will see he gets what he needs."

"Thank you, doctor."

Heads bobbed as they spoke in a language the doctor couldn't understand.

The sound of a circling plane reached his ears. He ran outside to search the sky then blocked the glare of the morning sun with a hand over his eyes. The buzz of an engine drawing closer finally helped him pinpoint the white plane descending to the calm waters of the snake-shaped Okavango River. A flock of birds near the water's edge flew up and away, adding squawking to the revved-up sound of the plane.

At a popping sound, the group of men turned their heads toward the noise. They cried out as they pointed toward the bush separating the village and the safari camp, some eight hundred meters away where a plume of smoke rose. They ran toward the village.

The doctor cried out, "What is going on? I need help carrying this man to the plane."

The son stopped, tears flowing down his cheeks. "I must go. Thank you for what you tried to do." Then he joined the others scurrying through the bush like impalas in fear of a stalking lion.

The doctor ran inside and recognized the death stare of a man gone to meet his chosen maker. He wanted to whisper a prayer, but the rapid popping noise drew him back outside where the sound of a plane touching water created a sense of hope for mere seconds. More disturbing noises—screams from the camp where he'd left his newfound friends—frightened him as he tried to decide what to do. More automatic gunfire followed.

A tall man carrying a bundle stumbled from the bush. Blood gushed from a head wound.

"Doctor!" It was John, their guide. "Doctor, help me."

"John, what on earth is going on? You're hurt." He tried to touch his head, but John jerked away. He smelled of smoke, feces, and fear.

"The government men are coming for me, for my village. They are killing everyone. You must escape." Dr. Girard followed John's gaze to where a man disembarked from the plane to the dock. John shoved the bundle into the doctor's arms. "Take my son, Doctor, and give him a life I cannot."

Before he could protest, more shots buzzed overhead, and both of them ducked.

"Please, Doctor." John ran back toward the danger as the doctor stared at the newborn squirming in his arms. The guide circled back, pressing an object into Dr. Girard's hand. "This is for my son—his legacy, his promise. Good doctor. I am trusting you with the future of my village and country." He bent to kiss the top of the baby's head and whispered, "You are the Kifaru."

Clive, the camp director, staggered out into the open, a dark spot spreading across his chest. He fell facedown onto the ground covered in elephant droppings. Dr. Girard whirled around to see the pilot wave him forward in wide desperate motions before hustling back on board. By the time the doctor swung open the door, the propeller spun.

The seaplane moved forward even as he slammed the door shut. The mewing of the newborn child brought an anxiousness to his heart, yet he couldn't resist looking down at the Okavango River, the camp, and the bush crawling with men carrying guns who surrounded one man he believed might be John. The muzzle flash of several weapons dropped the man to his back. When the soldiers ran away, the doctor believed he saw the fallen man raise his hand toward them, but the plane banked away, leaving the slaughter for the evening news.

In all the years since, the doctor had wondered if there was more he could have done. He had also pondered why he had been spared by the wings of an angel pilot rescuing him and a baby boy at the exact time when they needed help.

He'd buckled the seat belt and pulled the child to his chest. "Your father gave you to me for safekeeping. I will find out why."

With the story concluded, tears streamed down his face. "Your child did not fuss or demand to be fed. It was as if he knew it wasn't a time to protest what could not be changed. We stared at each other until the plane arrived in Maun." He squeezed Keeya's hand. "By then I knew I loved him and my life would never be the same. My wife loved him like no other until the day she died."

CHAPTER SEVENTEEN

Because Baboloki refused to leave Keeya in the care of the medical clinic, she ended up joining the others in the boats heading to the safari camp deep into the Okavango. The doctor explained she had been dehydrated and airsick. With a little rest and nourishment, she should recover quickly. The president thanked him and didn't bother to escort her to the boats.

"He walks like one of those pompous peacocks he's got walking around his house," Chase mumbled to Tessa as they climbed into the second boat. Handsome decided it would be better if he drove the lead boat with the president and his people in case they ran into trouble. Light was fading and he planned to take a shortcut back to camp.

"That woman, Keeya, seems to have bounced back. She was too sweet when she thanked Handsome for carrying her to the clinic." Tessa chuckled. "She's looking at him like he's a god."

Chase eased into the second boat. He took one of the blankets the driver passed out and opened it across them after taking the outside seat. The air would be chilly this late in the day as they sped through the waters.

It was amusing to watch Carter try to do the same for Sam who yanked it from him and completed the task herself, leaving him uncovered. When they pulled away from the dock, she seemed to have a change of heart and shared it with him but ignored the gesture by staring at the flock of marabou storks flapping their wings in a tree overhanging the far shore.

"Those are marabou." The driver pointed with one hand while

maneuvering out into deeper water with the other. Guides in the Okavango took every opportunity to share something about their delta.

"Their wingspan must be six feet." Tessa squinted to guard against the sinking sun. "Don't storks like to be closer to the ground?"

"Yes. Yes. That is true. When it is mating season, they nest in the trees. Usually they search for carrion, but during season they look for the babies."

"Why are they making so much noise? Are they scared of us?"

Chase enjoyed the sound of Tessa's voice. She was incapable of turning off the teacher in her, constantly searching for knowledge.

"They rattle their beaks to attract a mate."

Chase sat behind Carter and Sam. He watched him lean in to Sam, making a clicking sound with his teeth. She lifted her lips in a snarl then narrowed her eyes. The woman had the patience of a rattlesnake.

They sped up to keep pace with the lead boat. The chilly wind slammed into his face. He liked Tessa fussing over him more than he wanted to admit as she tucked the blanket around them. She mouthed, "Are you okay?"

Chase nodded when she timidly tangled her fingers with his. Normally, he would have recoiled at such a gesture from a woman. Touching hands with a female was another one of those taboos he'd set up years ago. Too intimate, too personal, too much like a commitment. He avoided it like the plague. Instead, he would fold the lady's arm through his, suggesting a warmth he really couldn't experience. But with Tessa, the forbidden fruit of his life, he found himself clamping his large hand around hers in a firm grip. She smiled up at him then turned to enjoy the beautiful sunset before them.

The quickening of his heartbeat whispered he should pull away, but instead, he recollected all the times he'd found ways to touch her over the last couple of years. Tessa was the one thing in his life that made him feel weak and frustrated. They'd become best friends, or at least it felt that way sometimes. The fear in her eyes when they first met had faded to admiration and mischief. Only once, in the middle of a night some time back, had she indicated a willingness to be with him in the way he envisioned.

Afghanistan had been a breeding ground for uncertainty, fear, and longing. That night had held promises of a forever love, but he chose to run toward duty rather than take a chance on a woman who could heal and love him unconditionally in spite of all his faults. Another man stepped in to steal that hope away and most likely, any chance of rekindling those emotions in her again. He'd decided to be satisfied with these moments.

Soon, something would need to be done about her husband who showed all the signs of a man who couldn't be trusted. Part of the reason they were in Botswana was the hornets' nest he'd stirred up with conflict diamonds. He didn't like Robert, but it was the tribesman from Afghanistan who really might stand in his way.

Tessa had little resolve when it came to the drug-running traitor called Roman Darya Petrov. He'd wormed his way into her psyche and still held a certain amount of power over her heart. Dr. Wu, the Enigma psychiatrist, called it Stockholm syndrome, where a captive embraces her kidnapper's motives and ideology. He suspected they'd been in touch, but she never brought it up and according to Dr. Wu, she hadn't with him, either, not that he would have shared the information. The doctor understood the importance of a healthy agent, so his focus remained on her well-being, not Chase's pathetic ego. Still, he wished he'd killed him when he had the chance.

"I'm exhausted." Tessa yawned. "Look at the camp. Isn't it beautiful with the lanterns all aglow? Very romantic." She released his hand, snapping him out of his tormented thoughts. "Why don't we go clean up then come back for some dinner. We'll turn in early."

Chase managed a grunt then pushed off the blanket. His side ached, and fatigue had overtaken him. "Don't really want to be sociable. Think I'll stay back tonight."

"I'll get a tray for us and stay with you." Tessa waved at Peter who helped the men tie up the boats. "I promised Dr. Girard I'd look after you."

"I'm fine. I don't need a nurse," he grumbled as he tried to help Tessa exit the boat. She turned and offered a hand instead. He reluctantly took it, just wanting to go to bed.

"I see that. And don't bite my head off. I'm only trying to help," she snapped. "You're such a baby."

No one had ever called him that before, and he wasn't sure if he should toss her in the water or laugh. He cocked his head to steal a look at Sam and Carter who had raised their eyebrows and grinned sheepishly. Several colorful comebacks were vying to spill from his mouth when Tessa laid a hand on his arm.

"I'm sorry, big guy. I'm still a little frightened at what happened to us. You must be in a lot of pain," she whispered. "You fuss all you want, but I'm sticking to you like glue."

Baboloki and his people already trudged toward the dining area. The president stopped long enough to allow Keeya to catch up with him. He gently touched her back then moved away, leaving her to follow again. She held her head high and moved with more assurance and strength than earlier in the afternoon. Did it have anything to do with finding out her son had been spared Baboloki's murderous hand?

Chase and Tessa caught up with Carter and Sam.

"You guys go on. We'll join you later to talk," Carter murmured. "Tess, no need for you to join us for dinner unless you want to. We'll shower and change then join the others."

Chase took a deep breath and agreed. "Be careful. Something is going on. I'll share with you later. Listen for anything unusual."

Sam chimed in as she and Carter split off to their tent. "I'll have Handsome send down a tray of food. You need to keep up your strength." The twilight of evening gave her glare at Tessa a sinister vibe. "No matter how much he complains about it, take care of him or there will be hell to pay. Got it?"

With a snap to attention and a military salute, Tessa barked, "Yes, ma'am."

Sam halted and twisted around with a threatening stance. Carter smirked at Chase then reached out and grabbed the senior agent, pulling her after him, even as she tried to jerk free. His laughter rolled across the open space. Chase let his guard down when Tessa slipped her arm through his.

"Are you trying to get yourself killed or do you like tormenting Sam?" He slipped free of her hold then placed his arm around her shoulders. The pressure on his wounds eased.

"I don't know what you mean, Captain Hunter," she chuckled. "I was being respectful of a senior agent."

"She pretty much ordered you to take care of me so I wouldn't want to cause more trouble between you two. It's for your own protection." They shared a spontaneous moment of light laughter and approached their tent. The effort to walk up three steps surprised him.

Tessa released him. "Oh right. I say I'm going to watch over you, and you get all Captain America on me." She unzipped the door and held it open for him to pass through then followed. "Agent Nymphomaniac spits a little venom, and you're amused." She helped him sit down on the bed and bent down to unlace his boots.

"What are you doing? Stop it."

Tessa straightened. "Okay. Do it yourself. I'm going to go take a shower. I was going to help you with that, too, but I see you're..." She laughed when he frowned up at her. He could feel his forehead pinch with indecision. "Your pride will be the death of both of us. It's okay to ask for help once in a while. All that talk at Enigma about how we're a family applies to you, too. Family takes care of family." She folded her arms across her chest and arched her eyebrows, speaking with her irritated-mom voice. "You can't fool me, Chase."

Chase tried to stand up, but she gently pushed him back down, aware taking orders from anyone else rubbed him the wrong way. "You are getting frisky because you think I'll balk and leave you alone with your macho crap."

"Frisky?" A grin toyed at the corners of his mouth. "Do I look like the kind of guy who gets frisky? I think I'm insulted. When I—"

"Yeah. Yeah. Yeah. I've heard all about your charms in the bedroom. If I have to suffer listening to one more of your brainy bimbos brag on the night they had with you, I'm going to--"

"What do they say?" he asked wolfishly. "Is that where you got the frisky idea?"

Tessa dropped her arms to her side, eyes batting. Once the nervous tic kicked in, her bossy demeanor collapsed. "They say you're an…amazing lover, but aloof." She shifted her weight to one hip, another sign of irritation. "You pretend to listen to them but won't do intimate things like hold hands. Some think you're a germaphobe. How do you ever expect to find Miss Right with that attitude? What are you afraid of?"

"And do you weigh in on these conversations?" Still amused, he managed to stand on his own.

"No. I mostly have overheard—"

"You're eavesdropping?"

They stared at each other. Chase loved backing her into a corner. She became vulnerable and wide-eyed.

"About that shower?"

The usual huff of disdain was followed by her trying to dart past him. But in close quarters she couldn't avoid him blocking her with a raised arm then jerked her body away. He swayed on unsteady feet and toppled backwards.

"Oh gosh!" Tessa tried to grab him with no success. "Are you all right?"

Flat on his back, he frowned up at her. "No thanks to you. You drive me crazy."

"I'll go get things ready for a shower." She extended her hand to him. "Then I'll come back to help you with things—if you need it—like unlacing your boots."

He avoided her hand and tried to sit then let her grasp his arm and help him.

"Chase, do you think I'm hitting on you? I'm trying to help."

Even in the dim light he could see her flushed cheeks.

He touched the spot on his chest that gave him fits during moments like these. "I'm not sure you are capable of hitting on a man, Tessa. So, no. I didn't think you were hitting on me." Part of him wanted to laugh but resisted. "We are friends." Cocking his head, he placed his feet to the floor. "I also forget that sometimes I go a little too far. And you do give the impression your hero worship is negotiable."

"Oh geeze," she moaned while avoiding eye contact.

"Our—friendship is complicated. But it is what it is. You make me laugh. Before you came along to be my pain in the neck, I didn't give a rip about anything or anyone. I want you to be happy and most of all, strong enough to defend yourself. I'm not going to rip your clothes off in a lapse in judgement, kick your husband to the curb—although it has crossed my mind—or force you to do anything to compromise your values. You are my best friend. That's it. Friends."

A slow smile spread across her mouth, forcing Chase to wish he hadn't promised he wouldn't have a lapse in judgement. It would be so easy to take advantage of her trusting nature and end this ridiculous pain in his chest.

"Now, as to the women I sleep with…"

"Too much information. No thanks. I don't want that mental picture."

He stared up at her. "Whatever we are to each other, it is safe ground for me. You expect nothing and give everything."

One corner of her mouth turned up. "And I appreciate that." She turned to leave.

"Tessa?"

"Yes?"

"You need to remember I'm also not a safe guy for you to be alone with on a regular basis. People like me do have lapses in judgement. Don't let your guard down. Okay?"

Tessa's lips parted.

"Do. You. Understand?"

She raised her chin. "Got it. Let's get cleaned up, and we'll talk about Handsome."

Chapter Eighteen

"Then Handsome knew all along he could easily take control of the country when the time came. All he needs is the diamond." Tessa sat down on the bed next to Chase. "Dr. Girard escaped with John and Keeya's child when the soldiers began killing everyone."

"Apparently Dr. Girard had no idea Keeya was still alive." Chase motioned for Sam and Carter to join them inside their tent and caught them up to speed. "I'm guessing they had met because she certainly knew the doctor when she laid eyes on him."

"It's been over thirty years." Sam sounded skeptical. "People change."

"If Robert tried to hide my son with someone I had met, I'd remember," Tessa interjected. "That poor woman. All these years, surviving in the presence of the man who she believed to have killed her family."

"Handsome still has no idea who she is?" Carter asked.

Chase shook his head. "No. Although I could have misunderstood the whole conversation. I need to talk to the doctor first. Handsome is a loose cannon we don't want going after Baboloki. At least with Baboloki we know who we're dealing with. The void he'd leave could put someone even worse in power. The country is fairly stable for the time being."

"Handsome has no special skills for leading a country." Carter pulled out a camp stool and sat. "In Africa, that seems to be the rule rather than the exception."

"What's to keep Keeya from breaking the news to him?" Tessa's comment paused the conversation. "If I'd found my son... I'd find it difficult not to blurt it out and try to make up for lost time. I'd become overprotective and give excuses for my absence, demonizing the kidnapper and in this case, murderer."

"We need to get Baboloki to admit what he did all those years ago." Chase fidgeted to make himself more comfortable. Exhaustion wafted over him. With a yawn, he continued, "Tessa, you need to talk to Keeya tomorrow and see if we're right. Let her know we want to help her. You're a mother so you understand how important it is to wait to reveal who she is even though—"

"I can do that. Don't worry. It might be difficult getting her alone long enough, but I'll do my best."

"Anything come up tonight at dinner?"

Sam shrugged. "President Baboloki bragged about what a great guy he's been for the country. The other guests ate it up, had their pictures taken with him and laughed at every little amusing antidote he shared."

"And, of course," Carter continued, "he wanted his picture taken with Sam."

Sam stood and moved to where he sat then pulled him to his feet. "Carter got his ego smashed because no one asked to take his picture or about his stupid time on the space station." She stuck out her bottom lip and rubbed his shoulder. "Poor baby."

"You can make it all better later," he quipped only to have her chuckle.

"Night, you two. Come on, Carter." She was already out the door when he turned to Chase and Tessa. He winked then caught up with his tent mate.

~ ~ ~

Baboloki stood on his deck that circled the baobab. It had stood like an upside-down tree for hundreds of years. The lavish accommodation connected to a bridge so as not to damage the rare tree. The camp had built only three of these VIP guest rooms. They towered in the air to get the best views of the delta.

A limited number of tourists got permission to enter the fragile ecosystem of the Okavango Delta each year. Some preferred a less Tarzan experience, one more like a five-star hotel. The president had secured one of those exclusive tree villas.

It resembled a tree house fit for a king, or president in his case. Indoor plumbing, the best safari-inspired furniture, faux-leopard rugs, and white bedding came with the hefty price tag Westerners appeared willing to pay in order to secure comfort and a romantic experience. A retractable staircase provided an element of safety when lions and elephants strolled through the camp at night.

From here, he could see the other tent structures and guests emerging for a breakfast of eggs, bacon, and flat cakes. If he was lucky, lekatane, or melon, would be served. Getting such treats out here might be too much to ask for on short notice.

Keeya, along with his secretary, stepped from their guest tent. There didn't seem to be a need to put a guard on her out here. Where would she go? It could be a dangerous place with hungry lions, ill-tempered Cape buffalo, and territorial hippopotami trying to force humans into the afterlife. Besides, Keeya's people died many years ago. Looking for a familiar face would be a waste of time. The few who escaped probably had started new lives elsewhere.

More than 150,000 people lived in and around the many islands of the Okavango. They moved with the fluctuations of the water levels. Villages could disappear overnight to find better fishing holes. Thatched houses remained a low-cost investment, one worth leaving for their food source.

Leaning against the railing with his cup of hot tea in hand, he watched Keeya stretch like a sleepy lioness on the savanna. Even from here, he caught the look of joy on her face. This place impressed upon her she'd come home to another life, another time. Was she thinking about her husband, John, or the child who died with him? Baboloki couldn't help but wonder if she might love him if he had saved the infant? Nothing he'd done over the years could rescue her from the memories of what he'd done to change her life. He realized that she would never love or forgive him.

But he continued to be smitten by her, even as she aged. The pretty young wife he'd chosen most recently could not compete with Keeya. The self-centered woman had decided after their child was born to make a life traveling with friends and continue her modeling career. She cared nothing about the boy. That would no longer be a problem.

Keeya, on the other hand, loved the child. He remained the one thing that brought her joy, and he'd gladly let her be the child's playmate and protector. The boy adored her as well. Understanding she'd chosen to be loving rather than cruel made Baboloki want her all the more. Why couldn't she let the past go?

With a casual turn of her head, she gazed up at him, still smiling, and then turned back toward the still waters of the blue Okavango. She hugged her bare arms against the frigid morning air. A battery-operated golf cart passed her. The passengers exchanged greetings before proceeding down the trampled path created by heavy-footed animals.

The dutiful secretary spotted him and waved. He lifted his warm teacup in acknowledgment before turning back to his quarters. A commotion along the riverbank caught his eye in time for him to see the escape of some carmine bee-eaters take flight off the brown banks. A blur of red and blue lifted to low-hanging branches. At the sound of laughter, he returned to the railing to see Keeya point with excitement at the birds. She looked his way and clapped her hands. Was that all it took to win her favor, bringing her to this wild place?

Baboloki finished his morning routine before joining the others at the dining pavilion. His security and the ladies had waited to walk with him.

"Keeya, you look very well this morning. This place agrees with you," Baboloki said under his breath. They approached the area where other guests stood at the buffet table.

"Yes. I think it does." She stole a glance at him. "This is my home. I belong in the delta. I will never go back."

Although her words were soft, the president frowned and clicked his tongue. "Don't be ridiculous. Your home is with me, and I will never leave you in such a dangerous place. What of my son? He needs you."

Keeya raised her chin and stared straight ahead. "He is not my son. You took that from me."

He turned to his security. "Take Keeya back to her quarters and bring her a tray of food. She will stay here today and rest."

"I do not need rest. I need to be free." She halted, displaying a stubbornness Baboloki recognized from other times she'd gotten out of control. "I will not be sent to my room like a child or bow to your orders any longer." She moved away with jerky movements and managed to avoid the president's touch. Running up the steps of the deck, she greeted the others. Baboloki swallowed his fury and joined her.

"Welcome, Mr. President. I was about to send someone to see if you'd like to take your breakfast in your accommodations." Peter pointed to the stack of plates on the buffet. "Please. Enjoy. We have some tasty surprises this morning."

"So I see. Ladies, please. You go first. They have some work to finish up, so I'm sure they will want to hurry along." He glanced at his secretary and Keeya.

"But of course." Peter moved to the coffee bar. "Tell me what you'd like to drink, and I'll bring it to your table."

Keeya offered a quiet attempt at conversation. "Can I sit over there by the edge? I'd like to see the delta this morning."

Peter nodded. "There is only a coffee table."

"That will be perfect, sir. Thank you for your kindness." Keeya filled her plate with the delights prepared for them then carried her plate to sit alone.

Baboloki's anger ebbed away, watching her obstinate expression become passive as she stared across the water. He would give her this victory, but at some point, he would need to teach her a lesson. It tended to get physical with her during those times, making her even more desirable. Even after all these years, Keeya remained an unobtainable prize. Maybe when he found the Kifaru diamond, his luck would change.

The Americans joined the group. He'd suspected from the day he met them that the man called Hunter and the State Department representative were more than friends or colleagues. He'd observed they shared a tent and the night of the Gaborone break-in, they'd ended up in the same room. Even though they seemed guarded about their relationship, their sideways glances indicated affection.

The man put him on edge. Being a military man himself, Baboloki recognized Hunter as someone who knew his way around trouble. He avoided eye contact but couldn't sidestep the muscled American when he cut him off at the table.

"Morning, Mr. President. Hope you slept well."

"Indeed. Are you better this morning, Captain Hunter? That was a nasty business yesterday. I've put my people on the incident. If there were poachers we will bring them to justice in short order. The Okavango must remain a safe place for tourists."

"Unlike years ago, when armed men murdered innocent guests and villagers?"

Baboloki tensed at the unexpected declaration. "Yes. Those were different times. Today, we are a stable country, thanks to my programs and repercussions for lawlessness."

Hunter grinned and narrowed his eyes to slits. "There's talk of a diamond that will bring a new leader to Botswana. Tessa is enamored by such stories. Have you heard anything about that?"

"Yes. Magical tales from an ignorant people who continue to live in the past. This diamond has no power. I read about it in the papers after Ms. Scott mentioned it at dinner the other day."

"Is it true that the one who possesses the diamond is the true heir to ruling Botswana?"

Baboloki didn't like the tone of the man or that he'd followed him to a table and sat on the opposite side. Must he endure this American's company? He took a spoonful of garlic potatoes and mixed them with his limp bacon before funneling it into his mouth. With his next bite held near his mouth, Baboloki sneered.

"Of course not. We are a democracy. Our elections are run fairly with the blessings of our people as well as the UN observers at every polling institution." He continued to eat before speaking again. "Do you think I want to be king, Dr. Hunter?"

"I think you enjoy your lot in life, and the threat of a diamond with such power could upset your rather perfect life."

A worker stopped to pour each man a fresh cup of hot tea then wandered off to help at the buffet. "Some men are destined for greatness, Captain Hunter. I have worked hard to make this country better."

"That you have, Mr. President." The man continued to exhibit a devious smirk that unnerved him more than he liked to admit.

"How long will you be with us?" The president hoped their departure had been moved up, considering his accident the day before.

"It's just now getting interesting. Besides"— he nodded over at Tessa Scott—"my friend is enjoying herself immensely." She sat next to Keeya and struck up a conversation. "She was shaken up a bit yesterday, what with getting stranded and a gunman on the loose. But it all worked out. She's a trouper. I promised her an adventure and"— he chuckled good heartedly "well, that is what I intend to give her."

"Could be very dangerous here, Captain Hunter." Baboloki spoke slowly, in hopes the man would pick up on his warning.

"Maybe. Or maybe I'll look into finding that diamond and see what happens." He nodded toward Tessa. "She would get a kick out of that."

"May I join you, Keeya?" Tessa looked down at the woman who stared across the calm waters of the Okavango Delta. The serene gaze vanished when Tessa didn't wait to be refused. The woman motioned for her to set her plate of fruit and eggs on the coffee table next to hers. "We met the other night. Remember?"

"Yes, ma'am."

"Please. Call me Tessa."

Keeya offered a tired expression then glanced over her shoulder at Baboloki who sat talking to other guests.

Tessa noted the concerned glance she gave her boss. "Is everything all right?"

Keeya turned back to stare at the water for only a few seconds before answering. Pulling her shoulders back, followed by raising her chin, the African beauty spoke in a hushed tone.

"I am in danger, Tessa. I must escape for the sake of my son. Please. Will you help me?"

Tessa set her coffee down and mimicked her interested look at the blue waters as she slipped her hand into Keeya's. "Yes. That is why I'm here."

Keeya turned eyes on her that seemed to hold back a dam of tears then laid her free hand on top of Tessa's and squeezed. "It will not be easy."

Tessa withdrew, in fear someone would spot them. "Things worthwhile are rarely easy."

CHAPTER NINETEEN

Dr. Girard finished vaccinating the last child in his tiny waiting room before checking outside in the spillover area where many people usually waited to see him on clinic days. Today it was empty except for a couple of nurse's aides who gossiped under one of the thatched pavilions. They spotted him and slid off the rough benches to meander back to work.

"Where is everyone?" he asked as the two women stopped at the bottom step. "Usually this place is a madhouse on open-clinic days."

The women surveyed the area and shrugged. "All healthy, sir. You have healed everyone." This was followed by a hearty laugh. Although the doctor joined in, an uneasiness came over him.

"Where are your husbands? They are usually here helping out."

"They are helping at the camp, sir. The president brought extra people with him, and they were understaffed. A big feast is planned. Lots of work to do with soldiers, security, and staff around."

"Yes. I got an invite, but I'm not going."

"What? I want to go but I have to watch my sister's children while she works in Gaborone. My mother will be tired." The young woman stuck her lip out.

The older woman gave her a playful shove. "You were not invited. You only want to see Handsome Jones."

Dr. Girard had spotted his son talking to her several times. "Handsome? He is a good man. Maybe too old for you." He guessed her to be in her early twenties and Louis, or Handsome was a good fifteen years older. "How about that young guide who takes out the big-game hunters?"

"He is stupid, Dr. Girard. I want a smart man. Handsome knows many things."

Dr. Girard only nodded and decided to speak to his son about the infatuated girl the next time they met. Everyone still believed the two of them were great friends, not father and son. Gossip traveled at the speed of sound in the Okavango, especially when rumors involved a relationship between a white doctor and a black son.

"Why don't you run along to your homes. You have been working very hard the last few weeks. I imagine someone is about if I need anything."

The women giggled. "Thank you, Dr. Girard. I'll come back in a while to see if things have changed. It is still early." Even as the older woman spoke, the younger of the two skipped happily away down the path leading to their village some three-hundred yards away.

"Be careful!" he called, watching them disappear through the trees. The village was a ten-minute walk, and rarely were there problems. But he never stopped worrying about the locals who supported his work and had become like family. Soon he would be here full-time to continue the work he so loved. Timing was everything. When the diamond returned to its rightful place among the people of Botswana, he could relax.

With Great Britain's young prince giving his fiancée an engagement ring with a Botswana diamond, the world now wanted to see what drove one of the royals to desire a stone from this small country. Maybe it had been a good time for his son to return to his birth home.

When the women disappeared from sight, he looked around the grounds. A lost baby baboon wandered around aimlessly then scampered away when the doctor chuckled at the sight. Only the warm noon breeze rustling through the palms broke the silence. Even the birds had stopped their lazy calls to mates. Uneasiness washed over him. He decided to call it a day and had turned to go inside when a uniformed man holding a rifle across his chest stepped in front of him.

Dr. Girard stepped back and grabbed the doorframe to keep from falling. But the menacing man stepped closer, and the doctor's foot slipped. In an instant, the doctor tumbled backward down the steps and hit his face on a shiny boot at the bottom.

He moaned but tried to push himself up enough to see the person before him. When he could only get to his hands and knees, a command was given and two strangers in uniforms jerked him to a standing position to confront a familiar face.

"You seem to have had an unfortunate fall, Dr. Girard." The deep voice sounded wise and reassuring.

He blinked to clear the blur, or was it blood running into his eyes?

"P-President Baboloki?" he stuttered then squinted against the afternoon sun.

"Yes," he spoke matter-of-factly. "I wanted to have a conversation about a few things."

Dr. Girard was handed a hand mirror and a rag. He tried to wipe the blood from his eyes, making his face resemble a Sioux warrior headed off to war. "I need to sit down," he mumbled. His legs wobbled, but the soldiers caught him under each arm and shook him until he stood straight.

"You hit your head several times, Dr. Girard. I hope you don't have a concussion." President Baboloki twisted his mouth into a wide smile revealing yellow teeth. "Or worse," he chuckled. "My men are going to take you inside then set up a safe perimeter against unwanted visitors."

"Unwanted visitors?"

"We wouldn't want to be interrupted by some of the locals coming for medical care." The president folded his hands in front of his body.

"That is why I am here, to take care of the sick," he mumbled as he turned to look at each soldier holding him up. "I am a doctor."

"And I want to talk to you about that. It seems you have a personal interest in this village." He swung out his arm as if taking in the whole compound. "I've heard you have a history of saving lives, even before you opened this clinic." He patted the doctor's shoulder. "So unfortunate this place is constructed of shoddy materials." Baboloki sighed and took a moment to scope out the surrounding area. "I've never been a fan of thatched roofs. Looks like a fire hazard."

"Thatch was used only on the small pavilions for patients to wait out of the sun."

"Yes. I see the roof of the clinic is metal. Very proactive in dry seasons when fires sometimes sweep across the savanna and delta."

Dr. Girard shook off his guards. "What do you want?"

Baboloki leaned closer and pulled at the doctor's ear. "The truth."

~ ~ ~

Tessa observed how Baboloki's secretary invaded Keeya's personal space as the three of them walked back to their tent. She likely spied on her for the president, further proof Keeya was not a willing member of his staff. But if true, why hadn't she escaped years ago? Surely there were times his guard had been let down or opportunities presented themselves.

"Keeya, I'm doing some work on a book called, The Women of Africa. Can I interview you on tape, maybe use my phone to record?"

Keeya glanced at the secretary who halted in front of their tent with an announcement. "We have a lot of work to do today before the president returns from his hunt."

The president had left earlier, taking his secretary aside, both of them speaking in hushed tones. His exit seemed to carry a lot of fanfare with his staff. The camp director passed along the information that the president would not be returning until late afternoon.

"I promise I won't be long. I'd also like to interview you," Tessa chirped enthusiastically. "After all, you work for the president and see lots of history-making events. The State Department needs to see how the women of Botswana are changing the face of Africa. Oh, please say you two will do it," Tessa coaxed.

"We go together," the secretary snapped. "I promised the president I'd make sure Keeya would be looked after in case she had another spell like yesterday."

"Sure. That would be lovely." Tessa beamed. The disappointed expression on Keeya's face broke her heart. "Naledi, I'll interview you first since you have the ear of the president." The ego stroking seemed to be working on the woman. Tessa pulled out her phone and punched the record app. "Shall we sit on the deck?" The woman nodded, and the three went up the steps.

"Don't you have a tour to do?"

"Yes. They said it would be a short wait. The president pushed off first, and our guide needs to finish up the breakfast cleanup. This is a great time. Thank you for helping me out."

The secretary offered an apathetic nod. "I'm very busy, so let's begin."

"Of course."

Tessa asked the secretary what she felt were benign questions about her work, where she came from, and her family. She even let her voice turn a little squeaky and asked a couple of dumb-blonde type questions. The woman nodded and gave a thin smile then pointed at the phone to start the interview. With a giggle and flipping her hair out of her face, Tessa believed she'd pulled off the picture of a stupid American who had too much money and not enough to do except write a book nobody would read. The only down side of the interview was Keeya grew solemn with a look of panic in her eyes. She must have feared she'd confided in the wrong person about her predicament.

Tessa sighed with relief when Chase ran up the deck steps. "Hey, there you are. Ready to go?"

"I sure am. Maybe today won't be as exciting as our little adventure yesterday." Tessa laughed like she didn't have an ounce of sense.

"I'm sure our guide won't let that happen. Besides, the president said his men are all along the way looking for trouble." Chase winked at the other two ladies. "Oh, Naledi, the cook and Peter want to talk to you about tonight's dinner for the president. I told them I'd tell you. They've been waiting a while because I couldn't find Tess."

The secretary stood and brushed down her simple cotton dress. "Thank you, Ms. Scott." She turned to Keeya. "You've got work to do."

Keeya's round eyes narrowed with an icy calm. "Yes. Right away. Sorry about the interview," she addressed Tessa.

"No problem. I got what I needed," Tessa said happily as she looped her arm through Chase's.

The secretary disappeared down the steps and walked briskly toward the camp facilities.

Chase turned to Keeya and dropped the jovial tone. "Come with us."

"What?" Keeya took a step back.

Tessa moved to her side and laid a hand on her arm. "I'm not as dumb as I pretended. We're getting you out of here, Keeya. We can talk later."

"Then you believed me when I said I was in danger and that Baboloki wanted to kill my son if he found him?"

Chase pulled Keeya down the steps after him. "Yes. We need to get you to a safe place, Keeya."

"Dr. Girard might be able to hide me," she said easing down the stairs hand in hand with Tessa.

"Maybe, but not today. That is an obvious place to look since your old village is nearby. You're going to have to trust us." Chase pulled Keeya behind Tessa then stepped in front of both women. He hurried them toward the boat dock where a man waited. "This is Joseph. He works for Dr. Girard."

The man nodded to Keeya.

"You can trust me. My parents were killed by Baboloki's soldiers years ago."

"And you survived?" Keeya sounded amazed.

"Barely. Several of us were playing down by the delta when they came. We hid in the papyrus at the water's edge. When they left, we slipped back into the village to see everything on fire."

Keeya took his hand and got in the mokoro then wiped at her eyes. "So young to see such horror. I'm sorry you had to suffer."

"I saw you that day."

Keeya covered her mouth to cover a whimper.

The man went on. "Baboloki beat you then forced you to go with them. I wanted to help, but…"

"You were a child." Tears squeezed from the corners of her eyes. She swiped at her tears. "How did you survive?"

"My friends and I waded across the delta then took the long way to another village to warn them. They all escaped before Baboloki's men caught them, but their village was also burned. They took us in and raised us."

"You two can catch up later. Joseph needs to get you out of here. We'll meet up later, Keeya." Chase tilted his head in the direction for them to go then looked over his shoulder. "We need to slow things down here so you can get a head start."

Tessa waved goodbye and searched for some encouraging words to offer, but the truth loomed over the situation like a dark cloud.

Even before the boat disappeared into the channel of tall grasses, Tessa and Chase strolled back toward the dining area where Carter and Sam waited. The secretary continued to listen to the cook and camp director discuss plans for the evening meal. A couple of times, Naledi interrupted them with a shake of her head and spoke in a firm voice.

"Where's Handsome?" Tessa inquired as she scanned the area. "He is making me really nervous. Do we tell him about Keeya?"

"Not yet. We need to talk to Dr. Girard and find out what happened on the day Baboloki raided the camp and village. Maybe it wasn't Baboloki but someone else in charge."

"I believe it was. Too many coincidences."

Sam put her hands on her hips. "If you found the trail, then Baboloki can, too."

Tessa ignored the dig and tried not to let Sam's snarky remarks cloud her ability to think.

The agent went on. "With that article in the news about the lost Kifaru being found, the president has to be feeling a little insecure."

Chase retold the conversation with him from breakfast. "He didn't like my interest very much. I'm not comfortable with Handsome being here, either. We've got to get him away from the president before he finds out the truth. Hell will break loose if he realizes Keeya is his mother and has been held prisoner all these years."

"Where did Baboloki head off to so early this morning?" Carter poured himself another cup of coffee and offered to fill Sam's, but she waved him off. "There were some new guys I hadn't seen before. Looked military."

"Not sure. They arrived in the motorboats shortly after breakfast but never disembarked. His security team met them on the dock. The head guy, Dage I think, gave orders to some of the locals. Looked like they were loading coolers like we had yesterday with soft drinks, maybe some lunch. If they're big-game hunting they won't be coming back in like us."

Chase nodded to the secretary when she saw him chatting with the others.

Naledi kept turning her head as if searching for someone then headed back toward her tent.

"Guess she's afraid Keeya cornered us."

"Ready, folks?" It was Handsome. "Our chariot awaits. That means we're in the Land Rover today. Lots to see and no hippopotamus to worry about. Well, unless we get between them and their favorite watering hole." They moved out behind the dining area to the vehicle.

"What are those marks on the side of the car?" Tessa touched the indentions.

"A hippo was on one side of the road and the water on the other. I drove between them, and she took offense at that."

Tessa gasped then shivered. "I'm thinking those dancing hippos in Fantasia were a little overdone."

Everyone found seats in the vehicle that resembled an open-air truck, the back slightly higher than the front seats.

"Meanest creatures on God's green Earth." Tessa sat in front with Handsome, camera at the ready. "Not to worry. That disgruntled hippo moved on to another part of the delta. Today we'll see lions and if we're lucky, some giraffes."

The engine roared to life, and a cloud of dust kicked up when he moved down the open road. "There are reports of a pride of females stalking some impalas not far from here. With any luck, you'll get to see a kill up close and personal."

Tessa experienced both a thrill and a sense of foreboding at the thought of seeing a lion bring down a defenseless impala. She'd watched such moments on numerous nature programs over the years without batting an eye. The parallel of Keeya trying to escape Baboloki reminded her of the wilds of the Okavango.

The car veered off the road with a bounce then pulled up under a mopane tree. A swirl of dust followed them as Handsome killed the engine. He used his index finger to push back his ballcap before looking through his binoculars. Handing them to Tessa, he pointed to something in the distance.

Squinting first, Tessa then looked through the binoculars.

"Over there at your ten o'clock." Handsome pointed as he leaned forward.

"I see them," Chase whispered.

"I don't—" Before Tessa could finish, a heavy thud hit the hood of the Land Rover and black spots filled her vision. She screamed and dropped the binoculars and tried to backpedal out of the seat. A large arm slammed her back in place.

"Sit still." Handsome spoke between clenched teeth.

A magnificent leopard stood like a statue, gazing out at the impalas who had started to leap in a desperate attempt to escape the approaching lions. Then, suddenly, the leopard turned his head and stared at Tessa.

"Whatever you do, don't look him in the eyes," Handsome whispered. "Don't look. Him. In. The eyes."

CHAPTER TWENTY

Keeya sat quiet, her back straight as an ironing board while Joseph poled her through the swamp. The tall grasses waved gently in the morning breeze. Her grandmother used to say it was God's way of saying goodbye to the cold air in the morning so the sun could do its job. Closing her eyes, she lifted her face to the sun and listened to the nothingness that filled the Okavango.

So very quiet. The beauty of no sound let everything else be experienced; the movement of water, the flight of birds, the brittle grasses touching the papyrus along the bank and even the voice of God whispering in her ear. If she were to die this instant, her heart would be free of the trappings of Gaborone and her jailer.

"We will pull in soon, Miss Keeya," Joseph spoke almost too low to hear. Voices carried far in the Okavango. "Someone will be waiting for us. You will be safe."

She could never repay this kindness from strangers who believed in her. The only thing she could offer Joseph was a smile of gratitude, as she watched him move the mokoro through the channel through the tall papyrus. The sound of motorized boats roared like giant pterodactyls across the water.

"What is it, Joseph?"

"Boats are coming in the open water. We hide so they not see us, Miss Keeya." Soon the sounds faded. "They go another way, I think."

"Is that a problem?"

Joseph waited before poling back into the channel. "Baboloki has men patrolling the waters. He is a suspicious man. Guess he has enemies and must be careful."

Keeya loved how quickly the quiet swallowed up the sounds of progress and left the Okavango as it had been for hundreds of years. She drew strength from this place. Once all was lost and now there might be a future for her, for her son. If she could only hold him, kiss his cheek and tell him about his father who gave his life so he could carry on the work of the people of the Okavango and Kalahari. All people in Botswana needed a voice. The breath of life whispered on the warm breezes touching her face.

"We are here, Miss Keeya." Joseph let the mokoro coast to a sandy beach hidden among the tall grasses. He jumped in the water and grabbed the bow of the boat to walk it in. Two men rose from the shelter of the grasses and waved at Keeya before helping her out onto the sand. "These are my friends, Miss Keeya. They are the ones who escaped with me so long ago."

"Where are we going?" It had been a long time since she trusted anyone and in less than a day, she found herself daring to believe in the kindness of strangers who could set her free. They motioned for her to follow. "Wait!" she begged.

They halted.

"I. I could be putting you in danger. Tell me where to go, and I will go. You need not trouble yourself with an old woman."

Joseph pulled the boat into some bushes and covered it with fallen palm leaves and brush. "No. You are our family left behind and taken from us. There are others who survived that day of murder. They are waiting for you, Miss Keeya. You are the mother of the Kifaru."

The men stared at her in anticipation, waiting for some word of encouragement to continue.

Keeya longed to cry tears of joy but raised her chin in a show of stubborn resolve. "Let's go home, my children. I want to see my people."

Joseph nodded to his friends. "So be it, then."

~ ~ ~

Baboloki stared out the tiny window of a room Dr. Girard used as an office. Besides a small rickety desk, painted red, and a rusty file cabinet, a cot rested against one wall, topped with a folded sheet and a small pillow. The information about the doctor said he slept in the clinic, refusing more comfortable accommodations in the bunkhouse used by doctors and other medical staff visiting from the West and Europe. The locals took good care of him. His needs were few. Only a hot plate, a tea kettle, and a coffee can filled with cutlery adorned a lopsided cart, indicating this must be his kitchen.

"I found this, Mr. President." Dage, his chief of security, handed him a picture. "The doctor has bandaged his own cuts, sir. Do you wish to speak to him?"

Baboloki stared at the picture. "In a minute. I want to think."

"Yes, sir."

The president held the picture closer to the window where the light could brighten the fading snapshot. The picture revealed a younger Dr. Girard and a woman who held a small black child in her arms. Dr. Girard eyed the woman who was kissing the child of about two years of age. He slept against her shoulder, so most of his face remained hidden.

A chaotic sense of panic jolted the president. He froze, not liking what this sense of limbo and inability to think straight meant. Was it possible the doctor indeed saved a child that day the village was attacked? Were the ridiculous stories the heir of the Kifaru diamond had survived true?

His men never found a baby the day of the attack, although he was believed to have been hidden. With the scent of blood in the air, it didn't take long for hyenas and lions to enjoy the flesh not burned in the fire. How could a baby have survived?

The few who escaped were later rounded up and executed, their corpses thrown to the crocodiles. If there were others, they would have been gobbled up by the beasts who ruled the Okavango. No one would have dared shelter them, risking their own villages' safety. Not even a weathered local could have lasted for long.

Then there was the plane spotted flying away that day. Records showed the manifest listed only the pilot, no passengers. It had been the pilot who'd reported the fire and alerted the authorities something was wrong. Baboloki had returned later to be the savior and report the massacre. His was the face presented to the media, promising justice for the Okavango. His efforts had rounded up poachers and troublemakers then quickly extinguished the movement of outrage.

Once more Baboloki examined the photograph. He turned and stormed out of the tiny office to find the doctor sitting on the edge of a cot with his head cradled between his hands. Taking a deep breath, Baboloki entered the room and dropped the picture on the cot.

The doctor glanced down at the picture then picked it up and sighed. "Where did you find this?" His voice remained calm.

"No matter. Who is the child?"

Dr. Girard lifted his eyes, confusion stopped his attempt at denial. "The child?"

Baboloki snatched the picture and pointed to the child the woman held. "Yes. Who is it?" He dropped it on the floor, and the doctor reached for it only to have the president ram his boot on top of his hand. The doctor cried out and pulled free. "Who. Is. It?"

"I don't remember." The doctor shook his head, and tried to rescue the picture.

Baboloki grabbed him by the throat and jerked him to stand on wobbly legs. "Then why did you save this picture for so long? Clearly it is old."

"My house burned after my wife died. That is one of the few pictures I have of her."

The president released him with a shove so he fell back onto the cot.

"The child, Dr. Girard." The slow burn inside him simmered in his tone.

"I think it was a clinic in Birmingham, Alabama, where I volunteered. My wife lost our only child seven months into her pregnancy. Any child who needed comfort, a kiss or holding, my sweet wife took it upon herself to be the angel they may, otherwise, never have. She believed that was the reason God did not bless her with a child." His voice broke. "All I needed was her and, in the end, I lost her, too."

"I do not believe a place like Alabama would approve of your concern for black children."

"We were Canadians. Americans were going through a change of attitude toward racial equality. Volunteers were welcomed. We took many of these trips in those days and in every clinic, we found a child who needed us, needed a home, a life. When my wife became ill, we were denied adoption time and time again. Finally, we gave up."

"When was the first time you were here, Dr. Girard?"

The doctor rubbed his smashed hand and touched his head. "Decades ago."

The president smacked him upside the head with the palm of his hand. "How many years? Ten? Twenty?"

"Closer to forty, I think." His voice trembled. "Before the troubles with rebels and poachers. It was a peaceful place."

"So, you weren't in the Okavango when villages burned and the tourists were killed?"

"I came several years earlier with Doctors Without Borders. My wife and I planned to come before we started our family, but then she miscarried our child. We decided to try another time. But it never happened."

Baboloki listened without showing emotion. There were no records on who came to the Okavango from forty years ago. Passports could be altered and replaced. The only reason he knew the identities of the others who'd stayed in the camp that day was because family members had inquired. No one asked about a doctor. None of the people he'd captured knew of any doctor, but then again, none of them worked at the camp.

The doctor took a deep breath before confronting the president. "What is this all about? I have given my savings to open this clinic. I work hard for these people. I have done nothing wrong."

"I am looking for the Kifaru diamond. Have you heard of it?" The president wanted to pounce if the answer were a lie.

"Yes."

"How?"

"These people speak of it in their stories, how it has the power to lead a nation. But they are told to the children as myths, legends, nothing more. No one believes in this nonsense, not even these simple people. Before I left my clinic in the US, I heard stories of this diamond. I think it all came up because some British prince gave his fiancée a ring with a Botswana diamond. People like to glamourize such things in America. I expect they've already made a television movie about it." The doctor frowned. "That is all I know, Mr. President."

"Do they say there is someone who will come with the diamond and take my place?"

The doctor chuckled and tried to look amused, but touched his head and cringed instead. "That is ridiculous. The diamond, if there ever was one, is gone or broken up into many pieces. As to a new leader, why would that happen? Elections decide the leaders, not a lump of pressed carbon."

Baboloki tapped his mouth with his index finger and walked around the examining room as a guard stood rigid near the door. "Have you seen anyone new in the village, say between the age of thirty-five and forty?"

"There are always new people who come to the clinic once and never return. They come from many island communities in the Okavango. No one new in the village nearby that I've noticed, though. Most either work for me, the camp, or contract out for hunts with a British company. I would have met them by now in any of those cases."

"Why is that, Dr. Girard?"

"They are required to get a physical, immunizations, and first aid training from me before being allowed to work with tourists. It protects both them and the guests. When new people arrive from across our borders, they must run their cars through solutions to protect our cattle from disease and wipe our shoes in the same solution. I would have been told if there was someone sneaking in illegally and threatening the livelihood of the people."

"Yes. I implemented that practice after cattle traffickers slipped across the border." He smirked. "They will not be returning—or leaving, for that matter. But I'm not looking for a thief. I'm looking for someone who has an ax to grind. Someone who can blend in."

"No one comes to mind. I have watched many of these people grow up. I come every year, but I suppose someone could have come many years ago or when I was absent."

Baboloki experienced a moment of acceptance then the relief evaporated. He motioned for the guard. "Take the doctor to the airstrip about forty-five kilometers south from here."

The guard nodded as he waved to some more men in the hall to join him. "I know it, sir. There is a small transport station there for tourists to wait."

"Yes. Make sure the good doctor is comfortable but out of sight. This time of day, I doubt there will be much activity."

"No. I've done nothing wrong, and these people need me," the doctor insisted as he struggled to stand.

"It is for your own protection. I wouldn't want you to further injure yourself. I'll make sure you get to a doctor in Maun. If they decide you require more medical attention, then I'll have you flown to Gaborone." Baboloki forced himself to be civil even though rage brewed inside him. "Besides, my men are much better at deciding if you have told me the truth. I tend to be a little easy on people I think are lying to me." He shrugged. "I have too much faith in mankind, I guess." He turned to the guard. "Isn't that right, Lieutenant?"

The soldier pulled back his shoulders. "Yes, sir!"

"This place looks like an accident waiting to happen," he mused. "If you know what I mean."

"Please, Mr. President. These people need this clinic. I have told you the truth."

The president walked to his side and gently patted the doctor's cheek. "And I appreciate that." He pivoted and growled to the lieutenant, "Get him out of here."

CHAPTER TWENTY-ONE

"Easy," Chase whispered when the leopard turned to stare down at Tessa. Handsome pressed his arm against her upper chest to keep her from moving. A list of possible solutions to this new problem infiltrated his brain like wet cement. He was too frightened, watching the large animal move a step closer to the windshield, to come up with any reasonable idea of what to do.

Tessa gasped for breath. Even sitting at an angle, he could see beads of sweat forming on her brow. Handsome warned again not to stare at the leopard. She squeezed her eyes shut to comply, but opened them enough to form a squint.

Handsome made sloth-like micro moves when he took hold of the steering wheel. Was he going to lay on the horn? Maybe the loud noise would frighten the beast enough to run away.

His thumb went to the center of the wheel, producing a sound more like a child's toy car than a badass Land Rover. Handsome removed his arm from Tessa's chest, pulled a pistol from between the seats, and raised it in the air. Before he could pull the trigger, the leopard swiveled his head toward a giant anthill some eight feet away then jumped down.

Gulping air, Tessa faced Chase who touched her shoulder then lifted a finger to his lips. The leopard glanced back at the vehicle and focused on Tessa, who sat the nearest to ground level and to him.

With a sudden burst of speed, a warthog bolted from a hole at the base of the anthill. The leopard leaped after him and paused when a second warthog shot out of the same hole. In seconds, all three animals were far enough from them to allow them to take a deep breath.

"Holy cow," Tessa moaned, laying her head back against the seat. "I could have been on his lunch menu."

Handsome grabbed the binoculars and stared into the tall grasses. "We'd better find a place to park out of the sun. Our buddy will want his tree back after not catching his pork sandwich for lunch. We might smell like bacon by then." He put the vehicle in drive and chuckled, looking over at Tessa. "And I thought you couldn't get any whiter."

Everyone laughed when Tessa slammed her fist into his massive arm. "You looked a little pale yourself and not nearly so handsome."

This amused him as he slowly pulled forward into the grasses where the impalas ran for their lives.

The morning continued without serious incident, except for when a herd of elephants crossed in front of them, forcing them to back up. The matriarch charged then halted, stirring up a cloud of dust. Handsome stopped and waited for them to move on. The click of cameras didn't seem to bother the giants. Several kudus, a herd of zebras sharing a watering hole with some marabou, storks, and four giraffes found themselves in the crosshairs of Enigma cameras.

After a time, Handsome found a shady area and let everyone out for a short rest and some refreshments.

"Damn, this place is amazing." Carter removed his hat and wiped his brow with his sleeve.

Sam glanced up toward the branches of the trees and accepted a cola from Handsome. "At least it isn't so hot today. Good decision to come in winter. I imagine Sacramento is roasting."

"You all right, Tess?" Chase handed her an orange soda. "I hadn't counted on an up-close- and-personal visit with a hungry leopard." He took a swig of his own drink.

She removed her pith helmet with her free hand and fanned it out toward the savanna. "I was terrified. I never imagined we'd be able to interact so closely with these animals."

"Tessa, look there," Handsome called. "Watch how the giraffe is getting a drink. This is their most vulnerable time. See how they spread their legs and bend down?"

"Good time for a lion to find his next meal." She lifted the binoculars to her eyes.

"Exactly."

"Their tongues are blue!" She laughed and handed the glasses to Chase.

"How did you get us today, Handsome?" Carter asked, lifting his own binoculars. "You draw the short straw?"

"This is a good time to talk without being interrupted. I volunteered. Several of the people from my village came to help out today. The president invited some of his protection detail for dinner."

Sam leaned against the car. "Looked a lot like military to me."

Chase slipped the binoculars around his neck and let them rest on his chest. "Me, too. I don't like it."

Handsome took a deep breath. "He calls them his 'chosen ones.' In truth, they are a collection of ex-special forces, rebels, thugs, and criminals. You can put a monkey in a suit but it's still a monkey."

"He doesn't like me very much." Chase took a long drink of his soda then crushed the can in his fist.

"Neither do I," Handsome smirked. "Who knew Baboloki and I would have something in common? He puts them in his military guard to make sure they keep an eye on his officers. In the past, the officers had complained about some of their duties, and the president took offense to that."

"What kind of duties? A soldier obeys his commander-in-chief." Chase didn't always agree with his orders, but he did his best to follow them.

"Rounding up student protestors, ranchers who complained about having to put their cattle down when there was no hoof-and-mouth disease in their quadrant."

"Why would he do that? Economically, the ranchers could have established a sense of calm when other quadrants suffered. I remember how Europe boycotted all meat coming from Botswana." Sam's PhD in world economics once again brought new insight to the situation.

Handsome passed around a trash bag for their empty cans. "Another way to show that Westerners, Europeans, and others couldn't be counted on. "Even though putting all the herds down did, in fact, eliminate the disease, ranchers had to start over and found themselves borrowing money from the government to do so. Even though loans were at a reasonable rate, they ballooned five years in. Hard to get your herds profitable in that length of time, at least for the small ranches. No doubt some of that interest went into Baboloki's pocket."

"What about the people of the Kalahari and Okavango who aren't ranchers. Did they suffer from Baboloki's suspicion?" Tessa leaned on the vehicle next to Sam.

"More like emotional blackmail. The threat of allowing a dam to be built could most certainly affect their way of life. Some of the younger ones embraced the idea, but their families refused to accept it. During the times when big-game hunts were stopped, the people went hungry. They poached for food and for a livelihood. Keep in mind, the horn of a rhinoceros can support a family for a year here."

"But Baboloki ended that practice in spite of environmental groups protesting around the world." Chase crossed his arms on his chest and stood at ease like a soldier often does.

"Naturally. He made a deal with the villages to stop poaching, and he would allow the

big-game hunters who often dropped fifty-to seventy-five thousand dollars each when they came back in. That provided jobs for many people along with schools for the children, medical care like my father's clinic, and better roads that connected to Maun."

"And he got the credit for ending poaching and the improved economic stability, at least among the rural communities," Chase added. "How is he any different than every other politician in the world? They all take credit for fixing a problem they created in the first place."

"Maybe none." Handsome shrugged. "His military guard has taken advantage of this and hunted at their own pleasure, selling elephant ivory, rhino horns, and other trophies to supplement their salaries. When the villagers complain, they are beaten, shot, or disappear. After a while, they stopped complaining. The numbers of endangered animals, according to Baboloki's statistics have increased, but who knows if that is really true?"

"Wasn't Baboloki supposed to be hunting downriver today?" Tessa asked as she straightened and looked toward the watering hole where a few giraffes still meandered. A military-style truck eased up and stopped. Several guns slipped out over its back railing. A shot rang out, and one giraffe dropped then another, until three of the four lay on the ground.

The Enigma team gathered together watching five men jump out from the back and run up to the fallen beasts. One brought along an ax and hacked at the large bull's head while several others took to removing the skin.

"I think I'm going to be sick," Tessa moaned.

Someone revealed a cell phone and took pictures of themselves with the giraffe that hadn't undergone their attempt at butchering.

"Are we going to do something?" Sam bristled.

"Like what?" Handsome said, throwing the trash bag in the cooler then loading it into the Land Rover. The team kept an eye on the mayhem while trying to get back in the vehicle.

"Stop them," Tessa demanded, climbing into the front.

Chase pushed her over and pointed to the back where he'd sat earlier and took the front passenger seat. "You got any weapons besides that starter pistol you waved around earlier, Handsome?"

"Well, since you asked."

Handsome pulled a small semi-automatic handgun from under the seat and handed it to Chase. "There's another one under your seat,

Carter, in a holster attached to the metal frame.

"Got it," he quickly announced.

"Let's go have a little chat, shall we?" Handsome turned on the engine and put the vehicle in gear.

The soldiers stopped their excited laughter and machete wielding when the safari vehicle approached. Two of them moved back toward their truck in a calculated, slow movement. The others waited by the downed giraffes. Pulling up alongside of the watering hole, Handsome let the vehicle idle as he stared at the bloody carcasses.

"Looks like you've been busy," Handsome said offhandedly.

One of the soldiers looked at his two buddies then over at the truck where the others had disappeared. "Is there a problem?" he asked, his face becoming a mask of temperamental impatience.

"Do you have a permit to hunt out here? This area has a lot of tourists coming and going." Handsome pointed to the giraffes.

"We don't need a permit." He smiled devilishly.

"Yeah," he joked back. "Here you do. What are you going to do with all that meat?"

"Leave it. We only want the head and hide. Makes a good rug for some rich man's wall in Moscow or London."

Handsome whistled. "How much do you get for one of these?"

"Plenty."

"Maybe since you don't have a permit, I'll just take it off your hands." Handsome let a chuckle escape from deep in his throat.

The soldiers came closer and eyed the women. "Maybe you're showing off for the pretty ladies."

A sense of alarm came over Chase when the men who had disappeared into the truck returned carrying some fancy firepower. "Nice weapons. That military issue?"

The soldier cut his eyes to Chase and frowned. "Not exactly." Then he twisted his lips in a show of impatience. "We got them on eBay."

All the soldiers found this amusing and laughed with each step they took closer. They tapped the side of their weapons with what seemed to be nervous anticipation.

"Do you have a problem with this?" he asked then looked back over his shoulder at the bloody animals.

"Probably not as much as the giraffes," Handsome laughed.

"President Baboloki gave us some time off to hunt."

"Did he now?" Handsome chuckled then smiled broadly.

"Where is the president? I thought he planned to hunt, too. Why aren't you with him?" Chase tipped his wide-brimmed hat back with one finger. "He doesn't strike me as someone who could find his way out of a paper bag without some help."

Whatever amusement the soldiers had enjoyed a moment earlier vanished. "Maybe you should keep your mouth shut."

"Maybe you should lower your weapons," Chase added.

"And maybe you should get the hell out of here before there's an accident," the leader snapped, his eyes bulging.

"Let's go, Chase." Tessa leaned up and touched his shoulder. "Please."

"The lady makes sense." The leader nodded her way.

"I'll check back later to see how you're doing here." Handsome's face appeared frozen with a plastic smile.

The soldiers pointed their weapons at them. "Or maybe not. Trust me. We'll be fine."

Two of the men seemed to decide a little more encouragement was necessary, pulled up their rifles, and aimed.

"Guess we're not wanted. The camp is expecting us back anyway. We're already about twenty minutes late. You know how the camp directors get when their bread and butter doesn't arrive back on time." Handsome put the vehicle in reverse. "Especially after yesterday."

When Tessa's hand touched his hip, Chase heard her suck in her breath. Both he and Carter stood, brandishing their weapons.

"You boys take care. I'll be sure to let the president know we crossed paths." When he backed the vehicle from the scene, Chase eased down into his seat but kept his weapon leveled at the leader. Carter angled himself forward in order to keep his weapon ready.

Handsome continued to back the vehicle, using only his side mirrors, until they returned to the shady spot where they'd taken a break. Stopping, Handsome called the incident in to camp, at Chase's suggestion, in case the soldiers decided to follow up on their threats.

Even though the soldiers were not hidden, they continued to load what they could of the giraffes into the back of the truck, leaving most of the bodies intact.

"Guess we made them nervous," Handsome speculated, looking through the binoculars.

"Must have forgotten something," Chase said watching through his own binoculars.

Just as the driver, or leader, exited the cab and ran back to one of the giraffes, the leopard came bounding out of the tree line and grabbed him. He fought while the cat grabbed the back of his neck and dragged him with ease toward the trees. His screams were terrifying.

"What is happening?" Tessa stood up with Sam, trying to see the carnage they left behind.

"Poetic justice, I think," Chase answered calmly. Some of the other soldiers shot their weapons after the disappearing cat. He put away the gun and relaxed.

Carter pulled Sam down to sit next to him. "Mother Nature always finds a way, they say."

Tessa groaned and shook her head. "Let me out. I have to throw up."

CHAPTER TWENTY-TWO

Peter stood next to another Land Rover. Chase suspected he was moments from coming to search for them. When Handsome put the vehicle in park, the camp director sighed then approached to help the ladies down.

"That message scared me. We haven't had any trouble in forever, and in two days we've had a shooting, poaching, and a missing person." Peter walked alongside Chase and Handsome.

"Missing? Who is missing? Not the president?" Chase already knew the answer but thought it best to play dumb.

"Keeya, the president's aide. We have looked everywhere for her. She has disappeared. This is no place to wander off. The secretary said you were still at the tent when she came down to talk to us this morning. Did she say anything?"

Tessa still appeared a little pale, so Chase took her small hand in his. The frightened look amused him.

"We made a quick stop at our own tent then came straight here. I told her I'd interview her later today, maybe at lunch." If Tessa could do anything well, it was tell a lie. He could spot her attempt at pulling a fast one, but that hadn't always been true.

At the beginning of their stormy relationship, he'd fallen for several of her lies and nearly been killed and nearly killed her. When she batted those blue eyes, people, men especially, believed her. She was an innocent. Or used to be. He wasn't so sure anymore.

"Last we saw her, she was sitting on the deck with some papers. She didn't look up when we walked by," Chase added for a little more reinforcement to the lie. "How long has she been missing?"

Handsome watched him and even slowed his long, leggy strides. It would be only a matter of time before he would need to be moved to a safer location if this whole Kifaru diamond thing really did make a difference in who led the country. The elections were not that far off.

"The president's secretary probably spent an hour with us then checked on tonight's seating arrangements." Peter rolled his eyes. "Everyone thinks they're important, apparently. We're in the bush. Who the hell cares?"

"When did Naledi go back to her tent?" Carter interjected as he slipped an arm around Sam who sidestepped him in time to resist being pulled in close to his side. He dropped his hand to hers, and this she didn't resist.

"Not sure. After another thirty minutes or so. She waited a while to come looking for Keeya, probably thinking she'd gone to the observation deck or down to the water. That in itself is alarming, if you don't tell someone where you are. In the daytime, it's not usually a problem. The secretary finally came to tell us, and we immediately began a search with no luck."

They ran up on the dining deck that looked out over the Okavango, where a buffet table filled with finger foods and fruit waited along with hot tea and biscuits left from breakfast.

"Could she be with some of the other staff?" Chase inquired as he passed out the plates to his friends. The British guests and Germans already sat at a table and sipped tea.

"That was where we looked first. This is a disaster. Out first visit with the president, and this happens. I understand some photographers from Geo-World magazine will be here soon to document the president's trip."

"Never heard of them." Tessa set her food on the table.

"I think they're European."

The two German men shook their head. "I've never heard of them, either, but if they're new, then I wouldn't have." They looked at the British guests.

They shrugged and went back to talking among themselves.

"Oh, I remember." Tessa waved her fork in the air. "They are a children's magazine. Daniel brought it home last year, thinking I'd want him to have it since it was geography based. Too pricey. Great pictures, though."

"Who is Daniel?" the director asked.

Chase leveled a warning gaze. "Isn't that your nephew? Cute kid."

Tessa choked on her tomato wedge.

With a quick smack on the back, Sam chuckled. "You eat like a kid,

Tessa. Remember to chew your food."

"Sorry. Too much salt I think." Tessa twitched away from Sam's touch. Chase imagined his senior agent hit her a little harder than necessary, but he found it amusing nonetheless. "And yes, Chase, that is my nephew. I'll have to tell him I met the photographers. Will they be here for the dinner tonight?"

Peter put his hands on his hips. "Yes. Coming in by plane. The pilot plans to stay the night. Not sure where I'll put him."

Handsome cleared away the plates from the British guests. "He can bunk with me. With Moremi in the hospital…"

"Great idea," Peter sighed. "Forgot about that. While you were gone, we got word he came through surgery without any issues and should make a full recovery."

Everyone sighed relief with the news and tried to ask a few follow-up questions, but the camp director hurried away to another area to solve a problem. The Europeans excused themselves to their quarters. This time of day usually meant the activity would be a nap. Tea time would be around four then a guide would take guests back out in the safari vehicles or the mokoros until sunset.

To experience sunset in the Okavango was almost a religious experience. Seeing it with Tessa at his side, created a deep desire to make some kind of romantic gesture toward her. Even when she walked away and stood at the railing around the deck, Chase found himself wondering about the possibility of plunging into a forbidden affair.

"You're staring, buddy," Carter mocked as he elbowed him in the side. "You're looking a little lovestruck." His gaze went to Tessa then back at Chase. "When are you going to do something about that? Or are you doing—"

"No. Nothing. This isn't the right time."

Carter smirked. "You know what? One of these days she is going to kick Robert to the curb and some yahoo good-ole boy is goin' swoop in and carry her off."

Chase couldn't resist a chuckle. "Is that a threat? Because if it is, I want to see how you react to rejection."

"I don't believe the two of you aren't a little more than friends, is all."

"Believe whatever you want."

"If you'd get off that high horse of yours and romance the lady, you might find out she has a thing for you, too. Sam says she and Robert are having some trouble."

"What kind of trouble?" Chase turned away from looking at her. "Since when does Tessa confide in Sam?"

"Beats me. I think those two are screwin' with our psyches." Carter stood and stretched. "Kind of makes a man all tingly inside, doesn't it?" He stretched his neck to look down toward where the tent accommodations stood. "About that. I feel a nap coming on." He slapped Chase on the back. "If you know what I mean."

Chase shook his head and pushed his chair back. "One of these days I'm going to have to plan a funeral for you. Be sure to write down your wishes."

In his deep Texan accent, he laid his hand on his heart. "Make sure I still have a satisfied grin on my face, good buddy."

"We're expected to go to our tents, Tessa." Chase walked up beside her and laid his hands on the railing. He wasn't sure why this feeling of time running out for what he wanted to say to her kept plaguing him with indecision.

The thought of breaking up a marriage and getting involved with an agent had always been taboo to him. That all changed the day Tessa opened her front door and invited him into her home. She had no idea what a rollercoaster ride waited for her in the following days. Her bravery and support impressed him so much, he failed to rid himself of her memory until they crossed paths a year later.

Somehow, she'd managed to worm her way into President Austin's good graces, and even the president decided she needed to stick around to help out his secret Enigma organization. Now here he was, standing like a schoolboy with his first crush, next to the woman he didn't deserve but wanted to take anyway, breaking all the rules he'd lived by for so long.

"Okay. Let's go." She turned away and turned back around when Chase didn't immediately catch up. "You coming?" Her eyebrows lifted.

There had been a time she would have looked terrified at the suggestion they be alone together. He wasn't sure when that attitude had changed, but her resistance to his presence was a great deal easier to take than her compliance. Her trusting nature managed to create a path of destruction on his morale high road.

He lifted his chin in acknowledgement and caught up with her.

"Are you mad at me for my forgetting about Daniel? I'm sorry," she confessed as she struggled to keep up with his long strides. "Slow down."

"No. I'm not mad. Just be careful what you say." He picked up the pace until Tessa had to almost run to keep up.

"Then what's going on?" She managed to grab his hand and tugged enough to slow his steps.

Chase instinctively looked down at her hand like it was a pair of restraints. She blushed then dropped his hand. He snatched it back in his and slowed down, turning his eyes to focus on their quarters.

"Sorry. I shouldn't have touched you. I know you hate that." Tessa entered the tent when he held back the zippered screen door. Tossing her pith helmet on the camp stool, she then flopped down on the bed, only to fluff her pillow over and over.

Chase stared at her lying on the bed, all relaxed with her hair twisting out of her ponytail on her neck. "I'm going to sit outside for a while. Try to get some rest."

She yawned and rolled away from him so he could no longer see her face. Looking at her form would be his undoing. He quickly returned to the deck to make a plan about Baboloki. Thinking about a pompous dictator seemed safer ground at the moment.

The warmth of the afternoon sun forced him to admit he needed a nap, too. He stretched out his legs and crossed his arms across his chest. Tilting his hat down kept the afternoon light from his eyes. The sounds of the Okavango were lulling him toward sleep when a hand touched his shoulder.

He bounded up so fast the man in front of him didn't have time to react. Chase caught him by the wrist and twisted hard enough the man fell to his knees.

"What the hell?" shouted Handsome.

Releasing him, Chase stepped back and stared at the giant pushing himself up. Handsome reminded him of a surprised Cape buffalo whose next move would be an attempt at murder. With no apology, he eased back into his director-style chair.

"Shouldn't you be working?" Chase said after taking a deep breath.

"Shouldn't you be on medication of some kind to deal with your passive-aggressive disorder?"

Chase pulled his hat down farther and smirked. "I decided I was fully functional without it. What do you want?"

"I want to talk to Tessa about the woman who is missing."

"Sorry. She is napping. And I have no intention of waking her up."

Handsome snorted. "You could have gotten us killed this morning."

"You mean when you went looking for trouble with Baboloki's thugs and suggested they give you their kill? Could it be you've gotten away with those antics before?"

"Maybe." Handsome dragged another chair up. When he sat, the chair groaned in protest. "I never pretended to be a Boy Scout."

"Your father seems to think otherwise."

"Yes. He prefers to think of me as his good little boy who will bring change to these people. Sometimes I think I do this for him. Sometimes I don't care." He narrowed his eyes and stared out at the waters of the Okavango that had turned silver in the afternoon sun. "But then I breathe in this place, and I want to be that boy my father believes me to be."

"What is the plan, anyway? Shouldn't you be a candidate or something, running a campaign or raising money to get yourself elected? Or do you think the Kifaru will help you skip all that?"

"Maybe."

"That's what this part of Africa needs, another idiot who thinks he's above the rule of law."

"I don't like your tone or insinuation." Handsome's voice took on a deep, sinister tone. Chase recognized it from months ago when he'd trapped him and Tessa in a cabin at Lake Tahoe. He couldn't be trusted to do the right thing.

"Let's face it, Handsome, you haven't done much to make me trust you."

"Pulled your butt out of Lake Tahoe and kept you from drowning."

"Are you sure it was me you were saving?" Chase watched Handsome turn his head to peer inside the darkness of the tent.

He shrugged. "Well, saving, you meant saving something of value."

"Are you talking about Tessa or your diamond?"

"Kind of the same thing, don't you think? You two sure are playing the part of lovers better than I expected. And here I thought Tessa was the smart one of your ragtag bunch of assassins. How did she come to be mixed up with you, anyway? Does she understand what you do for a living?"

"My relationship with Tessa is none of your business. She thinks her coming to us was divine intervention." This never failed to amuse him. "I guess the president thought we needed a moral compass. Who am I to disagree with the most powerful man on Earth?"

Handsome grew silent for a few minutes before continuing, "The missing woman."

"What about her?"

"Something is wrong. She and my father were chatting like old friends. I caught them holding hands, smiling. It even looked like she had tears in her eyes."

"Doctors have that effect on their patients. Saw it with my own folks who were doctors."

"Your parents were doctors?" Handsome asked in disbelief. "What happened to you? At least I have an excuse."

"They were medical missionaries in China. Some military officials...maybe the government, didn't like them giving the villages a sense of hope as they healed them. They killed them. My sister and I only escaped with the help of some Christians and Buddhist monks."

Handsome rubbed his face. "Sorry. Guess that's why you're such an asshole sometimes."

Chase laughed. "Sometimes. Other times it's because I have to deal with people like you. As to Keeya, I think she isn't a big fan of the president and doesn't necessarily follow orders very well. She and Naledi, the secretary, didn't seem to be getting along this morning."

"Why doesn't Keeya leave?"

"Maybe she needs the job." Chase wasn't ready to tell Handsome the truth. "It's my understanding she's from the Okavango, someplace. You know how it is, you come home and forget why you ever left?"

"No. I don't. We moved around a lot. My parents were afraid someone would find out the truth about me. This is the first place I dared let myself feel anything."

"You need to be sure what it is you want. These people deserve a leader who can protect them from money-driven companies that don't give a rip about this land. I mean, you hate Baboloki because he killed your father. Maybe there is something else here for you. Don't screw it up."

"I don't need advice from you," he snarled.

"You always want to get in the last word don't you, Handsome? I'll tell Tess you dropped by. Beat it. Your rattling on and on has nearly put me in a coma."

Handsome stood. "One more thing. Two of your snakes slithered in posing as photographers for some kid's magazine. They asked for you when they spotted me. I told them to check in, and I'd come get you."

"I'm not leaving Tessa alone."

"I can stay until you get back."

Chase pushed his hat back with his index finger and slipped on his sunglasses. "The last time I left Tessa in your care, she disappeared to parts unknown. No thanks. They're big boys. Point them in my direction."

Handsome lumbered toward the steps. "I'll think about it."

CHAPTER TWENTY-THREE

Baboloki admired his kill as it was loaded onto a truck. The kudu was a nice specimen. He gave orders for the meat to be given to a local village and sent the head to his taxidermy in Maun. The head would be displayed in the capital or perhaps the national museum.

"Be sure my name is attached." He nodded toward his head of security. "Can you do that for me, Dage?"

"Yes, sir. With the shooting yesterday, and endangering the camp guests, I'm not comfortable leaving your protection to anyone else." Dage wore light-colored khakis and a safari vest, taking the edge off his usual military appearance. He could have been one of Baboloki's pals who had come along on the trip.

"I see your point. Very well." Baboloki listened patiently to Dage give orders to the driver of the truck and then the president allowed one of the guards to tag along with them. "I believe we have a boat to catch. Our guide headed that way an hour ago."

A Jeep with one of the locals who drove them to the rendezvous point followed. Dage forked out some money in appreciation. Baboloki watched at a distance when his security officer leveled a warning about mentioning the rhino brought down and left for someone else to deal with the carcass.

The horn was smaller than Baboloki hoped. Game wardens and veterinarians often removed rhino horns to keep the animals safe from poaching. Since the horns are keratin, a type of protein found in human hair and fingernails, they grew back. Why should he be denied such a treasure when a mere kilogram of the horn went for sixty-thousand dollars on the black market? A little retirement money in a Swiss bank account might come in handy someday.

The president could see the boat and their guide waving to them. He recognized him from the camp. Although it was nice to be admired in spite of the constant babble of the man in Tswana, Dage intervened and carried on the conversation so he wouldn't have to.

He wanted to think about the Kifaru diamond and the possibility it had returned to Botswana. And what about Keeya's child? Had he survived? If so, where had he been? Had the doctor rescued the baby and carried him off to a safer locale? Why wouldn't he have shared the story? What would make him keep such a secret? Perhaps by day's end there would be answers.

After glancing up at the afternoon sun, he realized they'd missed the lunch hour back at the camp. Box lunches had been prepared for them in case the hunt went well and they couldn't get back for the usual noon meal. He hadn't wanted to visit with the guests, especially the Americans. He found them more than annoying, and speculated again if they were CIA. Captain Hunter caused him to feel cautious with his words and temper. The man was tough as nails even when he attempted to put on gentlemanly airs.

"What's wrong?" he asked the driver of their boat.

"There is smoke in the distance, Mr. President. It's coming from the direction of the medical clinic."

Baboloki and Dage shaded their eyes in pretense of interest.

"When I dropped you there this morning, was all well?"

"Yes. We said hello. The doctor was busy, so we didn't stay long. Our ride arrived earlier than expected for the hunt. We ate the lunch you packed. Delicious, by the way," Dage commented. "I'm sure things are fine. They were building a fire in some kind of pit."

The guide nodded as he revved up the engine and pulled out into the wide part of the river. "Maybe roasting meat. The doctor built a stone firepit for the village, so they could work and cook for their people during celebrations."

"Probably nothing," Dage insisted as he found a seat next to his boss and met his gaze.

The guide continued to stand at the wheel, turning the boat in the direction of the camp. Several times, he glanced over his shoulder toward the plume of smoke rising in the late-afternoon sky. Baboloki knew it was only a matter of time before news would fill the Okavango that the medical clinic lay in ashes. Maybe this would flush out the troublemaker trying to take the presidency away from him.

~ ~ ~

It wasn't long until Chase watched Zoric and Vernon pass by his tent. The two Enigma agents offered a casual nod of recognition and a friendly hello. Their quarters were on the other side of Carter and Sam. Since they didn't stop, he guessed Handsome had lied earlier about their interest in order to get Tessa alone.

Another hour passed before he stood, stretched out his arms, and cringed. The wound in his side burned. Instinctively, he laid a hand on it and pressed gently, as if by doing so, the sudden jolt would ease.

He entered the tent and tried to zip down the door quietly so as not to wake Tessa. But when he turned around, she stared at him with her luminous blue eyes that switched the pain in his side to the one in his chest. "Did I wake you?"

She pushed up on her knees and moved to the edge of the bed nearer him. She beckoned him closer, and Chase sucked in his breath and obeyed.

"You overdid it this morning. I knew you should have stayed put. I would have been glad to babysit you," she mumbled, lifting his tee shirt. "I'll change your bandage."

Before she could swing off the bed, he grabbed the first aid supplies Dr. Girard sent with them. He liked having her on her knees on the edge of the bed. There was a familiarity about the gesture he wished would lead to other things. She didn't seem to notice. The easiness between them grew stronger with each passing day. Maybe she'd left the memories of Afghanistan behind.

"Can you hold your shirt up for me, or would it be better to take it off?" She removed several things from the supplies. When he didn't answer, she frowned. "Seriously? You think I'm suggesting something else?"

Ignoring the comment, he held his shirt up for her. "Of course not." Apparently, he managed to sound more irritated than disappointed.

She pulled away the bandage and stared at it before cleaning the area. "I saw you flinch when you stretched outside. You don't seem to have a fever," she said laying her palm flat against his midriff a little longer than he expected.

"Well I will be if you don't keep your hands off me," he said slowly.

A blush formed on her cheeks, as she proceeded to replace the bandage.

"Nothing to say?" He pulled the tee shirt over the clean dressing. "It's about time for one of your insults."

"You're despicable," she offered then rolled away and swung her legs off the bed. "How's that?" She didn't sound angry with him, and he took that as a good sign.

"I'm not up to going out for the sunset cruise. The mokoro is a little uncomfortable and tight."

"We could go out in the speedboat. I'm sure Handsome wouldn't mind taking us." She moved up next to him. When he didn't step back, she pushed by him. He caught her arm and tugged her back around. Surprise filled her eyes as they fell on the hand gripping her arm. "But if you don't want to, I understand. I'll stay with you. We look after each other."

The exhale he released came in a controlled, slow fashion. He remembered what Handsome had suggested about his identity. "Do you even know who I am, Tessa? What I do for a living and that I'm a poster boy for PTSD on a good day?" He stared hard at her and once again watched a flash of fear leap into her expression.

"There was a time I was afraid of you."

"And now?"

"There is no one in this world I trust more."

"Did it ever occur to you I'm getting tired of picking up your breadcrumbs for a rescue?"

The lightheartedness vanished. "No." She swallowed hard. "I'm. I'm sorry. I never, ever mean to put you or the team in jeopardy. Where is this coming from? Is it because I mentioned my son earlier?"

Chase circled her waist and pulled her tight against his chest. Her eyes went wide when he lowered his face so close his breath moved a wayward curl. Her body stiffened, and she pushed against his chest. "No. It's because I want—"

"Anybody home?" came the familiar voice of Vernon Kemp, his technical agent.

They were far enough into the darkness of the tent, Vernon and Zoric wouldn't be able to see them. Chase stepped away and let his hand fall down on Tessa's hip as he stole a glance outside then back to her face. She stared at him in confusion and bit her lower lip.

"You're not yourself. You know this is impossible," she whispered.

"I deal in impossible all the time." He stepped toward the screened door then turned back toward her. "When we finish this job, I want to put some distance between us. Understand?"

"Not really," she confessed. "Let's talk about it. Please."

"I'm not much of a talker and besides, that isn't what I want from you, Tessa."

"Aren't you glad to see us?" Vernon asked pushing his goofy face against the screen.

Zoric pulled the young agent back as Chase unzipped the tent. "No social skills," he declared when Chase and Tessa slipped out onto the deck. He and Chase locked eyes for a few seconds before the Serbian glanced at Tessa who managed to wear a guilty expression.

"Keeya is safe, for now," Zoric mumbled out of the side of his mouth then glanced down at the ground. "We saw smoke, flying in. Something is on fire."

"Could be anything."

"The pilot said it might be where the medical clinic is located, but since we were on a schedule, he didn't go check it out. He decided to return to Maun for the night after Baboloki's head of security wanted to run some errands for his boss. It's only about a half-hour flight."

"Guess that means the president returned."

"Not sure, since we didn't see him. We haven't been here long. Just headed down to the gathering place for afternoon tea. We did see Handsome, and he said he'd be our guide for the late-afternoon cruise. Taking the motorboat out, I think." Zoric rubbed his neck then his upper left thigh. "I don't think these stiff legs can manage that little mokoro thing they think is a boat. Looks like hippo bait to me."

"But think of the pictures we'd get." Vernon threw his arms out in exasperation. "Where's your spirit of adventure?"

"On the Discovery Channel. Grow up," Zoric snarled at his young friend then addressed Chase. "This guy thinks everything is a video game and he can either survive or get a do-over."

Tessa joined them. "Do we need to check on Dr. Girard?"

"We'll get Handsome to take us downriver if he can't contact the clinic by radio." Chase followed the three down the steps. "I think Baboloki is waiting on his tree house deck with his secretary. He doesn't look happy."

"Guess he finally got the bad news about Keeya." Tessa stole a glance toward the president's quarters.

"Keep walking. We'll find out soon enough what will happen next." Chase slipped his hand into Tessa's and picked up speed as they moved toward the dining area.

There continued to be a great deal of activity going on toward the preparation of the night's feast in honor of the president being a first-time guest. Peter joined them for tea and informed everyone Keeya remained missing. The president had returned and had been given the news.

"He is distraught," Peter added with a sigh. "He seems to care a lot about his people."

"Did he say anything about seeing smoke while they were out?"

Chase asked then let Zoric and Vernon relay what they'd seen and the pilot's comments. They sounded unconcerned even to him and expressed doubt whether it was anything to worry about.

"Nothing on the radio, and we would've heard by now." Peter chuckled. "It wouldn't be the first time the good doctor let one of his barbeques get out of hand. Last year, a bull elephant decided to nose around and sent everyone inside until a few other bulls came in and decided to add another couple of limbs to the fire when they pushed over one of the thatched cooling stations." He shook his head. "More smoke than fire. Haven't seen our bull, Rambo, in a few days. Might have decided to head that direction and cause a little trouble. I swear he enjoys it."

Peter stood up and moved away from the table before clapping his hands. "Time to head out, my friends. "The sunset should be spectacular—"

"Like always," interrupted the British lady.

"Yes. Indeed. No concerns about poachers. President Baboloki's people are keeping vigil in various places in case of trouble." He waved toward their exit ramp. "See you in a few hours. Expect a culinary delight tonight upon your return. So, off you go."

Handsome waited at the boat dock and assisted the Brits into their mokoros. The ladies squealed when the mokoro rocked suddenly, pitching the guide in the rear, holding the pole, into the water. Laughter erupted when Handsome pulled him out. The mishap had the ladies apologizing for their clumsiness. The two British men decided to travel together this time, saying they wanted to fish. Already out in the channel, they called back encouragement to the ladies.

Once the others had pushed off toward the narrow channels of the Okavango, Handsome helped the Enigma team into his boat. Sam and Carter were last to arrive. Carter whistled "The Yellow Rose of Texas" while Sam glowered at him.

Why Sam had been in a dangerous mood since they'd arrived still puzzled Chase. He hoped Carter wasn't taking unfair advantage of the situation with them being roommates. However, Sam could best the former astronaut any day of the week. The woman might look like a piece of fine crystal, but her resolve resembled steel. She squeezed in between Vernon and Zoric. The young tech immediately stopped his nonstop chatter and stared straight ahead. Zoric moved back next to Carter who pounded him on the back like a long-lost friend.

"Handsome, once you get out into more open waters, would you kill the engine so we can talk?" Chase sat up in the front seat next to him. The big man nodded and went only a couple of miles before stopping.

"What's up? Is it about the woman they call Keeya? She's still missing. I think it is odd she would walk away." Handsome kept his grip on the wheel as he sat.

Tessa leaned over the seat and laid her hand on his beefy shoulder. "Have you heard from your father today?"

"Come to think of it, no. Most days we connect, but I've been a little busy. We never miss more than a day or two. Why?"

Chase took a deep breath and nodded back at Zoric and Vernon. "They spotted some smoke coming from the direction of the clinic. We're a little worried is all. With what happened this morning and Baboloki being gone longer than the rest of us…"

Handsome located the radio in the console. "Baboloki was scheduled to be gone longer since he was on a hunt. Lunches were packed for them. And those poachers we ran into were a little far from the clinic, although I suspect they were part of the guard tagging along with the president. I'll call my father."

The static brought a silence to the team while Handsome continued to try and contact his father.

"Care if I head that way to make sure everything is okay?" Handsome fired up the engine.

Tessa patted his shoulder. "Go ahead. Sounds like a good idea."

In seconds, they were flying through the water at top speed. Chase moved back next to Tessa and pulled a thin blanket over them. The late afternoon had lost its punch of heat and soon the temperatures would tumble. The others also took blankets. Tessa nudged closer as he slipped his arm around her shoulders.

He planned to make this their last job. He considered a relationship dangerous ground with plenty of buried land mines to avoid. There weren't many things he feared. Rejection from Tessa Scott remained at the top of the list. She wanted to talk about what bothered him, and Chase knew himself well enough to reject such an idea.

Minutes from the landing point for the medical clinic, the smell of smoke was in the air. The boat idled slowly in when a smoldering compound appeared. People wandered around, crying and calling out words Chase couldn't understand. The men pitched in to secure the boat immediately.

"Go," Chase ordered Handsome. "Go."

The team followed Handsome who ran ahead to find Dr. Girard. Several of the villagers met him. In seconds, he took on the frightened look of a crazed man who had lost everything. He called out his father's name as he ran toward the main building, timbers still falling inside from the fire. Smoke curled upward and Chase didn't see how there could be survivors.

Handsome was rushing to go inside when Chase and Carter caught up with him, pulling him back for his own safety as a wall collapsed.

"No!" he screamed over and over then jerked free of the hands holding him back.

Tears flowed down his face. He staggered backward and fell to the ground. A group of villagers standing nearby also cried, some holding babies or propping up grandmothers who most likely were alive because of the good doctor's care.

The Enigma team stood helpless, watching the end of a man's life's work all because of the birth of a baby boy. Tessa was the only person who dared go to Handsome after he'd threatened several others to stay away from him. She squatted next to him and wiped his tears away. Her own trickled down her cheeks, flushed from the heat of the fire.

With the gentleness of a loving mother, she wrapped her arms around the giant of a man then laid her head on his shoulder. His arms went around her and hugged her so tight, Chase wondered how she could breathe.

Seeing give love and comfort to a despicable liar, crumbled Chase's resolve to send her packing once they returned to the States. He wanted that love for himself. The familiar pain in his chest returned, a reminder he actually had a heart capable of compassion and love.

Chase extended his hand. "Come on, buddy. Let's find out what happened."

CHAPTER TWENTY-FOUR

Tessa moved among the people, trying to comfort them. A woman with a baby struggled to keep her other two children close at hand while consoling an elderly woman.

"May I?" Tessa extended her hands out toward the baby girl who appeared to be around five months old. "I will stay close by." She cooed at the baby who returned the gesture then leaned slightly toward her. Tessa lifted her from her mother's arm. The baby pulled at Tessa's hair and pinched her lips with chubby fingers.

"She likes you." The woman revealed several missing teeth when she spoke. Her boys began fighting each other near one of the smoldering piles of rubble. With a look of panic and a few cross words at the boys, the mother offered to take back the infant.

Tessa tickled the baby into giggling then buried her head in her neck. She twirled around, enjoying the feel of holding a baby again.

"I need to get my boys."

"Go ahead. We are fine."

"Thank you, ma'am."

"Tessa. Call me Tessa."

The mother nodded then fussed at the boys who tried to escape her wrath.

"You're a friend of Handsome." A young woman in her twenties approached her timidly. "I saw him hug you."

Jealous girlfriend? Secret admirer? Her body tensed at the idea of another woman getting the wrong impression of her relationship with Handsome.

"Yes, we are old friends. He saved my life once, and I owe him big-time. He is part of my American family." The admiring glance the girl sent to Handsome, who spoke to Chase, told her she'd said the right thing. "So, you are Handsome's friend?"

"Yes." She looked around her. "The doctor is not dead like everyone thinks."

Tessa cringed as the baby yanked her earring. Gently, she removed the fingers and kissed them. "Are you sure?"

"Yes, ma'am. Very sure."

Tessa listened then insisted she tell Chase and Handsome. She called them over so the mother of the child could continue dealing with her boys. Handsome appeared to have pulled himself together, but his puffy eyes added to the sour expression and deep frown.

Chase tickled the cheeks of the baby, winning him a burst of laughter. "Who is this?"

"Part of your future fan club, I imagine." She landed a few more kisses on the baby's head before nodding at the young lady. "I think you need to listen to her story."

Handsome shifted his eyes to Tessa then the woman. "Taifa, what is it? Are you hurt?"

"No. No." The tears rolled freely while she threw her hands up. "Your friend, Dr. Girard. He is very hurt, very bad."

"He is not in the rubble of the clinic?" Handsome's hands went to the top of his head.

"No. I wanted to help. He sent us home because no one came to the clinic and the men were gone to help at the camp. My mother needed something for a headache, so I came back to beg for medicine," she wept.

"What happened?" Handsome gripped her arms.

Chase pulled him off the girl when she winced. "Taifa, you're hurt."

"I ran into the clinic to save what I could after they left," she sobbed. "I am sorry, Handsome."

"Taifa, you are burned." Handsome's voice softened. "What were you thinking, running into a burning building?"

"These people need medicine. Bandages. Things to make life easier. I got to the medicine cabinet and loaded up buckets. I went back three trips before the smoke got too bad." She pointed to some nearby trees. "There are the supplies."

Handsome got over himself suddenly and retrieved two of the buckets. "We need to fix your arms and hands."

"I used to be a medic. Let me," Chase insisted then motioned for her to climb up on a picnic table that had survived the fire. "Can you talk while I do this?" he asked. His knight-in-shining-armor grin wasn't lost on Tessa. It never failed. When he used his calm, cool voice in a tight situation, someone would fall victim to his charm. Taifa nodded sweetly and sniffed back the last of her tears.

"What did you see?" Handsome coaxed.

The baby nuzzled into Tessa's neck and dozed while Taifa stole glances at Handsome. She understood the young woman wanted to please him. "Tell them what you told me, Taifa."

"I heard men. They had guns. I had to hide to keep them from seeing me. I slipped to the back so I could look in the window."

She watched Chase for a few moments as he applied some ointment to her arm and added a look of endearing concern. Tessa tried to wrap her head around the idea, for the millionth time, how a man with his particular set of problem-solving skills could be so disarming. Watching him almost got her sidetracked from the seriousness of the situation.

"Did you recognize them?" Tessa adjusted the baby in her arms.

"No. They were not from the Okavango. They wore uniforms like some of the park rangers."

"How did they hurt the doctor?" Handsome asked.

"I don't know. His head was bleeding. I couldn't see his face. A man talked to him, but I couldn't see him. He wanted to know about the doctor's family."

Chase stood erect and leveled a serious expression at Handsome. "What about them?" he asked as he replaced the supplies in the bucket.

"Something about a picture they found of the doctor's wife."

Handsome shook his head. "He kept a picture of his wife and child in his desk."

Tessa and Chase met each other's eyes. That child stood before them. "What did Dr. Girard say about the picture?" Chase put his hands on his hips.

"She died. Good woman. Loved children. I don't understand why this made the man so angry."

"How many men, Taifa? Could you tell?" Handsome continued, his voice edged with irritation.

"I think five, six, maybe more, but I hid after that. I hoped they would leave him. I figured they want drugs. There is no money here. The doctor treats everyone the same. Good people. Bad people. Isn't that true, Handsome?" Taifa's voice quivered. "I am sorry I could not save him."

"What happened next?" Chase moved to Tessa's side and glanced down at the baby then at her.

"They dragged him out. Another man said they would make him talk when they got somewhere. They didn't say where. He cried when they set the fires." She burst into tears again. "I was so scared."

Handsome cupped her chin in his monstrous hand. "Thank you, Taifa. You have helped more than you know. And all this medicine will help people. We'll get it back to the camp where we have some refrigeration." He patted her cheek. "You did good. We will find him. Now, go home."

Chase gave her some care instructions for her arms and hands before she left. Tessa watched Handsome walk her to the trail leading to her village and considered whether there might be romance between the two.

"You look pretty happy holding that baby. You're a natural," Chase said, touching the baby's toes, so they would twitch.

Tessa took a deep breath. "I love babies. Makes me want another one." She kissed the child's head and wrinkled her nose at Chase. "Here comes her momma. Guess I'm back to wishing again," she said wistfully. The child never awoke in the handoff. A sigh escaped her when the mother walked away. A glance toward Chase caught him staring at her in a new way. "What? Why are you looking at me like that?"

"No reason," he said abruptly. He turned and motioned for her to follow. "We are under the gun." Carter and Sam joined them, the seriousness of the situation showing in their eyes. Chase retold Taifa's story. "Any guesses where Baboloki was this morning?"

"If he did this, history is repeating itself," Tessa whispered, watching Handsome approach. "What do we tell him? We can't keep all this from him."

"True enough," Sam interjected. "We don't want him turning on us. He's hard enough to handle. If we're not careful, he'll go on a rampage and try to kill the president."

"Agreed." Chase eyed Tessa. "You seem to be the only one to calm the savage beast. Are you up to telling him about his mother?"

Tessa took in each of her friends, knowing they counted on her to keep this situation from spiraling out of their control. "Okay. I'll call you over when you can explain some kind of plan."

"Don't take long. We need to get back before dark." As he spoke, the sun dipped toward the horizon.

Tessa cut Handsome off as he approached then led him to some tree stumps she'd seen used for stools. They stared at the smoldering building for a few minutes until Tessa got the courage to speak.

"Handsome, I have some things I need to tell you." She focused straight ahead but became aware when he started to watch her. "I understand you're worried about your father."

"Are you going to tell me this was Baboloki? Because if you do, I'm going to go kill him right now. I don't care about ruling Botswana. I want revenge. He killed my birth parents and he intends, if he hasn't already done it, to kill the only father I've ever known. He believes the legend of the Kifaru diamond and thinks he's being threatened."

"We don't know who did this, Handsome," she said, daring to finally meet his gaze. "I think there is a good chance you're right. But we have to be careful."

Handsome jumped up and doubled his fists. "No," he stormed.

Tessa sucked up her courage. Chase and the others were watching, and this was her chance to prove her worth to the team. "Sit down this minute," she growled in her best mom voice. "So, help me, Handsome, if you don't shut the hell up until I'm done talking, I'll do my best to make your life more miserable than it already is. Do you understand me?" Glaring up at him helped her feel one with the captive in King Kong, a love-hate relationship based partly on fear and a little respect. "Sit. Down," she repeated.

He glanced over her shoulder, and although Tessa had her back to the Enigma team, she imagined them poised for confrontation if this situation didn't go as planned. Slowly, he sat.

"You are not a very good badass, Tessa." His voice had returned to his normal level of unconcern.

"My children might disagree with that evaluation." This caused a slight upturn on one corner of his mouth. "Is this how you manage those jerks behind us, by using your mom tactics?"

"Yes. But let's make that our little secret. They aren't aware I think of them as spoiled little brats who need constant behavior modification. Probably why President Austin put me with them."

Handsome dropped his gaze to the ground and leaned forward to prop on his thighs. "Say what you will. I'm going to look for my father."

"They aren't likely to kill him, Handsome."

"And you believe this because…"

"Because we have something he wants." Tessa leaned toward him.

"And what would that be?" He turned toward her.

"Your birth mother. She's alive."

~ ~ ~

Dage paced outside the room where Dr. Girard slept then stepped inside to evaluate the doctor's condition. He couldn't justify having his men beat the man further. With a probable concussion, he had suffered enough. Dage needed to return to inform the president no new revelations about the Kifaru diamond or the child in the photo had been revealed.

The doctor moaned and tried to sit up, squinting when his gaze landed on Dage.

"You are one of the president's men."

Dage moved closer and spotted the dried blood on the man's forehead and around his ear. With one eye swelled shut, he resembled a cyclops.

"Yes. Would you like some water?"

"Yes. Please," he answered in a gravelly voice.

Dage retrieved a water bottle from the room next door and twisted off the cap when he returned. "I need some information first." He moved to stand before him and poured a fourth of the bottle on the floor.

Dr. Girard watched with his one good eye until Dage stopped. He cocked his head so he could stare up at him. "You've been rubbing your neck. Is it stiff? Sore?"

Dage hadn't realized he had rubbed the ache that plagued him of late. "You are the pain in my neck, Dr. Girard."

"I don't what this place is, but I noticed some sacks of rice over there," he said pointing to some dusty metal shelves. "Remove one of your socks and fill it three quarters full with the rice."

"And why would I want to do that?" Dage sniffed back a chuckle.

"Tie a knot in the end of the sock." The doctor pointed to a table. "I think that is an old microwave. It seems this place has electricity. Maybe it still works. Hopefully, mice haven't eaten the cord."

This time, Dage did laugh. "So, if I do this?"

"Cook it for a minute and a half. Gently put it around your neck. The heat will ease your pain." The doctor lowered his head into his hands. "Make sure it isn't directly on your skin. It might be too hot."

Dage decided to humor the old man and followed his instructions. It took him several tries to tie the sock after spilling rice on the floor. With the heat came a relief Dage hadn't expected.

"You probably can buy a ready-made heat sock in Gaborone. They carry them in pharmacies."

Dage removed the sock and stared at the man who shivered in the room constructed of concrete blocks. He went into the next room and retrieved a blanket from one of bunks.

"Here," he said wrapping the threadbare fabric around the doctor. His next gesture was to hand him the bottle of water. "Drink." The bottle wobbled in his trembling hands, so Dage held it to his lips for him. "Why did you help me after what we've put you through today?"

"I am a doctor, and you needed my help." His wobbly smile revealed a newly chipped front tooth. The water trickled down his chin.

Another guard entered the room. "Should we try and question him again?"

Dage stared at the doctor who lay down on his sagging bed then over at the guard. "No. You and your men can go. I'll wait for the next shift and inform Baboloki you tried."

The guard raised his chin in acknowledgment and exited the room.

"Dr. Girard?" Dage walked to the door and checked to see if the others had left. "I think it is time for a change of scenery."

CHAPTER TWENTY-FIVE

Tiki torches placed strategically around the campground blazed with flickering flames. The heavy dose of African romance wasn't lost on Chase. Tourists paid good money for this kind of atmosphere, and Camp Kubu had mastered the brand beautifully.

Quiet laughter floated intermittently into the darkness, followed by the roar of a distant, hungry lion. The cool breeze forced him to admit not wearing a jacket over his long-sleeved tee shirt might be a bad idea. He leaned against the railing constructed of twigs. Folding his arms across his chest, he continued to listen to the friendly chatter.

The meal turned out to be a nice surprise for the guests. The British anticipated creepy- crawler cuisine and expressed pleasure to the camp director.

"What was the meat entrée, Peter?" the younger of the two British women asked.

"It is a traditional Botswana dish called seswaa. It's a meaty stew served over thick polenta or, as some locals call it, pap."

"Explain polenta. That actually sounds Italian," one of the German men chuckled.

"Could be. It's a paste or dough made of cornmeal. Some bake it, but we fried it. Quite a process."

Tessa laid her hand on her stomach. "Well, I want the recipe. Is it labor intensive? I'm afraid I'm not a very good cook."

"I'll second that," Chase chimed in. Tessa shook her head.

Peter continued, "It's boiled stew meat with plenty of onions and pepper. Once the meat has cooked for two hours, it is shredded and pounded with salt to add more flavor." He lit his pipe. "The leafy greens we call morogo."

Baboloki twirled his wine in a glass with the Okavango logo stenciled on the side. "I appreciate the traditional foods of my country."

Chase wedged himself in next to Tessa, who scooted over on the rattan settee. "The mopane worms were a little out there, but I've had worse."

"Yes. These beautiful multicolored caterpillars are a local delicacy. I haven't had them for a long time." Baboloki drained his glass. "It is an acquired taste." The ladies cringed and shivered almost in unison. The president chuckled and smiled broadly. "Thank you for sharing your portions, ladies."

Stretching his arm to rest on the back of the settee, Chase toyed with Tessa's hair, when she shifted her questioning eyes to him. To jerk away would indicate displeasure, and they had already established they were involved. Hair like hers begged to be touched. His wolfish expression led her to lay a hand between them. In seconds, she'd managed to pinch him so hard, he jerked his leg to the side.

"What's the matter?" To an outsider, she'd appear genuinely concerned.

Chase squeezed the back of her neck. "Got a cramp in my leg. I'll take care of it later." This time he sent her a warning glance, drawing a serious expression. Her mouth appeared pouty. She drove him crazy.

Tessa chose to pat his thigh at that instant. "I think he overdid it today. Still thinks he's twenty-five." A light chuckle went through the group. She turned to the camp director. "Any news on Keeya? I'm worried. This is hostile country at night."

Peter nodded after puffing on his pipe. "I got word someone saw her with a man later in the day. I'm assuming she found friends to stay with. The Okavango is one big family at times."

"I'd like to see that information, Peter," the president interjected. "She has been an employee for a long time. I want to make sure she is all right. This is not like her to take off without telling anyone." Chase noted the concern in his voice, but guessed the president made a habit of putting up a good show for others.

"I didn't write it down, Mr. President. All I got was she seemed to be following the man and in no way seemed coerced. At the time, no one knew we were searching for someone, and I got the information secondhand. We have had workers wander off from time to time without giving us warning. Some of these people decide they are done for the day and leave if their job requirements have been completed. I wouldn't worry too much about it. Sounds like she is safe."

Baboloki nodded then stood. "I'm calling it a night. I have some paperwork to attend to before retiring for the night."

"Where is your security guy? Dage I think was his name?" Chase withdrew his arm and wove his fingers through Tessa's so she would stop patting his thigh to irritate him.

"I told him to take care of some things in Maun. He'll be back tomorrow if there's a plane available. If not, he'll have to find another way."

"Good show. Don't want to lose any more guests." Peter stood and accompanied the president to the steps. "I'll have someone walk you to your quarters, Mr. President."

"Headed that way, too. We can escort the president, Peter." Chase stood and leveled a look at Carter who pushed himself up then pulled Sam to her feet. Extending his hand for Tessa, resulted in her ignoring the offer and scooting to the edge of the cushions herself. Before she could ignore him further, he grabbed her elbow. "Night, everyone. See you in the morning." Chase pressed a finger to Tessa's back then ushered her near the president.

"You don't mind, do you, Mr. President?" Tessa cooed, taking the arm he offered her.

"I never mind two beautiful ladies walking me to my quarters."

Sam stepped up on the other side and slipped her arm through his as well.

"Besides, these two gentlemen look like they are used to protecting what is important."

"I think we'll tag along, too. Long day," one of the Germans announced as they meandered up.

By the time they'd started down the path to their tents, the British guests called after them to wait up. Flashlights shone like beacons of safety.

Even though the group surrounded the president, flashlights revealed guards stationed nearby with appropriate firepower to dissuade intruders or hungry animals.

Chase's thoughts turned to Handsome since he presented a bigger danger than a Cape buffalo or a sneaky hyena. He'd helped behind the scenes with the dinner, but Chase preferred him to be visible. There were still trust issues concerning his loyalty, methods, and future plans.

Dr. Girard's disappearance under mysterious circumstances left a lot of unanswered questions. This alone might cause Handsome to blame Baboloki but not enough evidence indicated his guilt.

"Good night, Mr. President," the group, one by one, offered.

Chase could see the lights on in his fancy apartment-style quarters and several guards waiting for him. When he stepped onto the deck, his secretary joined him, said a few words then came downstairs to head to her own tent.

The Germans and British split off next, leaving the four Enigma agents to go it alone. Zoric and Vernon stayed behind to keep an eye on Handsome's coming and goings under the pretense of a nightcap with the camp director who appeared willing to talk about the job bestowed upon him. Nothing like being told you'd appear in a magazine spread to open a person up.

Chase invited the other two agents up onto their deck. "Looks like the president has plenty of security in case Handsome decides to do a little investigating on his own. His intimidation techniques can be a little overwhelming."

"Sounds like Dage may have been sent back to check on the doctor," Sam offered.

"I figured as much. Too bad we didn't find out sooner." Carter nodded at Sam.

"I'd say we'd go have a look, but we're trapped here in the middle of nowhere. I wouldn't want to be in the Okavango, trying to navigate my way out, in the dark with hippos leaving the water to graze on land." Chase gritted his teeth, trying to come up with a solution.

"It's late," Tessa added. "Even captors need to sleep. Wherever he is, they think he can't be found and have lots of time. I'm betting they'll be careful once the word spreads about the medical clinic and the missing doctor. That will be all over the place by dawn."

"She's right," Chase agreed. "Someone always sees something around here. We'll probably never know who spotted Keeya this morning. At least they didn't recognize who she was." He couldn't stop a yawn. "See you guys in the morning. Zoric and Vern hope to remind Handsome of his promise not to go crazy until we can sort this thing out."

"It seemed to have a calming effect on him when I told him his mother was still alive." Tessa unzipped the tent door while Chase waited for his agents to leave.

"Wrapping your arms around him didn't hurt, either," he said, joining her inside. "I swear we need to bottle whatever it is you have to calm that beast."

"It's called kindness." Tessa removed her sweatshirt then searched through her bag. "I could have sworn I put my pj's in here this morning." She sighed spotting a lump under the covers. "Robert always complains I leave pj's and socks under the sheets."

She started to pull back the blanket when Chase jerked her back into his arms.

"Excuse me," she snapped. "You've been a little too touchy-feely all night. Keep your hands to yourself," she warned as he pushed her aside.

"That lump moved."

"I'm not playing that game tonight, Chase." The beam from the flashlight picked up movement where her hand had touched moments earlier. She sucked in her breath and grabbed the hem of Chase's tee shirt.

"Give me that flashlight, Tess," he ordered in a low voice. She obeyed without question. He hammered the moving object several times then retrieved his hunting knife from his duffel bag. He stabbed the lump over and over then slit the blanket open to find blood.

"Oh my gosh. Oh my gosh." She covered her mouth as if trying not to scream while stomping her feet in a nervous dance.

Chase pulled the dark-gray creature out slowly to make sure it could no longer strike. "Well aren't you a bad boy?" The snake lay limp. "I believe we have a young black mamba." With his free hand, he pulled back the covers and laid it on the sheet he'd ripped with his knife.

"Young?" she squealed. "It's six or seven feet long." Her voice pitched near hysteria.

"They can grow as big as fourteen feet. These guys are one of the most poisonous snakes on the continent. We would have never made it to a doctor in time for an antidote. And he most certainly would have struck both of us. They're known for striking multiple times."

"I am terrified, Chase." She doubled her fists over her heart. "Those things can slither in and out of our tents?"

Chase exhaled slowly to control his rapid heartbeat. Once again, Tessa had been on the brink of disaster. "Like most snakes, they tend to stay away from people. I can't imagine this guy lived around here."

"Are you saying someone brought it in here and wanted me dead?"

"Kind of looks that way."

CHAPTER TWENTY-SIX

Dage helped Dr. Girard into a small apartment on the outside of Maun. Not even the president knew of its existence. A second cousin had purchased it five years earlier and died suddenly, leaving it to Dage, his only living relative. He rarely came here and when he did, there remained a certain sense of concealment since it had remained in his cousin's name all these years.

Although he'd been loyal to the president, a certain amount of caution padded his common sense. The ruthlessness of his boss became mundane over the years. Most of the time he looked the other way in order to keep his position at the top of the favored list. Somewhere along the line, he'd begun to question the man's mental state.

"Where are we, Dage?" Dr. Girard obeyed his instructions to the letter as he slipped into Maun by hiding in the floorboard of the back seat. The tan Jeep, although old, retained a certain well-cared-for appearance. He had saved a long time to purchase it and knew buying another one would be almost impossible for him. He'd parked the car at a friend's house who owed him a favor. With a little money incentive, his friend handed over his own car keys. Dage reminded him of his power in the government and left him a promise to return in a few hours.

"A safe place, Dr. Girard." He pulled down the shades of the ground floor apartment. Most of the other units in the building were visiting teachers from Gaborone. Efforts to make the building hospitable enough to attract people to work here guaranteed Dage a safe hideout for the doctor.

"Thank you. You are a good man," the doctor said pulling out a folding chair from the table. "Why are you helping me?"

It took only seconds to secure the five-hundred-square-foot apartment. He ran the water in the sink until it cleared. "I'll make you some tea then clean your wounds."

Dr. Girard remained quiet until the chipped china cup of steaming tea was set before him. Dage returned from the bathroom with a first aid kit and true to his word, cleaned his wounds then administered some antibiotic cream before bandaging his ear and head.

"Let me make you more tea, Dr. Girard. I'll see if I have something to cook. There may be noodles or rice."

The doctor watched him, reminding him what he'd done. President Baboloki would kill him if he found out. He needed a way out if this went sideways.

He cooked without another word until he set a plastic plate filled with brown rice before the doctor. "It's all I have."

The doctor took a moment to say a blessing over the food and finished by asking for protection, not for himself, but for Dage. "This is delicious. I'm in your debt."

"No. You are not. There was no need to burn the clinic down to get answers. Those people in the Okavango need you."

The doctor continued to eat slowly. His swollen lips prevented him from putting too much in his mouth at any one time. He could barely open it. "Yes. It will be difficult to raise money for another one. It took many years to get this far." The doctor's eyes watered.

Dage regretted being a part of this madness. "Dr. Girard, I need to know. Has the Kifaru diamond returned to Botswana?"

A sudden look of terror crossed the man's face. Did he expect another beating?

"I'm not going to hurt you. I'm trying to protect myself. If the president suspects I have double-crossed him, then I'm a dead man. So, I'll ask you again—is the Kifaru in Botswana?"

Dr. Girard pushed his plate away and motioned for Dage to sit down. "I have a story to tell you. You have done me a favor tonight."

"Sir, I was in charge of your poor treatment. I did you no favor. I have a responsibility to right a wrong done to an innocent man. I'm tired of being the muscle behind a monster. Talk to me."

"The story began over thirty-five years ago." He squeezed his one good eye shut. "Or was it longer?"

"Take your time, doctor."

~ ~ ~

Tessa stretched out on the king-sized bed like a spoiled feline then threw her arm out to touch Chase. Rolling over to watch him sleep in the first rays of morning light, she discovered him gone. A wave of panic engulfed her, and she sat up with such speed, her hair fell from her rubber band into her eyes.

"Chase!" she called while moving the covers off her body. Cold morning air slammed against her bare arms and neck as a figure moved to her side.

"I'm here." He sat on the edge of the bed, not close enough to touch her, but near enough to let her know there wasn't anything to worry about.

Tessa eased back under the covers and stared at him. She managed to stack up some pillows behind her back. "I thought you'd left me."

"Not a chance." He offered his boyish charm and grabbed at her covered foot like he might tickle her. She pulled away. "Pretty nice digs, huh?"

The night before, Chase had hurried to warn Carter and Sam of their uninvited guest. They were okay. Since Carter had a radio, he contacted Vernon and Zoric. Handsome came almost immediately after informing the director of what had transpired. They were escorted to one of the tree house villas, much like Baboloki's, for the remainder of their stay.

Tessa tucked the covers around her chest after noticing Chase's glances lingered on her body a little too long. They'd slept in the same bed without touching most of the night, thanks to an abundance of pillows. Once she'd heard an unusual sound and snuggled closer to his back.

"I fixed coffee. Want some?" he announced. "This is not the cheap stuff, either."

"Yes. Thanks." At least the job took him away from the bed. Talk about a knight in shining armor. "Does the inside bathroom have hot water, or do we have to wait until night for this one, too?"

"I took a shower, and the water is not hot but quite warm. I'm going to miss taking you to the bathroom." He laughed when he brought her the coffee on a small woven tray.

"Ha. Ha. I don't believe that for a minute." Taking a sip of the hot brew drew a sigh of pleasure. "Is it early?"

"Yeah. I couldn't sleep. You're such a bed hog. You'd think with a king-size bed, you'd stay on your own side." One of his eyebrows went up.

Tessa glared at him over the rim of her cup, trying to pretend she didn't care anything about his opinions. "I. I." It was hopeless. That big bad wolf attitude got her every time. She decided to try flippant. "None of my other husbands complained."

His demeanor immediately changed from playful to sullen. Maybe she shouldn't have tried this kind of attack.

"I only know of two others. Are there more?"

"I had a weakness for this lead singer at a county fair talent contest. Oh. And I never told anyone, but I eloped to Las Vegas my freshman year of college. Annulled it the very next day. Elvis was not happy."

One corner of his mouth lifted in amusement. "I bet. You are getting so good at those lies, you might get recruited by the CIA before long."

"And leave all this? Never." He continued to stand rigid, staring down at her in half amusement and half something else. "Besides, you're the only one I can count on to protect me. I doubt anyone at the CIA would give a rip."

"Now you're flirting with me, Tessa." He jumped on the bed next to her on top of the covers. She splashed a few drops of coffee on her pajamas and released a disgruntled yelp. "Maybe we should talk about something besides your tribesman from Afghanistan."

She hadn't mentioned Darya, yet he always seemed to come up at times like these. He hated the man who'd saved her life from unspeakable terror and even death. The tribesman continued to believe she was his woman, even after she'd returned home. Why Chase didn't drag Robert up, her real husband, still confused her. Why should he care in the first place?

"I never mentioned Afghanistan. Leave Darya out of our conversations from now on. Okay?"

Chase stared at her. His generous mouth suddenly turned down. Her heart skipped a beat watching him switch from white knight to the gunslinger. He didn't promise.

"I'm going to have Vernon and Zoric follow the president around today to see if they can find out any information. They're doing that magazine piece, so it shouldn't be a problem to shadow him. We need to also find out who put that snake in your bed."

Tessa shivered then handed Chase her cup to set on the tray resting on the nightstand. "Do you think it was Baboloki?"

"I believe he had someone do it. If one of us got bitten, then we'd have to leave. He doesn't like me and is suspicious of someone from the US State Department nosing around his country. With Keeya disappearing, it probably only adds to his paranoia."

"Any sign of Dage?"

Chase put his hands behind his head and crossed his legs. "Saw him slip in at first light. Not sure how he got back. I didn't hear a plane. Maybe by boat?"

"Handsome will be wanting to head out today in search of his father. No idea where to look at this point."

"My guess is Maun since the president sent his bodyguard there. The news about the clinic should be out now. We'll get to see what Baboloki does with the information. I'm also curious as to what he'll do when he sees you."

Tessa maneuvered away from Chase and stood up. The sensation of drowning washed over her when he continued to watch her with curiosity. Would he one day forget his good-guy manners and pounce on her vulnerable hero worship?

Agents in the field, or so she'd read, often got into romantic situations, parted, and moved on to other things. The idea remained completely foreign to her. Yet, it seemed he always tested the waters of some kind of relationship.

"Is there something else?" he asked, a bit too mischievously. "Weren't you going to take a shower. Do I need to go check it out first, in case there are snakes?"

"Not funny. I was thinking about the future."

"A lot of that going on these days."

~ ~ ~

Chase arrived at the dining platform and found Handsome setting up the buffet table. His scowl tipped him off not to mince words with the huge man moving about like an out-of-control tank. He poured his own coffee.

"Where's your boss?" Chase worried Peter would spill the news about the black mamba in Tessa's bed to his staff. He wanted to evaluate the expression on Baboloki's face when Tessa joined them later. Did he have a hand in the treachery?

"On the radio. Got the news about the clinic. He's upset." Handsome lowered his voice. "I put all the medicine we brought back in one of the refrigerators in the camp storage hut and made the assignments for the tours today. Peter will be out in time to get everyone on their way. I'll explain the meds later. He liked my father. I don't think he'll mind me using the refrigerator."

"Carter and Sam decided to leave. We think Dr. Girard may be in Maun. They'll spearhead the search."

Handsome stopped and leveled a stubborn glare at him. "I should go with them."

"And do what? You're like a bull in a china shop."

"If Baboloki—"

"We don't know who did this to the clinic," Chase interjected with a snarl. "Don't do something stupid. Let me handle this, will ya?"

With a reluctant nod, Handsome agreed. "How's Tessa? Why isn't she with you?"

"Pretending to be dead."

"Probably gets a lot of practice being around you," Handsome quipped as his bottom lip protruded outward. "Peter says he hasn't seen any reports of black mambas around here in several years. Too many tourists."

Chase drained his coffee cup as the other guests arrived. Baboloki enjoyed a big entrance, so he expected him to show up last. "Good morning, folks!"

"Where's your better half, Chase?" It was Carter.

"I left her sound asleep." He winked at one of the British ladies. "Too much excitement the last few days, I think." Moving to the buffet line, Chase handed out a few plates. It gave him a few extra minutes to stand and watch Baboloki arrive. "Mr. President, your timing is perfect. Handsome laid out all this delicious food."

Baboloki froze but recovered in short order and graciously took a plate from Chase's outstretched hand. "Where is your beautiful companion?"

Chase offered a pleasant laugh and filled his plate with runny eggs and limp bacon. The biscuits were hard as a brick. He hated the way they cooked breakfast here. "She was dead to the world when I came to bed last night. I don't think she moved all night. I let her sleep in."

The president offered a smug smirk and raised his chin in a kind of haughtiness. "Would you like for me to send someone after her?" He spooned a large portion of eggs onto his plate.

"No need!" Tessa bounded up the steps with her usual enthusiasm and rushed to Chase's side. "Sorry I'm late. What a night. Slept like a log," she laughed. "President Baboloki, are you, all right? You look like you've seen a ghost."

"Yes. Yes. I'm fine. You look lovely this morning."

The president nodded at one of his guards posted at the top of the steps. Chase found it amusing how quickly the guard excused himself. Someone else might find a snake in his bed tonight.

The camp director joined them and immediately came to take Tessa's hand. "Oh. My. Dear. I'm so glad you are well this morning," Peter gushed then turned to address the other guests. "Everyone needs to be very careful and check your beds throughout the day and especially tonight. Tessa found a black mamba under her covers last night."

The guests were noticeably shaken and asked Tessa what happened.

After her story ended, everyone offered compliments to Chase at his heroic rescue. She stood on tiptoe and kissed his lips so quickly, he later thought he'd imagined the whole thing.

"Yep. He's my hero." She patted his back then cheek and moved away. "Peter was gracious enough to upgrade our accommodations to one of the tree house villas. Very romantic."

A grumble of concern spread through the guests.

"Nothing to worry about, my friends. I'm having each tent double-checked today and this evening before you turn in. These animals are rare around here. We intend on making plenty of noise as well. If there are any more, they will quickly slither off."

"I'm out of here," Sam growled. "Carter, I want to go back to the city. Today."

"You're overreacting." Chase admired his friend's blasé attitude when addressing Sam.

"I'm leaving with or without you," Sam fumed before turning to Tessa. "I'm sorry. I've had enough excitement to last me a lifetime. Peter, how do I get out of here?"

He sighed. "I'll make some arrangements, Samantha. The medical clinic burned yesterday so we may be shorthanded on drivers."

"Was anyone hurt?" Chase sat across from the president once again in order to watch his reaction.

"No reports yet. Most everyone who helps out at the clinic had the day off or was here earning some extra money. Great people. The clinic had become quite a gathering place for medical care, education, and small-business opportunities for the women."

"Perhaps I can notify the authorities to make an immediate investigation." The president pushed his plate away.

"Smashing. Thank you, Mr. President." Peter turned to leave. "I'll say cheerio since I have some tasks to attend to this morning. Handsome has everyone's schedule. Mr. President, if you'll have Dage come by my office, I can go over your itinerary for the remainder of your stay."

"Thank you. I'm sure he'll have questions. He's very thorough."

Peter took his leave, and the staff served the guests then cleared the dishes as needed. Small talk continued for another thirty minutes.

"Handsome, will you send a fresh pot of coffee to my villa? I have a little work to do. I believe"— Baboloki glanced at Zoric and Vernon— "these two gentlemen would like to interview me before we go out today. Do you mind waiting an hour?"

Handsome pooched out his lips then shrugged a rude acknowledgement. The condescending stare-down between the two men forced Chase to rise from the table and intercept Handsome.

"Great breakfast. Why not let me take that coffee? I'm headed back that way in a few minutes. I want to check the villa for critters." A forced chuckle caught in his throat as he locked stares with Baboloki.

Baboloki nodded and motioned to Vernon and Zoric who gathered up their camera equipment. "Coming?"

In seconds, the president strode across the ground toward his tree house villa, surrounded by several guards. They scattered to allow Dage approach the president. The other guests met their guides and headed out.

"Boss?" Vernon mumbled as he slipped on sunglasses.

"You know what to do?"

"All set. No problem."

Handsome brought Chase a pot of coffee wrapped in a kitchen towel. "I would consider it a favor if you stumbled and spilled this on him."

Sam meandered up with Tessa at her side. "In that case you better take Tessa. She has the grace of a hippopotamus." She offered a thin smile then dusted off a bug from her jacket before locking gazes with Tessa.

"At least I don't look like one. Have you noticed your backside in the mirror?" Tessa started toward the steps then added in a syrupy voice, "I tell you this because I care, Sam."

"That's enough, you two," Chase chastised. He found it difficult to suppress a laugh. She'd bested his senior agent, and the sooner he put some space between them, the better. "We'll be back in a couple of minutes."

Vernon and Zoric were already setting up their equipment on the upper deck of the president's villa. Baboloki strolled up the stairs, stopping only to speak to his secretary coming down the steps. She waved her arms then her hand and rubbed at her eyes. The president bowed his head then shrugged before waving her away.

"I'd love to know what that's all about?" Chase mumbled.

"Whatever it is, it hasn't fazed him." She turned from her partner. "I need to get my camera before we head out." Tessa turned and ran up the stairs of their villa.

Chase let her run ahead. He paused when he noticed movement behind one of the pillars holding up the deck. He recognized Dage. "Go on up. I'll be there in a minute." Tessa glanced down at him and followed his line of sight.

The head of security leaned against the post and lit a cigarette. The smell of tobacco drifted in his direction as he decided to join Baboloki's head of security. The fact he didn't try to hide concerned Chase.

"Long night, Dage?"

"Very."

"Where'd you go?" Chase joined him in the shadows.

"The president sent me on an errand." He exhaled a puff of smoke.

"Care to share, or is it a secret? Maybe like you hiding Dr. Girard because you burned his clinic down and now you're trying to find out about the Kifaru?" Chase shifted his weight to one foot. "But I'm just guessing."

Dage threw his cigarette down and ground it into the dirt with the toe of his boot before lifting his bloodshot eyes to Chase. "Yes. Something like that."

Chase dropped his hands to his sides when Dage pointed an automatic weapon at his chest. "Sometimes I hate it when I'm right."

CHAPTER TWENTY-SEVEN

Tessa caught snippets of the conversation, at least enough to recognize when Chase was in trouble. Maybe, this once, she could save him. Going down the front steps would only put her in the same boat as her friend.

A quick survey of her villa revealed a rope ladder to use in case of an emergency. At the rear of the villa, a window, dressed with a thick mesh screen, opened to toward a stand of trees some fifteen feet away. A number of latches on the inside prevented curious monkeys from letting themselves in. Part of the front deck had a thick screened-in-porch area. This prevented curious primates from exploring.

She thought maybe she could slip out on the opposite end of the deck, but found a thorny crop of bushes that would discourage hippos out for a nightly stroll from getting too close and deter lions who figured a good back rub would be just the thing. Wild animals knew when to be cautious, so she decided to follow their example. The screen window would have to do.

Removing the screen took seconds. Securing the ladder so she felt safe required a little more time and courage. Heights created a certain amount of anxiety in her.

She grunted as she shoved an antique train trunk under the window. "Deep breath. Deep breath."

Tessa found several three-foot rubber bands in the trunk. She'd seen such items used for moving furniture and securing items on a truck, so they didn't end up scattered all over the highway in a sudden stop. Her father, a farmer, used them all the time. She looped three of them together, securing one end under the hook over the windowsill. She ran her belt through the opposite end so if she fell, she might keep from hitting the ground so hard.

The two-foot-long flashlight Tessa shoved into her waistband could be used for a club. Maybe she could sneak up on Dage and whack him on the head. The idea of rescuing Chase for a change encouraged her so much she easily swung out onto the floppy ladder to begin the descent. But once she looked down, fear welled up inside her.

The gulp in her throat drowned out the pounding of her heartbeat in her ears. She hugged the scratchy rope and squeezed her eyes shut.

"You're a pretty nosey guy," Tessa heard Dage say.

"Shooting me here would draw a great deal of attention, Dage." Tessa could imagine him with a cocky grin on his face and hands half-lifted in the air.

"Out here, anything is possible. Maybe another black mamba came under here and we both went after it. I tried to stop you…Well, accidents happen. Or I could haul you off a few miles from here and let you find your way back."

Tessa wasn't sure what Chase said next. Time meant everything. She couldn't let anything happen to him after all he'd done for her. Opening her eyes, she took a deep breath and started down, hoping her movements remained stealth enough to go unnoticed.

The rope ladder tapped against the villa for another two rungs then she could feel the air around her. "Oh gosh," she whispered. "Keep going. Don't look down. Don't look down."

But she did look down and found only another eight feet separated her from her first rescue for Enigma. With renewed confidence, Tessa accelerated her descent until something else moved on the ladder below her. A baby vervet monkey played on the rope, stealing closer to her in childlike curiosity.

"Go way," she fumed with a wave then nearly lost her tight grip and hugged the ladder for a few seconds. A squeal of delight from the baby drew her eyes back to the ground only to find an adult vervet scampering toward the rope like a crazed protective momma.

"No. No. No," Tessa mumbled then tried to wiggle the ladder enough to shake the baby off.

The mischievous little monkey swung toward her and squealed, with what Tessa imagined, was pure rebellious delight, at its mother. The angry mother opened her jaws and although she probably weighed no more than ten or eleven pounds, to Tessa she might as well have been a charging silver-back gorilla.

Attempting to move out of the way of the angry mother scooping up her baby, Tessa lost her balance on the next rung. Trying to right the misstep, one hand slipped, and her body to swung out like a ragdoll's. She hooked her foot around the ladder in hopes of pulling herself back, but managed to get tangled up even worse so that she had to try and free her foot by shaking her entire leg. With the awkward movement, her foot slipped out and she found herself dangling on the ladder by her fingertips.

No amount of grunting could position her back onto the ladder, and finally her fingers gave way and she plunged toward the ground with a scream. The screeching vervet monkeys escaped back into the trees. Bouncing up and down on the attached rubber bands, she kicked wildly to free herself. Then Chase walked out into her view, Dage holding a gun to his back.

Tessa pulled out her flashlight club and took a swing at him as she continued to bounce.

Chase's appeared wearing an expression of exasperation, she'd seen many times—not the reaction she'd sought. His jaw clenched over and over. "What the hell do you think you're doing, Tessa?" he growled.

"Umm. I'm trying to cause a distraction so he can take out Dage," she said, pointing her flashlight at something behind them.

Dage swung around to meet the hammer-like fist of Handsome against his jaw, dropping him limp to the ground.

Handsome stared down at Dage then gave Tessa a thumbs-up. "Thanks. I needed that."

Tessa's feet remained about two feet off the ground when suddenly the rubber bands gave way and she dropped in an undignified pile.

Carrying Dage over his shoulder, Handsome led the way to his small quarters at the other end of the camp with Chase and Tessa bringing up the rear. By the time he dropped Dage down on the cot, the man had moaned his way to consciousness. Tessa soaked a thin washcloth in some tepid water and folded it twice before laying it on his forehead. He bolted upright at her touch and swung his legs off the cot.

Chase pulled Tessa back before stepping up and leveling Dage's weapon at his head. "Some bodyguard you are," he quipped. "We have a saying in the States. You can't hoot with owls and expect to soar with the eagles."

Dage's lip curled up. "What does that mean?"

"Yeah. That is the stupidest thing you've ever said." Handsome glared at Chase. "Is that some of your Cherokee mumbo-jumbo?"

"I think it means," Tessa tried to speak softly, "Dage was out all night doing the president's bidding. He couldn't do his job so well in the day." She tapped her cheek. "That swollen jaw indicates you never even knew when Handsome came up behind you."

Looking more like a hungry pit bull than chief of security, Dage dragged the cloth across his face then lobbed it at Handsome, who let it fall to the floor.

"That was rude," he commented drily.

"I'll be leaving now." Dage stood without so much as a wobble.

"Before you leave, I want to continue our conversation about you burning down the clinic and taking Dr. Girard to what I hope is a safe place." Chase pointed down at the cot. "Sit down."

He cocked his head and let the news sink into Handsome. The expression on Handsome's face reminded him of things that go bump in the night; not something you really want to confront or discover that there really are monsters. The pinched forehead and wide eyes of Dage as he tried to slide further away from Handsome indicated the same thought might have crossed his mind.

"No," Tessa yelled trying to pull Handsome back. Chase waved her aside and smiled.

After several of Handsome's blows to Dage's gut, Chase stepped forward. "Ya know, Handsome, if you kill him, we're not going to get any information about Dr. Girard."

He dropped the bodyguard onto the cot again, clenching his fists over and over. "Where is the doctor? Tell me or I'll take you out into the deep water and let the hippos have your worthless body."

Dage managed to sit up enough to rub his midsection. Blood trickled out of his mouth and seeped through his shirt. "If you kill me you'll never find where he is."

"Then he is alive?" Tessa tried to pull Handsome around to face her, without success. She grabbed the cloth and wet it again. When she offered it to Dage, he snatched it from her hand.

"Yes. I think he has a concussion, but—"

Handsome grabbed him up by his shirt and shook him violently. Tessa covered her mouth, preventing a scream from escaping.

Chase handed her the gun and stepped forward to deliver a punch to Handsome's side. With an oof, he dropped the bodyguard to the floor and stepped back. The expression of violence still flamed in his eyes.

"We need him," Chase chided in a mild tone. "You've done enough. I think he gets the point you're bigger and badder than him." He pointed to the other side of the room. "Get over there. Better yet, don't you have something to do, like learn how to cook a decent breakfast? Gee, that stunk this morning."

"He didn't mean that, Handsome." She approached him carefully. "Let Chase talk to him. Please."

His breathing slowed, and his round eyes stopped bulging as they shifted to her.

She laid a hand on his forearm. "For Dr. Girard." She still carried the gun in her other hand and decided to hand it off to Chase, realizing Handsome could easily relieve her of it.

"I most certainly did mean it," Chase growled. "I paid good money to stay here, and you fed me crap this morning."

"Can we focus on the problem here?" Dage moaned removing the bloody washcloth from his face. "The doctor took a fall down the clinic steps when he discovered the soldiers there. He hit his head pretty hard on a rock at the bottom."

"So Baboloki is behind this?" Chase asked, cutting his eyes over at the mountain who had begun pacing.

"Yes. We went there yesterday. Baboloki received some information before we left that the Kifaru had returned to Botswana. Many people, these people, believe whoever possess it can rule the land or at least show the way to who should. It is nonsense for the president to use this legend to retain power. He is terrified of losing the election this time."

"Those rumors have always existed. Why is he afraid now?" Handsome snapped.

"The woman, Keeya, he keeps, gave birth to a son."

"The day Baboloki's men slaughtered most of those in the village where the clinic is located," Chase added.

Dage nodded as Tessa handed him a cup of water. "He kept Keeya all these years, in fear the child survived. He planned to use her as leverage." Dage rubbed his hand across his face.

"Who broke into Tessa's room in Gaborone? What were you looking for?" Chase kept stealing a glance at Handsome to make sure he continued to behave himself. Tessa stood near him, aware her presence had a calming effect on the man.

"I sent one of the guards. Your woman asked a lot of questions that day in the garden and brought up the Kifaru and the legend. She mentioned writing a book on some new information about the day of the massacre."

"And you stole the laptop and downloaded the information."

"Yes. Or someone did. I only delivered it. Whatever you wrote"—he glanced at Tessa— "disturbed him enough to insist Keeya come here with him. Now she's gone, and he is more dangerous than ever."

"Why burn down the clinic?" Handsome asked, stepping closer. Chase noted he focused on his father and his achievements rather than the woman Keeya.

"Dr. Girard made him angry. No other reason. He didn't want to hear that the black child held in his wife's arms was not Keeya's son. It is a loose end he wanted tied." Dage conveyed the story he'd witnessed the doctor tell Baboloki. "He tried to make him admit to being here the day thirty-seven years ago when life changed in the Okavango." Dage bowed his head. "But the doctor never wavered in his story, even after—"

"You hurt him." Chase's voice sounded flat, void of emotion.

It seemed the information about Keeya had sunk into Handsome's thick head. He stood rigid, his gaze slowly moving from Dage, to Chase and back again. His brow pinched and his thick lips parted as if he tried to speak then squeezed them together so tight they became a straight line.

"That came later. What broke his heart was to watch the clinic go up in flames. Baboloki gave orders for the doctor to be taken away and interrogated. After seeing the president returned back here safely, he sent me to Maun to check on the doctor."

"And then what?"

"I sent the soldiers away and hid him in a safe place."

"Why?" Handsome asked in a bewildered voice.

"Insurance. Baboloki's time will soon end."

"And you want to secure a place on the winning side." Chase moved closer, worried Handsome might lose control again.

"At first. The doctor is a good man. I told the president, burning down the clinic would only cause suspicion and distrust among the delta people. He removed the indigenous San people from their lands not so many years ago. They were denied access to water from their properties and faced arrest if they hunted. This was how they fed their families."

Handsome continued the story. "If I remember right, the land lies in the middle of the world's richest diamond field."

"The government has always denied that there was any link to mining. The president insisted the world know the relocation was to preserve the wildlife and ecosystem. It didn't matter the San people had lived in this area for a thousand years." Dage turned to Chase. "Your own country did this many times to native people, did they not? Baboloki moved them to reservations where they couldn't find work, and they turned to drugs and alcohol."

"Why should he worry? Nothing happened to him then or ever when he took the law into his own hands," Handsome complained, cocking his head as if to size up the man. "He wanted to send a warning."

"Yes. I believe he did. I also think he wanted to draw out whoever had the Kifaru or..." He stood up to stare Handsome in the eyes. "Are you that child?"

CHAPTER TWENTY-EIGHT

President Baboloki stormed onto the dining platform, followed by two of his guards. He paced for a few seconds before pouring himself a cup of coffee from the bottom of the breakfast pot. With a deep intake of breath, he moved to the railing and gazed over the beauty of the Okavango Delta. A saddle-billed stork moved along the edge of the water, dunking its red head beneath the surface to search for his next meal.

"Find Dage for me," he ordered a guard. "I have more things I need to have him do today."

The young man snapped to attention and ran off.

"I think he has already gone, Mr. President." Tessa walked up the steps ahead of Chase who bent his head over a brochure on local wildlife.

"Already?" Baboloki tensed in anger at not being told Dage was leaving.

"Handsome already had everything taken care of, coolers packed and a lunch if you want it. We'll be back by then, I think. Don't you think?" Tessa laid a hand on Chase's arm.

"Mr. President, I have everything right here." Handsome came from behind the partition separating the food prep area from the tables. "One of our people is headed to Maun. I told him I'd give you everything. Apparently, Dage already put one of your other people in charge while he is away. I can still call him back if you like. We needed supplies, and the plane couldn't return today. I'm taking the other two Americans downriver to meet someone who can take them closer to catching a plane. I'm afraid I insisted he hurry. Forgive me. It is my fault."

Baboloki took the outstretched itinerary from Handsome then stared at it for a few seconds.

"No. That won't be necessary." Baboloki waved him off like a pesky fly then turned his back to him and added, "Any news of Keeya?"

"No, sir." Handsome escaped behind the partition again.

"How did the interview go?" the American woman queried.

Even though he found the woman lovely, he also found her a little too inquisitive for his taste. He guessed that might be the case with Americans. Women, especially beautiful ones, should be seen and not heard.

"Well enough." He watched her over the rim of his cup. "I believe it is to be an ongoing process. The reporters will go with us today. Just a photo safari for me."

"No big game?" Chase prodded.

Baboloki set his cup on the bar. "I'd rather watch than shoot. I go on the hunts, but other than fish, I'd rather leave the beasts alone. Besides, tracking them is more sport than killing something which can't defend itself."

Chase took out his phone and scrolled through some pictures until he came to the ones of the poachers from the day before. "Ever see these guys? They were poaching and claimed you'd given them your blessing."

Baboloki took the phone to examine the pictures. "I did no such thing. These are some of my men, for sure, though." He handed the phone back to Chase then snapped his fingers at a nearby guard. Barking some heated orders as to what needed to be done with the poachers once found, the president tried to form an expression of disgust. "I assure you, this will be resolved by nightfall."

"They scared the hell out of the ladies. Now, our friends are leaving. The snake in our tent was the last straw."

"Very unfortunate. That kind of behavior affects the economic stability of the whole region." Baboloki offered a thin smile. "Africa is a dangerous place, Captain Hunter. It is best to remember when you look under a rock here, something might strike out. Some things don't like to be disturbed."

Chase returned a cynical expression. "I appreciate the warning. Good thing I'm a cautious guy."

"There is an African proverb we use here, 'Ears that do not listen to advice, accompany the head when it is chopped off.'"

"We have a saying, too," Chase sneered. "Two heads are better than one." He shrugged. "Or something like that."

Irritation flared up inside the president so quickly he decided to end the conversation. He pivoted on his heels. "Yes," the president said through gritted teeth, smoothing the front of his tan camo jacket before puffing out his chest. "You'll excuse me. I believe my guide is waving us over." He took his leave, followed by his guards.

"Are you trying to get another black mamba to pay us a visit?" Tessa mumbled to Chase. "He is really steamed."

"Good. People who make decisions when they're angry make mistakes."

"Another African proverb?" Tessa quizzed.

Chase was pleased with himself. "No. Experience. From what Dage says, we can expect that each day Keeya is gone and the diamond missing, the president will get a little more rattled. Things are out of his control. You can bet Keeya is a priority, and his people are searching for her."

Carter and Sam brought their luggage up onto the deck during the last of the conversation.

"You do understand you can't keep her hidden forever. Someone will make the mistake of saying too much. She's got to be moved." Sam put her hands on her hips and glanced over her shoulder.

Chase nodded. "We'll take care of Keeya. Carter, I need you to handle the Dr. Girard end of things."

"We'll take care of everything."

They filled the two departing agents in on the new information from Dage.

"He was vague about the location. I'm hoping some backtracking, security cameras, etc. can give us a strong lead. Dage is smart but may have made mistakes in his rush to secure the doctor." Chase scanned the area casually.

"I wish we could take him with us," Sam offered.

"Me, too. Not sure how you could explain his sudden presence, not to mention his colorful bruises Handsome gave him." Chase couldn't resist a grin.

"It's worth a try. From what you've said, he isn't a big fan of the dictator," Carter reasoned.

"Handsome has him secured in his quarters," Chase continued. "Carter is right. It's too risky leaving him here. Peter or even the secretary might stumble upon him. He might even escape, and I don't want to risk that."

"Can't we take him with us, Chase?" Tessa suggested. "Between you and Handsome, I doubt he'd give us much trouble. We will need to cause a diversion when we move him to the boat. The secretary is such a busybody, and Peter is always moving about, attending to the staff."

Vernon meandered up onto the deck to grab the cooler the guide had neglected to haul down to the Land Rover. After listening to a short version of Dage's story, he pulled out his phone. "I can't get everything you need to locate the kind of information you need right now, but I have someone who can. She's almost as good as me." He talked into the phone after a few seconds then clicked off. "Check your phones in a couple of hours. I woke her up. Middle of the night in California." He addressed Carter and Sam. "She knows the protocol for a secure call out here. No worries." With a salute to Chase, he grabbed the cooler and headed to catch his ride.

"You guys be careful. Baboloki is running on adrenaline and not the good kind. He's dangerous." Chase nodded to his two agents. "Make the doc your priority. We'll keep you informed about Keeya."

After he gave them some final instructions, Sam and Carter left Chase and Tessa alone.

When he rubbed the general area where he'd been shot, Tessa pulled his hand away. "Let me look at that," she insisted, trying to raise the tee shirt.

He sucked in his abdomen. "Do your hands ever get warm?"

She ignored him as she stared at the covered wound.

"See, I told you I'm good." He pulled down the tee shirt. "But thanks for the concern."

He could feel himself drawn to her mouth, parted in a mischievous tease that always managed to make his chest hurt. The way she gazed up at him forced him to gently pull her against him. When his arms circled her waist, he savored her blue eyes widened with anticipation. A hint of impending rejection of his admiration would soon follow. Her fingers lay flat against his chest and applied pressure to push him away. Casting his moral compass to the wind, he lowered his mouth to touch hers.

"Please tell me I'm interrupting something." Handsome lumbered out onto the deck with a backpack thrown across one shoulder. Tessa jumped back as if she'd been bee stung.

"No. No, of course not. I was checking on Chase's wound." Tessa rubbed her hands up and down the outside of her jean shorts. A blush touched her cheeks.

"Humph. Did he get shot in the nose because it looked to me—"

"Handsome, mind your own business," Chase growled. "You made your point."

Handsome glared at Tessa. "What are your kids up to while you're away? I don't think you said."

"They visit my parents in Tennessee every summer."

"What about Bobby?"

"Robert," she corrected. "He's setting up his new law business in Nevada City, a few miles from Grass Valley, where we live." She didn't make eye contact. "We're excited."

"Oh? We are?" With Handsome's condescending tone, Chase admitted the almost moment with Tessa had evaporated. And she'd be very careful next time. Probably a good thing.

"Can we go?" Tessa pushed by them both and ran down the steps toward the water.

Handsome's brow wrinkled. "Was it something I said?"

Chase jammed his index finger into Handsome's stomach. "Stop getting in my way."

"Aren't you two already playing house?" He nodded toward the tree house then cut his eyes back to Chase.

"Not even close," he fumed through clenched teeth.

A chuckle escaped Handsome's thick lips. "That would explain why you're such a—"

"Tessa and I are—friends. Nothing more."

"So that is what friendship looks like."

Chase eyed him from head to toe. "Tessa is…"

"Hot."

"She is that," he growled. "She's also a good woman."

"Are you trying to change all that?"

"Screw you. We wouldn't even be here if it weren't for you. She'll fall for a sad story every time. You're proof of that. When this is all over, I'm cutting her from field duty. She gets caught up in all this"—he waved at the surroundings—"and gets romantic notions in her head."

"Aww. Poor Captain Hunter. Hero worship is such a drag."

Chase noted the voice change from amused to cynical. There was no love lost between them. Handsome's interest in Tessa continued to be based on how she could help him. Maybe he felt an obligation to protect her at the same time. A sense of relief came over him. Someone else might need to keep an eye on her.

"Are you a little jealous, Handsome?"

Handsome chewed on his bottom lip. "You do appreciate you'll break her heart—and you're a total jerk? You're messing with pure gold. I would hate to have to feed you to—"

"Save the threats." Chase moved toward the steps. "Let's go. We've got things to do."

Handsome caught up and pushed in front of him at the bottom of the steps. "What Dage said, about Keeya giving birth the day of the massacre… Tessa told me yesterday you have my birth mother."

The time had come to let him in on the secret. "Keeya's your mother. We discovered this after we arrived. The day at the clinic when she saw Dr. Girard and you, the pieces came together for her. You must look like your birth father."

Staggering backward, Handsome took on a ghost-like gaze. "My mother? Keeya is my mother?"

"Yes. We had her taken away from here to protect her from being used against you by Baboloki. She's suffered enough over the years. She is free and is waiting for us." Chase took a deep breath and put his hands on his hips. "This has to be a shock. Dr. Girard never knew she survived. He was surprised, too, the other day when he saw her."

"Where? Where is she, Chase?" Handsome spoke so softly, Chase stepped closer to hear. "I-I want to see her."

"Then we need to get going. She needs to be moved to a safer place."

He never had believed he'd see the day when this giant of a man would stutter and take on the appearance of a helpless teddy bear. A fleeting ounce of sympathy touched him until he remembered all the times Handsome had put him in harm's way or tried to undo a plan, not to mention putting Tessa at death's door.

"You stay out of my way this time, Handsome. I know what I'm doing and if we're lucky, you and Keeya will come out okay."

"And my father?"

Together, they moved toward the dock where a speedboat bobbed and the engine puttered softly.

"Carter and Sam are on it. Vernon and Zoric are with Baboloki. There are a lot of moving parts here, so don't screw it up."

Chase tagged along with Tessa to finish up the interview with Baboloki's secretary. A good thirty-minute delay in her work schedule didn't appear to give Naledi any concern since she got to talk about herself. Tessa even took some pictures of her working. The woman shut down after Tessa asked about the earlier confrontation with the president.

Chase slipped away to corner Peter in his office and asked some rapid-fire questions about the area politics while Vernon got the president and some of his men moving away from camp in a government truck. Peter sat down at his desk and gave a dismissive glance toward the door.

"My staff is going about their daily chores of cleaning the quarters, laundry, and food prep for the day. While I have them occupied, I really need to get some work done."

When he exited the office, he saw that Handsome had wrapped Dage in a tattered bedspread and lifted him onto his shoulder. The man squirmed and moaned, frightening some plovers to fly up from the river bank. This in turn led to shrieks from tree-bound monkeys. On his way to the boat, he stepped a little close to a palm and banged his captive's head into the trunk. This took care of his squirming.

He laid the body next to Tessa's feet when he reached the dock then eased down into the boat, setting it rocking. After dragging the covered Dage after him without much finesse, Handsome secured him under a row of seats, unwrapping him enough to make sure he didn't suffocate.

When Chase ran up, Handsome lifted Tessa into the boat. With his hands still on her waist he winked at her seriousness and patted her cheek before turning his gaze back up to Chase who joined them by hopping on board then pushed in between him and Tessa.

"Let's go," Chase demanded with a shove against the man's chest. "Don't make me sorry I'm helping you."

"Whatever you say, Captain Hunter. Guess I'm in your debt."

"Again."

CHAPTER TWENTY-NINE

Baboloki beamed at his photographers who would be witness to a demonstration of how he could handle the male spotted hyena lunging at him from his chained post. A baboon, also chained to a post, bared his teeth with a shriek of displeasure. The Nigerian stood rigid, to the side, eyeing him, and waited for instructions.

"Are you familiar with the Hyena Men of Nigeria, Mr. Zoric?" It gave him pleasure to finally see some kind of expression on the ghoulish face of the photographer.

With narrowed eyes, Zoric offered him a look of contempt. "Barbaric treatment of animals can end up being a death sentence for the abuser."

Baboloki glanced over at the snarling hyena. "Yes. But in this case, I have a certain connection with these animals." He waved his hand in the air to show disregard for the concern. "The herbal medicine I take gives me strength, fortitude, and insight to handle these beasts."

"Insight?" Vernon lowered his camera after snapping several pictures of the president standing near the hyena.

"I become one with the hyena, and he believes I will not harm him while we perform." He removed his tan-colored vest and shirt then tossed them to one of his guards. His bare chest revealed impressive muscles for a man his age, along with some nasty-looking scars, perhaps from wounds inflicted by these very beasts he claimed to control. He snatched a red tee shirt from a nail near the hyena and pulled it over his head.

"What are these herbs, Mr. President?" Vernon continued. "Native drugs?"

Baboloki bristled. "I do not need drugs, you fool. The beast within me controls the hyena. My people will learn from me that all they must do to live a healthier, stronger life is to take advantage of the herbs and medicine that are all around them. This Nigerian sells his herbs to the locals when he travels after such a performance. It is a good living, or so he tells me."

The Nigerian helped the president into garb that resembled a long skirt-like apron over his short pants with layered strips of red leather around each edge. Gold and green tassels, tied throughout the design, caught the breeze and floated up like wisps of hair. After tying the costume in the back, the Nigerian handed the president some chain ankle bracelets that tinkled like they might have tiny bells embedded throughout the links.

"Doesn't using herbal medicines run the risk of a serious illness going untreated?" Zoric stepped back to set up his video recorder.

"Some of these herbs are for malaria, an illness not always treated properly out here in the swamp. There are natural remedies in every homeland. Even in your America, the weeping willow bark eases a headache when chewed. That is but one example. There is also the vinca used in the treatment of cancer."

"Are you afraid these humble people will think, they, too, can be a Hyena Man or approach another wild animal because of the herbs they buy?" Vernon snapped a quick picture of the Nigerian.

Again, he waved away the possibility of fear. "To be a Hyena Man, you must be either trained for many years or a descendent of these men."

"Which are you, Mr. President?" Vernon repositioned his camera, this time toward the hyena and baboon.

"I am both, of course. Although Botswana is my country, my home, I was born in Nigeria where I lived until I was ten. At that time, my family sold me as a slave to a military man in South Africa. He discovered my potential and raised me as his son until I entered the army." He smiled and spread out his arms. "The rest is history, as they say."

The president stood erect after attaching the chains on his ankles and slipping his bare feet into a pair of ragged flip-flops. The Nigerian retrieved a thermos from a backpack and handed it to one of the guards who poured a small amount into a disposable cup and drank from it then tossed it in the dirt.

"So, are we going to get a demonstration, Mr. President?" Zoric inquired, turning the camera toward the leader.

Another short cup was filled with the liquid and handed to the president who downed it in one gulp. He savored it momentarily and waited for some magical effect to empower him. The Nigerian easily approached the hyena and gave him a palm-sized piece of meat sprinkled with some wet herbs. When the jaws of the beast snapped at the food, the man dropped it to the ground where it was quickly scarfed down.

"The herbs help the animal relax and increase his interests in the performance." The president didn't hesitate to move alongside of the hyena who lay down then gazed up at his master. He reached down and stroked the hyena's back and spoke softly. "He enjoys this."

"Aren't you afraid he'll turn on you?" Zoric started filming.

"No." The Nigerian unfastened the chain from the post and handed it to the president.

The heavy-duty chain remained connected to the hyena who seemed to take his cue and jumped to his feet. He lunged away and Baboloki jerked him back. This went on for several minutes until the animal lunged toward the president and rested his front paws on his shoulders. Both Zoric and Vernon jumped out of the way.

The president understood they believed the hyena would rip his head off with the vise-grip jaws. Instead, the animal appeared to rest his chin on his shoulder. Baboloki rubbed his neck and under his chin. The macabre dance between the two continued until Baboloki dragged the animal back to the post and reattached the chain.

"You see, nothing to it," Baboloki panted, sweat pouring down his face and shoulders.

Zoric and Vernon stopped their filming and stared in awe at the dictator. In that split second, the hyena leaped toward Baboloki, growling with a viciousness absent moments before, and grabbed at his apron costume. He was jerked back under the strength of his jaws, but somehow reached behind him and untied the apron. The animal staggered back under the sudden release, and Baboloki rushed to get away.

His guards moved forward as did the Nigerian, terror in their eyes at what had nearly transpired.

"A-are you all right, Mr. President?" Vernon stammered.

Baboloki faced the animal and glared. He held out his hand toward one of the guards without ever taking his eyes off the hyena who tossed his head back and forth, the apron becoming a new toy.

A guard laid a revolver in the president's hand and in a blink of an eye, Baboloki unloaded it into the animal. He stared at the lifeless body for a few seconds then turned to Zoric and Vernon.

"And that is how I deal with traitors," he announced then sauntered back near the guard to return the weapon and spoke over his shoulder to the disgruntled Nigerian. "Get rid of it. Next time you bring me an untrained pet, I may have to shoot you."

The Nigerian nodded and set about removing the hyena. The baboon squatted and observed the hyena in a strange silence. One of the guards retrieved the skirt apron and placed it in a burlap sack before going out to the Land Rover.

Baboloki slapped his hands together and laughed from deep in his throat. "Shall we move on? Our guide looks a little anxious to stay on schedule."

~ ~ ~

The speedboat eased into the dock at the clinic location. The soft putter of the engine drifted with the ripples of the water into the tall papyrus grass across the channel. A large splash downstream revealed a bull elephant entering the Okavango. He disappeared somewhere on their side but seemed to be far enough away for little concern.

The scent of burned thatch caught the morning breeze, eroding the scent of simmering meat in cooking pots. Through the trees, a burned-out clinic lay in shambles like a dead cyclops, ugly and no longer of any use.

Handsome killed the engine and let the boat drift to the dock where he managed to tie it up. Chase put his hand on the weapon hidden under his safari vest to be ready in case they were surprised by poachers or Baboloki's goons.

Joseph emerged from the trees. "Welcome," he called. Several other villagers followed Joseph.

Chase moved his finger to the trigger of his weapon.

Joseph continued, "We have been waiting for you. Our other guest is safe and comfortable.

"How many people know about this?" Chase jumped up on the dock then extended a hand to Tessa.

Handsome pulled Dage to a sitting position and shoved him back against the seat.

"Everyone." Joseph's smile widened as he motioned for others to approach from the clinic grounds. "Yes. It was the wish of Keeya. These people have suffered much because of Baboloki. They will protect her. No worries."

Handsome lumbered up onto the dock and extended his hand. "Thank you, Joseph. She is a special lady."

The group of villagers gathered close, staring at Handsome as if he might walk on water any minute.

"Your mother is anxious to talk to you," Joseph chuckled. "We had to convince her not to be in such a hurry."

"You brought her here?" Chase fumed. "Joseph, we told you she needed to be in hiding. This was reckless."

"I tried to do as you ordered, sir, but Keeya would have none of it. Besides, she is safer with her people than hiding in the bush. The soldiers will not return because they have destroyed everything of value to them. They have even taken our good doctor." He shrugged.

"They are right." Dage moaned as he twisted in his seat. "They think they have Dr. Girard. How they will use him is yet to be determined. If they can prove he has Keeya's child some place, he is still of some use. When I released the soldiers so I could hide the doctor, my instructions were to find a connection between the child in the picture and the Kifaru. They are not stupid men but do not have the resources to pick up the trail of the child—in this case, Handsome. Hiding in plain sight is not such a bad idea."

"She will be discovered, Joseph," Tessa warned. "Where is she?"

"With my grandmother." A young woman glanced shyly at Handsome then focused on Tessa. "They were friends. My grandmother was working in Gaborone the day of the slaughter. She took my mother, then a child herself, to the doctor that day. That was the reason they survived. There were others."

"Like us," Joseph interjected. "But we were all afraid to say anything. We feared the soldiers would come back." He fanned his hands out toward the gathering. "We all have families, now. This is our home. We do not want to lose it again."

"I don't like it." Chase frowned.

"Is it true, Handsome? Are you the Kifaru?" the young woman asked shyly.

Handsome ignored the question and faced off with Chase. "These people cannot protect Keeya without more suffering. If Baboloki finds out, they will pay dearly. He is not one to forgive and forget."

"This morning"--Joseph stepped closer—"when I went to check out the fishing lines, I saw soldiers patrolling the waters. I watched them pull into shore, several times, and get out to search. They never stayed long. They pulled up alongside me and asked if I'd seen a woman walking about all alone or with someone unfamiliar."

Handsome ran his hand across his brow, wiping away sweat. "What did you tell them?"

Joseph laughed. "I told them if they were walking about in that area, then the crocodiles must have eaten them. It was an island and offered no shelter. They asked how to get back to the place with the airstrip."

"And you told them?" Handsome sounded cross.

"I told them where an airstrip was. Just not the one I'm sure they wanted. We'll see where they end up tonight." Joseph and the others laughed good-naturedly. "Those men were not from the Delta or the Kalahari. They could not find their way back to Maun without GPS." More laughter from everyone.

Tessa gently touched Chase on his lower back, drawing his sharp gaze. "Let's go talk to Keeya. Together with Handsome, she should make this decision as to what to do next." He reached back and grasped her hand before moving forward. She didn't try and twist free.

"Someone needs to stay here with Dage." Chase nodded toward the boat.

An elderly man stepped up and blew on a whistle. "Let me. I will use this if there is trouble. I owe Dr. Girard mine and my family's lives many times over. Now I know the truth. If it were not for him saving our Kifaru, this day would never have come. The good doctor tried to protect my father so long ago. I did not know it was our Dr. Girard until yesterday."

"You saw Dr. Girard the day of the massacre?" Handsome's eyes went wide.

"I was there. My father had been gored by a Cape buffalo, but he was already gone by the time the plane arrived. I ran with the others into the bush. I am ashamed I ran away after I saw John come running toward the camp."

"Tell me. What did you see?" Handsome lowered his voice in a comforting tone.

"I saw John, the camp guide, carrying a bundle. He looked frightened, pleading with the doctor who had visited our village several times during his safari trip. I hid behind some bushes. Gunfire hit all around. John shoved the bundle into the doctor's arms then ran back toward the village. I didn't stay. Later I found out almost everyone there had died. Some escaped. I believed the doctor was one of the camp guests who died."

"Thank you for telling me this. Dr. Girard told me that story many times. I am sorry for your loss."

"I'm glad my father did not see what we became, and suffer the end of what we held dear." The old man shook his head in sadness.

"Are you okay with this?" Chase asked Handsome.

"Yes. Let him have his moment. Dage is tied. Leave him in the sun. That will take some of the fight out of him."

"I am not the enemy here," Dage snapped.

Tessa nudged Chase's arm as she stared ahead. "Handsome?" He stepped up next to her. "I think someone has come to welcome you home."

Keeya stood at the end of the path leading to the burned-out clinic.

The delta breeze caught her plain brown skirt and moved it playfully to the side. She had placed some red flowers in her gray hair. The warm sun shining on her face gave her skin a radiant glow. Even from where Chase and Tessa stood, they could see tears of joy glistening on her cheeks.

Handsome stared at the woman. He appeared frozen in place, his face contorting with emotion. Chase tried to imagine what it must feel like to see your mother for the first time. He remembered his own mother and wished he had a second chance to see her, if only for a moment.

Keeya cocked her head to the side, and her lips twisted into a narrow smile. With confidence, Keeya raised her open arms toward her son. He ran toward her and scooped her up in his bear-like embrace before burying his face in her neck.

"My boy. My boy," she wept.

CHAPTER THIRTY

"That guy is a little scary," Zoric mumbled into Vernon's ear after stealing a glance toward the president. He loaded their equipment onto the truck then decided to watch Baboloki's movements.

The others stood to the side sipping on cold drinks and munching sandwiches. The Nigerian dragged the dead hyena out into the bush while the others chuckled at his efforts.

"Coming from you, Zoric, that says a lot." Vernon stole a glance toward the others to try and see the president. He seemed to be in conversation with one of the guards. It included some light-hearted laughter. "Look at them. Everyone is cool as a cucumber."

The president took a phone call on his cell. His jovial mood evaporated, and he switched from English to Tswana.

"Someone isn't happy," Zoric whispered out of the corner of his mouth.

The president clicked off and shouted orders to his men.

"Something wrong, Mr. President?" Vernon asked as he dropped his soda can into a trash bag offered by their guide who kept a fearful eye on the soldiers and the president.

"Nothing I can't handle," he snapped then jumped into the cab of the truck. He threw the phone in the cab of the truck. "Reception out here is unacceptable."

Zoric pulled the guide aside. "What's going on?"

The guide looked down at his feet then over his shoulder toward the others. "Something about his man Dage. He is nowhere to be found." He leaned in closer. "I think I did not understand all the words. He said the doctor escaped. What doctor? Do you think they were talking about Dr. Girard? Didn't he die in the fire at the clinic?"

The two Enigma agents locked eyes momentarily before Zoric offered an answer.

"No idea. Didn't Dage accompany someone who went for supplies?"

The man shrugged. "Handsome gives out the work schedules each morning. The supply truck left early. The president thinks something has gone wrong—or it seems so, from what I could understand. I should go. They are waiting for me. Be sure you stay seated in the back. The road is bumpy ahead."

The soldiers swung up into the truck and extended a hand for Zoric and Vernon. They were all solemn again and stared out across the savanna with a seriousness missing a moment earlier. The two Enigma agents grabbed hold of the bars surrounding the cargo area when the truck roared to life and shifted into gear. A belch of exhaust sounded like a gunshot as the truck bounced onto the dusty road.

Zoric elbowed Vernon and nodded toward the open space in front of the shed where the hyena demonstration had taken place. The Nigerian stood statue still, glaring at the truck.

"Somebody isn't happy about losing his pet hyena."

"Hey!" Vernon shouted at the driver, then banged a fist on the roof of the cab. "Forgot somebody."

The truck's brakes squealed to a jolting halt, creating a dust cloud to drift over them. The Nigerian ran to catch up, with his baboon in tow on a leash, and climbed on board. He met Vernon's gaze and nodded thanks. Vernon extended his hand in friendship. The Nigerian stared at it a couple of seconds, eyes full of surprise, until he grasped his hand and shook.

"Tough break on the hyena. Sorry." Vernon frowned and pointed toward the bush where he'd seen the Nigerian drag the animal.

Vernon wasn't sure the man could understand English, but his gaze went to the bush then to the bed of the truck. Zoric switched to the language the whole Enigma team were required to learn Russian. "We can use this guy."

~ ~ ~

Tessa choked up watching the tearful reunion. She put an arm around Chase's back. He responded by pulling her closer, touched by the moment as well. The wave of emotion gave him pause long enough to drop his arm around her shoulders and rest his chin on the top of her head.

"That is a beautiful thing, Chase." Tessa pressed her fingertips gently against his chest as her hand moved upward. He continued to stare at Handsome and his mother with an attempted stoic reserve, but his mind drifted to other possible pleasures. The woman had no inkling what chaos she stirred up inside him with her innocent touch.

He dropped his arm and stepped away from her to move forward. She didn't acknowledge his discomfort, just fell in step with him. There was a moment when her fingertips brushed against his him. He pulled away and checked his weapon inside his safari vest.

"Something wrong?" she asked, surveying the area around them.

"Stop touching me, Tess. It's a distraction I can't afford today," he sniped then leveled a frown at her.

Her eyelashes batted nervously, indicating she was either about to tell a lie or just got her feelings hurt. A wave of guilt washed over him, and he stopped short, only to have her plow into him.

She stepped back at her mistake. "What?" she growled. "I didn't know you were stopping. Sorry I invaded your space."

"If you want to invade my space then do it when we're alone and half-dressed."

Tessa sucked in her breath, her eyes turning to violet as they did when she'd lost her temper. "Not in a million years, you overgrown baboon."

He welcomed the confrontation. "And there she is, the insulting, unafraid Grass Valley commando who steps on my self-respect at every turn." He imagined steam coming out of her ears. Even though she resisted, he grabbed her arm and jerked her closer. "I cannot think straight when you touch me."

"Guess that is a holdover from your Neanderthal years."

This time, he chuckled wolfishly. "It most certainly is, Tessa Scott, and you'd best be remembering that part of me because one of these times you get all sentimental and touchy-feely, I'm going to eat you alive. You got that?" He released her so fast, Tessa staggered a step away.

"Got it," she huffed and doubled her fists at her side. "And you can go straight to hell."

"That's a given, I'm afraid. Let's break up this happy reunion before trouble arrives."

Chase regretted his rebuff instantly but knew it was the right thing to do. Their relationship needed something to cool them down. Earlier that morning, he'd become aware of her watching him while he shaved. Maybe he'd imagined it, but she displayed a curiosity and longing he'd not seen before. Her resistance to him had eroded enough that she touched him frequently and failed to withdraw from him even when no one was watching. Even in the king-size bed, the pillows she piled to separate them became fewer and fewer. This morning, most of them had been on the floor, and she'd curled up against his backside. If he hadn't slipped out and taken a cold shower… He didn't want to think about "what-ifs."

The other villagers milled around, watching Keeya and Handsome, some with tears in their eyes, but everyone smiling.

Keeya extended her arms out to Tessa then tilted her head toward Chase to come closer. She wrapped her arms around both of them, drawing the two agents to end up chest to chest.

"My heart is full, and you two had much to do with this moment. Thank you." She beamed releasing them to lay her hand on her heart. She looked up at Handsome. "Such a big strong man. I am so proud."

"Keeya, you are not safe here." Chase scanned the area, squinting. He slipped his sunglasses on to cut the glare.

"Please." She stared up at her son. "Just a few more minutes. I have waited so long for this day. If President Baboloki finds me, I may never have another chance."

"That is the whole point," Handsome chimed in. "Keeya, you must listen to the captain. He can protect you. I cannot."

"I won't be forced from my home again." Keeya pulled back her shoulders and raised her chin. "These are my people, and they will protect me."

Tessa stroked the woman's arm. "You put their lives at risk, Keeya. We aren't asking you to run away. Let us help you stay safe."

Keeya took a deep breath. "Give me a few minutes to gather the few things I brought.

"I'll go with you—" Tessa insisted, but the woman raised her hand.

"Please. I need to be alone so that I can pretend everything is normal and I am free." She patted Chase then her son. "My only request is I want to be free for a little longer."

Handsome frowned and let Keeya hug him before nodding at Chase and Tessa. "At least let some of these ladies from the village follow you at a distance."

Keeya waved them to follow, and they seemed to understand it was to be at a distance. They hung back, some walking arm in arm, whispering excitement at being a part of something special.

"Thank you," Handsome said watching his mother disappear around one of the still- standing supply sheds. He turned to Tessa and Chase. "We need to find my father. He is hurt and probably needs medical attention. How long before Carter and Sam check in?"

"Hard to say. It could take a while. They're dependent on satellite surveillance and the very few clues Dage provided."

"Maybe if you'd left me alone with him, he'd have been more willing to talk."

"Provided he can still talk," Chase added. "He doesn't trust us and fears Baboloki. If he really has hidden Dr. Girard, he's bought us some time. It won't take long for the word to get out that the doctor disappeared from wherever he was taken yesterday. I can't imagine there being many places suitable for him to use."

"What do we really know about him?" Tessa pushed some curls out of her face when the wind picked up.

"Not much. He's been with the president about ten years, loyal, protective, and acts like he may have some kind of interest in you becoming president. Does that surprise you?" Chase expected his voice might sound suspicious but cared little about Handsome's feelings in spite of the tender scene that had played out before them.

"Yes. I've been here ever since I landed several months ago."

"Except for the detour to Zimbabwe and South Africa you took when you left the States. What? Did you think we wouldn't be tracking your movements? Check out any of the diamond mines while you were there?"

"I see Enigma has been spying on innocent tourists again."

"We never spy on innocent tourists, only the ones who like to fabricate lies, steal, instigate coups, and use blackmail to further their own agenda. Any of those fit your description?" Chase winked at Tessa then glowered at Handsome. "Oh, wait. All of them."

"I am a changed man," Handsome declared in a holier-than-thou voice. "I want to make a difference. That's all."

"Yeah. That's what worries me," Chase snapped. "You have no skills to run a country."

"I have been preparing for this my whole life," Handsome snarled.

"So, shooting up a hotel in Tunisia several years ago prepared you how?" Before Handsome could answer, Chase poked him in the gut with his finger. "How about throwing in with diamond smugglers in the States or that woman who nearly killed us at Lake Tahoe. Let's not forget it was her people who did murder a couple of US Marshalls. You left us to dig out of an avalanche."

An anxious expression clouded Tessa's face. She was about to jump into the fight with some kind of excuse for Handsome. It's what she always did.

He addressed her before she could begin. "Didn't he persuade you to go with him to unknown parts and nearly cause you to drown because of his carelessness?" As she gaped at him, he refocused on Handsome. "Oh, you'd make a stellar leader. Honestly, I'm not sure anyone would notice the difference."

Handsome had pulled back his fist when the old man came wobbling up the path from the boat dock. Blood trickled down his forehead onto his white shirt. Handsome ran to him and caught him in his arms as he collapsed.

"I'm sorry. I failed."

Chase kneeled down and examined the cut on his forehead. Swelling had already formed a knot the size of a Ping-Pong ball on the back of his head. "I'll get the first aid kit out of the boat."

"The boat is gone," the old man declared. "That man managed to slip out of his ties and jumped me then knocked me unconscious."

With all the commotion over Keeya and Handsome, no one had noticed the sound of a motor turning over. The heated words had drowned out any idea of him escaping.

"We need to get him checked out." Handsome lifted him in his arms and carried him to a picnic table where he laid him down.

Screaming women came running around the distant shed with their children in tow. The few men left in the village appeared from the trees.

"Keeya!" Handsome breathed. Before he could run toward them, his young admirer raced to him.

She burst into tears. "That man in the boat. He had a gun pointed at us. He appeared out of nowhere."

Chase jerked her around to face him. "Where is Keeya, girl?"

"Gone. That man took her."

CHAPTER THIRTY-ONE

"There's a narrow canal around the back side of this area," Handsome huffed as he ran to where his mother had disappeared. "It sticks out like a peninsula. He could easily steer the boat there."

Quicker on his feet, Chase ran past him, leaving Tessa to bring up the rear. Several of the other villagers stayed with the wounded man. He spotted Keeya and Dage ahead, stepping into the boat.

Dage jumped down first and extended his hand to Keeya, who took it. She looked over her shoulder and spotted them but failed to call out to be rescued. A look of regret covered her face. She turned back to Dage and let him pull her into the boat. The boat sputtered to life and pulled out into deeper water.

Keeya found a seat and watched them approach. She kissed her fingers and offered them up toward Handsome. When Chase pulled his weapon and aimed at Dage, she stood up and blocked a clear shot.

"What the hell?" Chase fumed as he lowered his Glock. "What's she doing?"

"She's protecting Dage," Tessa panted, running up alongside the two men.

"Why would she do that?" Handsome whispered in disbelief.

Tessa shook her head. "Maybe she's leaving to protect you."

"Do I look like I need protection?" Handsome blustered.

She ran her hand down his arm. "To a mother, you do. Now what, Chase?"

Watching them disappear soured Chase's already-irritated frame of mind. "Is there a way back to camp from here, Handsome?"

"Not unless you cut across the savanna. The good roads lead to other small villages and on to Maun. It can be done, just slow going. Herds of Cape buffalo, impalas, and even the lions will find shade in an hour or so and will make it easier to travel. It isn't safe to walk until then unless we find another way out."

"Are there any other vehicles here?" Chase replaced his weapon and moved back toward the medical clinic area. "Surely the people who work have some means of transportation."

"A form of carpooling. Old vans, trucks, etc. There is one truck my father kept for emergencies." He pointed toward a lean-to with a tin roof peeled partially away. "In here. It's been a while since it has been out."

"Ya think?" Chase eyed the shed and another layer of pessimism flowed over him.

"A 1957 Chevrolet pickup," Tessa cooed. "My granddaddy had one of these."

He liked a woman who knew her vintage cars and trucks. "Help me get this stuff off that's stacked on it. Looks like the shed roof let some water blow in and rust some places out. Hopefully the engine is in good shape."

Handsome and Tessa helped Chase until some of the village men arrived and took over. "I'm going to try and contact camp to see if they have another boat, Chase. Tessa, see if you can help the ladies get some food and water for us. I'll check on our injured guy." Handsome backed away from her as he talked. "Looks like your boss has fallen in love."

Tessa flinched. "What?"

"The truck. Chase is smiling like a boy who just got his first kiss." He chuckled. "Hope he can get it running. This place needs a backup plan."

"Oh," Tessa mumbled.

"Are you two going to stand there and shoot the breeze or do something?" Chase turned back toward the cleared truck and ran his hand over the hood. "Got any gas, Handsome?" he called after him.

"I'll look around."

The big man moved away, leaving Tessa to continue to watch him, even after he'd heard Handsome ask her to help the ladies with some food.

Two men helped Chase push the truck outside the shed under some trees. "You know how to drive a stick shift?" Tessa took his question as an invitation to move closer. Maybe polite conversation would soothe her ruffled feathers.

"Sure. Grew up on a farm."

He raised the hood and frowned. "Looks like something has been having a picnic under here."

Tessa stepped up to have a look. "What a mess. This is going to take a while."

"Yeah." He straightened and turned to eye her. Words failed him, watching her walk around the truck, touching certain places and smiling. "Tess, I shouldn't have made that half-dressed comment. I'm sorry."

"I'm aware at how sorry you are, but I didn't ask for a character reference."

"Ouch." He grinned at her when she folded her arms across her chest and arched an eyebrow. "Let's--"

"Be friends? Buddies? Coworkers?" Tessa's voice took on a sarcastic tone. "You got it."

"That's not what I meant," he sighed.

"Really? You've made it pretty clear you are my boss, you have physical needs, that you somehow think, I'm a good candidate for a roll in the hay. Oh, and you will never take advantage of me, but continue to never miss a chance to make me feel uncomfortable."

"No. That's not—"

She stormed up to him and jammed her finger in his chest. "Listen to me, Captain Hunter. There is no way on God's green Earth, I have any interest in being on your brainy-bimbo wall of fame."

Chase looked down at the finger jammed in his chest. She twisted it in the spot that always hurt when he dwelled too much on what it would be like to have makeup sex. He loved how her eyes turned violet then her temper flared.

Jerking her hand back, she exhaled an impatient huff. "Excuse me for touching you again, Mr. High and Mighty."

She pivoted on her feet so fast they tangled and pitched her forward. Chase grabbed her around the waist and steadied her against his body. She tensed, and he removed his hands and stepped away to work on the truck. This time, Tessa didn't waste time leaving.

~ ~ ~

"Why are we stopping?" Zoric asked a guard who ignored him to hop down out of the truck and moved to the cab of the truck.

"These men will not answer you. We are to pick up another hyena to take back to the camp for some celebration." It was the Nigerian whose straight face indicated apathy.

"What?" Vernon squirmed on the hard bench. "We don't have a cage. Is there another truck or car?"

"No. This is my hyena. He will ride back here with us." The afternoon sun beat down on his sweat-stained hat. "Not to worry. He will be muzzled."

Zoric and Vernon locked concerned glares and squeezed farther down the already-crowded bench. The two men sharing the bench with them hugged their rifles a little tighter and rambled to the others with anxious tones in their voices. A lot of head bobbing followed, but no one moved as the Nigerian soon reappeared from a roughly pitched camp.

He prodded the muzzled animal to jump in the truck while holding tight to the leash formed of rope. The man jumped up into the back and pulled the animal closer as he sat across from the Enigma agents. With a wicked smirk, he stroked the animal like it was a fluffy Pomeranian. The beast thrashed his head back at the man in protest then sat and leaned against him. He spoke calmly to the beast when the truck started back down the road.

"I have seen everything," Zoric spoke out of the corner of his mouth without taking his eyes off the hyena. He pointed to the animal. "How long has the president been working with hyenas?"

The Nigerian scratched the hyena behind the ears and got a soft whine in thanks. His bloodshot eyes lifted to the agents and revealed a smile with yellow teeth. "Not long enough."

~ ~ ~

The street markets of fruits and vegetables had opened for business. A few people cast suspicious glances their way. Carter guessed they weren't accustomed to seeing white tourists in this part of town, especially someone who looked like Sam.

The unwanted attention led her to wrap a scarf around her head so only her face showed. Setting a wide-brimmed hat on top, shaded her catlike beauty. Her loose-fitting clothes hid the athletic body.

Carter wore jeans and a camo-green tee shirt that looked a lot like others he saw in the area. His faded ball cap, stained with sweat, gave him a rougher look than he normally wore. A cab driver stopped to asked if they were lost.

"No. Looking for an old college friend from Johannesburg. Told me to look him up if I got this way." Carter told him the street and continued looking over his shoulder as if expecting trouble. The cabby pointed him in the right direction then quickly pulled away.

Carter spotted the nondescript building where they believed Dr. Girard might be held. Vernon's colleague at Enigma in Sacramento had come through quicker than he'd hoped. Although the area appeared rundown from age more than lack of care, it might prove wise to keep a low profile.

"Locked," Sam whispered as she took a lock pick from her backpack. "Think there's a back entrance?"

"I would have to go around the block to find out. These places are butted up tight against each other. Let's try and get in this way first."

Sam withdrew her hands. "Done."

"Easy does it," Carter mouthed. Both pulled their weapons. Although the door creaked softly when the two entered, it might as well have been a sonic boom.

The interior remained dimly lit by morning sun pushing in through a few rear windows covered in screens and faded curtains sewn from Kenta cloth. There were two rooms, a gathering room in front with a tiny kitchen in back where another door led to a small fenced yard. A narrow set of stairs separated the two rooms. Carter and Sam navigated the stairs. He cringed with each squeak of a board.

At the top of the stairs, the gush of water running in the bathroom suddenly stopped with a high-pitched squeak of a faucet. To the right of the bathroom, light flooded into a bedroom. The air remained oppressive and stale, as if it had been closed up for too long. The agents stood on either side of the door, waiting for the person to exit. When the door swung open, a man shuffled out, rubbing a dingy towel against his face.

"Dr. Girard?" Sam asked as she holstered her weapon.

He flinched and took an unsteady step backward when Carter grabbed the doctor's forearm. "Whoa, Doc. It's us. Handsome's friends. Remember?" Carter pulled him slowly forward, seeing the look of terror in his eyes. "Remember?" he repeated.

Sam nodded for him to replace his weapon, and she threaded her arm through the doctor's. "We've been worried. Handsome is going crazy over this. Come on. You need to sit down."

"Where is Dage? Is he all right?"

"Dage?" Carter took the doctor's other arm and helped lead him into the bedroom. "Did Dage do this to you, Doc?" He eased him into a folding chair before taking a look at his cuts and bruises.

"No. Some of his men roughed me up when I was too slow getting out of their car. Also, I fell at the clinic when Baboloki came. I hit my head. Dage brought me here. He will be in danger when the president finds out it was him who relieved the others. Baboloki knows I was in no shape to escape on my own. Even if I were, Dage would pay the price for not leaving someone in charge of me."

"Why did he rescue you?" Sam found some antibiotic ointment and reapplied it to a cut over his eye.

"We all have secrets." The doctor winced. He touched her hand gently then removed it. "I'm fine, Dr. Cordova. Dage came in time to make sure there was no lasting damage. He took very good care of me. As to why he had a change of heart?" He stared at the floor. "Perhaps Keeya can explain everything at the proper time."

Carter frowned down at the text message on his phone. "The time is now, Doc." He showed Sam the message. "Dage has kidnapped Keeya."

The doctor sighed. "Yes. I worried he might try. I wasn't sure he'd be able to pull it off."

"You knew he was going to do this?" Sam squatted next to him. "Why does he want Keeya? Because she is important to the president?"

Dr. Girard shook his head and spoke matter-of-factly. "No. Because she is important to Dage's son."

"Dage has a family?" Carter sounded confused.

"The president married an international socialite who turned out to be a terrible match. He was too old for her, too controlling. The role of first lady didn't really appeal to her."

"You're saying when she gave him a son, it was her ticket to jet-set around with old friends instead of being a devoted mother?" Carter moved in front of the doctor, drawing his gaze up.

"Not exactly. President Baboloki thinks he has a son, but, in truth, the child belongs to Dage. Keeya knows this and has loved and cared for the child from the beginning. I'm not sure she would have loved a child of the president since he destroyed her family."

Sam stood to level a shocked look at her partner. "If Baboloki finds out the truth…"

"He'll kill the child, Dage, and most likely, Keeya, although I'm not convinced of that. From what Dage tells me, the president has a fascination with the woman and tried for years to win her favor. Maybe it was for the Kifaru diamond, to retain power, or remove the competition, I have no idea. But my son's life is in danger if Keeya is discovered with Handsome. She will not be able to protect him."

"Where will Dage take her, Dr. Girard? Did he say?" Carter demanded.

"In time, they will return home. We must go back."

CHAPTER THIRTY-TWO

The president's truck rolled back into camp in the late afternoon. They'd stopped in a couple of villages in an effort to campaign, and he had been well received by the people. One of his men had been left behind with the Nigerian and his beast. From what Vernon and Zoric could tell, those men would join them at the camp later. The hyena had thrashed his head and body the last several miles. The soldiers had grown afraid and threatened to shoot him if he didn't stay behind. Arrangements for them to come on another vehicle when it became available, satisfied their fears.

The president rushed to find his secretary upon returning to the camp. The camp director met him to inform him there was still no word of Keeya and added dinner would be ready at sunset. Everyone should have returned by then.

"Thank you, Peter. Has your man returned from Maun? I wanted to speak to Dage, my security chief."

Peter looked perplexed. "No. I wasn't aware Dage went to Maun. I guess Handsome handled that. He could almost run this camp himself. He also hasn't returned, but I got a message they had some problems with the boat they took out. We didn't have another one to send for him and the guests. Fortunately, they were near the medical clinic, and it seems the good doctor had some kind of car, or was it a truck?" Peter gave a chuckle. "No matter. They should be back anytime. I'll check with Handsome about your security person." He turned to leave but caught back up with the president. "We've fixed enough food for your men, too. Be sure to tell them."

The president nodded and continued with his brisk walk. He took the steps to his lodgings two at a time, proud his legs could bend so easily at his age. Hunched over the rattan desk, his secretary worked diligently on some accounting books and a calendar.

"Naledi, has Dage checked in?"

She jerked her head up, and tried to smother a gasp with her hand. "You frightened me. No, sir. I fear something is very wrong."

"Why? What has happened?" The president towered over her, preventing her from rising.

"Did you not get a call?"

"My cell phone doesn't work well out in the bush and besides, you forgot to charge it last night," he snapped. "What I got was a garbled message that there was trouble in Maun. What does that even mean?"

Naledi pushed her glasses up on her nose. "I'm sorry, sir. I got a call from one of the guards who kept an eye on Dr. Girard." She swallowed hard then licked her lips.

"Speak up, woman. I don't have all day."

"Dage released them last night and said he'd watch the doctor himself."

Baboloki frowned before squinting. "That is impossible. He was here with us."

"But he got here late."

"Why are we talking about this?"

"When the guards returned this morning, both the doctor and Dage were gone. He'd assured them he would stay until they returned so they could have a night off. Said the doctor would give him no trouble. They were very frightened."

The president paced with his hands locked behind his back. "I don't understand. Maybe they were lying to cover up their failure to carry out orders."

"Either way, the men questioned people in a two-block radius. There are not many businesses or houses in that part of Maun, mostly warehouses. But they did find some kids playing soccer in an abandoned lot. Said they saw a tall man help a white man into his car and drive off."

"Maybe the doctor took a turn for the worse and Dage tried to get him medical care." Baboloki suspected he had been double-crossed but needed to continue the line of questioning.

"Sir, I called several medical clinics in Maun and in surrounding areas this morning. No white man came in. They suggested I try Gaborone, and I did, but there was nothing." Naledi took a deep breath. "Besides, why wouldn't he have said something last night if the doctor got worse?"

"Maybe because he has moved the good doctor to protect him from me," he growled then stopped to look out across the Okavango as the sun lowered in the sky. He chewed the inside of his cheek. "The question is why would he do that? What does he know that I do not?"

"I never thought much about it, Mr. President, but it seemed to me Dage and Keeya were a little too friendly."

Baboloki chuckled. "Naledi, she is an old woman. Dage attracts many young women to his bedroom on a regular basis. I doubt there is something—"

"No, sir. I do not mean romance. Something else." Her voice quivered as her gaze lowered to the floor.

"What?" Baboloki jerked her to a standing position. "What?"

"It was always when Keeya had charge of your son, sir."

Baboloki didn't like surprises.

"I mean, sir, Dage shows too much interest in the boy."

"He is supposed to protect him, and if that means helping the boy trust him, then what is the harm?"

"I guess nothing, sir."

Baboloki squeezed her arm. "What are you hiding?" he demanded, and shoved her down in the chair. "Tell me if you have suspicions. No harm will come to you. You have been my loyal aide for too many years."

"I cannot say for sure, sir. But…once, when your wife came home unexpectedly and walked in on them, they argued about the boy."

"Again. Dage believed my wife should be a mother, not a socialite."

"When Keeya tried to take the boy from the room, your wife slapped her so hard she fell down."

Rage welled up inside the president. Keeya had shown the boy nothing but love from the day he was born. The child gave her purpose and a will to live. For that, he remained grateful. The image of his spoiled wife slapping the woman who had been the one thing he desired, wiped away any moments of regret he had at disposing of her.

"Go on, Naledi. You've nothing to fear from me."

"Dage helped Keeya to her feet because the little one cried so hard. When his mother tried to take him, he threw himself at Keeya and hugged her legs. Your wife was furious and started to hit the child, only Keeya grabbed her hand and shoved her aside."

Baboloki admired her audacity. "Please tell me she returned the slap."

"No, sir. Something worse."

"Worse? What?" He could sense trouble.

"Keeya raised that arrogant nose of hers and threatened to tell the truth about what she'd done to you if she ever struck the child or tried to take him from her care again."

"What did Dage do then?"

"He kneeled down by the boy and hugged him then escorted your wife out. I heard him ask her if she was trying to get herself killed as they left the room."

The president patted his secretary on the shoulder with fatherly affection. "Thank you, Naledi. I can always depend on you." He stared into space, entranced with the possibilities of Dage's actions. "Were there other times you saw Dage and Keeya together?"

"Only a few times. Your son was there each time. Dage always played with the boy."

"And Keeya?"

"She would laugh and tease them for being silly. At the time, I thought it nice the boy had a mother figure…"

"And a father figure?"

"I didn't mean that, sir."

He waved his hand in the air. "I am a busy man."

"You have been a good father." She swallowed hard before her trembling voice squeaked out the news. "There is more, sir. Your wife has not reported in since she left. The pilot's family says he never arrived at their destination. I fear something is wrong, sir. The plane is missing."

He didn't bother to show surprise or concern but couldn't resist letting one corner of his mouth turn up in a satisfied smirk. "All good things come to those who wait, Naledi."

"Sir?"

The president didn't respond further. He turned back to her earlier words. Hadn't he set aside time each day to interact with the boy? Or had he forgotten most days and left it up to Keeya? When he sent word, affairs of state interfered, he sent Dage to explain.

There were even times he'd sent the security guard to his wife when he chose other endeavors to prop up his rule of power. In the end, she'd had enough and left for longer and longer periods of time. Had there been something between her and Dage?

"Have you tried calling Dage?"

"Yes. Nothing." Naledi pursed her lips and shook her head before speaking. "Keeya is behind this, Mr. President. She has poisoned your son and your most trusted guard and friend with her lies. She only cares about herself."

Baboloki jutted out his bottom lip and narrowed his eyes again as he strolled onto the deck. Bringing Keeya back to the Okavango may be his undoing. Why did she think this time escape would be successful?

She might be dead unless someone helped her. More than thirty-five years had passed, and in that time the delta had changed; eight to ten-foot crocodiles swam the channels, unlike when she left. Hippopotami, never friendly, could easily kill her if she wandered into the wrong pools. If she was still alive, then someone helped. But who?

The reputation he'd created over the years convinced people of his powerful reach to loyal citizens and to those who were not. The people in this area of the country would have heard from fathers and grandfathers of his first visit to their precious Okavango. Maybe a child had survived, like the Kifaru boy he sought to capture.

Naledi brought him a pack of cigarettes and waited to light his first smoke of the evening. He nodded thanks, and she scurried back to her work. She soon gathered up her things and escaped to her own tent. Why couldn't everyone on his staff be like her, devoted, dependable, and loyal?

This last bit of information, concerning Dage and Keeya, perplexed him. He searched his memories for clues. Had Keeya won Dage over to helping her escape? Why would he do that? Had she promised him a reward if her son really returned to take his place as a possible leader of Botswana? Again. Why would he jeopardize a sure thing to help an old woman who had been his prisoner for years? Something wasn't right.

Voices lifted from below, bringing him to the railing. He spotted the Americans walking hand in hand. Nothing had gone right since they showed up. It seemed a little convenient, things spiraling out of control from the moment they arrived in Botswana.

He speculated who they really were, or at least the man called Hunter. The woman's credentials checked out, but his, not so much. All he really knew about him was that he worked for a protection service hired by the State Department. Somewhere along the way, they'd developed more than a business relationship.

Baboloki decided he'd have to find out more about these two. Their friends had left earlier in the day, complaining of the place being unsafe. Then there were the two video magazine reporters following him everywhere. Too many clever coincidences for his liking.

He puffed on his cigarette as his eyes fell on Hunter who chose that instant to look up. The woman looked tired and didn't seem to notice the man's diverted glance at Baboloki who lit another cigarette as Hunter raised his chin in a snide greeting then moved on to his own tree house quarters. Retrieving the cell phone from its portable charger, the president called Kirk Opperman of the Camelthorn Mine Company.

"I have a problem, Kirk. I need some information on a Chase Hunter escorting Ms. Scott from the State Department." He gave the names of the two men who had been creating a video profile of him for several days as well as the American couple who left earlier in the day. "I need that information immediately. Something is not right. I think they are planning on preventing me from being elected."

He listened intently to the voice on the other end of the phone then replied, "Do it, Kirk, or you'll be the next one on my hit list. Do you understand me?" Before his puppet could answer, Baboloki clicked off.

~ ~ ~

As Chase and Tessa ran up the steps to their tree house, she squeezed her fingers out of his tight hold. She pushed back the bamboo and mesh doors, leaving Chase to linger in his misery on the deck. He'd been sullen all day, and her mood matched his in spite of the children who came around to sing songs for her. She enjoyed the women when they took her to their homes and shared a part of their lives. But having Chase reprimand her for paying him too much attention both embarrassed and humiliated her. She couldn't drop the romantic hand-holding charade fast enough.

Had she really let her feelings rise to the surface, or did she overplay her role as lover? Who was she kidding? They were partners, agents, not romantic buddies looking for a fling. He made that pretty clear with his short-tempered attitude toward her.

She wanted to go home. Get this over with, whatever this was, and return to her life in Grass Valley. Kidnapping, arson, and theft laced with poachers and attempted murder made the risky business of keeping Handsome safe enough to run for president seem like a walk in the park. Why were they even here?

With regret, she had to admit part of the reason they were here was a result of her involvement with Handsome. She owed him her life and her children's lives. That was water under the bridge. Once again, she'd let her emotions get the best of her. Every word out of Handsome's mouth she'd bought hook, line, and sinker.

Chase walked in looking down at his phone. "Got a call from Carter. They found Dr. Girard. He's going to be okay." He tossed the phone on the desk and approached Tessa, stopping about three feet away. "I got a text from Vernon, too. They had quite a day." He told her about the Hyena Man and Baboloki's performance. "Sounds like Baboloki intends a second performance tonight. Word is he invited everyone along the way to watch."

"Those animals are unpredictable. Convenient time for an accident."

"Like the black mamba in your bed."

Tessa shivered then hugged her arms. "Any word on Keeya and

Dage?"

He shook his head. "The nice thing about out here is you don't leave a big social media footprint, and our satellites have bigger fish to fry than a disgruntled employee."

"But Keeya?"

"She went willingly and even protected him."

"Why would she do that?"

"Maybe she's bat crazy," he huffed.

"That's your answer? How in the world did you get to be a captain in Delta Force or even the Rangers?"

He smirked. "Even Rangers have a difficult time reading women. Probably why so many of us get divorced. Why do you think she left with Dage?"

Rubbing her arms and turning her back on him, she searched through her suitcase for something to wear for the evening. "It's not just protecting Dage. She wanted something else."

"Well her disappearance is driving Baboloki crazy. That has to be worth something."

"But what would be a bigger punishment for all his sins?"

"You mean besides death?"

"Yes. Death would be too good for him. She needed him alive in hopes the Kifaru existed and would return. It was a farfetched dream, but she never lost hope. What could she do to Baboloki to make him feel all the pain she'd experienced over the years?" He continued to give her a blank stare. "Baboloki's son. How better to show him a lesson, than to take his son. In the process, she could barter for her own son's life."

Chase ran his hand over his face then pinched the bridge of his nose. "I'm not sure if I should give you a promotion or a hug."

Tessa jerked her head around. "You see," she fumed. "There you go again. One minute we're solving problems, and the next you're flirting. Most of the time I think we're kidding around. But when I do the same thing, you turn into the by-the-book guy and make me feel like I've committed some kind of sexual harassment." She slammed her suitcase shut. "Either we're friends who have some moments of mutual tenderness and respect, or we're a couple of robots who go through the motions of being human. Let me know what you want, and I'll do it."

She didn't expect what happened next.

CHAPTER THIRTY-THREE

Slipping back into the presidential compound with little interference worked to Dage and Keeya's advantage. No one questioned their sudden arrival. Dage had cleaned himself up enough to not draw undue attention, and Keeya relaxed once she saw the president's son.

"Imari," Keeya exclaimed as she opened her arms for him. She kneeled before him in the foyer. A nurse had been put in charge of his care in her absence, and Keeya bombarded her with questions concerning his well-being.

Another servant appeared. and Dage ordered her to pack a bag for the boy.

"Where are we going, Keeya?" Seven-year-old Imari asked. Then he looked up at Dage. "Are you coming, too?"

Dage tried to erase the scowl he'd learned to wear for his job. The boy stared up at him and leaned into Keeya for comfort. He stroked the top of his head. "Yes, son. I am coming. What do you say we take a little trip?"

The boy clapped his hands. "Where are we going? Will my father be there?"

Keeya hugged him and stood up. "The president is busy, Imari. I do not know when we will see him."

"But you and Dage will be there. Right?"

He squatted to level a serious gaze at the child. "I will always be there for you."

The boy let go of Keeya and stepped closer to Dage. His lip jutted out in some unknown disappointment. The words whispered when he leaned in, warmed Dage's heart. "I wish you were my father."

The man patted the child's cheek. "You must never say that where anyone but Keeya or myself can hear you. Do you understand?"

Imari nodded enthusiastically. "Yes, sir."

"Very good, then." Dage stood up. "Are you brave enough to go on an adventure?"

The boy straightened like a soldier waiting for orders. "Yes, sir."

"Excellent. Take care of this woman for me until I return, Imari. I have some business to attend to before our journey can begin."

Imari grabbed Keeya's hand and pulled. "Come, Keeya. Let's play."

Keeya winked at the boy then focused at Dage. "Hurry, my friend."

He nodded and moved down the hall just as Opperman stepped out of an office and leveled a gun at his chest.

~ ~ ~

"So, what's the deal?" Tessa shifted her weight to one hip and put her hands on her waist after pushing her hair behind her ears. "Tell me," she demanded. "Robots or friends?"

Chase's eyes narrowed the way they did when masking anger or impatience. His nostrils flared, and he straighten his six-foot-one frame. His jaw tightened and released. Tessa decided she might be in not just deep water, but shark-infested waters.

In that split second, he focused on her body, letting his gaze wander recklessly, then on her mouth. When she shoved her hands in her vest pockets and tried to speak, he stormed toward her.

Taking a step back, Tessa found herself pressed up against the small nightstand with no escape. He stood so close, his breath touched her face.

"Stop," she demanded forcefully, although later she realized it had only been a whisper, a half-hearted whisper, at that.

"No." Chase lowered his head so his nose almost touched hers. "There is no being friends with you."

Tessa could not stop the habit of her eyes batting ninety to nothing when scared. "Why not?" She tried to push farther back so that she sat on the edge of the nightstand. If he'd been a dragon, fire would be coming out of his mouth about now. Why was he so mad?

"This is why." He grabbed her by the shoulders and pulled her into his arms. Before she could protest, he captured her mouth and kissed her hard. At one point, her knees gave way, and she remained upright only because he held onto her. The kiss stopped as suddenly as it began. "Half the time I don't know if I should wring your stubborn neck, or rip your clothes off and..." When he stepped back, his mouth went to a pouting position.

"And what?" she mumbled. For crying out loud. Why couldn't she have said something sultry and tempting, like, "Tell me, big boy, and make my dreams come true." Did anyone ever really say such ridiculous things? Oh, for heaven's sake! She was losing her mind.

He pivoted on his heels and headed toward the bathroom. "I'm taking a cold shower, so you'll have plenty of hot water tonight." Tessa stared after him even as he turned back toward her and frowned. "When we get home, you're on desk duty. No more field work for you."

This did make her angry. "Why not?" she fumed. "You can't do that to me."

"I can and will. If you don't like it, then quit. Makes no difference to me." With that, he walked into the bathroom and slammed the door.

Tessa could not resist getting in the last word. She went to the door just as the shower faucet turned on. "Okay. I quit," she yelled. "I don't need you or your band of misfits."

Jerking the door open, Chase stood there in nothing but his boxer shorts. "You need us a lot more than we need you. Go back to your boring life. Waste that brain of yours on church bazaars, school committees, and little league. But I venture to say you wouldn't last two days in that life."

The second slamming of the door and her quick exit were simultaneous. She shouted over the sound of water. "I never want to work with you again, Chase Hunter. Do you hear me? Never. You make me so miserable, I…"

She couldn't finish the sentence because anything she said would have been a lie. You make me miserable because you're a jerk, a Neanderthal, a chauvinistic baboon, and I hate you. The truth was she was miserable because she wanted to release the uptight woman caged inside her and fall helplessly in love with the man she admired more than anyone on earth.

The kiss. What did it mean? Had they gotten too close and physical desires were just that, carnal desires on the most basic of levels? Chase had never pursued her in that fashion. She guessed maybe he'd been without the physical comforts of one of his brainy bimbos far too long. It had not been a kiss of passion, more like he might be teaching her a lesson. Nonetheless the sensual sensation lingering in her body, from his touch, smoldered like a fire.

She struggled to pull up a mental picture of her husband back home. Their relationship had been on defrost ever since she'd returned from Afghanistan. Then, when all the Kifaru mess flared up, they grew further apart. Normally, she would pray about her problems. Not this one. The reality of what needed to happen and what she wanted to happen remained unthinkable to someone like her.

Her mind briefly escaped to the Wakhan Valley where the tribesman had taken her and introduced her to a new kind of love. He, too, remained a problem that most likely would reappear. Unlike Chase, the tribesman would not have any qualms about taking her a second time.

"What are you doing?" Chase's voice cut into her reverie.

She whirled around and saw him standing with a towel wrapped around his lower body and another he used to rub across his head. When she didn't move, he threw the towel he'd used on his head, at her.

"Are you going to watch me get dressed? I mean it's fine with me, but I figured you were a little uptight about that kind of thing." His eyes were wide, now, and his lips formed a perfect straight line.

Tessa caught the towel and huffed past him. "You're insufferable, you know that?'

"I certainly do. And you are kidding yourself if you think I buy into you being incensed."

It was all Tessa could do not to slam the door. The evening would be long and awkward. When she got under the hot spray of water, she remembered she'd not brought any clean clothes with her into the bathroom. The ones she'd discarded were soaking wet from the spray splattered on the floor, and the dust had turned to mud.

"Great," she moaned.

Chase strolled onto the deck and turned so he could see into the suite. Knowing he'd provoked her again, he expected a cold shoulder for the rest of the trip. He'd meant to give her a good dressing down, but that turned out to be a little bit different tongue-lashing than he'd planned. He didn't regret it. It was ill-advised and the planning sucked. Keeping his hands off her when she was such a gullible target, kept getting him sidetracked. He couldn't think straight.

"Keep it down, will you?" Handsome said from the bottom of the steps. "You want to argue, do it on your own time. You scared the fruit bats into yapping."

Chase nodded and waved him off.

"I mean it, Chase. Play nice with the lady."

"Or what? You going to teach me a lesson?"

"I'm looking for a reason to feed you to the crocodiles, so whatever is going on between you two, get it solved. It's like I've been taking care of a couple of spoiled brats all day."

"I'll pass the word along. Now, beat it. I'm waiting for Tessa to get ready. We'll be down soon." He smirked. "Maybe."

Handsome pointed his huge finger at him as if in some kind of warning then turned and left.

Chase focused his attention on the bathroom door. She'd left her clothes on the far side of the bed. The soft touch of darkness caressed the Okavango. Only small artificial candles on timers lit the suite. Chase thought about his next move considering the abundance of romantic ambiance.

One of the reasons he was good at what he did in the special forces was the ability to assess the situation, devise a plan, and wait for it to happen. He slowed his breathing and took in his surroundings, the smells, the sounds, and even the way the air felt against his skin, all the while focusing on the woman who would need to come through the bathroom door in a few minutes wearing nothing more than a towel.

"Chase?" she called in a calm, cool voice.

He ignored her.

"Chase, can you bring me my clothes? I left them on the bed."

Darkness covered him enough that his form would be no more than a shadow. He'd experienced this kind of anticipation many times when he waited to encounter an insurgent. They never knew what hit them. A ribbon of candlelight flickered from the cracked bathroom door. He remained in the shadows then stepped back inside.

~ ~ ~

The sudden appearance of Kirk Opperman stopped Dage in his tracks. The Camelthorn owner showed a crooked smile when Dage raised his hands carefully. Opperman tilted his head to steal a glance at Keeya who had pulled the boy behind her. His young arms wrapped around her lower body, he buried his face against her back. Extending her hands behind her, Keeya appeared to pat him lovingly.

"This is an unexpected surprise," Opperman volunteered.

"Put that gun away before you hurt someone," Dage spoke in a flat voice. "You shouldn't be here."

"I might say the same thing about you, Dage. As a matter of fact, I believe your boss is looking for you."

"He sent me here to pick up his son."

Opperman chuckled. "He must have forgotten that when we talked earlier. He's a little confused as to why you've disappeared." His eyes shifted to Keeya. "Now I see why. You're a dead man, Dage."

"I found her wandering in the bush. She was hungry, thirsty, and alone. I brought her here to refresh herself."

"Guess she was lucky you came along. Why not take her back to the president? He is extremely worried about her welfare."

"I plan to take her back tomorrow, with his son. It was too difficult to return Keeya to Camp Kubu then come here. We, or I—"

"Maybe I should give him a call to tell him you are here." A narrow, almost-ghoulish clown appearance came over his face. "Why would you take such a chance?"

"I've done nothing wrong," Dage offered with confidence. "I tried to contact the president that I had found Keeya and was headed here, but unfortunately, cell service is not the best."

"Yet the president had no problem calling me earlier."

Dage leveled a cold stare at the bald man in front of him.

"No matter. I really don't care why you're here."

Dage cocked his head in interest.

"That's right. I am sick and tired of Baboloki's lavish lifestyle, promises he never keeps, and his threats of violence when he doesn't get his way. The country is primed to be more on the world stage, an economic powerhouse that all African nations can model. Baboloki is so afraid of losing his grip on the people of Botswana, he refuses to be a part of the future."

Dage lowered his hands until Opperman waved the gun at him. "Then why are you here?"

"He said you'd been compiling a file on the Americans, especially the man called Hunter. I came to get it."

"No need. I can tell you what you want." He raised his chin. "Let Keeya take the boy to his room. He is frightened."

Opperman nodded at Keeya, and she led the boy away. "You look like hell, Dage. What happened to your face?"

"The man called Handsome Jones didn't like the way Dr. Girard was treated."

"You needed some of the pretty knocked off you anyway. Who is Handsome Jones?"

"Keeya's son."

Opperman lowered his weapon. "Keeya's son survived? I never believed the story of a diamond in the possession of the true leader of Botswana. Are you telling me the Kifaru is really a man?"

This time, Dage managed to lower his hands to his side. "I'm telling you it is time to get on the right side of what is inevitable."

CHAPTER THIRTY-FOUR

"Chase?" Tessa tried to use her calm voice when she cracked the door open wider to stick her head out. Letting her eyes adjust to the dabbled light before she dared to step outside her safe place, she quickly found Chase leaning on the doorframe directly across from her. "Chase." She stuck a finger out the crack and pointed to the bed. "Get my clothes. I forgot to bring them with me."

He moved panther-like to the end of the bed. "And why was that?"

Tessa hesitated, thinking maybe she needed to admit to some kind of lesson learned. "Because," she spoke slowly, trying to make her words drip with honey, "your masculine presence erased all common sense from my thought processes?"

The wolfish chuckle in his throat did not sound like he believed she'd learned any kind of lesson at all. His next words came out a bit more impatient. "I know that isn't true, Tessa."

"Fine. I let my anger cloud my judgement. If this was a do-or-die situation, I could be in a world of hurt."

Snatching up the clothes, he lifted them in slow motion. "I'm sure being naked under a towel would play in your favor." The mischievous grin came into focus as he approached the door. "I know it gets my heart pumping."

"Well, praise be. The man has a heart," she snapped, no longer able to fake being a devoted student to lessons learned. "You're doing it again," she growled. Chase halted and pulled the clothes behind him as she reached through the door. "Give. Them. To. Me, you big…"

"Ah, careful. I wouldn't be calling me names, Tessa. As a matter of fact, I think I need to let you figure this out on your own." He tossed the clothes back on the bed and moved to a rattan chair near the bathroom.

"Fine."

"Another 'fine'? Third time's a charm. Women love that word. Fine. One of these days I'm going to have to try and figure out what it really means when a woman says 'fine.'" The inflection in his voice hinted he had lost interest in baiting her.

She swung the door open. "I'm sure in your case, when a woman says it to you, she is referring to your feeble attempt at romance." She had wrapped the oversized towel almost two times around her damp body. Wet hair hung like ropes down on her chest. She padded across the floor, leaving a trail of wet footprints.

If she hadn't been so angry, Tessa would have seen Chase push himself out of the chair because he now blocked her retreat. He braced his feet and he crossed his arms across his chest.

"Get out of my way," she growled through gritted teeth.

"Say. Pretty. Please."

"Why are you being such a jerk? What happened to the gentleman who always makes sure I'm safe and protected."

Chase scrunched his mouth together tightly and squinted like he might be turning into a cyborg. "He left with the Grass Valley housewife who used to be scared of her own shadow, modest beyond compare, and stuttered at the slightest confrontation. I came in his place."

"You think you're being clever, but you're really being obtuse."

"Obtuse. I like that."

"Really? Because it means annoyingly insensitive or slow to understand."

He dropped his arms, and a narrow smile spread across his face. "I'm aware of what it means, Tessa. I'm also aware you like it."

Tessa jerked her chin up and swallowed, noting it sounded like a nervous gulp. If she didn't stand up to him, he'd never let this go. Whatever this was. "Move." She stepped forward, and her bare foot slipped on the wet trail she'd left. She squealed before pitching forward.

Chase rushed to catch her and hit the wet floor with his bare feet. He slammed her back onto the bed with him on top of her. Her arms flung out at shoulder height, clean clothes in one hand. Their noses touched while he seemed to be waiting for her to speak.

"Another successful rescue," he declared, his lips moving against hers.

She glared at him, afraid to speak, afraid to acknowledge she didn't want him to move.

"You're welcome," he teased.

He pushed himself up with one awkward motion then extended his hand to her.

She checked to make sure the towel remained secure before letting him pull her off the bed. "Are you done having fun at my expense, or should I expect some more boyish maneuvers?"

Chase took one of his dirty shirts and mopped the water off the floor. "Oh, I'd definitely expect some more boyish maneuvers. I'm trying to work myself into your heart."

"Like a worm into an apple." Tessa escaped to the bathroom and closed the door. For a few seconds, she allowed herself to replay the back and forth between them. When she got home, things were going to have to change. Either she would choose this crazy life, or keep on the safe path, with Enigma in the rearview mirror.

~ ~ ~

Carter and Sam helped Dr. Girard out of the rented Jeep. They'd returned to the medical compound as the sun appeared to sink into the Okavango Delta. They'd been lucky enough to have him checked out at a local clinic, whose staff promised not to put the visit on record. One of the male nurses knew the doctor.

"Without Dr. Girard's help, I would have never had the opportunity to go to school," he said, hugging the doctor. "I will drive you back if you can find a car."

The doctor shook hands with the two Enigma agents. "God has provided once again."

Sam grimaced. "Do you think God can provide us with weapons in case we run into some of Baboloki's men?"

"Or one of those angry hippos," Carter laughed nervously. "I don't really want to be in the bush as the sun goes down and depend on my good looks to get us through."

"Like they ever have," Sam mocked.

Upon arriving, the people from the village welcomed the doctor with singing and applause. One after another, they approached him with their story of fear that he'd perished, and how those who had not gone to work had tried to extinguish the fire. He shook hands and embraced the people to offer comfort. His eyes filled with emotion at seeing the destruction left behind by the president's men.

"Will you leave us for good, Dr. Girard?" one of the women who was heavy with her first pregnancy asked.

"No. No. We will rebuild. My home is here. With all of you."

Carter led the doctor to a picnic bench so he could keep his strength.

"Doc, you need to take it easy for a few days."

"Yes, of course." He patted Carter's hand on his arm as he eased down.

Children surrounded him with their gifts of stick creations and rocks. He accepted them and bragged on each one.

"When Nyack sent someone ahead to tell us the good news, we prepared a place for you to stay." The old gentleman who'd let Dage escape stood proud before the doctor. "We cleared out the tool shed and have a comfortable place for you to rest."

"That will do nicely until we can rebuild. I guess all the medical equipment and supplies will need to be replaced."

"We saved what we could," the old man continued. "Handsome took the medicine to Camp Kubu to keep it cool and safe. It has only been a few days. No emergencies."

The news seemed to comfort the doctor until he was informed about Keeya being taken by Dage. Even though it wasn't unexpected, the doctor worried what the man might be plotting. He remained grateful for his help in the escape from Baboloki's men. When his friends lit cooking fires, he turned to the Enigma agents.

"What of my son? Is he safe?"

"Yes. Unless Baboloki finds out the truth, he has nothing to worry about. We want this election to be a choice of the people. Most people may not even care about a myth about a diamond." Sam sat next to him.

Dr. Girard nodded and gazed out over the compound. "But these people care. They have suffered greatly. Whatever will be, will be. But it is time for the truth. They deserve to know."

~ ~ ~

"The meal was delicious, Peter. You outdid yourself." Baboloki leaned back in his chair and rubbed his stomach. "The dancers were very entertaining, too. Where were they from?"

Peter threw another log on the firepit situated in the stone part of the deck. "A village about fifteen kilometers from here. They drove in early this afternoon. I didn't want them on the road tonight so they are staying in some of the tents we have for the workers when they need to sleep over. Doesn't happen often."

"Why is that?"

"Most of the men and women who work here are from the medical compound. Sometimes they walk. It is only a few kilometers, and they have a truck, not unlike the one our American friends fixed and drove back today."

Chase slipped an arm around Tessa when she pulled her jacket closed and shivered. "Hopefully it's in better shape. I'm not sure that old rattle trap will make it back to the compound." He rubbed Tessa's arm then pulled her closer. She remained a trouper and leaned in to him, playing the part of lover. She played it a little too well for his liking. But what did he expect?

"Tomorrow I have a surprise for everyone," the president announced. "I'd hoped that we could do it tonight but—"

"What surprise?" the British couple chorused.

"Come on, Mr. President," one of the German men coaxed. "Don't keep us in suspense."

He told them about the Hyena Men of Nigeria and their ability to control terrifying beasts.

"I have been learning this remarkable gift from them. Not anyone can do it. It requires a special temperament and concentration. Apparently, I possess both," he bragged before chuckling. "Since tomorrow is usually when these people come home from their jobs in the city, I have sent my men out to invite them to the demonstration."

"Impressive." One of the German men nodded. "I suppose it is also a good motivation to vote for you in the upcoming election." Although his voice sounded encouraging, his eyes told another story. The German men's comments had taken on a little more condescension after being in the president's company for a few days.

"These people want a strong leader. I have always tried to be the man they can count on."

"Mr. President, what of the Kifaru diamond? The people were talking today about its possible return." Tessa laid a hand on Chase's thigh and squeezed until it pinched.

He flinched and moved his leg. She was toying with him. Getting even with his boyish maneuvers. Without skipping a beat, he removed his arm from around her shoulders then laid his hand on hers with a vise-like grip. He could feel her try to withdraw, so he lifted her hand to his lips and kissed her palm.

"That is a myth that keeps popping up during every election season. I'm not sure why."

"Maybe they are hoping for something you aren't giving them, Mr. President," Chase interjected.

The president frowned and appeared to offer a fatherly expression through gritted teeth.

"Something to consider, don't you think?" Chase continued.

"Of course, but there is no Kifaru, nor will there ever be, Captain Hunter." His eyebrow arched. "It is my understanding you have a history in America with someone who claims to be the Kifaru. What can you tell me about that?"

Tessa's fingers laced in his. "Yes. I did meet someone who offered a ridiculous story about the Kifaru. The reason I got interested was because a couple of US Marshals got killed by someone looking for it. Turned out to be a woman from South Africa."

"Is that why you are here? You hope to find the diamond for yourself?"

"I came with Tessa because the State Department sent her to talk to you about women and health issues. I thought it would be a good time to look for the woman who disappeared from custody."

"So, you are law enforcement, not an academic?" Baboloki lit a cigar.

Tessa kissed his cheek. "Chase and I work very hard and hardly ever have time alone. I invited him to come with me." She smiled up at him then to Baboloki. "It wasn't until we got here, our friendship turned in a different direction." Chase slipped an arm around her shoulders. "I wasn't aware of the Kifaru until I read about it in the papers. I contacted the State Department, and they had some information but didn't seem concerned about it. I, on the other hand, was fascinated by the mystery. Sorry if I, rather we, stepped on your toes. We meant no disrespect." The woman was a master at diverting his anger by her silky touch and voice. "You should have told me about that woman," she whined.

"I couldn't talk about it. Besides, I didn't find out until after we'd plan to come here."

Tessa smiled up at him then over at the president. "Divine intervention. I'm always telling Chase that." She laughed quietly. "He never believes me. Do you?"

Chase couldn't resist landing an unexpected kiss on her upturned mouth. Her eyes flashed violet, alerting him he'd crossed the line. Retaliation could be sweet. He stood and pulled her to her feet. With a yawn and exaggerated stretch, he nodded toward Peter, who sat stone-faced.

"I for one am exhausted." He grabbed Tessa's hand. "Time for bed. See everyone in the morning."

The others stood and joined them on the walk back to their quarters. Safety in numbers with lots of flashlights was the best course of action in the bush.

"Baboloki knows who we are and that we are up to something," Tessa said walking through their suite door. The night sounds of the bush surrounded them with their raw music. "Did Handsome take the workers back to the village? Shouldn't he be back soon?"

"Yeah. I think so. I told him to come by when he gets back if it isn't too late." Chase zipped the door closed. "We have a lot of loose ends." He watched her remove her sweater then sit down on the bed to untie her boots. She struggled to pull them off. Crossing the room, he lifted her foot and pulled. He caught her foot in one hand and ran his finger down the bottom, creating a powerless kind of laughter.

Tessa caught her breath. "Stop it. You know I'm ticklish there. I hate that." She tried to sit up, but Chase ran his finger down the middle again. She tried to kick him with her free foot and connected with his private parts.

As he hunkered over in pain, Tessa escaped to the middle of the bed. "I told you to stop. I'm sorry. It was a reflex. I didn't mean to hurt you."

He tried to straighten and glared at her amused face. "Lesson learned."

"Promise?" she said in a flippant tone.

He hobbled to the bed and sat. With each deep breath he took, he rubbed his face and moaned. All he managed to do was nod until he felt the mattress move and her presence behind him. When she slipped her hands onto his shoulders, he grabbed her and pulled her into his lap.

"Time for that spanking I've been promising you. And no, I won't promise any such thing because I like doing it and let's be honest. You don't really mind."

Tessa stared up into his eyes. She didn't try to fight, escape, or argue. "Chase," she whispered. "Please. Stop."

Chase pushed her off him. "Desk duty. No more field work until we sort this out. One of these times—"

"I won't cheat on Robert, so treat me like everyone else. Please."

"I don't want you to, Tess. Get ready for bed. I'm going out on the deck to wait for Handsome. I need to cool off."

She swung her legs to the floor. When she stepped away he pulled her back so he had to look up at her.

"Don't get the idea I'm some kind of knight in shining armor, Tessa. I'm not, and you of all people should know that. Wanting you is not the same as loving you. You deserve a forever love, not someone like me. Being friends with you has gotten a little more complicated than I'm used to."

"I think being here with all that has been going on—things have gotten intense between us, and the lines got a little blurred."

Chase pushed her back and stood up. "Intense? I break out in a sweat when I look at you," he admitted. "The lines aren't blurred for me, Tess. I know exactly what I want and how to get it. You're the one who can't decide what you want because deep down I'm too big of a risk. And you're right. Go to bed. Talk to you in the morning."

CHAPTER THIRTY-FIVE

Handsome gathered his father in his massive arms and lifted him off the ground. Bursts of laughter rose between them as Dr. Girard rubbed his head then patted his back like he did when Handsome was a boy. The emotion welled up inside the doctor as he stepped back. He stroked his son's face.

"I am glad to see you. I worried I might never again." Dr. Girard let his son guide him to a chair in his new accommodations. "Your friends found me." The doctor nodded at Sam and Carter standing in the doorway. "And a former student drove us back. I wish he didn't need to return to Maun so soon."

Handsome checked his father's wounds and bruises. "I'm going to kill him," he growled.

"Most of this was because I fell down the steps and hit my head. The president never struck me, son."

"I can't believe you're defending him." Handsome pulled the one chair in the tiny quarters closer. "This is his fault. The clinic, all you have worked for, destroyed."

Dr. Girard took on a concerned look before he cupped his son's chin in his hand. "Listen to me. You are going to be a great man, a great leader for these people. Do not muddy up your future with revenge. Do not become the man Baboloki is. He is afraid of me. If he discovers you're my son, you'll be killed. You must tread lightly."

Carter looked over his shoulder and pushed into the room. "Let's not get ahead of ourselves. Handsome will have to go through the same process as any other candidate, get funding, campaign... You can't depend on the legend of the Kifaru to get you the presidency. The world has changed. Even out here in the bush, people have access to the modern world. I saw a satellite dish in the medical compound the other day."

"I'm not sure I even want the job," Handsome sighed.

"But your mother…Keeya. We must talk to her before Baboloki finds her. If Dage still has her, then she will be safe."

Handsome caught his father up-to-date about the way Dage managed to outmaneuver them all and take Keeya. He still didn't understand why his mother would leave with him until Sam informed him about the child.

"The young boy was the child she never got to raise, love, or guide through life. That little boy means the world to her. Sounds like Dage kept a dangerous secret."

The four explored where Dage may have taken Keeya to keep her safe and decided nothing could be done until morning. Handsome accepted Carter and Sam's offer to stay the night with his father so he could return to Camp Kubu to try and continue acting normal.

He'd witnessed the evening's festivities and felt enraged at the smug expression on Baboloki's face while the food was served and then at the entertainment that followed. He'd nodded approval and clapped calmly, even though the dancers had gone above and beyond to perform. At least the guests showed their appreciation with their applause and kind words afterward. The president on the other hand remained in his cushioned rattan chair near the fire and smoked a cigar, observing everyone with squinted eyes.

Handsome became aware he also followed his movements while serving and cleaning up. The crooked snarl the president offered when they'd locked gazes gave him pause. A chill pinched the nape of his neck.

Old habits die hard when you've had to hide the truth most of your life and be suspicious of anyone who appears confrontational. Therefore, he couldn't bring himself to look humble and nod a sign of respect. He stopped, straightened to his six-foot-six height and glared back, with what he hoped, was a darkness the president needed to heed.

The other person the president appeared to observe more closely was Chase Hunter. The man took pride in baiting the president on a number of occasions and came across as an ugly American without social skills. He played the part well by offering inappropriate comments along with questions about things that didn't concern him. Even in the darkness, touched only by the light of tiki torches and a campfire, Handsome could see the flame of irritation wash over the president's face. Only when

Tessa spoke did the president divert his interest from the captain.

Maybe Enigma kept Tessa in the mix for just this sort of thing. She certainly wasn't a killer like the rest of them or possessed of any special skills, other than creating a kind of chaos that the captain clearly enjoyed.

He'd met the man a few years back and had to admit he'd feared him. Back in the Old West days, he would have been one of those sheriffs who shot first and asked questions later. His attention to details added to his lethal demeanor and could manipulate any situation to a successful outcome.

Back then, Handsome would have sworn the man lacked a conscience and even got off on putting a would-be terrorist out of his jihadist misery. Few words, no sense of humor, and by all accounts, little to no expressions of remorse, made up the man who had him thrown him into a Tunisian jail, an experience he would not soon forget. He could still remember the smirk on Chase's face when the rusty door slammed shut on his cell.

Now, something had changed in the man. Was it the Grass Valley housewife who tagged along after him like a faithful puppy? Although well-liked among her fellow Enigma team members, well, except for Samantha Cordova, she wielded a presence that had softened the mighty Captain Chase Hunter.

The senior agent, like a lot of men in his profession, went through women like other people went through socks, discarding some, wearing others out until they were no longer of any use to him, and even buying new ones when he had no use for the old ones. And like socks, they meant nothing to him except for a little comfort in times of need.

Tessa certainly wasn't a worn-out sock. Pretty, smart, and brave to a fault, a man could get lost in those blue eyes. She was American apple pie, the Fourth of July, and Christmas rolled into one innocent academic who happened to have the ear of the president and the notorious Captain Hunter.

At first, he believed she and the captain were having a fling, but time had erased that opinion. He wondered how the former Delta Force captain managed to keep his hands off her or better still, how she kept him in line.

When the three of them nearly met with an untimely death at Lake Tahoe, it had been Chase who threw caution to the wind and saved Tessa along with Handsome's chances of becoming the leader of Botswana. Even then, when he could have taken advantage of the woman's naked body after saving her from drowning, he remained the model of chivalry. Handsome could still remember the look of terror in the man's eyes as he dragged Tessa from the icy waters. For the first time since he'd encountered Chase, he witnessed fear in his dark eyes. The woman was definitely his Achilles' heel.

Although the hero worship of the captain was obvious, there remained little indication they shared a sexual relationship. Since he'd known her, Tessa appeared to be a devoted mother and wife. Was it an act?

Whatever the reason for Chase's guard-dog mentality, Handsome knew still waters ran deep, and if anyone threatened the safety of his charge, he would revert back to the monster slayer he'd become years earlier—a man of no mercy and the ability to bestow unimaginable pain without batting an eye. Chase Hunter was a rabid dog on a short leash held in the hands of Tessa Scott.

That could be bad news for Baboloki since he definitely had an eye for the ladies. He wasn't shy about checking out both Sam and Tessa whenever it suited him. Even though his cold observations of Tessa's backside concerned Handsome, knowing the explosive consequences of crossing Chase and that the captain watched on in quiet aloofness, gave Handsome reason to be on the alert for trouble. However, the president remained a gentleman to her and even tried to engage her in pleasant conversation about her work at the State Department.

Handsome admitted to himself, even he possessed a kind of need to be protective of the woman. Gullible, naïve, and refreshing as a spring rain, Tessa believed in him when no one else did. She trusted him when the smart thing would have been to run away. Even though she'd been frightened of him, she followed him to danger and nearly lost her life. Could be why Chase still didn't trust him and looked forward to the day when he could bring this little party to an end.

How could one piece of carbon turn so many lives upside down? Kifaru should have been called Toxic or Nightmare. Even so, the idea of living up to his birth father's expectations, and now his mother's, inflated his pride in the hopes of making a difference for these people. If not for the example of his adopted father, his life might have been very different.

"Why are you sitting out here all by your lonesome, Captain Hunter?" Handsome asked as he climbed the steps to the deck surrounding the tree house suite. "And why, pray tell, aren't you in there with that woman who clearly thinks you walk on water?"

Chase cocked his head at the giant then nodded toward a chair next to him. "That woman is the reason I'm here making sure you don't cause a fairly stable African country to go off the rails."

He plopped down and sighed. "That wasn't really my question."

"What is your problem?" Chase sulked.

Handsome looked over his shoulder into the suite where he could see Tessa propped against several pillows, sound asleep. "Seems to me you're the one with the problem. The Chase Hunter I used to know took whatever he wanted and left the world in ruins when he finished with—well, you get my point."

"Talking about Tess is off-limits. Understand?"

"Probably more than you'd like. Your pet do-gooder is helping me, and you're jealous."

Chase cut off a chuckle in his throat that sounded like he might choke. "Keep telling yourself that. I like Tess. We all do. And yes, I watch her back."

Handsome gave a dog howl. "We all do that, Chase. Even Baboloki."

"I've noticed. He's a little too engaging when she's around. I'm not sure if it's because she's a babe, or if he thinks he can get under my skin."

"I'm betting on both. Any word on Keeya?"

"No. The president's secretary brought him several messages after you left. We were sitting around the fire talking. He waved her off the last time. But his demeaner got darker as the evening went on."

Handsome shared the latest news about Baboloki and the child he claimed as his son. "Poetic justice if you ask me."

"The only one who loses in that game is the little boy. Keeya is your mother, but don't do anything that would hurt that child. She is more attached to him than to you. Her loyalties could jeopardize everything you're trying to accomplish."

Handsome stared out into the night, listening to the sounds of the delta. "When this started out, years ago, all I wanted was revenge."

"And now?"

"Now I want to come home, to be a part of something bigger than myself. I want to help my father with the clinic. He's the one who makes a difference. I'm nothing. I have nothing but a diverse education and a questionable history of lending my skills to the highest bidder." Handsome sighed and tried to adjust his large frame to the tight chair. "I love this country as I've loved America and Canada. I've been blessed with seeing both the best and worst humanity has to offer."

"I get that," Chase said looking back into the suite to see Tessa roll to her side then stretch her arm where he should be laying. "Some things are worth a gamble, Handsome."

"I'm clueless about politics. Why did I think I could do this?"

"Things always look easier when you're standing on the outside looking in. Besides, Tess likes to say things that are worthwhile are never easy."

"Didn't figure you for a philosopher."

"I'm trying to say you know enough about the right way to do things and can avoid the traps of corruption and deceit. Surround yourself with good men and women. You haven't been part of a tribal society, so you don't owe anyone any favors. Be your own man. If you aren't elected, then you can still work with Dr. Girard. He's going to need you more than ever. Don't leave destiny up to a legend."

"Are you encouraging me to run for president?" he gasped before landing an easy punch on Chase's arm. "I'm touched."

"Doesn't mean I like you," he offered, shoving at his fist.

Handsome stood and turned to look inside the suite. "Well, I will be needing a first lady to be at my side. I'm thinking—"

"Over my dead body," Chase frowned up at Handsome, who continued to look amused.

"In our line of work, the Tessa Scotts of the world get killed if they fall in love with the likes of us."

"Not this time." Chase stood and turned away.

~ ~ ~

Baboloki paced in the treetop suite with his cell phone to this ear.

"And where are they now, Opperman?" His voice grew low and deadly.

"Under surveillance, Mr. President. I didn't know there was a problem until they'd left. They are headed back to the Okavango. Apparently, the Kifaru is already there. I guess you didn't know that."

Baboloki fought the rising panic in his chest, the need to take deep breaths, and then exhaled in frustration. "I did not. Why were they there?"

"Hard to say for sure. Since both of them packed a bag, I assumed you decided to extend your stay and needed a few things. Dage didn't expect me, of course, and questioned me like the relentless jerk he is, and—"

"About what?" he interrupted.

"Why I was in your office. I told him you asked me to get Chase Hunter's file and go over it with you, that you had some concerns."

"Did you have a chance to read it?"

"He's a professor at some California college. Teaches literature, some online courses. Former army captain. Does some work for the State Department when someone needs muscle. Pretty unremarkable. No red flags. Couple of speeding tickets five years ago. His grandfather is an old Washington diplomat, and that is probably how he got in with the government work. Some family on his mother's side lives on an Indian reservation. I'm not sure what you're looking for with this guy. When I met him, I got the impression he was more interested in the State Department woman than anything. Just an American wise ass."

"Anything else?"

"Those magazine guys check out. Nothing jumped out at me. I didn't get very far before Dage walked in on me."

"Then finish it, and keep me informed."

There was a pause. "Dage insisted I give it to him since he would see you tomorrow."

"You really are worthless."

"I wouldn't get too insulting, Mr. President. It seems you could soon be replaced. And I, on the other hand, will need to be supportive of anyone who wishes to usher in a new Botswana. Something you have been reluctant to embrace."

"Are you threatening me?" he quipped.

"No. My interests are in Camelthorn Diamond Industries. I want to make sure it lives beyond any future changes that may or may not occur. You still have my full support, Mr. President."

"Until I don't. Am I right?"

"You need to take care of this," Opperman warned. "There is a rumor your wife is missing. Any truth to that?"

"She'll turn up."

"Aren't you concerned about the well-being of your son?"

"What about Imari?"

Opperman cooed. "They took him."

The president clicked off.

Opperman chuckled and hung up the phone. He rolled his shoulders then turned his head back and forth until his neck popped. "Happy?"

Dage stuffed the file on Chase into his duffel bag. "I don't trust you."

"I lied for you. There's no need to rush off tonight. I have my plane on standby for you. There's a landing strip a few kilometers from a medical clinic."

"The one Baboloki destroyed?"

"Don't forget you were part of those actions. Add kidnapping a respected doctor, Keeya, and now his son"— Opperman offered the hostile observation then raised an eyebrow— "or the child he thinks is his son, and you are in way over your head. I see you've got two choices. One is, take Keeya back to Baboloki, who seems to have an unhealthy attachment to the woman."

"And the other choice?"

"Find the Kifaru and kill him. And do it soon."

CHAPTER THIRTY-SIX

Chase accepted the tray of hot tea and biscuits from the two young women who came each morning to wake them and offer something to get them moving. Each day, he requested coffee, and each day they brought tea. Fortunately, a fresh bottle of water, a battery-operated coffeemaker, and some African brand coffee packets ended up on the dresser each evening. He'd already fixed the coffee and gently set the tray down next to the cosmetic bag Tessa left open enough for a lipstick to poke out the top.

The early morning mist reminded him of something from a Terry Brooks fantasy novel, as it moved along the waters of the Okavango Delta. Sunlight divided the mist periodically, giving the impression God might be slicing the beautiful fog into smaller pieces to leave you breathless when the beauty of the river revealed itself.

He took a sip of the hot brew and compared the Okavango to his mother's home on the Qualla Reservation. The Little Pigeon River, cold and crystal clear, had been a place to go tubing, fish for trout, and learn from his Cherokee grandfather. The old man would like it here, with the animals, tribes and traditions, and the smell of life. When he returned to the States, Chase promised himself to go for a visit. Maybe a little trout fishing would ease this ache in his chest. Then he glanced over at the bed where Tessa stirred.

After setting his cup down and pouring her hot tea, he moved to the side of the bed and decided to take a moment to let his eyes feast on the woman who had become so intertwined in his life. He found he could hardly breathe when they were apart. Maybe a heart-to-heart talk with his grandfather could put him on the straight and narrow.

When had this out-of-control emotion swallowed him? Was it the day they met under the spell of a terrorist attack? The show of bravery she demonstrated when faced with the possibility her family had been killed? Maybe it was in an alley when he took advantage of her innocence to lure some Egyptian into thinking he'd cornered his prey in Washington D.C.

He still remembered how her drenched clothes clung to her body from the outer rings of an incoming hurricane. The firmness of her lips, the unquestioning belief in her eyes that he meant her no harm, as he explored what didn't belong to him under the badge of national security—or so he convinced himself. Because of him, Tessa had nearly died on several occasions. Kidnapped by a tribesman in Afghanistan, followed by the likes of Handsome Jones and his pretty story.

He knew he should fire her, send her back to Grass Valley to a life of church suppers, school fundraisers, and her cottage garden. Something always got in the way so that he delayed cutting her loose. Was it because of his selfish need to be near her, her ability to see geo-political conflict with new eyes for Enigma, or the fear the tribesman would return and finish what he started with her in the wilds of the Wakhan Valley.

The tribesman, Roman Darya Petrov, had brainwashed her in those days of captivity. The Enigma shrink had called it Stockholm syndrome. It took months of therapy to get her back to being her perky, happy self. The man was a lot like himself, in that he could be a ghost when need be and a dangerous weapon when push came to shove. The tribesman was one of the few men on earth who wasn't afraid of him. And the half Afghan, half Russian, in truth, continued to be one of the few men he respected and despised at the same time.

He feared Tessa had no willpower against him. Getting her out of Afghanistan proved to be tricky and he nearly failed at the rescue. The tribesman had followed her to the States, and now he didn't know where he was or if he kept in touch with Tessa. He suspected she knew plenty about his whereabouts but never mentioned it.

The best course of action was to get her so entrenched with her family's life again, that nothing seemed more important than raising three kids, keeping the garden up, and doting on the needy guy she'd married. Turning her back into a regular wife and mother might be hard on him, but it was the only way to keep her safe from people she'd encountered through Enigma.

"Are you going to sleep away the morning?" He watched her stretch and nearly changed his mind about cutting her loose. "Brought you tea."

Tessa rubbed her eyes then took the cup. "Thank you," she mumbled. "How long have you been up? When did you come to bed last night?" She took the first sip and then gazed over the rim of the cup at him.

"You slept in the middle of the bed again. I almost had to sleep in the chair. Bed hog."

"Poor guy."

He recognized the snarky tone. "Well, you rewarded me, so I guess we're square," he teased.

Her eyes opened wider as she took another sip but remained quiet.

"What? No comeback?" He sat on the edge of the bed, forcing the tea to slosh over the edge of the cup. She sucked in her breath as the liquid touched her fingers.

"Sorry." Still nothing.

When she'd finished the tea and handed the cup back to him, Tessa pushed the covers off and exited the bed on the opposite side from him. Chase resisted a rising impulse to pull her back and waited until she circled around. Her bare legs appeared tan and firm so that he contemplated the sanity of letting her go.

"You're staring." Her voice was void of emotion.

"Sorry."

"You've been saying that a lot lately." She went to the coffeepot. Like him, that was her preferred wake-up call.

Chase chewed the inside of his lip to keep from blurting out how he really felt about her.

"Refill?" She pointed to his cup. When he shook his head, she continued, "Did Handsome come by?"

"Yeah. Seems to think you'd make a good first lady of Botswana." He couldn't hide the sarcasm until she laughed out loud the way she did when she was totally thrilled and amused.

"I would at that. But I think Baboloki is taken," she teased. "Oh, he meant himself." The innocent expression on her face caused Chase to let one corner of his mouth lift.

"I told him that could be dangerous considering someone from Afghanistan might take offense." Chase waited for a reaction. But like always when he brought it up, there was none.

Tessa set her cup down. "What did the big boy have to say. Really."

"He really thinks you'd be a good first lady." Tessa rolled her eyes before leveling a no-nonsense gaze his way. "And you were right about Keeya. There's a child involved. Apparently, Baboloki has no idea Dage is really the father of that little boy he thinks is his son."

Tessa sucked in her breath before joining him on the edge of the bed. "Sam and Carter are at the village watching over the doctor."

Chase let his gaze drift over her body as she turned to stare out to the vista outside. He straightened quick enough when she turned back.

"Any word from Dage and Keeya?"

"I talked to Vernon earlier this morning while you were imitating Sleeping Beauty."

Another eye roll.

"He hacked into the presidential compound and saw a lot of activity last night and this morning. The images weren't clear except that one person was a whole lot shorter than the others."

"The little boy."

"That's my guess. A lot of arm waving and cars. No one seemed to be forced into the vehicle. Then there was a report of an unscheduled takeoff from a private airstrip. No flight plan was filed, but three adults got on that plane."

"No little guy?" Chase shook his head and clamped his lips tightly. "Suspicious. Who owns the plane and airstrip?"

"Camelthorn."

"Mr. Kirk Opperman, the sleazy South African. I didn't like him."

"Can't be sure right, but the question is whose side is he on, and where is that kid?"

"Either he's a bargaining chip, or being kept in a safe place until they return. Was there any indication of who the passengers might be?"

Chase decided another cup of coffee sounded good and left the bed to escape Tessa's proximity. "From what Vernon could find out from his contacts on the ground, one of them was an older woman. A white man gave orders like Patton, and no mention of the third. He also was able to find out Baboloki made a couple of calls last night, one to Camelthorn headquarters that lasted about a minute and another to his residence. The second lasted about twenty minutes."

"They're coming here."

"How you figure that? For Dage and Keeya to return is a death sentence."

Tessa shrugged. "Only a hunch. Maybe they found out something about us and the Kifaru and plan to confront us with spying or some other offense." Tessa slid off the bed and palmed her cheeks. "Oh my gosh! We're going to be thrown in jail!" She started to pace. "I won't last two minutes in jail. I'm a big cry baby and will spill my guts at the slightest threat of violence!"

"Calm down," Chase offered in a no-nonsense voice before draining his cup. "They're not going to throw you in jail when you could be crocodile bait. Much neater and cheaper in the long run." He watched her stop her terrified march across the floor and glare at him with violet eyes.

"I can tell by the color change of your lovely blue eyes, I may have said something that ticked you off." He raised his eyebrows and tried to appear confused.

"Crocodiles," she fumed. "Is that supposed to be funny?"

"I thought it was hilarious. Guess I don't have a good read on you yet." Chase set his cup down and moved toward the bathroom, but she cut him off. "Yes?" he said in a long, drawn-out voice.

"I need to be comforted about this." Chase laid a hand on his chest. "Be still my heart."

"You're impossible," she snapped, pushing him aside, and made a beeline to the bathroom. Then she came back, dug through her clothes, and returned to close the door with a bang.

"I could have brought those to you," he called innocently then chuckled as he listened to her ranting on the other side of the door.

~ ~ ~

The usual group met for a breakfast of runny eggs, limp bacon, and some kind of sweet roll. The leftovers from the night before had been sent home with the staff for their families. Peter tried to show his appreciation to them when he could, knowing many of their families could use a little extra food for their children. They never asked him for a handout but appreciated his kindness whenever he offered.

Chase took his time walking to the observation platform where meals were served. The view across the delta was breathtaking this morning with a herd of elephants moving slowly along the far bank then lumbering into the water to cross. The guests leaned against the railings to snap pictures. Tomorrow, everyone would leave for home or other countries in Africa.

He observed Tessa beaming when she paused to watch the giants swim the river to enter their camp. A hush fell over the group. Watching them sway away and lift their trunks to touch the babies, while others seem to test the air, kept even him, spellbound. The matriarch shook her head and emitted a low rumbling sound. Right on cue, all twelve animals moved simultaneously through the brush and disappeared. This really was an amazing country.

Since Baboloki hadn't arrived, he surmised he watched from his own deck. Guests were warned each day to give the animals, especially elephants, plenty of room. Chase asked Peter if someone should go check on the president.

"Several of his men have already done that. He'll be here shortly, I'm told, along with his secretary."

Peter then encouraged the guests to begin serving themselves. This morning, some fruit and pancakes had been added. The melted butter would have to serve as syrup, but Chase didn't care. He had tired of their breakfast style the first morning, and the pancakes were a nice surprise.

"Morning, everyone," the president greeted the group happily. The man liked a grand entrance. "I'll have only coffee this morning, Peter, and maybe some fruit. Since I'll be giving a demonstration soon, I want to be alert."

"I can hardly wait," Chase said flippantly. The president smirked for a few seconds before taking a sip of his coffee.

Handsome set the bowl of fruit in front of the president then poured him a cup of coffee.

"Thank you. I'm sorry. What was your name again?" Baboloki asked, looking up at Handsome with a bewildered stare. When he didn't answer, Peter spoke up.

"This is Handsome. I mentioned him to you yesterday. He's been my right-hand man since he came here several months ago."

"Oh yes. I remember now. You gave me the day's schedule. Where are you from, Handsome?"

"My family is from Maun. I lived with an American family and traveled with them most of my life."

"Interesting." Baboloki connected his gaze with Chase. "You two seem like old friends. I saw him join you last night on your deck."

"I promised Mr. Hunter I'd bring him some homemade lager the villagers make."

"Damn good stuff, too. Wasn't expecting that." Chase gave Handsome a nod of appreciation. "Tell your old friend I'm impressed. That's one recipe I would like to take back home."

Handsome chuckled good-naturedly. "That will never happen. It is passed down from generation to generation."

"Kind of like the Kifaru, don't you think, Handsome?" Baboloki held his coffee in midair, waiting for an answer.

"I wouldn't know, sir."

"That was quite an opportunity you got, traveling with Americans," Baboloki continued. "Did your parents sell you? I ask only because sometimes there are too many mouths to feed."

"My parents died, and some American missionaries took me in. When they returned home, they adopted me so I could go with them. I decided to return and reconnect with my roots."

"Peter tells me you live over at the medical compound when time allows." Baboloki held his cup up to be refilled. Handsome set the coffeepot down, refusing to comply.

This line of questioning could ignite an already-explosive situation if Handsome lost his temper and spilled the truth about his heritage, Chase needed to be ready to knock a few heads of the guards with itchy fingers and Billy clubs.

Tessa smiled sweetly then dabbed at her mouth with one of the cloth napkins. "Oh, it is such an inspiring story, Mr. President. Handsome is so modest."

Baboloki shifted his eyes to her. "Really?"

"He volunteers there because he promised his adoptive parents wherever he went, he'd find a way to share God's love and give his time and money if he had it. I listened to sweet stories yesterday while we were trying to get back. How he taught the children to read, carried the old people to the clinic when they couldn't walk, and even gave his entire salary to those in need." Tessa pretended to wipe away a tear. "Now, that is being a Christian, don't you think?"

"Handsome, that is amazing," the British woman said, touching her heart.

"Ms. Scott makes me sound like I have wings and a halo." Handsome looked down at Tessa. "I am only serving God with my actions. Nothing more. Please. Do not fuss over me. I have been blessed. It is the right thing to do."

"It must have pained you to hear of the attack on the clinic and the death of Dr. Girard." He turned to Peter. "I'm sorry to ask, but did they ever find his body?"

"I'm afraid that part of the building burned completely down. He must have fallen asleep in there. Such a shame. He was such a good man." Peter shook his head in dismay. "I don't how those people will do without a clinic."

Baboloki set his cup down and clapped his hands together. "After the coming election, I will make sure it is rebuilt," he proclaimed. "These people are the life blood of the delta. We must keep it filled with their traditions, and knowledge of the Okavango." Baboloki turned back to Handsome who remained solemn. "We will catch these men who did this. I promise you that."

When Handsome took a threatening step toward the president, Chase diverted the attention to himself. "I guess you are the real deal, Mr. President. I've misjudged you. I'm looking forward to your demonstration later today. Perhaps you'd like to share our boat for our last ride in the Okavango?"

"If your lovely companion doesn't mind sharing, I would enjoy that."

Peter laughed. "I have secured several drivers for three boats, so everyone can go. Our guides were told about some young cheetahs down river and a herd of wildebeest crossing some shallow waters. It's not the great migration of the Serengeti, but I'm sure you'll enjoy the show nonetheless. We've packed some fishing poles for those of you who'd like to try your hand at catching a tiger fish. Ugly rascals, but a good photo op."

Peter ordered the servers to clean up and told the guests to prepare to leave in fifteen minutes.

"Get a handle on yourself," Chase mumbled as he walked past Handsome. "You were letting him bait you." He took Tessa's hand and pulled her after him. At the bottom of the steps, he put his arm around her neck and pulled her in tight to whisper in her ear, "You are getting too comfortable telling lies, Tessa Scott. Good job back there."

She elbowed him hard enough to make him flinch and whispered back, "If I'm going to be first lady, I've got to protect my future, don't I?"

CHAPTER THIRTY-SEVEN

There passengers disembarked from the small-engine plane to find a late-model Land Rover waiting for them. A driver leaning against the tailgate waved a greeting. Landing had taken two tries since the first try met with a herd of slow-moving elephants crossing the runway into the bush, followed by some baboons who decided to sit for a while. The sound of the plane hurried their decision to scamper away in agitation.

Dage assisted Keeya to a comfortable position in the Rover and brought her a bottled water. She'd gotten a little airsick but hadn't complained. He took note of how Kirk Opperman gave some instructions to the pilot about returning, and soon the plane disappeared over the tops of the trees. The driver stowed what little luggage they'd brought and waited for Kirk to settle in before heading out.

The driver played some African rap music on the radio until Kirk turned it off. The drive to Keeya's village took almost an hour and a half, part of the time spent waiting for zebras to get out of the way and a limping wildebeest being stalked by a couple of hungry lions. Dage was grateful Keeya didn't complain. The sparkle in her eyes indicated her enjoyment of the trip.

Dage, on the other hand, wanted protection, not stopping out in the open where some of Baboloki's hired mercenaries could pick them off. He wasn't sure how many he employed, but he didn't trust them. They spent their time poaching, drinking, and giving compliments to the president with disregard for the common people. Whenever Baboloki traveled outside of Gaborone, these men were dispatched along the way to keep an eye out for assassins or thieves who might put his life in jeopardy. Dage had warned him on numerous occasions they were more of a threat than the Botswana people.

Then he'd hired the Hyena Men from Nigeria, a group of circus performers in his mind. Only one of them remained. Baboloki liked to fancy himself as being one with the beasts. His plan consisted of convincing the people of his ability to control such creatures to show them his strength and power. The Nigerian took good care of his beasts and often tried to instruct Baboloki he needed to connect on a primal level. He wondered if the Nigerian might decide to turn the beasts against the president someday.

Besides the hyenas and baboons Baboloki trained with, he had moved to black mambas, most unpredictable creatures. He once overheard the Nigerians try to tell their boss that the cobra was a much better animal to manipulate, but it fell on deaf ears. He was fascinated by the deadly animal and studied them relentlessly.

Kifaru meant black rhino, a strong and powerful animal that the world respected and loved. The black mamba represented death to those who didn't tread lightly. If Baboloki could demonstrate his control over such a dangerous and feared reptile, he could also convince the tribal people of his divine power.

The Land Rover rolled past the village and onto the medical compound. The smell of burning embers still lingered, and thin tentacles of smoke twisted upward with the morning breezes. Kirk exited the vehicle to survey the destruction then removed his hat to wipe his forehead on his sleeve.

"What a mess. You did this?" Kirk asked Dage then stepped forward to help Keeya out of the back seat.

"No. I advised against it."

"But you gave the order," Kirk accused drily.

Dage didn't answer. He wasn't proud of not standing up to the president. Many things haunted him the treatment of Dr. Girard, working for a man who destroyed the home of the San people where he had lived. He had carried out other acts of violence to insure Baboloki remained in power.

Then there was Imari, his son. The truth would have gotten him tortured and killed, not to mention the life the little boy might endure. So, he confided in Keeya, who he knew had been wronged, enslaved to a monster, and given no choice but to spend her years serving the man she hated.

The child brightened her days and gave her a chance to love again. Somehow, they'd become friends through it all. It took some convincing, but Keeya agreed to let the boy go to Kirk's home in another part of the city after they left. One of his trusted employees would take the child and the nurse to a compound in an exclusive gated community on the outskirts of Gaborone. After talking to the man, Keeya promised Imari it was only for a little while and she would soon come back to take him on a fantastic journey.

Dage wasn't sure that would happen, or if he'd ever see his son again. Putting his faith in a man like Kirk Opperman did not sit right with him. Left with few choices, he handed him over to a stranger and prayed for his safety.

"Put those hands in the air," came a disgruntled voice behind them.

The three turned to see a man and woman pointing rifles at them. Dage recognized the pair from Camp Kubu who traveled with Chase and the State Department woman. He raised his nose in the air and sobered.

"I should have known you weren't innocent friends of Chase Hunter." Dage lifted his hands higher when the woman waved her rifle at him. She didn't look so helpless and frightened now. A beautiful woman will make a man gloss over details. "Are you even an astronaut?"

Carter smiled. "Not anymore. NASA seemed to think I took too many risks."

"Shocking," Kirk Opperman quipped. "And you, my dear, who are you?"

Sam kept silent as her frown deepened.

"Oh, she isn't much of a talker," Carter laughed. "But she is really good at other things, like slicing through a man's neck with a Samurai sword, taking out a kneecap with her foot, and convincing men it was all worth it to be with her." He sighed then eyed Sam. "I can't tell you how really incredible she is." He winked at her as she leveled a dangerous glare his way. "Anyway, here we are. Maybe you'd better tell me why you're here and what your future plans might be. I have a lot on my plate today and want to make sure I schedule you in—if you know what I mean."

Dr. Girard came hobbling out of the shed and waved to Keeya. She ran to him until Sam blocked her path and bounced her back with her rifle.

"Keeya," Dr. Girard called. "Put those things down, Carter."

"Stay back, Doctor. Sam?" Carter threw out one arm to stop the doctor as Sam leaned her weapon against a tree. After a quick body search of all three, Sam nodded to Carter then retrieved her weapon.

Keeya ran into Dr. Girard's outstretched arms. "Dage told me what happened. I'm very sorry. This is my fault. If I had not run away, the president would not have come here looking for me."

"He suspects I was the one who took your son."

"Our son, good doctor. Our son." Keeya stroked both his arms.

Carter continued to smile wickedly at the other two men. "I'm waiting."

"The president plans to do one of his ridiculous demonstrations with those god-awful hyenas today. I talked to him last night." Kirk tried to lower his hands, but Carter shoved his rifle forward to cause him to lift them again. "Several villages have been invited to watch. He's thinking this will put to rest the Kifaru nonsense."

"It isn't nonsense if it's true," Dr. Girard warned. "I was there the day Baboloki entered the safari camp, killing the guests and the people of the nearby village. The village where Keeya and her husband shared a life. I watched them kill her husband."

"Yet, you escaped." Kirk's comment was edged with skepticism.

"Yes. Barely. A plane arrived as the area became overrun with rebels dressed like soldiers."

"And what of the Kifaru? How does that fit in?" Kirk chuckled. "I mean, this is preposterous."

Keeya stepped forward and spoke softly. "You know my husband was the rightful heir of the Kifaru diamond?"

Kirk nodded.

"And that whoever possesses it is destined to lead the country?"

"I've heard the story, Keeya. Fairy tales don't impress me."

Dage growled. "Listen to her."

Kirk puckered a sour expression. "Why should I?"

"Because that day I gave birth to a son. My husband ran to the safari camp to find Dr. Girard." She extended her hands to the doctor and pulled him forward. "Tell them."

"John and I had become fast friends. He was a brilliant young man. He found me that day and handed me his newborn son."

This time Kirk dropped his hands in spite of being held at gunpoint. "Are you telling me the heir to the Kifaru diamond survived?"

"I raised him as my own son. It is time the people of Botswana knew the truth of that day." Dr. Girard pointed a finger at Opperman. "Were you a part of the massacre? Did you sanction it?"

Opperman's left eye took on a nervous twitch. "No. But my father supported it as did other mining operations in the country and South Africa. They were heavily invested in prospecting and sinking mine shafts. When the previous leaders wanted to explore other environmental options for the country, a lot of money poured in to change stubborn attitudes."

"Why here? Why did they choose this village to destroy?" Keeya whimpered.

"Because your husband tried to make a difference. Showing the villages through education and tourism, they didn't need to risk their lives in the mines. He led an underground movement for change." Opperman paused and licked dry lips. "And he carried a lot of weight because everyone knew the story of the Kifaru. People listened to him. He had their best interests at heart."

"That he did care," she cried. "Now, for decades, we've lived under the rule of a dictator who pretends to the world we have a democracy and that he has the best interests of his people at heart. When it is really the mining industry that lines his pockets and threatens the small villages with poverty if they complain. We are better than that."

"Things won't change overnight, Keeya." Opperman kept trying to remove the sweat from his brow and neck. "I'm on your side. Remember?"

Dage lowered his hands and wasn't threatened this time. "Time will tell. You have brought us this far. I think you are only trying to cover your ass."

Opperman took a deep breath. "True. But as a businessman, I understand when the winds of change can't be stopped. I have investors to look after and a company to run. I don't need chaos running rampant in the capitol or a leader with an inflated ego making us look like baboons on the world market."

"News flash," Carter offered. "The world already sees you that way. But you have all the elements of a great nation here." He lowered his weapon. "I'm not sure Keeya's son is going to be able to lead this country, but he can help unite it."

"My son wants Botswana to be a model for Africa," Dr. Girard pleaded. "Support him in his efforts. He has the education and training to help find the right people. Others will listen because, like his birth father, he is in possession of the diamond. He is the Kifaru."

~ ~ ~

The delta sun touched Chase's bare skin like warm fingers when he and the other Camp Kubu guests returned for the noon meal. This would be everyone's last day in the delta, and no one hurried up the path to the observation deck where meals had been shared.

Guests shared how the idea of leaving caused a kind of sadness in them. Chase, who'd never imagined a place could make him feel a connection to anything, realized he had mixed emotions about leaving. Was it his Cherokee heritage, or his aversion to Botswana's pompous President Baboloki who governed by greed and murder? Did the endangered wildlife remind him of himself, therefore instilling a desire to help these people inherit a better life?

He glanced over at Tessa when her musical laughter drifted his way. She and Vernon, thumbing through a guidebook, appeared to share something amusing. The two of them had a special relationship, one he envied. The shy nerd had barely been able to make eye contact with a woman before she came into their lives at Enigma. There were still issues in that department, but his respect and admiration for her left him vulnerable to her charms and mothering instinct. Chase envied their friendship at times—so carefree and innocent, a lot like the two of them. Although Vernon was a monster behind the computer, he was a babe in the woods when it came to women.

When she strolled past, Chase pulled her back next to him. Vernon continued on without skipping a beat, Zoric hustling forward to catch up with him. Tessa made no effort to escape, stepping back into her part as lover.

He spent way too much time in thinking how things would be different if Robert, the inattentive husband, were out of the picture. He felt like a Dateline episode waiting to happen.

This little trip had forced them to share an abundance of time together, pretending to be something they weren't. At times, the relationship almost seemed real, until Tessa pulled on the reins and got in one of her snarky, temperamental moods to ignite both their dark sides.

In her case, those moods became a cloak of defense against the inevitable. His, on the other hand, only managed to make him aware of how much control she had over him. He hated not being in control. Either way, the time was up on what to do about it. She would be gone when they got back home. This madness in his head, the ache in his chest, needed to end—one way or another.

"Penny for your thoughts." Tessa elbowed him good-naturedly.

Chase responded with a deep frown. "Do you really want to blush in front of all these people?"

"Do you ever think about anything besides sex?" she whispered. "Well, and, besides killing someone?"

"No, that's pretty much it for me."

He touched her back to guide her ahead of him on the narrow path, only to feel her straighten then shiver. A sensitive spot. He committed it to memory in case the opportunity arose to explore it again. Almost immediately, her muscles relaxed, and she tilted her head to send him an interested gaze. Was she really that sensual? She extended her hand back, and he reluctantly took it as they entered the campgrounds.

A commotion greeted them. Chase spotted Peter holding a rifle and several workers moving nervously behind him. Movement near the riverbank revealed a man tying a huge hyena to a tree. Although muzzled, the growl the animal emitted and swaying of his head, lent a chill to his spine. The beast leaped at the handler several times, but whatever he said to the animal, drove him to retreat on his hunches then bounce up again in seconds.

Once the handler had him secure, the hyena lay down and looked up at him. He reached down and scratched behind the hyena's ears then rubbed his back, all the while, talking calmly to him in some language Chase didn't understand.

Tessa stepped back into Chase's body, and he put a protective arm around her. "That is horrible," she moaned. "I don't know whether I'm terrified or feel sorry for that thing."

Baboloki walked up and stared toward the beast. "I wouldn't feel too much concern for him. He'd rip your pretty throat out if given the chance." He smiled over at Tessa who retreated deeper into Chase's embrace.

"Tess, go up on the deck. I need to change my socks after wading in the water to untie your fishing line." Chase kissed her temple and walked her to the steps. "Need anything while I'm up there?"

As he stepped away, she grabbed his hand and pulled him back. "Be careful. I don't like this."

Chase patted her on the cheek and headed off to their tree house to get his Glock. He also had a sense of foreboding.

Chapter Thirty-Eight

Tessa watched people meander into Camp Kubu from the bush on foot, the delta by mokoros, and as well as a couple of trucks. The happy chatter sounded like children anxious for a festive event about to occur. Their expressive faces varied from surprise to joyous smiles. These people were wide-eyed and full of anticipation. Some ventured near the chained hyena only to be frightened away by its lunging, or by the Nigerian who stood straddle-legged nearby with his arms folded across his chest.

His muscled black arms glistened with perspiration in the afternoon sun, giving him a magical aura as he glared out from under his dirty ball cap. He stood like a magnificent statue at times with only his eyes glancing around the area. His downturned lips and flaring nostrils indicated to Tessa the man was also on a short leash, beautiful and dangerous at the same time. Perhaps he hated not being in charge of such an event and agreed to do this only to protect his animals.

Several soldiers brought a cage with a baboon that bared its teeth and blended with the beautiful sounds of the Okavango birds perched in the trees. The erratic behavior chilled Tessa until another closed metal container arrived, secured by clamps on each end. Dread filled her. These animals were never meant to perform for man. Whatever was in the box couldn't be good. Why else would it have such security and only a few small holes at the top like something an ice pick might make?

"Come on, Tessa." Handsome had come up beside her and stared down at the crowd. "Have something to eat." He wore a serious expression. "I don't like this."

"Handsome, promise you'll stay away from the president. I want you safe." She was surprised at his narrow smile, but continued, "Please."

"Your concern touches me. You have believed in this from the start."

She whispered a response. "Not true. I was terrified of you."

"Yet you followed me into danger with the hope of finding truth." Handsome lifted his hand toward her cheek then let it drop as he glanced around the deck.

"I followed you because you protected me and my children. I owed you." Tessa also looked around, watching the others fill their plates with fruit, cheeses, and strips of dried meat.

"Captain Hunter is good at what he does, Tessa. He won't let anything happen to you, so stay close to him."

She nodded.

"It is none of my business, but be careful with your…"

She refocused on his large eyes.

"Don't let him talk you into anything you don't want to do. Understand what I'm trying to tell you?"

Tessa nodded. "I won't." She laid a hand on his arm. "And thanks."

His chin went up then he glared down at her touch.

"I'd vote for you. Good luck."

Watching him stride back toward the area where servers waited on the guests, Tessa was reminded what a giant of a man he was, both in statue and determination.

She spotted Chase walking through the men and women who'd arrived to watch the president perform. His long strides and laser-like focus hypnotized her common sense. No matter what she'd promised Handsome, her heart was a goner. Watching him work, even if it was on the lookout for trouble, drove her to evaluate why the chemistry between them continued to grow.

Captain Chase Hunter was a badass fixer for Enigma who didn't care how a problem got solved if it resulted in a safer America. His patriotic calling was above reproach. Those dark looks and chocolate-colored eyes could force a speedy confession. She guessed, a female admirer fell victim more often than not. Even she had stared at him in admiration when he wasn't aware. Why had God thrown him into her perfect little world to stir up chaos and the impure thoughts she fought desperately to repress?

"Everything okay?" he asked as he took the steps two at a time to join her.

"I'm half convinced this is to show these people how powerful Baboloki is so if the Kifaru becomes known they will not be so inclined to throw their support behind him." She pointed to the metal container.

"What do you think is in that?"

"One of the guards said some kind of snake. Cobra would be my guess. They've been used for tricks like this for centuries. In India, they lure them out of baskets with a flute."

"Yes. Most people think the music charms them, but snakes don't have ears."

"Right. They follow the swaying movement of the flute, probably thinking it alive. People think it's magic. Truth is, some snake charmers break off the fangs and sew their mouths shut. Their cobras evidently die of starvation."

Tessa took a deep breath, not sure if she hoped this would be the case for whatever was in the box. "Well, don't do anything heroic today, Chase."

He chuckled. "Me? Never." His hand rested on her back. They stepped toward the buffet. "Come on. I'm starved."

~ ~ ~

The uninvited guests arrived amidst the converging villagers from around the area. Several of the older women wore Herero dresses, a tradition begun under the influence of nineteenth and twentieth-century missionaries. They were long and Victorian-like with full petticoats and worn with matching flat hats. Others wore long dresses with colorful blankets around their shoulders and beautiful turban-like head coverings for their heads.

Samantha Cordova chose to wear a blanket so her weapons wouldn't be exposed. Her long dark hair, tucked beneath a midnight-blue turban created a shadow on her olive skin that almost appeared like the other women in spite of being taller. She cradled a wrapped bundle resembling a baby in her arms and walked confidently into the crowd with her new friends.

The doctor and Carter had ridden to camp in Joseph's small motorboat, a ramshackle affair that had the former astronaut afraid they might sink before reaching camp. Each of them had borrowed a kaross, an animal skin blanket, to throw over their shoulders. Instead of traditional skull caps, they wore ball caps to shade their faces.

Although the doctor wore dark clothing underneath his kaross, Carter managed to wear his safari vest to have plenty of weapons and ammo if needed. Because of his healthy tan, no one seemed to suspect he was a white man. The villagers surrounded him enough to keep the secret. The young woman who fancied Handsome took charge of the doctor and kept him steady on his feet.

Kirk Opperman, dressed similar to the doctor and several of the men who gave tours, took charge of him in case he decided his alliance changed.

The former security chief had turned into an asset to the group, considering his loyalty represented a safe outcome for his son. He, too, carried weapons and wore the Camp Kubu uniform with the addition of a gun with limited ammunition. His job was to make sure nothing happened to Keeya, who walked among some of the women dressed in Western clothing. Even so, all of them wore a turban-like hat of colorful material for the special occasion. It was a custom. She held her head high, as if unafraid of being discovered by Baboloki's people. Other than his secretary and the camp director, no one should recognize her. Few of his soldiers had ever seen her.

Both Carter and Sam wore earwigs to stay in communication with the other Enigma agents. "Okay, boys and girls, we're in place," Carter said good-naturedly. "Let's get this dance started."

"Copy that," Chase said close to Tessa as if whispering something in her ear. She smiled then looked away as if listening to the excitement.

"Peter, you look a little distressed," Chase said, handing his plate to one of the servers. "I'd like a look at that rifle. I consider myself a pretty good bird hunter. We use shotguns for pheasant back in the States, but still…"

"Maybe later, Chase. I'm not liking this whole hyena thing."

"What's in the metal box?" Chase wiped his mouth then took a swig from a water bottle.

The camp director rolled his eyes. "The president thinks he's going to control a snake. I'd rather just shoot the metal box up right, but I'd run the risk of being thrown in prison for the rest of my life for ruining a good time."

"Baboloki is dangerous, Peter." Chase threw his legs over the long bench at the table and stood. "I'm afraid some of these people are going to get hurt. Look at them."

"Can't do anything about it. You've seen how he is. This is what Botswana has had to put up with for almost four decades. I think he's losing his grip. Why else would he do this hyena madness? I've seen these Hyena Men before. Look at that Nigerian standing guard over his animals. He's probably been doing this since he was seven. He's half Baboloki's age and by the looks of him, strong as one of those wretched creatures."

"Better not say that too loud. Here he comes."

"Good heavens. What is he wearing?" Peter fumed.

The crowd formed a circle of sorts around the open area as Baboloki pranced out in his colorful costume covered in red and green tassels and a skirt-like apron tied in the back. The red tee shirt stretched across his torso showed off his still-fit body. A bandana tied around his head was topped with a cap that boasted the national soccer team, a fashion choice that got some cheers from a few young fans in the crowd.

He removed it then tossed the scarf their way. A scramble in the dirt between two youngsters ignited a great deal of laughter among the people.

The chain ankle bracelets tinkled when he stomped forward. The thigh-high leather boots he'd sported for the last few days had been replaced with flip-flops.

"Is he crazy?" Tessa pushed between Handsome and Chase standing at the railing.

Chase stole a glance at Tessa and noticed Handsome had done the same. She looked tiny sandwiched between them. He realized that in spite of their differences, she had managed to bring Handsome and himself together. It was a heady feeling knowing the three of them stood on the threshold of change for Botswana.

Chase took out a handkerchief and rubbed it across his brow then held it out to Handsome. "Take care of this for me, will ya?"

Handsome frowned down at the damp rag. "If my boss wasn't watching you, I'd shove this down your throat."

"Now, boys," Tessa reprimanded in a silky soft voice. "I think the show is about to begin."

Handsome placed his hand on Tessa's where it gripped the railing. "Don't take any unnecessary chances."

"Heck of a time to be concerned about that, don't you think?" Chase growled under his breath, fixated on the beat of a drum the Nigerian held. But Handsome had already disappeared.

The drum tempo increased, and the president danced around hypnotically with the villagers cheering and clapping along. Some began to sing and sway, creating the feel of a festive celebration. Tessa felt her body join in the rhythmic dance until Chase turned raised eyebrows her way. He slipped an arm around her waist and pulled her in to his side before turning back to the scene below.

She relaxed against him and let her palm go to the middle of his back. Tessa closed her eyes and fell in love with the magic of the music. She laid her head on Chase's chest and listened to his steady heartbeat.

"Stop it, Tess," Chase warned without taking his eyes off the president. "We've talked about this." A hot blush of embarrassment creeping up her neck and face, caused her to slowly withdraw and push away. He did not stop her.

Baboloki stopped dancing and received an enthusiastic round of applause. He took a few minutes to catch his breath before giving a political speech about all he'd done for the people of Botswana and especially for the delta tribes. People were eerily quiet but listened politely.

Many of these people remembered the violence that occurred decades ago and the changes to their way of life. Everyone had lost something or someone during that time of cleansing. The man spoke as if he were one of them and with powerful words of hope and change.

He explained about the Hyena Men and what they represented: strength, power, and spiritual gifts that only a few possessed. Watching him walk toward the hyena, Tessa wondered about the docile animal, when a short time ago it had been ferocious. Had it been drugged? It watched the president with devilish eyes of gold and lifted its nose to sniff the air.

The Nigerian unfastened the chain from the tree, careful to leave it connected to the leash. It immediately jumped to its feet and tried to shake loose of the muzzle in a spastic show of anger. Without the Nigerian holding the end of the chain, it would have lunged at some nearby children. Even so, they fell back as if they'd been attacked, and scurried behind their fathers. Baboloki laughed loudly and grabbed the chain from its handler.

Beast and man performed as one, the hyena trying to escape only to be dragged back by the president until the animal would jump at him and rest his head against his shoulder in surrender. There were some gasps, applause, and shouts of encouragement as the two did their magical dance that, accompanied by the drum beat, wove a magical spell.

Then Baboloki passed the chain leash back to the Nigerian. The animal immediately hunkered down and emitted a low growl toward the president. He motioned for the guests on the deck to join them.

Tessa slipped her arm through Chase's and clamped her free hand over his. "Chase?"

"Come on!" Baboloki called enthusiastically. "Nothing to fear."

"No thanks," called the elder British man as he wrapped an arm around his wife.

The president nodded toward some soldiers who rushed upon the deck, their rifles cradled ominously. Their demeanor forced their bodies to become rigid as they pulled themselves to their full height. The expressionless faces indicated these men meant to bring the guests to the ground below.

"Now see here," the elder Brit complained, looking to Peter for help.

"I think we'd better go down." Chase cocked his head toward the president below. "It'll be all right. Move slowly. Smile."

The two British couples clung to each other, while the Germans frowned and conversed with each other in their native tongue. They all followed Chase and Tessa and huddled together once they left the deck area. Even Peter was forced to join them, a soldier removing his gun from his hands with a jerk. The Germans complained only to suffer shoves so hard one of them fell with a thud.

Chase quickly offered his hand and helped him up, surprised at the muscle tone in his arm. "Easy. You okay?"

He nodded and dusted himself off. The glint of fire flared in his eyes.

"Intimidation. Keep cool. They aren't the only ones with guns here," he mumbled. Both Germen men shook their heads in understanding and allowed their eyes to travel around the circle as if they might be trying to find someone they knew.

"That is better," Baboloki proclaimed then pivoted toward the hyena. "Today is a special day. You will see that it is I who should lead this country." He fanned his hand out toward the beast that leapt to his feet and once more, tried to free himself of the muzzle. The Nigerian held the leash so tight, the veins showed on his arms. "I have the power to control even these disgusting beasts that prey on the helpless, the weak, and the sick." His eyes bulged and blasted out his promise. "With me, I'll destroy anyone who tries to take your way of life."

A deep voice from the crowd called out, "Don't you mean you will destroy our way of life if we get in your way?"

Baboloki whirled around, furious he'd been challenged. His cheeks flushed red as he shouted back. "Who said that? Show yourself!"

Tessa spotted Handsome's larger-than-life body push through the crowd and glare at the president.

"I said it. I seek only the truth. I do not see it here today."

Baboloki sniffed. "And who are you? A simpleton who serves tourists. What makes you think someone like you can change what I have created?"

Handsome removed a rag from his pants pocket. Chase had given him the rag earlier and unfolded it carefully. Then, with the care of lifting an infant into the air, Handsome Jones held up the Kifaru diamond.

CHAPTER THIRTY-NINE

A hush fell over the crowd then a low shocked, rumble of disbelief ebbed through the villagers. Baboloki watched his admirers fade away with each second that Handsome stood like a giant, holding up the Kifaru.

"Nothing to say, Mr. President?" Handsome prodded. "You killed my father thirty-seven years ago because you were afraid of a little piece of carbon, a rock that meant nothing to you and everything to the people of Botswana."

"I did no such thing. Where is your proof?"

Another man pushed up alongside Handsome. "I am the proof." Gasps and guarded conversations came from the crowd. The surrounding villages had no doubt all heard of the death of Dr. Girard. "I was there that day. John, Handsome's father who some of you may remember, handed him to me to protect until the day we could return and end the stunted form of democracy this president pretends to believe in."

The president's face flushed with anger. He pointed an accusing finger at Handsome. "Liar," he accused. "How dare you. You two aren't even citizens of this land. Why should anyone here believe you?"

"Because," came yet another voice behind him on the edge of the crowd, "I am his mother." Keeya glared at the president as she stepped forward with Dage at her side. "I am Keeya." She looked around at the people who had arrived to see the president's demonstration. "You knew me long ago. My husband escaped the village the day of the massacre and ran to the old safari camp, but it, too, was burned to the ground. He took our newborn son in hopes of finding Dr. Girard, our friend."

The crowd suddenly lost the festive vibe and began to shout out memories of that day. Several called out stories of other villages being torched and destroyed from unknown rebels. Some argued they were not soldiers, but rebels.

Fuzzy details remained to this day about what had really happened. What had been consistent was the stories of how John, the respected engineer who helped build schools, purify water, and teach conservation had been brutally murdered.

"Keeya," Baboloki whispered sadly. Then he turned around to confront the crowd. "This woman is a worker in my home. She came to me years ago, lost and half-starved. I know nothing of this son or husband she speaks of. I took her in, showed mercy and kindness all these years. This is treachery!" He puffed out his chest and laid a fist over his chest. "This breaks my heart."

"You have no heart, Mr. President," Dage commented as he pushed in front of Keeya. "You have held this woman against her will since you kidnapped her the day of the massacre. The child was never found, and you feared he survived."

"Lies," Baboloki said coldly, having regained some composure. "All lies. You have shamed me, Dage. I gave you chances to improve yourself and this is how you repay me?"

The crowd nodded and pointed at Dage in disgust then shouted sympathetic remarks to the president with this new information.

"You will be defeated in the election," Handsome proclaimed. "I will be running against you this time. The people will have a choice." He tucked the diamond inside his vest. "I am not afraid of you. And people will no longer be held hostage to your threats of draining the Okavango if someone other than you is elected." Handsome extended a hand toward Tessa. "My friends from America have encouraged the World Heritage organization to make it a protected waterway, I plan to keep it that way. And I think my DNA will prove I am John and Keeya's son. Dr. Girard took a sample of Keeya's blood the day you came to the medical center. I am a citizen of Botswana, Mr. President, and will oppose you in the election."

"You will never win."

"But I will try and not be afraid to challenge you."

"You have no support."

Handsome looked over his shoulder as yet another man moved through the crowd to come alongside him. Kirk Opperman glared at the president. "I've warned you for years this time would come. My money will support the man who pushes Botswana forward, not keeps a strangle hold on her beautiful throat."

Baboloki sneered. "You are a fool, Opperman."

Chase spoke into his hidden mic, hoping everyone hadn't forgotten to listen to their earwig. "Be alert. This guy is about to come unhinged."

"Roger that," came from each agent one at a time. "Moving forward."

Tessa released Chase's arm and took a step forward, cocking her head as if to catch every word. Her wide eyes darted between Handsome and the president.

The two Germans caught Chase's eye as they tensed in a stance recognized as military. Their hands nonchalantly slipped into their safari vests, eyes narrowed, nostrils flaring—ready to for action.

While Chase considered the possibility his team members weren't the only ones armed, Baboloki nodded to his men and shouted, "Take them!"

Several soldiers shoved their way toward Keeya and grabbed her from behind. She called out to her son to be careful. Dage pivoted to protect her and was met with a rifle butt that smashed into his face. She collapsed out of the soldier's grip onto the ground next Dage, covered in blood splatter from a broken nose. One of the soldiers planted a boot down on his chest as Dage struggled to rise, only to receive another blow to the head.

"Please. Stop," Keeya begged with outstretched hands over his face.

The soldier grabbed her hand and jerked her up then dragged her to Baboloki where he shoved her down at his feet.

Dr. Girard and Opperman tried to run but were quickly captured, in spite of Handsome stepping forward to stop them. There were too many men for him to knock down, even after he shoved several to the ground. A gun pointed at his back and head, slowed him down enough to face the president once again.

"Boss?" Vernon's questioning tone came through on the earwig.

"Easy does it, guys."

Carter and Zoric emerged from the crowd and created a diversion for Vernon who managed to slip onto the deck without being seen. Samantha stood a head taller than some of the women Chase recognized from the village where Keeya had disappeared. She briefly made eye contact, and he felt reassured she was one person he didn't need to worry about.

The president motioned widely with his hands for the Nigerian to bring him the chained hyena again. With the commotion and smell of blood on Dage, the beast jerked and pawed up a cloud of dust. His growls filled the circle when he jumped and thrashed his head back and forth. The Nigerian struggled to contain him as Baboloki moved toward the two entangled in a dance of rebellion.

In a show of impatience, the president grabbed the chain from the

Nigerian then wrapped it around the neck of the beast, and in seconds forced the animal to lie flat and stare up at his new master.

"You see, my friends. Even the beast fears me. His rebellious behavior will never be tolerated." He reached down and patted the hyena's head, drawing a contemptuous growl.

Some villagers slipped away, while others appeared frozen in place. The women grabbed the hands of children who tried to get closer. Some burst into tears of protest as they were pulled back toward the bush.

Baboloki pointed to Chase and revealed a smug smile then laughed. "These Americans know nothing of us, how we live, what we need or even want. They bring trouble, trying to force their way of life down our throats, use up our resources, kill our big game for trophies they aren't even allowed to display in the States."

Some of the remaining villagers nodded, casting cautious glances at Handsome, who stood tall and unafraid.

"Give me the diamond," Baboloki commanded, holding the hyena tight with one hand and stretching the other toward the man who threatened his future.

When Handsome stood firm, Baboloki pulled the hyena close to Keeya who scrambled backward like a crab. She fell again and crawled toward the area where the tourists were being corralled by armed soldiers.

Chase stepped out to help Keeya when Tessa ran to her and tugged her to her feet. Before Chase could intervene, two soldiers closed around both women. Tessa struggled against being manhandled and was finally subdued by a rough shake from one of the soldiers.

Another soldier ran up to the tourists and demanded they show their hands. The Germans and Brits complied slowly, but Chase's hand remained closed around his weapon inside his jacket. He leveled a deadly glare at the soldier who shouted orders again at Chase. He recognized him as one of the poachers from a few days earlier.

Recognition flashed in the soldier's eyes and reached to search Chase. In the blink of an eye, he'd grabbed the man's hand, twisted it back so fast, the soldier dropped to the dirt. Another twist snapped the bone. Chase caught up the rifle even before it touched the ground and fired off a shot at the guard on Handsome.

Soldiers all around the circle stepped forward leveling their weapons at the enemies of the president. Villagers cried out and collided into each other in a mad rush to escape the camp. In seconds, the only ones left were camp employees, tourists, Baboloki's enemies, and Enigma.

"Guess this didn't go exactly like you planned," Chase said offhandedly, stealing a glance at Tessa who had her arms wrapped around Keeya. The fear in her eyes gave him hope she wouldn't try to be a hero.

"I think it's turned out pretty well," Baboloki spoke with the confidence of a loved savior of his people. "These simple people understand both my strength, my willingness to suppress dissension, and that the Kifaru really possesses no real power." He turned to Handsome as one of the guards brought the president the diamond. "You said so yourself—it's just a piece of carbon. No magical powers. No sign of divine leadership."

"I don't need the Kifaru to beat you in the election. Take it. All it has ever done for me is keep me in hiding. If I had known you imprisoned my mother all these years, I would have killed you long ago."

Baboloki pooched out his lips then revealed a devilish smirk. "Sounds like a threat to my well-being," he said to his men. "Since you claim to be a citizen of Botswana, you should know it's against the law to say such things about your president." Baboloki looked over to Chase. "Even in your country when threats are made against your president then the Secret Service takes them into custody." One of the soldiers prodded Handsome forward with his rifle.

"Then arrest him and put him on trial," Chase suggested.

"Trial? Don't be ridiculous. That's a little too risky with Opperman's people jumping ship and switching sides. They have friends in low places, and I don't want this troublemaker to become a national hero." He lifted the Kifaru and eyed it carefully. "But you're right. Who needs the Kifaru?" He hurled it into the Okavango. The splash sounded like a 6.9 earthquake to Chase, but Handsome didn't bat an eye.

The hyena lunged at the president. He lost his grip of the section of the chain wrapped tightly around the animal's neck, leaving it a loose leash attached to a collar. Baboloki shouted curses at the animal shaking his head as it tried to back away with erratic jerks. With one last powerful pull on the leash, the collar broke and the hyena was freed.

Employees scrambled up trees or clambered onto observation platforms near the river. Even the soldiers turned away from their duties to see how best to protect themselves or the president.

"No!" the president demanded as Chase fired his rifle at the hyena but missed. Baboloki spun around toward Tessa and Keeya.

Chase wanted to fire a second time but didn't have a clear shot because the women were between the animal and him.

Handsome snatched the rifle away from his guard who then fled immediately. Baboloki's eyes bulged at the sight of the freed hyena who jutted out his tongue and ran it across his mouth.

"Do something," Baboloki ordered.

Several of the soldiers took nervous shots at the beast and managed to hit Opperman in the shoulder and grazed the doctor's ear.

"Stop shooting," Chase yelled. "You're going to kill the innocent."

The hyena bolted toward the women who both screamed in horror. Keeya ran sideways, only to fall at Carter's feet. He grabbed her arm and jerked her up and behind him.

Tessa took small backward steps, murmuring, "Good boy. Nice hyena."

The hyena pawed the dirt and salivated white foam as it circled her. She might as well have been a wounded wildebeest calf. He lunged at her but not close enough to catch her. Tessa screamed and ran toward a set of side steps to the deck. Chase sprinted toward Tessa and caught foul stench of the hyena's filthy body.

The hellish growls mixed with Tessa's screams drove Chase to throw caution to the wind. He lifted his weapon even as the animal ripped into Tessa.

CHAPTER FORTY

Tessa continued to scream as she clawed her way up the steps. The hyena's teeth sank deeper into her leather boot then tried to pull her down the steps by shaking her violently. Four shots rang out. She lay still, face down on the steps as Chase and Handsome ran up and dragged the beast off her lower legs. Blood covered one leg on her motionless body.

Chase passed his rifle to Handsome then gently rolled Tessa into his arms and lifted her off the steps. In the last seconds of the attack she'd fainted. Laying his hand on her chest, he found her rapid heartbeat. His team formed a half circle in front of him to shield from further attacks. He gently laid her on the ground.

Her eyes blinked open as he pushed the blonde strands from her face. Tears oozed from the corners of her eyes as she circled his neck with her arms to give him a reassuring embrace.

 Chase's gaze narrowed when he jumped to his feet. Tessa's blood now covered his clothes when he looked to Handsome. "Let's finish this."

Handsome rose like a sleepy giant and turned toward the president. He handed Chase his weapon.

The soldiers lifted their guns, but the Enigma team anticipated the move and put them down one by one.

Peter, also covered in blood from his wound, jumped into the fray by taking back his weapon. He tried to put himself between the villagers and the soldiers, and sprayed a round of bullets toward the attackers. He took another hit to the leg and fell back.

In a surprise move, the two Germans pulled their weapons and took up where Peter left off who gave them time to escape to the deck.

The rest of the Enigma team picked off the soldiers hiding behind trees. Several had taken a hostage and used them for protection but to no avail. One by one they were eliminated.

It took seconds for the area to be filled with the smell of gunpowder tinted with the smell of blood and death. Baboloki retreated behind the large crate that had held the hyena. The baboon had managed to get shot and now lay with his arm shoved through the bars of it and lay dying.

"You've got no one left, Mr. President," Chase shouted. "No one will hurt you. You have my word." He got an accepting chin tilt from Handsome. "It's over."

The president stood holding a large metal container the size of a mechanic's tool box. He surveyed the carnage without any show of emotion. The Enigma team checked the wounded and found several soldiers still breathing. Baboloki's gaze fell on Handsome and Chase, his thick lips forming a sneer of contempt.

"You will die for what you did today. Such fools." Baboloki pulled back his shoulders. "Without the Kifaru, you are nothing."

"I do not need the diamond," Handsome spoke with self-assurance. Silence fell, everyone still conscious faced the president and the man who would become their new leader.

"And why is that?" Baboloki scoffed.

"Isn't it obvious?" Chase holstered his weapon. "He is the Kifaru."

"Not for long," Baboloki growled as he opened the box then dropped it in front of the two men.

A ten-foot black mamba uncoiled itself. Chase and Handsome jumped sideways and let out a frightened shout of warning. They waved their arms as they staggered back.

The deadly creature slithered toward Tessa who remained on her back.

"Tessa, be still," Chase shouted as she tried to drag herself away. He would never forget the look of terror in her eyes.

Handsome and Chase created a kind of dangerous dance of stomping, kicking, and waving to distract the snake that raised a third of its body length to strike. Her hands slipped so that she fell back down on her back. Pulling her bloody knees up, Tessa sobbed and shook her head no at the impending attack.

Baboloki's satanic-like chuckle unnerved Chase long enough to take his eyes off the snake and glance at Tessa's pale face. Her eyes widened, frozen in terror. Her lips trembled. Her wounds prevented her from moving any further.

"Be still," Dr. Girard called to them. "Let the snake pass, and you'll be in no danger. He will avoid conflict."

Baboloki picked up a rock and hurled it at the snake. It reared back slightly then lunged forward as a scream escaped Tessa. Chase dove in front of her, landing on her hip when she tried to turn away. He took the first strike on the arm.

"Handsome," Sam called. She tossed him an ordinary garden hoe laying on the ground someone dropped in the chaos. "I'm out of bullets. Cut its head off," she demanded as the snake reared back with lightning speed.

Handsome swung the staff like an agile ninja and managed to distract the black mamba long enough for the Germans to pull Tessa and Chase out of harm's way. The venomous monster lunged at Handsome, striking him twice on the thigh.

Dage scrambled to his feet and pulled Keeya back. Dr. Girard stumbled forward, but Carter grabbed his arms and held him in place.

Chase felt a wave a pain in his chest, but croaked out instructions to Carter when he bent down to check on him.

"We put some of the meds in the camp cooler. Go look for the anti-venom."

Carter jumped to his feet and pushed Dr. Girard into one of the workers. "Take him now! Go before it's too late. We only have about fifteen minutes before the symptoms become excruciating."

The weight pressing on Chase's chest didn't cause him to take his eyes off the president. He was still a dangerous man. The sound of Tessa crying and stroking his face did little to comfort him when the snake was still at large.

Baboloki kept an eye on the snake. It moved swiftly away until a sudden flight of a marabou stork, flying up from the water's edge caused the snake to circle around erratically.

This time it headed toward the president. He pivoted too quickly and stumbled into the crate with the dead baboon. The snake raced toward him.

The president cried out, "Someone help me!" But no one moved, in fear the black mamba would turn in their direction. "Please," he yelled as his foot hit the root of a giant Baobab tree and fell across the dead hyena.

A shot rang out as the black mamba connected to the president's chest. Dage staggered forward, a rifle cradled in his arms. He approached the president and bent down to throw off the snake.

Dr. Girard returned, panting but holding up two needles of anti-venom. He fell to his knees next to Chase. He knew he must be in cardiac distress. He'd seen it on the battlefield many times when he was a medic. He could hardly breathe more than a shallow breath.

"You're in serious trouble, Chase. I'm giving you the first shot." Chase tried to nod but couldn't even manage to do that. "Lucky we had two of these. You'll feel better in a few seconds, my boy."

The doctor pushed himself up and hurried to Handsome only to trip over a soldier's rifle.

The needle of anti-venom flew in the air. Dr. Girard scampered to grab for it.

Dage reached and caught it midflight. His eyes went to Handsome who was being cradled by his sobbing mother. Standing, he glared down at President Baboloki.

"What are you waiting for?" the president pulled at his chest. "Give me the shot."

Dage moved toward Handsome and handed Dr. Girard the shot. "Do it, Dr. Girard. Save your son. Save our leader."

"No!" Baboloki gasped. "I'll give you anything you want."

Dr. Girard injected the lifesaving anti-venom into his son. Together, the doctor and Keeya clung to Handsome until he breathed easier. They remained terrified he might not live. "I would suggest everyone be moved out of here. This will be a horrible death for the president."

Several of the village men and employees who had remained turned their backs on the president. The pain started immediately then the shortness of breath. Death would be a release in less than an hour. No one tried to make him comfortable.

The Nigerian approached the president and sat cross-legged in front of him. He watched with the curiosity of a child, turning his head to the side when convulsions rippled through the president's body. Chase watched until the Nigerian stood and dragged the hyena out from under the president's body, to his side. He placed the hand of Baboloki onto the head of the hyena.

When the weight lifted off his chest, Chase could focus on Tessa. He laid his hand on her as she continued to pour water on a towel to wipe his face. When his pulse stabilized and he could breathe more easily, he gazed up at her and wanted to smile but failed. She kissed his face multiple times and whispered how much he meant to her, not to ever do another stupid thing to save her, how she couldn't go on if he died.

"Tessa?" he said licking his lips and closing his eyes.

"Yes, Chase?" she said running her fingers down his cheek.

He tried to sit up, but she grabbed him around the shoulders and pulled him into her body to cradle him as he lost hold of consciousness.

~ ~ ~

Peter watched the darkness swallow the Okavango Delta just like it had been doing for hundreds of years. The fruit bats' puppy-like barks, along with the angry lions fighting with hyena over a crippled Cape buffalo on the edge of camp, continued to put the guests on edge. Elephants trumpeted, not liking the smell of blood in the air.

The entire camp was under lockdown after the death of the president. He helped Kirk Opperman contact the proper authorities and several seaplanes and helicopters came in to remove the bodies. Statements were taken and the story told too many times to remember.

The only one who tried to tell government authorities a different story as to the chain of events was Naledi, the president's devoted secretary. Too many refuted her story to be believed, but her statement was taken nonetheless. Peter made sure Opperman and Dage remained in camp, and retold the story of the president trying to tame a hyena and a black mamba. They carried the most weight. They expressed concerns about the late president's mental health.

The soldiers turned out to be no more than mercenaries who tried to take down witnesses so they could ransack the camp and cover up their poaching enterprise. Dage informed law enforcement they were also responsible, at Baboloki's blessing, for burning down the medical clinic. Peter was promised they would be rounded up and punished.

Chase listened to Carter catch him up on the camp activity. His enthusiasm almost made him chuckle.

"Opperman offered the secretary a lucrative deal for her silence. Guess there won't be more than one version of the truth," Carter said as he placed his hands behind his head.

Dinner had been served on the deck of Chase and Tessa's tree house suite. Torches burned below while officials continued to collect evidence and interview a few witnesses. One of the government officials brought word the vice president had been sworn in earlier in the evening.

Girard, although still not 100 percent himself, cared for the injured. Along with Keeya, he got to talk to Handsome and discuss the future.

"Dage dropped by earlier and said Opperman had made arrangements for Baboloki's son to be kept hidden until he and Keeya could break the news. He'll arrive in the morning. That is going to be rough." Chase liked the updates, but felt the pressures of the day weighing heavily on him. "Where are the rest of the unlikely heroes?"

"Peter is hobbling around giving orders to his crew about making

Baboloki's suite ready for Keeya and the boy."

"And Handsome? How is it he got the anti-venom instead of the president? I could have sworn Dage and Handsome were on the road to killing each other a day ago."

Carter chuckled. "I think if it weren't for knowing Handsome was Keeya's son, he might have given the shot to the president. But then again, he's free to raise the boy."

"The wife will probably come in for the funeral and take off again. I'm sure Opperman will make restitution to her as well, in order to have her gone." Chase couldn't imagine her wanting to leave her child behind.

Sam popped a piece of potato in her mouth and chewed before speaking. "News came in a little while ago that the wife's plane had been found, crashed in the rainforest around the equator. No survivors. Opperman will make sure right is done by the child. Keeya and Dage have nothing to worry about there. Hard to believe he's going to support Handsome."

"After today"— Chase stretched—"I think Handsome could be king if he wanted."

"And I don't want that," came Handsome's booming voice from the direction of the steps. They twisted around in their seats to see Handsome carrying Tessa like a ragdoll. She had her arms around his neck and waved happily.

"Put me down, Handsome," she demanded. "I'm fine."

He carried her to one of the camp chairs at the table and settled her next to Sam. "She's not fine. Badly sprained ankle with ten stitches. Another twenty on her leg. Not too bad, I guess, considering."

"You need to take it easy, too, Handsome. I'm beat. How can you walk around like nothing happened?" The guy was a rock. "That snake got you twice."

Handsome arched an eyebrow and in a deep voice intoned, "I am the Kifaru."

The group burst out into moans and insults. Even Handsome smiled for once.

"Go on and laugh." Handsome pulled up a chair. "Seriously. I want to thank you for all you did for me. I didn't deserve it. There were times I never believed the story or in myself."

Chase narrowed his eyes at the man and landed a punch on his huge arm. "We still don't, so get over yourself and prove us wrong."

"I believed in you, Handsome," Tessa chimed in and winked at him before giving a wrinkled-nose look to the others who frowned or dropped an eye roll.

"I know, Tessa. And I'd like to offer you a position as first lady of

Botswana if I'm elected." Although Handsome spoke to Tessa, his eyes were on Chase.

"Well, good luck with that. She is bad luck from the get-go. You owe Enigma. Take her," Chase quipped as he pointed to her.

"Well, thank you for the offer, Mr. Future President of Botswana. But I already have a husband. If only you'd spoken up twelve years ago." Tessa threw her hands up in a show of helplessness.

Handsome laughed so loud the others joined in, and they finished their meal with talk of the future as dessert.

The camp quieted down around midnight, even the warring lions and hyenas silent for once, or perhaps they'd moved on in search of prey. Vernon and Zoric gave access to their information and photos for the authorities to demonstrate the possibility the president had been unstable. They turned in first after checking in with Chase and bringing him up to speed. Before Carter and Sam left, they asked Tessa several times if she was all right.

"I'm touched." Tessa blinked innocently up at Sam who loomed over her with a stoic posture and sour expression.

"You're touched all right." Sam pinched Tessa on the shoulder, and she quickly slapped at her hand.

Tessa smacked her lips together to make kissing sounds then smiled wickedly. "I know you love me, Sam." She made her voice sound like she might be talking to a toddler.

Sam cut her eyes to Chase then Carter. "I'm going to bed. You coming, Carter?"

He hopped up out of the chair and slapped his hands together before pretending to yawn. "I'm beat. Think I'll turn in, too."

Tessa chuckled and landed a fist on Sam's leg. She reciprocated by shoving Tessa's head forward. It would be the closest thing to friendship either would be willing to admit. When they left, silence followed for a few minutes until Chase took a deep breath then slowly expelled it.

"Handsome, there is going to be a media storm headed your way. Are you ready for this?"

"I've been preparing for it my whole life, so we'll see. This may not work out, but at least someone worthy may have a chance to make a difference."

Tessa patted his hand. "Well my money is on you." She stood. "I'm going to bed. Thanks for packing me up those stairs, Handsome." He pushed up halfway out of the chair when she motioned for him to sit down. "You're not going to carry me inside. I can manage. See you in the morning, Handsome."

After she left, the men continued their conversation in low voices.

"Keep us informed, Handsome. Enigma will be watching," Chase warned.

A hard glower of rebellion washed over Handsome's face. "And if I find out you've done anything inappropriate to the lady's husband or her children or basically her life, I'll be in touch with you. You keep that in mind."

"I'm a freakin' angel."

He nodded. "I'm sure. Possibly one of those with a forked tail and horns. This isn't a threat."

"She's a big girl, Handsome, capable of making her own decisions about—life. Besides, we're friends. Nothing to be concerned about."

Handsome rose and moved toward the stairs. "I'll see you in the morning. Opperman is sending his helicopter to get you to Gaborone on time for your flight. I'll send someone with a wake-up call around six."

Chase watched him disappear into the night before entering the tree house suite. Tessa had already rumpled the covers into chaos and was tossing and turning. He slid in next to her, fully clothed. She woke immediately.

"I had a bad dream," she whispered into his face inches from hers.

"Probably going to be a lot of those for a while. Dr. Wu can help when we get back." He dared push her hair out of her eyes. "Are you still scared?"

She laid a palm on his cheek. "You could have died protecting me."

He yawned. "All in a day's work, ma'am."

"You're impossible," she said, patting his cheek before withdrawing her hand. "And I adore you."

"I'm here for you, Tess. Always. Now, go to sleep. I'll wake you up if you have more nightmares, and you do the same for me."

Instead of rolling away and shoving pillows between them, Tessa remained in the crook of his arm and slept against him the rest of the night. He was too tired to do anything about it. Maybe it was for the best, this time around. When they got stateside, he'd see where things were headed between them. But deep down, Chase knew in order to do that, he would need to help her get rid of the ghosts Enigma had laid at her feet.

WHAT YOU SHOULD KNOW ABOUT BOTSWANA

First of all, the country described in this book is not unsafe or run by a corrupt dictator. Botswana is actually one of the safest countries in Africa. A little-known fact is that street crime is rare in this amazing country which is a welcomed change in Africa. Botswana is the continent's longest continuous multi-party democracy. Unlike the story I've just told, it is relatively free of corruption and has an excellent human rights record.

Botswana is known for protecting some of the largest areas of wilderness. The Okavango Delta, where most of the story takes place, is a vast inland river delta, located in the north. With sprawling grassy plains, there is an abundance of wildlife; hippos, elephants, crocodiles as well as, lions, leopards, giraffes and rhino. It is a dream for those wanting to go on a photo safari.

Most people live on the fringes of the wetlands in towns and villages. Since the country's independence it has become one of the fastest growing economies in the world. Botswana is wide open for a new life and full of opportunities. With a good educational network and transportation system, it is an excellent place to get lost for the adventurous.

My time in Botswana was nothing short of magical. The quiet is deafening when poling through the Okavango Delta. I tried to weave some of my experiences into Tessa and Chase's adventure.

The Hyena Men of Nigeria do really exist. You can find videos about them on YouTube. It is one of the most interesting things I discovered in my research and wanted to incorporate it into the story. It was an unexplained surprise when I started writing. I first found them on Pinterest of all places.

There are numerous videos on YouTube about the Okavango Delta. I recommend you trying a few of them out before deciding on an overseas vacation. I found the people to be welcoming and eager to share their amazing country. Everyone speaks English and are interested in people from the west.

The tent I described where Tessa and Chase stayed was very much like the one my husband and I shared. Fruit bats really did bark at night and a resident hippo named Amadeus visited in the middle of the night. A bull elephant I mentioned by the name of

Rambo visited the camp during the day with a couple of his buddies. Just the week before our arrival he pushed a tree over on a tent one night. The guests had turned out their lantern at bedtime. Poor Rambo just didn't know they were there. The incident with the leopard was part of my trip. Even now when I look at those pictures I get the shivers. Today a lot of the accommodations are lifted up like a treehouse.

Going to Africa was a dream come true for me. At the time I taught World Geography and wrote a classroom thematic book for teachers. I realized that children can go through their entire educational experience without ever learning about this continent. Never miss an opportunity to teach them about the world.

I've made some collections on Pinterest if you are interested. It is a great place to escape.

https://www.pinterest.com/ptierneyjames/africa/
https://www.pinterest.com/ptierneyjames/enigma-5-black-mamba/

ABOUT THE AUTHOR

Tierney James decided to become a full-time writer after working in education for over thirty years. Besides serving as a Solar System Ambassador for NASA's Jet Propulsion Lab, and attending Space Camp for Educators, Tierney served as a Geo-teacher for National Geographic. Her love of travel and cultures took her on adventures throughout Africa, Asia and Europe. From the Great Wall of China to floating the Okavango Delta of Botswana, Tierney weaves her unique experiences into the adventures she loves to write. Living on an Indian reservation and in a mining town continues to fuel the characters in the Enigma and Wind Dancer series.

The love of teaching continues in her marketing and writing workshops along with the creation of educational materials and children's books. Try some of her other books to bring a little adventure to your life. http://www.tierneyjames.com

Books by Tierney James

Enigma Series
- An Unlikely Hero
- Winds of Deception
- Rooftop Angels
- KIFARU

Stand Alone Novels
- The Rescued Heart
- Dance of the Devil's Trill

Wind Dancer Series
- Dark Side of Morning

Education
- African Safari

Children's Books
- There's a Superhero in the Library
- Zombie Meatloaf
- Mission K9 Rescue

ENIGMA #6 COMING 2019

THE TRIBESMAN

The cold winds brought ice crystals to hit the tribesman who stood taller than the other Kyrgyz. His shoulders were wider and more muscled, and a hint of mixed parentage showed in his thicker lips and wide mouth. But the almond-shaped eyes labeled him from Central Asia. These treacherous mountains and plains reminded him of another home in Montana.

"It is good to have you back, Darya." The old Kahn remained wiry at the ripe old age of fifty-five. In this land, years beyond forty were considered ancient. "How long will you stay?"

"I need to find someone?" He led his horse into a lean-to protected building of mud.

"And the woman? What of her? Is she dead?"

Darya rubbed down the horse. "No. She will be with me soon."

The old Kahn smoked his pipe of heroin to relieve the pain in his spine. "Who do you seek?"

"I want to make sure Masood, the Taliban leader, is dead. The woman will not be safe until he is."

"Then where will you go?"

"To Russia."

The Kahn spit on the ground. "You walk in danger. Why not stay with us?" When the younger Kyrgyz didn't explain, the Kahn continued, "It's because of the woman." He nodded with understanding.

"Yes. This time, the American captain cannot interfere."

"How do you know this?"

"Because I will kill him if he tries." The old Kahn sighed with resignation and moved away to enter his yurt.

Darya moved to look at the desolate land marked with raw beauty and lost himself in the memories of the woman. He whispered the words, "I'm coming for you, Tessa Scott."

~ ~ ~

Tessa bolted straight up from another nightmare. Gasping for breath, Tessa lifted her hands to her throat then her chest. With a glance to the man next to her, she realized her husband had not been awakened by her distress. She left their bed and moved to the frosty window then laid her cheek against the cold glass.

His image could not be erased, even after all this time. A sense of foreboding washed over her when his memory filled her. The wild freedom he brought to her life on the rooftop of the world still remained so fresh. The man had enslaved her heart to a life of incredible adventure and danger. This kind of life old women retold in stories to their children and grandchildren around cooking fires on winter nights or in grassy meadows during times of summer heat when all work ceased.

There would be no escape this time, nor would she try if he ever dared show his face again.

"Darya," she mouthed, resting her face against the cold window pane. "Darya."

9 781965 460184